CONTEXT

THE CROWN ROSE *Fiona Avery*

THE HEALER *Michael Blumlein, MD*

GENETOPIA *Keith Brooke*

GALILEO'S CHILDREN: *edited by Gardner Dozois*
TALES OF SCIENCE VS. SUPERSTITION

THE PRODIGAL TROLL *Charles Coleman Finlay*

PARADOX: *John Meaney*
BOOK ONE OF THE NULAPEIRON SEQUENCE

CONTEXT: *John Meaney*
BOOK TWO OF THE NULAPEIRON SEQUENCE

TIDES *Scott Mackay*

SILVERHEART *Michael Moorcock*
& Storm Constantine

STARSHIP: MUTINY *Mike Resnick*

HERE, THERE & EVERYWHERE *Chris Roberson*

SILVER SCREEN *Justina Robson*

STAR OF GYPSIES *Robert Silverberg*

THE AFFINITY TRAP *Martin Sketchley*

THE RESURRECTED MAN *Sean Williams*

MACROLIFE *George Zebrowski*

CONTEXT

BOOK TWO
OF THE NULAPEIRON SEQUENCE

JOHN MEANEY

an imprint of Prometheus Books
Amherst, NY

Inquiries should be addressed to
Pyr
59 John Glenn Drive
Amherst, New York 14228–2197
VOICE: 716–691–0133, ext. 207
FAX: 716–564–2711
WWW.PYRSF.COM

09 08 07 06 05   5 4 3 2 1

Library of Congress Cataloging-in-Publication Data

Meaney, John.
    Context / John Meaney.
        p. cm.
    Originally published: London : Bantam Press, a division of Transworld Publishers, 2002.
    ISBN 1–59102–335–1 (alk. paper)
    1. Wounds and injuries—Patients—Fiction. I. Title.

PS6113.E17C66 2005
813'.6—dc22

                                                                2004027137

Printed in the United States of America on acid-free paper

For *Yvonne*—
always and forever

1

NULAPEIRON AD 3418

This was the view from inside the long passenger cabin: glowing orange mists, redolent with inner fires, which billowed and swirled beyond the clear membranous hull. In dark gaps amid the pulsing orange vapours, glimpses of cavern ceiling high above, of rock-strewn floor below.

On distant walls, black teardrop shapes hung, their strong tendrils splayed against the raw, cold stone. They were armoured arachnabugs: military-grade, single-occupant, and armed.

The passenger-transport was a long shuttle-bug, currently holding still, poised at the vast cavern's exact centre. For security scans? None of the passengers seemed worried.

"Why we did stopped?" A child's voice, plaintive.

A lurch, and the long shuttle-bug slid forwards along its longitudinal filament, thread-like braids flowing across the hull. Adults laughed, and the child gave a gap-toothed grin.

Tom was slumped in the soft seat, and his pale skin was etched with unvoiced suffering. Unseen beneath his dark trews, amber gel—sprinkled with healing silver motes—encased his left thigh.

Above them, on the cabin's furry ceiling, big purple servolice crawled, offering snacks. One paused overhead, but Elva, beside Tom, waved the thing on. Few passengers wanted refreshment; they were nearing journey's end. The plush cabin was filled with bright excitement at entering a new realm, or the sweet pleasure of returning home: many people, recently, had been granted wander-leave for the first time in their lives.

But in Tom's injured leg, dark pain crouched like a venomous spider.

"Are you OK, my—Tom?" Elva looked concerned.

Don't call me Lord. His rank meant nothing now.

But he said only: "I'm fine."

It was a lie. His leg wound was serious, maybe mortal, but pure agony defined his missing left arm. In the thirteen Standard Years since it had been severed, never had the nonexistent limb burned more painfully than now.

"Good security." Elva stared out at the unbreathable orange vapour.

Always the tactician. Years ago, Tom had learned to count on her.

Then the glowing clouds were gone, and polished walls were sliding past, tessellated with intricate square-patterned mosaics in bright primary hues. Crystal and bronze sculptures stood in white-lit alcoves.

A huge platform, of pale marble with pale grey swirls, drew close. At its rear stood ornate high archways filled with shimmering scanfields: entrances to the rich, fabled realm which lay beyond.

The shuttle-bug whispered into position, and docked.

And as the transport's doors dissolved open, a long row of mirror-masked soldiers in tan capes hoisted shining grasers, snapped bootheels together, coming to sharp attention.

Huge holos glimmered into being above the exit arches:

*** WELCOME, HONOURED GUESTS ***
*** TO THE ***
*** AURINEATE GRAND'AUME ***

Alongside the disembarking passengers, soldiers—uniformly tall—remained unmoving at strict attention. Watching, from behind their faceless mirrormasks.

"Tasteless." Elva nodded towards the giant holos, then handed Tom his cane.

But Tom knew her trained awareness was centred upon the soldiers, evaluating the threat. Tom drew his cloak close, limped slowly towards the shimmerfields.

Were there always troops to greet new arrivals? Or was there conflict nearby?

Other passengers streamed past, rushing for the exits. Floating mesodrones bore their luggage; but everything Tom and Elva owned fitted into the one small bag she carried.

"Ahem." Elva cleared her throat.

Up ahead, near the shimmerfields, stood a slender woman robed in black. Decorative fronds sprouted cowl-like from her collar—black, in contrast to her triangular, bone-white features—moving slowly, as if stirred by unfelt breezes. Black cuffs trailed to the floor.

A bronze microdrone hung above each shoulder. Behind her stood an honour guard of twelve soldiers: bare-headed, stone-faced, formal scimitars fastened across their backs.

"I see her," murmured Tom.

They had wanted neither fuss nor ceremony. Had thought that, in the Aurineate Grand'aume—one of the few major realms with neither Lords nor Ladies—they could arrive incognito.

"It's all right," said Elva. "No-one else cares."

A tight grin stretched momentarily across Tom's face. She was right: they were anonymous travellers, unnoticed amid the crowd.

They headed towards the waiting woman.

*** INDEPENDENCE & COMMITMENT ***

Another holo shone its greeting.

"Let's hope their medicine"—Tom stopped, pointed at the holo with his cane—"has more class than their advertising."

Elva looked away. It was nothing she could joke about. Inside

Tom's infected leg, a colony of femtocytes was growing. Engineered pseudatoms, replicating fast, threatened to phase-shift into action and dismantle his cells.

If the Grand'aume's medics were not as advanced as their reputation suggested, then Tom would very shortly die a quick but agonizing death.

The black-robed woman curtsied.

"I am Nirilya." She spoke in accented Nov'glin. "Your guide, Lord Corcorigan."

Tom appreciated her effort: speaking his native tongue.

Beyond the marble platform, the floor was purple glass, the exact colour of orthoplum wine. On it, the twelve-strong honour guard stood to attention. Overhead, near the gilded ceiling, rosy glowglobes floated.

"And you"—Nirilya's tone was cold—"must be Captain Elva Strelsthorm."

Elva's hands tightened into half-fists, then relaxed. Such stark words, in another place, would have borne grave insult. Had Elva been noble-born, they would constitute a death-duel challenge. But this was another culture, and Nirilya was not speaking her own language; they would have to make allowances.

Nirilya was staring at Tom: another breach of protocol.

"If you'll permit me"—she gestured towards the purple glass floor—"my Lord."

It rippled.

A deformity spread across the floor. Then a two-metre swelling grew, morphed into a lev-chair, and detached itself with a gentle *pop*. It slid towards Tom.

He glanced at Elva, then surrendered, and eased himself inside the chair.

Fate . . .

A spasm shook his leg, and he briefly closed his eyes.

"Are you—?"

"Let's go."

The chair rose. Inside, Tom tried to relax.

He was twenty-nine Standard Years of age, athlete and warrior, but he felt like an old, old man.

It was a rich realm. They passed through corridors of solid sapphire; tunnels of stone carved with microscopic intricacy, lit by familiar fluorofungus upon the ceilings. Walls were panelled in milky jade, or polished granite across which ALife mandelbroten pulsed.

Surrounded by the honour guard, Tom's chair skimmed across the floor. Nirilya and Elva walked side by side, like old friends; only the tension in Elva's shoulders indicated otherwise.

They crossed a noisy, energetic boulevard whose pearly ceiling glowed with opalescent light. Everyone here wore blue, yet the variety was immense: diamond-crossed doublets, loose jumpsuits, trailing robes.

There were no discreet passageways for servitors. A demesne where everyone was equal?

I wanted to achieve something like this.

They traversed a series of crystal lev-steps, over a copper fountain, to a low balcony where Nirilya dismissed the honour guard. The officer-in-charge bowed, then the men wheeled away, and marched into a transverse corridor.

A doorshimmer evaporated at Nirilya's gesture.

"Your apartments, my Lord."

Inside: sweeping buttresses of dark blue glass; glassine columns, slowly morphing; holoflames dancing above hexagonal flagstones. And for rehab, there was a chamber with a laminar-flow strip for running, and a glassine wall sloping inwards at forty-five degrees and covered with tiny knobs and protuberances, some shaped like miniature whimsical gargoyles.

"You'll need a climbing wall," said Elva. "As soon as you've recovered."

Tom, still in his lev-chair, nodded silently.

A large reception chamber, a dining chamber, a small art gallery and library, and half a dozen sleeping chambers completed the ensemble.

Elva turned to Nirilya. "This is quite satisfactory."

Her words were a dismissal, and Nirilya's face tightened.

But her voice was steady as she said: "We can go straight to the medical centre, if you wish."

Tom, standing in the med centre's reception chamber, watched his lev-chair melt into the glassine floor. Elva, looking more relaxed since Nirilya had left, examined their surroundings.

"Here we are."

A barefoot young woman, shaven-headed and clad in a russet tabard, came into the chamber. She genuflected.

"Please follow me, my Lord."

Then she retraced her steps . . . walking *backwards* into the corridor from which she had come. Tom leaned on his cane, glanced at Elva, and followed.

Twin rows of arches lined the long corridor. To the left, the first chamber contained a semi-translucent clone/regrow vat. All around the vat, a circle of barefoot men sat cross-legged, watching and waiting.

"A moment." Tom halted.

"Sir?" The young woman stopped, trembling. "Have I given offence in any—?"

"Not even a tiny bit. Are you a servitrix?"

"My Lord? I'm a vassal in the ownership of Malfax Cortindo, who is owned by Dr. Xyenquil himself."

There was pride in her statement.

I should have known.

In the realms of Gelmethri Syektor where he had lived, servitors were owned only by nobility. His own years of servitude were etched forever in his soul. But there had also been opportunity; finally, the joys of logosophical discovery in the Sorites School.

Yet here—he understood immediately—a vassal could be indentured to another vassal, held to merciless account for the most trivial
of offences, restricted in education and work, in living quarters and
even in marriage. So easily abused, beyond even the immense range of
privileges which the law accorded any vassal's owner, knowing there
was no redress: receiving the misery passed down from their owner's
own suffering.

It was an endless hierarchy of manipulation and cruelty, of all the
capricious, devastating acts which follow when human beings are held
to be no more than property.

No matter that such propensities come from neural patterns laid
down by primate genes, and that Tom could have written the logosophical equations to prove it. When ethical systems become possible,
they also become *necessary*, and that was why Tom had once been part
of a revolution which aimed to bring liberty to all of Nulapeiron's ten
billion diverse souls.

But now that seemed a time of almost child-like innocence.

So arrogant—to think that I could change all this.

In the last chamber on the right, a grey-haired man with no legs was
struggling to cross the floor, walking on his stumps. Pain and
determination etched deep lines in his sweat-drenched features; his
breath came in painful rasps.

Sweet Destiny. Tom could only stare. *Be strong, my friend.*

He almost asked the female vassal to explain, but then he realized:
clone/regrow vats could regenerate damaged cells, but the processes
were expensive. Reserved for whatever élite held sway here: Lords and
Ladies, by another name.

"They can fit prosthetics," Elva murmured, "once he's able to walk
like that."

Hardening the skin on his stumps, learning to use his hip flexors
to maximum effect.

Often, Tom had run and climbed for hours—had once ascended, as a solo free-climb, the outer surface of a kilometre-wide terraformer sphere hanging in the clouds above the surface: the day he killed the Oracle. That same day, he had run sixty klicks in one long, unbroken ultra-endurance session, after escaping in a drop-bug to the ground.

But he had never pushed himself as hard as this poor injured vassal struggling to cross a modest chamber, forcing himself to walk upon legs which did not exist.

2
NULAPEIRON AD 3418

Hard blackness pressed heavily upon him from all directions.

Receding now . . .

Tom struggled awake, panicking, wondering what had happened.

"You're all right, my Lord. A touch of retrograde amnesia: nothing to worry about."

A *thing* was bent over him—humanoid, glistening purple—and then it shed its skin in sections, some kind of protective suit, revealing a slight man with frizzy red hair, dressed in ordinary clothes.

"My name is Dr. Xyenquil, sir, and you exhibited a reaction to the scan—"

As Tom sat up, cold sheets of blue gel slid from his naked body.

"—but the crisis is past."

Tom groaned. His talisman, a small silver stallion, was hanging from its cord round his throat, and he clutched at it for comfort.

"Reaction?" His mouth felt dry and fuzzy. "What kind of . . . reaction?"

"The femtocytes didn't like being scanned. But"—a quick, professional smile—"we can cope. In any other realm, though . . ."

Unspoken: *You'd be dead.*

"That's comforting."

"It would help," said Xyenquil, "if I could see the original infecting rod."

"Sorry. We left it behind." Elva glanced at Tom. "It's a bit far to go and fetch it."

Elva had in fact commissioned the femtocytic security, never suspecting that it would one day be turned against her Liege Lord who had disappeared into exile four SY before, running from the clandestine revolutionary alliance of LudusVitae in which she, too, was a senior executive officer.

The first two years were a black, fragmented haze in Tom's memory, clouded by alcohol and sordid grime, when he wandered as a broken derelict—there had been a head injury when he fled his LudusVitae comrades, and perhaps that was the beginning of his destitute madness—descending through poverty-stricken strata until he found himself at the edge of a deep-buried sea on the lowest level of all, knowing he could go no further.

And the slow recovery: working in Vosie's café, then teaching school, in the peaceful community he had grown to love. But then, less than sixty days ago, soldiers had come: sent by Lord Corduven d'Ovraison, whom Tom had known since his days of servitude in Palace Darinia.

For a thousand years, the nobles' power structure was upheld by Oracles. Tom, who had devised a way to subvert Oracular truecasts, might be considered a prime architect of the revolution which had exploded across Nulapeiron while he tried to live a quiet life far from the Prima Strata of distant realms, and a struggle which had ceased to hold any meaning for him.

But there was another noble he had known for nearly fifteen SY, and it was she, the Lady Sylvana, whom Corduven was desperate to rescue from a pogrom court.

So fifty days ago, with Corduven's commandos, Tom had infiltrated the court, found the beautiful Sylvana suspended at the centre of a vast spherical hall, trapped in a cruciform structure formed of conducting rods, held in place by a lev-field, ready to impale her—slowly—when the court passed sentence.

Then the rescue team had struck, while Tom, descending from the ceiling, pulled Sylvana from the cruciform, and got her away just before the thing exploded, long rods lancing in every direction, impaling hundreds, including Tom.

Since then, even those who had appeared to be only slightly wounded had perished, screaming in agony, weeping blood from every orifice, from their very skin, as their bodies inexorably dissolved.

Every one of them, save Tom, whose desperately coded counter-measures fought a holding battle, broadcasting do-nothing commands to the infecting 'cytes: commands which could not be sustained.

There was nothing to do but wait. Xyenquil had implanted antiphages; he told Tom to go home and rest.

Wearing a new lev-support, like a cummerbund around his waist—"Very stylish, my Lord," said Elva, not quite keeping a straight face—Tom walked stiffly to a high balcony overlooking Os-Vensum-brae Cavernae.

Down below, towers and colonnades of smartnacre and mor-phmarble cycled, slow and viscous, through their changing forms. Beside Tom, Elva, accustomed to more static surroundings, started to look queasy.

"Tom? Why don't we go somewhere else?"

A wide black lake, with ice patches floating. Overhead, among twisted stalactites, snowy edelaces fluttered and glided, hunting for blindmoths.

Away from the quickglass and the ornate boulevards, this was a raw, natural cavern. The air was cold; wild fluorofungus grew splashed across the ceiling, keeping the air fresh with its characteristic woody scent.

On the other side of the lake, on a beach-like scree, a small party moved: a white-bearded man with a staff—a teacher, perhaps—fol-lowed by nine children, wrapped up in red insul-suits against the cold.

"Better." Tom's breath steamed. "Good idea, Elva."

He was leaning on the cane. There were no lev-fields; the waist-support was rendered useless here.

But Elva was shivering.

"Are you sure you're not cold, Tom?"

He shrugged in reply. If anything, he was sweating more than earlier.

"Perhaps we should go back," said Elva. "If you're getting a fev—"

A sharp cry echoed across the icy lake, and Elva crouched by reflex in a combat stance.

Edelace.

A white shape had dropped from the ceiling, and covered a small, struggling boy like a lacy shawl. But this was deadly, a hunting edelace, laden with toxins.

The old man moved surprisingly fast, swinging his staff round to point at the boy. Then a strange dark fire—*black* flames—sprouted from the staff's metal-shod point.

He touched the edelace with that negative fire, and it shrivelled.

"Are you OK?" called Elva.

For a moment Tom thought she meant him. The sight of black flames had struck a deep, frightening chord inside him: a wave of cold fear. It dissipated, leaving a strange fatigue in its wake.

What does it mean?

Tom stood swaying, trying to remain steady. Perhaps it was a fever: infection and counteragents waging war inside his body.

What am I supposed to remember?

Across the lake, the old man gave no sign of having heard Elva. He used his staff to carry the wounded edelace, draped across the tip, down to the lake's edge. Then he flicked it onto the black waters, left it floating where it might regrow.

Strange enough. Yet it was the manner of the party's leaving which affected Tom profoundly.

The nine boys were seated here and there, on flat stones or shale, staring in different directions. Chewing food, acting like normal children of their age, if perhaps a little quiet.

But as the old man turned away from the lake, all nine boys stood in perfect unison. Silently, blank-faced, they formed a single file. As the old man led the way, using his cane to help him up the slope, the nine boys followed soundlessly, climbing without effort.

Into a dark tunnel mouth, they disappeared one by one. It was impossible to tell which had been attacked by the edelace.

Then the silent boys were gone.

"Wait and see," Dr. Xyenquil had told him. *"That's all we can do."*

"And if your antiphages don't work?"

There had been no comforting reply.

It was in Eskania Broadway, a place of glassine blue and polished granite, that Tom gave Elva the slip. His thoughts swirled; he knew only that he had to be alone.

He left her apologizing to a food vendor. The scallop-shaped lev-stall had descended from the ceiling, and Tom had picked a red confection, expecting sweet redberries, then spat it out upon the flagstones: some fishbloc derivative, salty and strong.

"Yes, I'll pay you." Elva was saying.

Feeling dizzy, Tom slipped into a side tunnel. The air was cold, and yet he was sweating as he took a series of turns guaranteed to confuse. He came out into a low-ceilinged plaza.

There were bright-garbed Laksheesh monks, an accountscribe symbiont group—asthenic spindle-armed men, torsos rising from the living emerald gelblock which had long since dissolved their lower bodies—and a squad of bannermen. And a throng of ordinary vassals and freedmen, going about their business.

There was a dark tunnel entrance which seemed to beckon him. Checking that Elva was not following—though he could not have said *why* he needed to lose her—he took that route, and came out beside a polychromatic stream over which a footbridge arced.

Overhead, fluorofungus shone a surreal indigo, almost invisible. Beneath him, swirling bright colours: acid stench like a Vortex Mortis.

It drew him.

And then he was standing on the railing, sweating and shivering, staring down.

What's wrong with me?

Death beckoned. The acid stream called to him, whispered surcease, promised a peaceful alternative to the horrors which lay ahead.

He remembered the funeral: Father's corpse dissolving, knucklebone plopping into the Vortex Mortis, the red-eyed mourners looking on.

End it.

He bent his legs to jump.

End it now.

"My Lord!"

Her hand caught his cape, and he toppled back onto the bridge. Pain slammed into his injured leg, bringing him into the moment.

"Nirilya?"

Concerned white face, framed by cowl-like black fronds.

"Lord Corcorigan. You'd better come with me."

Interlude, unknown or forgotten. Amnesia must have taken hold, for when Tom's awareness returned, he was in a chamber he had never seen before, and Nirilya—

They were twisting apart, those long black ribbons which formed her garments. Her robe dropped away. Revealed, she was white-skinned and almost gaunt: areoles prominent on small cupped breasts. Cascading black hair.

The treatment. It's another reaction . . .

Ice and fire.

Hallucinating? But I saw—

There was a vial of scented lev-gel, and she smeared it on, slowly, across Tom's bare torso—though he could not remember undressing— then used her fingers and her warm tongue: soft liquid sensations more real than he could possibly imagine.

Floating in mid-air, gel and lev-field holding them aloft, amid a swarm of circling flitterglows in the shadow-shrouded chamber, he and she became one: entwined, combined, as though their very cells would merge. Drifting, pulsing, until Tom's entire being burst in silver crescendo and flowed outwards eternally, forever.

Jerked into wakefulness.
Oh, Fate.
Lying on the cold stone floor, lev-gel sliding from his body.
"Nirilya."
She was pulling her robes together, her green feline eyes warm with satisfaction.
"My fine Lord. How are you?"
"Er . . ." He looked around for his clothes.
"Over there." Nirilya pointed. "I need to get to the Bureau. I'm late."
"I . . ."
She leaned over, kissed him.
"Nirilya. We have to talk."
What the Chaos happened here?
Growing very still, she stared at him. Then, carefully: "We don't have to meet up later, if it's inconvenient. My Lord."
Tom, pulling on his trews, shook his head.
"I didn't mean for . . ." He stopped, helpless.
Nirilya clicked her fingers, and a black drone floated into the chamber.
"It'll get you breakfast. I've, ah, got to . . ."
She turned and moved at a run, slipped through the frosting door-shimmer, was gone.
Chaos!

Halfway through his meal of nut omelettes, krilajuice and boljicream —sitting outstretched, bare-chested—Tom stopped, stared up at the floating black drone as though it had forced the food on him, then resumed eating.

His normal breakfast was fruitbloc, perhaps a cup of daistral.

What's wrong with me?

But he was ravenous. An aftereffect of yesterday's fever? He forced himself to slow down. Here he was, enjoying breakfast in Nirilya's chambers, after a night of . . .

Rubbing his face, he felt sinking dismay. Satisfaction, yes, and those charged erotic memories . . . but last night was nothing he had intended.

I nearly killed myself.

It could have been a fever, a mind-altering hallucination from bloodstream debris—fragments of warring femtocytes and antiphages. Or perhaps a rogue femtocyte, gaining access to his logotrope-enabled mind, had fired up his death wish.

But there was a deeper part of him which knew that these were rationalizations, and that he had received formless, nameless visions born of Chaos, swirling fast and strong in the dark mind-waters which lie beneath the fragile illusion human beings term consciousness.

At last, he pushed the food aside. His stomach was flat and ridged with muscle, but if he continued to eat like—

No!

He leaped to his feet, scattering dishes, recoiling at the sight of his own shoulder.

It's an illusion.

But he knew, even before he felt with trembling fingers, that it was real, not holo. The stump, protruding from his left shoulder, looked as it always did—save that, from the end, half-formed, a tiny hand was growing. Miniature fingers curled like soft pale baby worms.

A flesh-bud, awaiting growth.

3

NULAPEIRON AD 3418

He wanted to weep: great aching tears of bitterness and regret; and he wanted to laugh: loud and echoing in celebration.

Instead, Tom stood upon the viaduct which crossed Eskania Broadway, and his hand—his good, right hand—clutched the dark blue balustrade until the knuckles whitened, until it seemed that either frozen quickglass or his tendons must shatter or snap.

"Are you all right, young fellow?"

The man was white-haired and bent with age or injury, and a freedman's narrow bracelet encircled his bony left wrist.

"Yes, I'm—"

For a moment, Tom swayed beneath a wave of weakness.

I've lost my cane.

The old man's weight was half upon his burgundy glass walking stick. Tom realized that his own cane was gone, that his lev-support was back in the apartment, and that his leg was almost free of pain.

"Good, good." The old man turned away, muttering. "Good, good, good . . ."

Xyenquil . . . He did this to me.

Feeling oddly disconnected, Tom made his way to the helical down-ramp, let the laminar flow take him slowly down to the boulevard's marbled floor. It glimmered with inner life, beneath amber glowglobes floating near the opalescent ceiling.

He walked then, almost without volition, cocooned from the passing throngs by a muffled sense of dislocation, until he reached the square archway leading to the med centre.

They had gone too far.

There was a floating tricon, complex yet discreet, by the glassine arch. The motile holo ideogram was dense with meaning: a clumped configuration overall, redolent of strength; calming pink/gold facets of a hundred hues, denoting care and healing, while the complex folding/unfolding of its topology furnished staff résumés and the med centre's prestigious history.

Tom pointed at a facet, made a *show-me-more* control gesture.

Rectilinear facets, indicating a lack of irony, laid bare the facts of Xyenquil's expertise. Elva had chosen well: Xyenquil was more than capable of implanting regrowth factors while combating a life-threatening infection.

Damn you—

Tom's fist (his proper fist) tightened, and for a second killing rage swept through him. Then it was gone, and he turned away, deliberately relaxing the hand, trying to recall the way to his apartment.

I have to talk to Elva.

She was performing triceps dips, hands on a glassine chair and heels on a desktop. Purple dark-stained leotard top, revealing creamy skin: athletic shoulders, strong upper body. Sweat plastered strands of hair across her forehead; her jaw was hard with determination.

Her long trousers were baggy, pale grey, and her feet were clad in training slippers. A discarded skipping rope lay in twisted loops upon the black polished floor.

"Don't stop," said Tom, standing in the chamber's archway.

She pumped through the remaining repetitions, her core muscles tight with strengthening tension, in perfect form.

"Not bad." Tom smiled, a little.

"Thank you."

Icy words, as exact and correct as her exercises.

I never realized how disciplined you are.

He'd known she spent less time than he on endurance conditioning, but had not factored in the intensity of her workout period, and the daily weapons training. She had been his chief security officer, back when he had a demesne to command—a shorter rule than most— but in those days he had appreciated her intelligence work (and her eidetic memory) more than her warrior attributes.

When he had met up with her again in Darinia Demesne, five ten-days ago, he realized just who it was he had always depended on, however much Sylvana's unattainable beauty had entranced him.

And the last forty days, spent travelling in each other's company, had shown him her true sterling worth, wrapped up though he was in the misery of his hurt.

"I hope," he began, "you weren't worried when I—"

"My Lord can spend his nights"—with an unaccustomed flatness to her tone—"wherever he pleases, of course."

"Perhaps it pleases me to explain."

"Sir." Standing at ease, her chin raised. "But Grand'aume Security informed me of your whereabouts, when I considered initiating a search."

"I—That's good."

"Their having you under constant surveillance? A double-edged sword, if I may venture an opinion."

"Elva . . ." Tom was exasperated. "Of course you can speak freely, whenever you like."

"Thank you."

Silence rebounded off the cold elegant walls.

Chaos, this is hard.

Aware suddenly of the closeness of the chamber, the slick high-lights of her sweat-damp skin, her exertion-soaked tight leotard top. And her infinity-gaze—pale grey eyes: strong and unambiguous— directed away from him.

He took a deep breath, then asked the question he could no longer contain.

"Elva, what did you do to me?"

"I'm sorry?"

"I thought—" Tom shook his head, turning away. "Xyenquil's achieved . . . more than I intended."

"And you're not—"

What? he wondered. *Pleased?*

Very softly: "So was his femtoregime to your specification?"

"Sir." Her tone was formal, and pulled him round. "I ordered full healing capabilities, regardless of cost."

After a moment, "You're not just my servitrix," Tom said. "Don't call me sir."

But she was hurt, and a scowl lurked beneath the controlled mask of her features.

"Yes, my Lord."

Damn it!

"For Fate's sake, Elva. You think I haven't had the chance for cell-regrow before?"

"What?"

"Lord A'Dekal, did you ever meet him? No . . . Crusty old bastard, presided at my ascension ceremony. Offered me the use of his med facilities, at a price."

Elva said nothing.

"He wanted," Tom continued, "my support for his reactionary think-tank, the Circulus Fidelis. The cost"—grimly—"was too high."

"You could have found a way."

The chamber seemed to spin.

"What are you talking about?"

"To use the facility, and infiltrate A'Dekal's group."

"This was earlier . . . Before you recruited me into LudusVitae."

"Before you killed General d'Ovraison's brother?"

"*What?*" Sudden rage, his words bouncing back from the glassine walls. Logically, she had always known about the Oracle; yet her raw

words now—answering back, in this place, after what she had done—
flayed like a deadly insult. "You *dare?*"

All his anger and frustration expanded, ballooned, and blood-rush
pounded in his ears.

", . . dare to help you, Tom, with no strings att—"

"Silence."

And Elva was rigid then, locked into her attention stance; her contained fury seemed to swell and coruscate around her. Her jaw muscles
flexed with tension.

But perhaps it was not just Elva who had gone too far.

"By the fourteenth article," she said stiffly, "of the Artifex Con-
junctonis, I formally request allegiance-transfer—"

"*No.*"

"—to General d'Ovraison, who has already indicated his willingness to recruit me into the new Academy. Failing that—"

"Don't push me, Elva."

"—to Darinia Demesne's interim governing—"

"Request denied." Tom reined in his anger.

His words seemed to hang in the charged air between them.

Then she gave a small formal bow in salute. "Yes, my Lord."

Elva turned on her heel, and marched towards her chamber, as
though her sweat-soaked training clothes were full military uniform.

Damn you, Elva. Why did you have to force the issue?

For some words, once spoken, can never be retracted.

And behind it all lay an old, old knowledge: that he was Elva's
Liege Lord, a position he had seen abused too many times to count.

Frost-sparkle. Evaporation.

There was a message-chime, which Tom accepted. Now, in the
archway, where the doorshimmer had stood, waited Nirilya and the
red-haired medic, Xyenquil.

A wave of tension washed through the chamber.

"Come in."

Tom perched on a lev-stool, and directed the visitors to a couch. Nirilya gathered her black robe and sat; then Xyenquil, fidgeting with his tunic's silver clasp, took his place beside her.

Elva entered, stood at the chamber's rear with her arms folded, leaning against the glassine wall.

Xyenquil cleared his throat. "Nirilya's reported some fever-like symptoms in yourself, sir. And, ah, we've completed our post-op analyses."

By the wall, Elva unfolded her arms, re-crossed them.

Holding out an infocrystal, Xyenquil gestured to the chamber's systems, and a holo grew into being:

Splayed shapes, like alien creatures torn inside out: bright beaded lines forming streamers, spirals, twisted glowing knots.

Xyenquil rotated the image—a shining jagged landscape—then froze it.

"These are the result of Calabi-Yau transformations, my Lord."

The holo showed atom-sized femtocytes, ripped apart in ways beyond imagining.

"Is this"—Tom looked up at Xyenquil—"some kind of logosophical metaphor?"

"At first I thought . . ." Xyenquil swallowed. "No. They really have been twisted through the hyperdimensions. I'm sure of it."

It was as if something had reached inside Tom's body, torn open the hidden dimensions of spacetime, and destroyed the femtocytes in the process.

"And I know nothing," added Xyenquil, "in myth or reality, capable of that."

Elva stepped forward. Where she had been leaning against the slow-morphing wall, a shallow Elva-shaped depression marked the surface.

"Just what"—her tone was flat, professional—"is the significance of this?"

Xyenquil shrugged helplessly. "I don't—"

"Wait a moment." Tom held up his hand. "Are you saying, Doctor, that it's not your treatment which has destroyed my infection?"

"My Lord, I'm not—Yes, sir. That's what I mean."

Dark fire . . .

In the cold cavern, the black flames which sprouted from the old man's staff . . . that was the moment when a strange change had overtaken Tom. And there was something he was supposed to remember, but could not.

". . . on your behalf, my Lord. Haven't we, Nirilya?"

"Yes." Her feline eyes were unreadable. "We have an appointment with the Seer."

"An audience," said Xyenquil, almost stammering, "is quite unheard of, for, um, outsiders."

A Seer?

There was a hint of triumph in Nirilya's eyes, but it was her words which captivated Tom. Was this some kind of Oracle?

And if so, he could see no reason why this Seer would help Tom Corcorigan, whose last memory of an Oracular visit was his redmetal poignard rammed to the hilt in Gérard d'Ovraison's side, and the hot cupric stench of the surprised Oracle's death.

"We should go"—Nirilya stood, robes rustling—"straightaway."

We're going to consult an Oracle?

4
NULAPEIRON AD 3418

The threadway hung in a long catenary across the abyss, spanning the endless drop from tunnel's end to the great silver-grey sphere which hung at the vertical shaft's centre. The sphere itself was fifty metres in diameter, maybe more; the shaft in which it floated was immense.

Even Tom felt vertigo when he stared down.

Behind them, in the tunnel, Nirilya and Xyenquil waited with an honour guard of Core Dragoons. Only Tom and Elva were invited into the Seer's dwelling place.

"Why are you doing this?" she asked.

Tom shook his head, unwilling to share his half-formed thoughts, his strange presentiment about dark fire.

I'm afraid . . . With ruthless self-honesty. *But of what?*

"Tactically," Elva added, "I don't like this."

She grew silent.

The threadway was a narrow flexible tunnel, quite transparent save for a too-thin strip which ran along its floor. It was one of thirteen, hanging above the abyss: there was no other way into the Seer's sphere.

Elva stepped inside first, with no trace of nerves, and Tom followed. The threadway swayed from side to side as they made their way down the curved interior.

"I dare say"—with a trace of Elva's usual irony—"the Seer knows we're coming."

Inside the hollow sphere, sapphire lightning flashed and cracked. At the globe chamber's centre hung a complex silver platform; above, skull-like, an ornate silver throne was floating: armour-encased, helm-like overhang, bristling with inbuilt weaponry and controls.

And inside its heavy carapace, in a small soft seat, a tiny wizened figure sat, peering at the two visitors with bright, startling eyes.

A Seer?

Tom, like Elva, stood frozen on a floating lev-step.

Like no Oracle I've ever seen.

And it came to him then that he had no idea what he was doing here, what madness—beyond courtesy to his hosts—had drawn him to this place, except perhaps a strange unfocused fear, and the notion that the world was slipping away from him because of his own inadequacies. He had only a local medic's word that spacetime had unravelled in his vicinity, that some influence had reached beyond reality's constraints to tear apart the tiny invaders inside him: a cure more mysterious, potentially more dangerous, than the original infection.

So he shivered, although the air was not cold, while all around the chamber blue lightning danced and played, spat and coldly burned.

Finally, the helm-throne moved through the air, drawing closer, and they saw more closely the small lined figure which might have been a mortally sick child or an old, old man.

GREETINGS, LORD ONE-ARM.

The message grew in huge bright holo-tricons, animated and complex, changing as the Seer's lips moved, voice unheard.

WELL MET TO THEE, LORD ORACLE KILLER.

"Well met yourself," Tom called across the gap between them, voice raised above the lightning's crackle.

"We've met too many like you," murmured Elva, very low.

OH, NO . . . A trace of smile on the young/old wizened face. **YOU'VE NOT COME ACROSS *ANYTHING* LIKE ME.**

Elva swallowed.

Then she leaped lightly to the next step, deliberately away from Tom, untagging her graser pistol.

"No," said Tom. "Not yet."

He feared there might be defensive femtotech, perhaps a smartmiasma. It would be in defiance of the Comitia Freni Fem'telorum, designed and codified to prevent humanity's destruction with its own weaponry, but there had been violations other than those of Elva's former comrades—beyond the destroyed infection inside his body—and there was so much about this place which did not seem right.

And so, addressing the Seer: "You're not an Oracle, then?"

SEE FOR YOURSELF, MY LORD.

The entire chamber flickered.

And what happened next went far beyond the abilities of any Oracle that Tom had ever met or heard of.

First vision.

Tom saw:

A kaleidoscope of **busy bazaars** . . . **crystal ballrooms with nobles dancing** . . . **thermidors flaring in lava** . . . **deserted thousand-kilometre tunnels where only blindmoths move** . . .

It was a flickering montage of everyday life throughout the world, from every stratum and sector of Nulapeiron.

Second vision.

A dizzying switch to other worlds, whose very existence had been mere legend, a fantasy, during Tom's impoverished youth: **mist-borne cities above silver seas** . . . **antlered bipeds communing in an amphitheatre beneath a violet sky** . . . **bewigged tripods dancing on razorstone while their voracious seedlings wait with fangs bared** . . .

"What are you doing to him?"

Elva's voice, sounding from a distance.

Tom reeled at the sense of limitless space.

I have seen the sky.

No more than a few dozen people—among ten billion inhabitants—had seen the world's surface, but Tom was one of them, was conditioned against the agoraphobic response which could reduce an unprepared person to catatonia.

But, lost amid the Seer's visions, Tom felt a sense of unremitting emptiness, the insignificance of life amid the vastly greater, infinite universe, and it pressed inexorably down, saddening and over-whelming him.

Third vision.

He saw **the creamy nebuloid drifting in space as flame-tailed comets, the tiny males of her species, wheel inwards to her core . . .**

"Last chance, Seer. Release him."

He whimpered before the immensity, the vast interstellar scale of his forced perception.

Fourth vision.

Changes coming faster now . . .

Angular lightning, dancing gavottes on a salt-white desert . . . fat green toroids rolling, with tiny bipedal corpses trapped on their digestive rims . . . a newborn spindlebug drops screeching from its cocoon . . .

"I said . . ."

Gasping, Tom held up his hand.

He shuddered, blinked moisture from his eyes.

"It's all right, Elva."

It had begun as revenge, for the loss of his mother and his father's death. He had studied all the logosophical disciplines—*"For you, logos-*

ophy is a weapon," Sylvana once said—including all he could find on the forbidden topic of the Oracles.

Time flowed both ways in an Oracle's brain, past and future inter-mixed, with no tangible difference between past memory and prescient vision—of their own personal future—save that Lords and Ladies could use truecasts as the basis for their formidable political power.

Poor Oracles.

They spent most of their time watching and reading news reports and analyses, to be reported (subjectively later) as future-memories to their constant entourage of analysts. Sometimes, now, Tom could see the Oracles as tools, as pitiful victims who were scarcely human, and rarely benefited from the privileged strata their existence helped to maintain.

But not one of them could see things which did not occur before his or her own eyes at some point in their life, or force their strange disturbing visions into another person's mind.

"Seer, what exactly are you?"

It seemed no coincidence that Dr. Xyenquil had lately been talking about Calabi-Yau transformations, and the use of spacetime's hidden hyperdimensions. If the Seer could truly perceive distant places and times . . .

AND WHAT IS THE PURPOSE OF EXISTENCE? A mocking smile crossed the Seer's features. **BY ALL MEANS, LET'S ADDRESS THE BIG, ETERNAL QUESTIONS WHILE WE'RE HERE . . .**

Sapphire lightning continued to dance.

An image grew between Tom and the Oracle, and for a moment Tom thought it was another vision. But it was merely holo. Elva, too, was frowning at the sight.

A membrane separates the chamber from the glowing blue fluid. Inside, drifting shapes move slowly: humans, connected by tendrils to some shadowy central mass.

Two youths watch, horrified, from the observation chamber ... And one of these youths is Tom, visiting his imprisoned schoolfriend Kreevil ...

The holo dwindled, faded, was gone.

Tom remembered the occasion, and how it had been his fault that Kreevil was among the schoolboy thieves. Poor unlucky Kreevil: imprisoned for a crime he had not wanted to be part of.

That was real.

Could the Seer really pluck images from the past, and cause them to be reproduced?

And why that particular image?

He noted then that the lightnings and the glowing blue fluid were of the same electric hue. He had seen other hints of it in the past ...

"What is that fluid, Seer?"

A strange expression masked the Seer's face, was gone.

Keep your secret, then.

But Tom was far too familiar with burning, long-held hatred not to recognize its obsessive presence in another human being ... if this Seer could be termed human.

"Just what are you, Seer?" he asked again. "An experiment gone wrong?"

Silence, while the lev-throne rose higher, almost to the domed ceiling, then dropped down closer. The Seer's lips moved; Tom could not quite hear his whisper.

YOUR REPUTATION AS A FIGHTER IS WELL EARNED.

A half-smile.

BUT ARE YOU THE LOGOSOPHER THAT PEOPLE CLAIM?

"Try me."

Then five, twenty, a hundred holo-manifolds blossomed into being, tesseracts with equations scrolling past at breakneck speed. It was genuine, and it was new, and Tom tried to slip into full logosophical trance, to merge with the gestalten-tao . . . but it was too late, and the tantalizing images minimized to dots, and vanished.

Timewave engineering? Damn you . . .

It was some kind of cruel joke, to allow a glimpse of the workings behind an Oracle's mind, then to take that insight away.

DO YOU KNOW WHAT THE COLLEGIUM PERPETUUM DELPHINORUM WOULD DO, IF THEY KNEW YOU HAD SEEN EVEN THAT MUCH?

Tom shook his head.

"*Sweet Chaos.*" Elva. "Do you have any idea how valuable—?"

On the next lev-step, Elva went down on one knee, and turned towards Tom. Her eyes held an expression he had never seen: a hunger, a despair, a great depth of sadness.

"Tom, I'm sorry . . ." She paused, then: "I've another loyalty, and this one goes right back to childhood."

Tom stared at her. Beyond, at the edge of his vision, the Seer's spherical lev-throne dropped, came hurtling downwards.

NO! STOP HER!

It shot towards Elva.

DON'T YOU KNOW WHAT SHE IS?

"I never thought I'd be the one to do this. Oh, Tom, I never once woke up without wondering if this was the day everything would just end. It was always Litha who was the important one. I thought, I really thought—"

STOP! DON'T LET HER DO IT!

"Tom, you must know how I feel about—"

Confused, Tom leaped to Elva's side, almost sliding off the lev-step before he caught his balance. He grasped her arm.

"What's going on?"

But her only answer was a gasp.

"Ah . . ."

She shuddered, eyes already growing opaque.

Thanatotrope.

Suicide implant. Self-immolation by conscious decision: undercover operatives used them, choosing death over torture.

"Elva! No—"

The Seer spun away, silver highlights sliding across the helm-throne's polished dome.

I SHOULD NOT HAVE REVEALED SO MUCH.

Blue lightning coruscated angrily.

MY SCANFIELDS CAN'T DETECT—BUT IT'S TOO LATE NOW.

Elva's body was growing slack and heavy in Tom's arm, her eyes half-lidded as though sleep was upon her.

"*My love* . . ." Shaking, she reached out, touched Tom's mouth with a gentle fingertip. ". . . *always* . . ."

The most important words he had ever heard: they changed his life in an instant.

I'M SORRY . . .

"Forever," he said, meaning it.

And kissed her soft lips as she died.

5

NULAPEIRON AD 3418

Pale, triangular face. Green eyes, dark with concern.

"Go away." His voice was a distant grey whisper.

Her soft touch against his cheek.

Elva, dying . . .

"I think you should leave"—the red-haired medic, Xyenquil—"for now, Mistress Nirilya."

Vassals stood statue-like against the plain polished wall, staring straight ahead.

"He needs me."

Tom's face was like stone when he turned to look at her: "Go away. Now."

A faux-comic moment: in the med hall's main corridor, a long bundle slipped from the lev-pallet as it bucked—"Watch out!"—but one of the attendants caught the thing just in time: Elva's corpse, bound in russet cloth.

"Where are they taking her?" Tom asked.

"Sir—"

"I'm her Liege Lord."

Xyenquil sighed. "For autopsy. By our laws, we can—Lord Corcorigan, it would be better if we have your authorization."

Tom stared at him for a long moment.

Then, mechanically: "Proceed."

His thumb ring sparked, recording the agreement.

Back in the apartment, he looked inside the chamber which had been readied for his rehabilitation. The laminar-flow running pad, the adjustable slope of the carefully designed climbing wall, with its jokey gargoyle-featured protuberances.

Prepared to Elva's specifications. Who else could know him so well?

"Elva . . . I'm sorry." Too stunned to sob, he stood with tears tracking down his face, making no attempt to brush them away. "Nirilya was . . . a mistake."

He gasped, and leaned against the doorway's arch, feeling his legs about to give way.

Please come back.

But no-one knew better than he the futility of prayers to Fate.

There was no sleep that night.

Instead, he sat facing Elva's chair—the one she had used most often over the past few days—with glowglimmers tuned almost to pitch darkness, wrapped in deep shadows, remembering the past, picking over every mistake he had made.

Too many . . .

He and Elva had never even kissed, until the moment of her death. There were so many times he could have spoken up, could have done things differently. So often, he had seen Liege Lords abuse their privileges . . . but he had broken so many other precedents, so many other rules. Surely he could have managed this properly. And their backgrounds, his and Elva's, had been the same.

As far as he knew.

"It was always Litha who was the important one."

It was what she had said, before death came to shut her down at her own command.

Who is Litha? Or who was she?

Someone that important to Elva, someone she would mention in her final breath . . . And Tom had no idea who Litha might be.

Elva. There's so much I need to ask you.

But death is the final stripper of illusions. It cuts away the pleasant images we use to cocoon ourselves during the everyday, the insulating fluff of social interactions and light-hearted entertainments, leaving bare the starkest of realities: that every life must end, and in its wake leave survivors to contemplate their loved one's passing, the inevitability of their own extinction.

And worse: that even initial grief-heat passes, slowly cooling as the survivors' energies begin to ebb, leaving stunned acceptance in its wake, and unwiped tears which grow as cold as death.

There had been a brother: Odom Strelsthorm, whose wedding Tom had attended, four Standard Years ago. But Odom and his wife Trilina would be impossible to find—even by courier—given the conditions in Gelmethri Syektor.

It had taken Tom and Elva four tendays to reach the Grand'aume; and it had taken all of Elva's skills to make the arrangements, to get them here. Yet she had not once complained.

Damn it all to Chaos . . .

Gritty-eyed, Tom waved open a series of displays and traced through news-holos, using his noble-house access rights—valid even here, in this realm which boasted no Lords or Ladies of its own—to trace the revolution's path. Wondering if he could search out the family Strelsthorm; knowing it was impossible.

It was not just an academic exercise. For most of the four SY since Elva's brother had married, Tom had lived in exile, far from the revolution which suddenly seemed as arbitrary and meaningless as the cruel and overbearing system it was meant to replace.

Tom wiped his face, tried to focus on the holo reports.

Half-melted corpses; smoke-blackened tunnels. "Sources implicating the White Glowclusters have disappeared in mysterious . . ."

Gesturing, he interrogated the *White Glowclusters* tricon. The three-dimensional ideograph changed shade, unfurled like a blossoming flower, revealing intricate inner facets which read:

. . . a secret society of Zhongguo Ren origin, affiliated with the Strontium Dragons and known to be responsible for the following atrocities . . .

Enough.

He had friends among those secret societies.

Tom explored another link.

Consul Populis, a breakaway LudusVitae action brigade, came to power in Luftwin Sectoris during the second putsch. They discovered documents implicating revanchist noble houses, led by Lord Delivglan, in the arming of General d'Ovraison, the notorious Butcher of Lenkilion . . .

"Stop."

He waved the holos away.

It was a nightmare.

Corduven's bias, briefing Tom, had been different—he hardly considered himself a butcher—but the facts remained as he had outlined them: for two Standard Years, since the abortive global action code-named Flashpoint, there had been bloodshed and confusion in hundreds of realms. Widespread so-called revolution . . . yet nothing had changed for the better.

Nobles and repressed commoners . . . They could all go to Chaos and Perdition, if only Tom could have her back.

Elva. I need you.

But there was no-one there to answer.

A low chime sounded.

Elva's back!

Then he shut down his emotions, cursing himself.

No, I don't think so.

Grimly, he waved the doorshimmer away, and saw Nirilya standing there.

"I don't"—he spoke quickly, before she could interject—"want to see you just now."

"I know." Nirilya bowed her head. "But the . . . the Seer is expecting you. In three hours."

Expecting me?

Tom remembered Elva's ironic comment: "*I dare say the Seer knows we're coming.*"

Half-laughing, half-sobbing: "You mean, it's my Destiny to go?"

Nirilya stared at him, confused.

"Leave me, Nirilya. Now."

"All right." Stepping back into the corridor outside. "I—"

Doorshimmer, coalescing into place.

Ice bitch. It's all your fault.

But he would not have felt such rage if it had been even remotely true. For there was only one person responsible for Elva's death; and now it seemed that he was the one who lacked the strength to carry on alone.

He reached inside his tunic, pulled out his stallion talisman. He made the control gesture—a conjunctive sequence of protokinemes, a compound order: a substitute for a left-handed gesture—and it fell apart into two neat halves.

Black nul-gel coated the crystal.

"This was my real advantage. Not ability."

He had been fourteen SY old when a renegade Pilot—a figure out of legend, until she proved they were real—had given him the comms crystal. It had acted as a teaching document, and more: a communications conduit to mu-space itself, until the last occasion of use had burned it out. Scorch marks marred the smooth curves of an equine body: a stallion, a mythical creature.

Perhaps some functionality remains.

Before, he had been given logosophical puzzles to solve, to extract the next portion of a tale whose exact relationship to historical truth he had never determined. Even with the comms resonator damaged, perhaps those old tales were in there still: a comfort, a link to his past.

An escape. Or a reminder of the first time he had seen Elva, when she was part of the hunt for the Pilot: though the authorities never admitted just what kind of person they tracked down and killed.

And it was Father who had carved the stallion from a solid ingot. Tom could still see those blocky hands guiding the cutting graser with practised skill; hear the spatter of molten metal; taste the hot acrid tang upon the air.

I miss you, Father . . .

Tom inserted the copper download needle, and began the sequence: expecting a replay of earlier modules, but finding instead something new —a continuation of what went before—and in its own way disturbing.

6

TERRA AD 2142

<<Ro's Story>>

[1]

"Race you!"

Albrecht's white lanky body arced through a competent dive into dark waters.

"Bastard." Ro crouched on the old stone jetty, careful of its slippery moss, then swung her arms forwards, propelling herself, and cleanly entered the lake.

He's never won yet.

Swimming fast: freestyle-racer dolphin-crawl.

Faster.

Speed through superior technique: the ongoing mathematical self-analysis of attack angle on the stroke, body alignment cutting turbulence, propulsion from the feet.

Albrecht reached the orange hydroplatform a second before her, caught it just right. By the time she hauled herself up beside him, he was whistling nonchalantly, staring at the pine forest beyond the lake's edge.

Above, jagged white-capped mountains looked serene, majestic.

"You must be getting old." Albrecht spoke in English, as always when he was with her.

"Getting cold." She shivered, aware of her bathing suit's flimsiness and his proximity.

They were both nineteen years old.

"Ro, I've been wanting to ask—"

A flyer was hovering over a clump of pine.

It moved. Ro watched, analysing its parabolic descent, its minute non-automated corrections.

"Oh, God," she said. "It's Gramps. With Mother, I'll bet."

An old-fashioned gull door swung up, and two people alighted onto the stone beach: a slender grey-haired woman, and a stocky, ursine—like a big old Kodiak bear—white-bearded man with wide shoulders and powerful forearms.

"As I thought." Ro double-blinked her left lens to max zoom. "Gramps was flying."

By hand, too. Good for you, Gramps.

Albrecht sucked in a breath.

"Father Mulligan's waving," he said, and lifted a tentative hand in Gramps's direction.

Mother waved too, though facing the wrong way. Nothing new: Karyn McNamara had been blind since before Ro's birth.

Your timing sucks for once, Mother.

"Listen," she said, as Albrecht was preparing to dive. "I've got to tell you—"

"What?"

In a rush: "I'm going to DistribOne, Arizona. An UNSA internship."

Albrecht stopped. The hydroplatform rocked, and for a moment it looked as though he might fall in. Then he sat back down.

There was so much he could say: that she had tagged her name onto the h-mail petition going around the schoolNets in protest at the United Nations' growing power; that signing on with their space agency smacked of hypocrisy. And he knew her mother well enough to realize that Karyn would not approve. But all he managed was:

"That's in AmeriFed."

"Yes." Ro felt miserable. "My exam results were good enough—"

"But you're just starting your second year."

"The internship runs in parallel."

She was studying with the Technische Netteninstitut von Zürich, but it was instantiated in EveryWare: location was irrelevant.

Albrecht blinked rapidly.

"Shit." Ro swallowed. "This isn't easy."

"It seems easy enough for you." And then a bitter non sequitur, designed to hurt: "Violet eyes are passé, you know."

He threw himself into a graceless dive, splashing her.

"Al—"

Hugging herself for warmth, she watched him strike out for the shore.

"I'm sorry." Grandfather spread his hands wide. "I didn't think to bring a towel."

"That's OK." Ro stood on tiptoe, kissed his leathery cheek.

She had swum directly to the beach; her clothes—a bright pink jumpsuit, neatly folded—and towel were on the stone jetty, half a klick away.

"How was Adelaide?" she asked.

"Getting hot. We trained on the beach."

He had the thick wrists and forearms of a lifelong aikidoka.

"For God's sake." It was Mother, trying to get a rise out of Grandfather. "Ro? Shall we meet back at the school?"

Grandfather—Father Michael Mulligan SJ, PhD, DSc—grinned, and shrugged his heavy shoulders. He really looked like a friendly bear.

"Your fault," he said. "She's annoyed because your strand's offline."

Ro nodded towards the jetty. "I left it with my stuff."

They would in fact approve: both reckoned that young people leaned too much on EveryWare.

"So you missed the news." Mother stood with her hands on her hips.

Silver sockets, where her eyes should have been, glinted in the September sun.

"What news?"

"Your canton-reg has come through."

Ro fell silent.

So I'm a voting citizen now.

And she no longer needed anyone's approval to work abroad.

At the jetty, she performed a towel dance: wriggling out of her swimsuit, kicking it aside, pulling on the pink jumpsuit. Grandfather had flown Mother back to the school, and there was no-one else in sight, but you never—

A bush rustled, and she grew still.

Nothing.

Shaking her head, Ro slipped her boots on, then wound her golden infostrand necklet wise round her throat. Picking up her towel, she began to climb the uneven hillside path.

It passed close to dark rhododendron bushes and *someone grabbed her* but she moved very fast, clamping the wrist and dropping him—*watch it*—ignoring her attacker's yell as she struck hard with her knee, tracking the vectors by reflex—*no!*—and pulled down at the last moment, smashing collarbone instead of throat.

You moron.

If she had struck a few centimetres higher . . .

"Christ!"—Albrecht, down on his knees, his face white—"Ach . . . I think you've broken my wrist. And my chest . . ."

"I nearly killed you." She turned away from him.

"But you have to—"

Over her shoulder: "*Help is EveryWare.* Isn't that what they say?"

And Albrecht's strand was a subcutaneous implant.

She began to climb.

"Come back!"

White buildings, low and square beneath the Alpine sky. Deserted gardens: the nuns must be at prayer. The Angelus.

Will I miss this place?

Through the Zen garden—always, the Fibonacci swirls leaping into her mathematical awareness—and into her room.

"Damn you, Al."

She threw her damp towel into a corner.

Making me feel like a freak.

In the bathroom, she thumbed on a mirrorfield.

Violet eyes—no longer fashionable, apparently—stared back at her. In the irises, minuscule Lissajous figures slowly orbited. Hiding her true appearance. Albrecht was one of the few who knew . . .

"Damn you all."

She dabbed at her eyes, and the contacts came out.

"Every last one of you."

And stared at herself: her eyes their natural jet-black—no surrounding whites, just pure obsidian—then smiled, entirely without humour.

Black on black, like the depths of space.

Inhuman eyes.

<<MODULE ENDS>>

7

NULAPEIRON AD 3418

Sturmgard, with its dark, high caverns, lined with statues of the warrior dead: seated rows of brooding figures, their stone broadswords splashed with incongruous bright shades of mutated fluorofungus.

A light drizzle fell.

Looking up, it was impossible to tell where the rainfall began. Somewhere between the black shadows crowding the ceiling's apex and the brighter lit alcoves below, silvery drops condensed into existence, slid down towards the walking pilgrims.

"But the district legato approved my—"

Behind Tom, an unfortunate freedman's complaint was shut off. The hall's guards, not known for their tolerance, barred whomever they pleased.

Tom limped into the Dringhalle, leaning heavily on his black cane. The leg was hurting again, but Xyenquil had assured him the femtocytes were destroyed; it was merely muscle damage and ordinary infection, responding to treatment. In the meantime, having found his cane, he made use of it; in his current weakened state, it could also be a weapon—

Tricon projection.

It leaped out at him, though the pattern was subtle: a mere scratching in frost, a sketched outline upon a rime-coated shield. Already, soft steady rain was dissolving it while Tom watched; the sign must have been laser-etched within the past minute.

It was crudely two-dimensional—any tricon needed volume and colour and movement to convey true meaning—but this was a projection, an ideogram aspect, and it scared the Chaos out of Tom.

Danger.

His skin crawled.

Trying to be subtle, Tom scanned his surroundings, focusing on the people, knowing that femtotech-array surveillance was impossible to detect by unaided sight. Near the Dringhalle's main aisle, off-duty militiamen in uniform were handing around a ganja mask within their group: illegal as Chaos in public, but they could get away with it.

Pilgrims, other travellers, passing by . . . One richly garbed merchant flanked by copper-helmed housecarls . . . Nothing suspicious.

No-one even glanced at Tom.

It could be anyone.

But the melting frost symbol was a code aimed specifically at him: a LudusVitae cipher, active four SY before—when Tom was part of the movement—and surely not used since then. Despite the intervening years, Tom recognized the code tag immediately.

Request immediate rendezvous.

While the angled outline modified the content with its own additional warning:

Fully urgent.

There were directions encoded in the now dissolved sign, and Tom followed them. Turning right, he followed a tessellated pathway—burnt orange and off-white mosaic—into raw natural caverns which sparkled with mineral seams.

The air was moist and warm, heavy with vapour. By a bubbling mud pool, a wide raised platform offered bright refreshment tents, and pastel pink and blue ceramic tables at which travellers might sit.

Tom took a seat with his back to the safety rail, beside a big, painfully fluorescent orange tent.

"Sir?" A vassal with stunted limbs and heavy brow. "Anything to drink, good traveller?"

"Daistral. Any flavour."

"Can I offer—?"

"Just the daistral."

As the vassal went away, Tom watched the other resting travellers. Two matronly women seated nearby, one with a leashed vrulspike at her feet, were giving their order to a barefoot female vassal.

". . . of krilajuice for Bubbsy. He's very thirsty."

The reptile's forked tongue licked the vassal's bare ankle, leaving a red acidic mark.

"*Makes you wonder*"—the whisper came from Tom's side—"*why we bothered, doesn't it?*"

But he could not turn; the vassal was returning.

"Ah, thank you."

Tom passed over a cred-sliver.

Then he leaned back as the vassal left, stared up at a purple moss-coated stalactite, and murmured: "Sentinel. How have you been?"

For there was no mistaking that patrician voice.

If he wanted to kill me, I'd already be dead.

He had been highly placed in Ludus Vitae's senior command, this Sentinel. Highly placed in society too, presumably, though Tom knew the man only by his codename.

"My state of health is irrelevant." The voice came from the tent. "But you . . . Have the years of schoolteaching dulled your . . ." Sentinel stopped, chuckled. "Apparently not, given recent events in Darinia Demesne."

There was a narrow slit in the bright orange tent fabric. Inside, a hint of blocky features, cropped white hair.

"What do you want?" Tom spoke with minimal lip movement. If Sturmgard Security had them under surveillance . . .

But Sentinel had never been careless. Grant him that much.

"To offer you a job, Thomas Corcorigan. Perhaps even a new life."

A life without Elva.

Using the cane, Tom levered himself upright without a word, and walked.

Glowing hexagonal flukes—mating thermidors—arced briefly through the air, dropped back into glowing lava with a liquid plop.

"Look out!"

Lava splash, but the spectators moved back in time. It hissed, cooled, grew dark, and somebody laughed in relief.

Maybe I should have said yes.

Tom stared, uninterested, at the lava pool, at the travellers enjoying their too brief wander-leave. He was blanketed in a thick fatigue that had nothing to do with physical illness or its aftermath. For someone who had killed an Oracle by playing tricks with Destiny, it was stupid: he was trapped in a Fate whose meaning was lost beyond redemption.

"Perhaps even a new life . . ."

In four tendays of travelling, Elva had become so much a part of his existence that her absence was like a vacuum: impossible to breathe, and ultimately fatal. Leaning on the cane, Tom watched the bubbling lava without thought, aware only of the pressure of his loss.

"Help me!"

A heavy woman, gesticulating.

"My bag . . ." Breathlessly: "He's got it . . ."

He came fast, weaving through the crowd: a lithe youth, narrow legs pumping, a dark bag clutched in his grip.

Thief.

Tom tried to react but it was too late. The youth was already past him—*I'm supposed to be a fighter*—and Tom had to turn, hoist his cane, and break into a slow jog. Pain flared in his left thigh.

And then it became obvious that there was no need to push himself, and he slowed down, coming to a painful stop, and stood there with the cane's support, wondering what it was that he had just witnessed.

They moved so fast.

The trained perceptions of a phi2dao fighter, the art in which he had trained since his early servitor days under Maestro da Silva's exacting tutelage, were suddenly rendered useless by four young men who reacted more quickly than he could apprehend, in a way which seemed entirely mysterious, beyond any rational or sensible understanding.

"Let me—*Mmph.*"

The thief's face was pressed into the hard ground by a heavy bootheel. He writhed once, tried to buck his captors off; but his wrists and ankles were held in unbreakable grips.

With the struggling thief locked into place, prone and trapped, the nature of those wrist and ankle holds became clear. What Tom could not understand was the way the four men had materialized from the crowd, shifted into existence around the fleeing thief, and slammed into him in synchrony.

The thief stood no chance against a sixteen-limbed organism which moved at lightning speed, with absolute determination and not a microsecond's hesitation.

Then two more stepped forward from the crowd; one of them picked up the fallen bag and returned it to the woman who had cried out. Another stabbed down with a foreknuckle, and the thief lay still.

"Don't hurt him . . ." the woman protested, too late.

Her saviours stood around her, their faces stony blank, with signs of neither victory nor remorse. And Tom could see, as he limped slowly past, that though the men were dressed in drab-coloured mufti, each wore a shining scarlet cravat tied in military fashion round his throat.

It was bright red, that fabric: the shade of oxygen-rich blood spurting from a dead Oracle's arteries, or of scarlet jumpsuits worn by children beside a black icy lake, who demonstrated the same ability to move in unison without spoken command, betraying no sign of individuality or weakness, and raised the same sensation of creeping dread in any rational onlooker.

Tom passed a gloomy corridor, alcoves covered with stained and faded drapes, where a hand-scraped holosign read *Scragg's SleepEasy*. Tom would have smiled; but the name was not meant as a joke. Drudges, with careworn faces, walked by: barefoot, every one.

So much for the revolution.

There was a short cut, unlit: no fluorofungus on the ceiling. Tom held his breath, walked through the dead-zone, and took a shuddering breath of fresh air when he reached the bright cross-tunnel at the end.

No sign of anyone following. Shivering, he walked, pain throbbing in his thigh.

He knew that psychopaths, born without the normal modalities of consciousness and conscience, were neurologically different. Before his logosophically trained analytical abilities, it was impossible to deny the darker aspects of his own obsessive, driven, often violent past.

But he knew that the men he had seen today were something other than social outcasts, or unfortunate individuals damaged in the womb. Their strange abilities stemmed from more than military training.

They might be more or less than human, but they were certainly *other*. Even now, concerned only with Elva's loss, when geopolitics and eldritch phenomena had never seemed less relevant, Tom feared them.

Checkpoint.

*** AURINEATE CORE ***

Militia squad. Stone faces, gleaming graser rifles.

*** TRAVEL-TAGS REQUIRED ***

Tom's tag sparked with ruby light, and then he was out of Sturm-gard and back amid the rich security which pervaded central Aurineate Grand'aume.

A patio led to moss gardens, overlooking a broad boulevard running crosswise. Tom walked to the balustrade, leaned over. There was plenty of foot traffic—freedmen, vassals and servitors dragging smoothcarts —and, in the central aisle, slow-moving levanquins encrusted with baroque ornamentation. The soft lyrical mating songs of caged blind-moths floated upwards.

A few lev-cars glided just beneath the marble ceiling, and some of them were studded with precious rubies and sapphires, their interiors rich with exotic fabrics, perfumed with exquisite scents from Sectorin Fralnitsa or the blind chemist sages of Rilkutan.

The Aurineate Grand'aume was possibly the most prosperous realm Tom had visited. But he could not help wondering if scarcity and squalor were likewise absent from the lower strata, and whether their inhabitants knew anything of the wealth and luxury enjoyed by those who dwelt above.

Emerald lights strobed.

Tom stepped back from the balustrade just as a lev-car drew level, hovering, while fluorescent emerald-green rings pulsed along its hull. Its membrane-door softened and liquefied; a man poked his head through.

"Lord Corcorigan?" The driver was blond, lightly bearded, with an amber ovoid set beneath his left cheekbone. "My name is Ralkin Vel-sivith. I'd be honoured, sir, if you would step aboard."

No weapons were visible, but there were other means of coercion and Tom could not be bothered to argue with someone who flew an official vehicle but used the polite forms.

Instead, Tom laid his black cane on the balustrade, swung his legs over so that he was standing on the lev-car's vestigial stub wing, retrieved his cane and climbed inside.

The cabin was small, furnished in black: comfortable, but not luxurious.

"What does the flashing green indicate?" Tom gestured at the sliding green pulses outside, now appearing muted: filtered out to avoid distraction. "Security services?"

"Oh, no." Velsivith took the car down a few metres, then stepped up the speed. "That's for civilian use: anyone can turn on their emergency strobe."

But Velsivith was not a civilian. No ordinary inhabitant of the Grand'aume's highest stratum would travel with a blatant silver dagger sheathed hilt forward at each hip, in a double cross-draw position designed for speed and misdirection.

"So if you're late for dinner"—despite himself, Tom was intrigued by the notion of emergency signals for everyone—"you just turn on the strobe and redplane the speed."

"Ha! No . . . There's a specified list of valid domestic emergencies."

"Even so." Tom looked out at the boulevard flowing past below.

"The penalty for misuse"—with a glance at Tom—"is amputation of a hand. First offence."

"Really." And when Velsivith's face tightened in silence, Tom added: "Interesting realm you have here, sir."

The lev-car banked left, accelerating hard.

They touched down in a holding bay lined with marble, where each wall bore a shield-like crest wrought from iron, surmounted by spikes like black metallic thorns. They descended from the lev-car and Velsivith led Tom to an octagonal reception chamber.

Silver security mannequins stood in all eight corners, their liquid silver skins filled with twisted reflections of their red granite surroundings, and distorted images of each person who entered here.

From behind a marble-fronted desk, the duty officer, a pretty plumpish woman, told Tom to take a seat.

"They'll be with you shortly, sir."

The Aurineate Grand'aume's official seal-of-the-realm, a complex tricon of two hundred hues and convoluted topography, rotated endlessly above her desk.

Velsivith touched finger to forehead in salute. "I'll take my leave, Lord Corcorigan."

The amber ovoid inset in his cheek, catching a spark of golden light, seemed to wink at Tom. "Good luck." And, to the duty officer: "See ya later, darlin'."

She sighed and shook her head, more from tiredness than annoyance.

Tom sat down, and watched Velsivith leave. He leaned back.

And waited.

Then, driven by a feeling he could not have named, he stood up with his cane's assistance, avoided the receptionist's gaze and walked slowly out through the square archway which Velsivith had used. The silver mannequins remained unmoving as he passed.

Outside, Tom found himself in a ring-shaped chamber around a central well. In the atrium below, Velsivith was greeting a slender, dark-cloaked, pale-eyed woman, kissing her with the ease of long familiarity.

They left together, hand in hand. Tom pondered on them, on the way the woman had moved, the way she cocked her head at Velsivith's approach. It came to him that the woman was blind, and intimate with Velsivith yet not dependent on him.

It gave an interesting insight into the man, a contrast to his breezy flirtation with the receptionist. Smiling sadly, Tom returned to the reception chamber and regained his seat.

His injured thigh began to ache once more, but this time the pain seemed almost welcome: like an old friend dropping in for a visit, unannounced and with no indication whether this was a brief reunion or an extended stay.

They were very respectful. When they showed him into the low-ceilinged chamber, motioning him towards a plain but comfortable lev-chair, they used polite forms of address, and couched every order as a humble yet formal request.

But it was clear nonetheless that he was not at liberty to leave without answering their questions, and that if he tried he would learn the difference between a social occasion and an interrogation.

There were three of them, and they introduced themselves in turn. Feldrif sat to Tom's left: lean and black-skinned, his pale silk tunic adorned with ruffles whose frivolity was in sharp contrast to the gauntness of his face, the watchful intelligence in his amber eyes.

On Tom's right, Altigorn was a plump white man in burgundy robes, with fat-folds squeezing his eyes almost shut. An off-cycle eunuch, whose implants could flood his body with testosterone and adrenaline at will, his bulk comprising muscle as well as fat: not to be underestimated.

While in front of him sat Muldavika: scalp shaven on the left, straw-coloured hair hanging to her right shoulder, a row of ruby stars across her forehead.

"I'm an Iota," she said, noticing his attention. "Don't worry, I won't try to convert you."

"I'm sorry?"

Feldrif's laugh was not entirely pleasant.

"She's a warden," he explained, "in the Church of the Incompressible Algorithm. No-one holds it against her."

There was no way for Tom to interpret this comment: one culture's insult is another's irony. Muldavika's expression was unreadable, hard as stone.

After that, they got down to business.

"The first commoner to be elevated to Lordship in Gelmethri Syektor for nearly a century." Holo-tesseracts delineated Tom's biography; Feldrif read the highlights aloud. "Remarkable logosophical ability, by all accounts. Ruled Corcorigan Demesne"—he looked up, amber eyes filled with private speculation—"for only two SY, before disappearing without explanation."

Tom said nothing.

"And you reappeared, after four SY," Feldrif continued, "just a few tendays ago. Believed to have assisted in a special forces operation which ended a show trial of captured nobles. And which somehow"—frowning now—"seems to have led to the cessation of violence in that sector."

Fate, I hope so.

"We're not altogether clear, Lord Corcorigan, just how that was accomplished."

"Just lucky, I guess."

Muldavika's face tightened. In her church, *luck* was blasphemy.

"You'll understand," said Altigorn, his jowls wobbling as he spoke, "that the Seer is a most, er, valuable resource within our realm. Any unexplained death in his presence is a matter of grave concern."

Elva.

Tom blinked, unable to speak.

Why did you do it?

But then he regained a measure of composure, and answered: "Your Seer was never in any danger. Not from me, and not from Elva."

His three interrogators exchanged looks.

An hour later:

"You have our full sympathy"—Feldrif, speaking smoothly, was covering the same ground yet again—"Lord Corcorigan. You'll appreciate our concern."

"I don't know . . ." Tom clenched his fist, released it. "Why she had to kill herself."

"*Had* to, my Lord?" Muldavika leaned towards Tom. "You make it sound like a duty."

"How else do you interpret what she said? The way she—"

That was when he stopped, realizing what was wrong with their line of questioning.

"Why don't you know this already?"

Feldrif: "What do you mean?"

"If the Seer is that important, you have his chambers under surveillance."

A long silence.

Then Muldavika said, "Captain Elva Strelsthorm's final words were, near enough, *'I've another loyalty, and this one goes right back to childhood.'* What do you think she meant by that?"

Tom looked away.

"I've known her," he said finally, "since I was fourteen SY old. But I have no idea what she was referring to."

A deeper layer of questioning:

"Did you work with many agents, my Lord, who bore thanatotropic implants?"

That told him all he needed to know about their background knowledge, of both him and Elva.

"No," he said after a moment. "But I knew of their . . . Look." He stopped, wiped perspiration from his forehead. *"I don't know.* You commit suicide to avoid torture, or out of despair, but neither one applied to Elva. She—" He choked then, and could not continue.

"Take a minute, my Lord."

"No . . ." Tom blinked, essayed a humourless smile. "Your own deepscans didn't work, did they?"

"My Lord?"

"You didn't detect Elva's implant . . ." But his voice trailed off as he registered the odd expressions on his three interrogators' faces. "What is it? Am I missing something?"

It was Muldavika who let out a long breath, and told Tom more than he wanted to know about the manner of Elva's dying.

"Tanglethreads are undetectable even by deepscans, Lord Corcorigan. As I'm sure you are aware."

"What?"

The term she used was one he had not heard beyond the realm of fiction, and never within the ranks of LudusVitae.

"You weren't aware of this." Feldrif was reading from a lased-in display: Tom's physiometric readouts. "Which means, of course, you are free to go, my Lord."

His tone was polite enough, but still a dismissal.

"Thank you."

There was little else to say.

But as he was starting to walk away, it was Altigorn who said:

"One other thing, Lord Corcorigan. What does the term *Blight* mean to you?"

Tom turned, frowning. "Nothing at all."

"Or"—Feldrif, this time—"*Dark Fire*, my Lord?"

What?

There was a sharp intake of breath from Muldavika. Tom's heart pounded; surely his telemetry readings had leapt off the scale.

"All right . . ."

But the answer he gave must have satisfied them even less than himself.

". . . I've been dreaming of black flames. Every night since Elva . . . since it happened. It scares me, but I've no idea what it means."

It sounded insane; but their own scanners showed that he did not lie.

Elva . . . What was this other loyalty you held?

None of it made sense.

I would have helped, if you'd only asked . . .

But there was no-one to hear his devastated grief, or to frame a reply which might seem remotely rational.

8

NULAPEIRON AD 3418

The one who is gone
(Now she's no longer here)
Her dark memories torn
Leave dry tunnels sere.
You see it, don't you?
How the void lingers through?
. . . Now Elva is gone.

Cold ice, solid stone
And maha *pervades all:*
Now we are alone
Thin illusion must pall.
Only twists, superstrings—
Mathematical things—
Since Elva is gone.

Fluorofungal shine
And glowcluster shimmer
Flood entropic time:
Die Zeit tot uns immer.
Just interstices—
Empty space, if you please—
For Elva is gone.
Shadows, pale shade
(Empty core, surface hard)
By consensus made
Our atomic facade.
It's reductio
Ad vacuum, *I know—*
But Elva is gone.

Emergent conceit—
Warmth, love: obsolete
Now Elva is gone.

She would have wanted a funnier epitaph. But every attempt at whimsy seemed odd and painful, incongruous in a world drained of colour and warmth, left hard and brittle in the aftermath of her passing.

Tom hugged his cape about himself. The time for tears was past: death was too enormous, too implacable, for such fragile shows of emotion.

Icy mist, black lake. Above, the shadowed ceiling, the half-glimpsed edelaces.

A blink of time, and our cosmos ends.

And now, and forever: a universe without Elva.

We never even kissed, until the end.

Yet he was her Liege Lord: a position he had seen abused so often that . . . But the thought brought no comfort.

Tom shivered.

And heard. "They come."

The priestess prayed.

Eight russet-liveried vassals slid the white cocoon out onto the water. The black lake was flat and silent, and there was no draught in the chill air, as though the cavern itself held its breath.

Beside Tom, Xyenquil formed a prayer-mudra with his fingers, accompanying the priestess. Rows of vassals stood to attention. Nirilya remained well back, near an exit. Her hood was black; her dark robes fluttered, in a breeze which did not exist.

Tom watched the cocoon drift towards the lake's centre. Inside, teloworms would already be at work, digesting the flesh that had once borne Elva's spirit.

". . . *our daughter, that was instantiated, is now complete. Solved and demonstrated: the algorithm of her life is worked out, and honours thereby the greater whole . . .*"

Above, among frost-rimed stalactites, edelaces fluttered. Others glided in from shadowed tunnels.

"... *the nöomatrix, whence the Omega Singularity comes, to collapse the holy cosmic function, observed by Its omniscient love ...*"

A fragile edelace drifted down, and draped itself across the white cocoon. Tom shivered, but could not look away.

Another edelace dropped.

"... *to the depths, conjoining her remains ...*"

More descended, fragile and fluttering, blanketing the cocoon with their lacy forms.

Elva. Please come back ...

It began to sink beneath the dark waters.

The edelaces would digest the cocoon and absorb the teloworms which had fed upon Elva's body and broken down the bones; the teloworms themselves, as parasites, would live on inside the edelaces, to catalyse their hosts' reproduction, bringing forth new life in white fragile forms whose beauty was legendary and whose toxins were deadly.

Elva.

The cocoon sank, disappeared. Recitation over, the priestess bowed.

Elva, my only love.

The lake was black and still.

Suddenly *it moved* and he sat bolt upright in his sweat-soaked bed, surrounded by gloomy darkness, breathing hard as though sprinting for a long race's finish line.

When he looked down at his stump it was shrouded in shadows and then *it moved again* and he jerked back in fear. It was a tiny motion. The bud-hand, centimetres longer than yesterday, had only twitched, but the sensation was massive and electric.

A gift from Elva?

He lay back down, head turned to the right, away from the new growth, and wondered what kind of world it was when even his body and his dreams were not his own. And prepared for a gritty-eyed, sleepless wait for the morningshift to come.

Walking, at random. He carried the cane, but as precaution, not necessity.

Floor hatch revolving, slats falling into place.

Tom followed the spiral stairs down to the Secundum Stratum. Checking his travel-tag—making sure he could return—he walked to the nearest hatch and descended again, down to Tertium.

It was like a scene from childhood, though richer: an Aqua Hall, silvery streams tinkling, a ceramic sculpture fountain. Queuing vassals, empty containers in hand, ration-spikes tucked into their belts. In the corridor beyond, two white-haired women were struggling with filled containers.

"Please," said Tom. "Allow me."

He used his cane as a yoke, slinging it through the carry ropes. Then he laid it across his shoulders and stood upright.

"Ladies?"

"I'm Eta," said one of the women. And, "I'm Ara," said the other.

Sloshing water made the burden awkward.

"My name's Tom. Er . . . Which way?"

Terracotta-walled corridor. He deposited the containers just inside the indicated alcove: a plain, clean dwelling.

"Thank you, Tom."

"Would you stay, Tom, for some daistral?"

Tom wiped his forehead. His thigh was beginning to throb.

"I must go. But thank you."

As he left, pulling the curtain closed behind, he saw the two women clasp hands, and wondered at their relationship. Tom had lost too much not to recognize love when he saw it, and he smiled wistfully, just for a second, before walking on.

"Spare a sliver, noble giver?" An urchin, cap in hand. "Grant a mil for our thespian thrill?"

Tom stopped, leaning on his cane.

A troupe of mummers, amid a ring of spectators up ahead, was giving a performance. One holomasked player, with two faces staring in opposite directions, represented an Oracle.

"Please, noble sir. A small donation fends off starv—"

The urchin's voice trailed off.

One of the mummers, blunt ceramic dagger upraised, had his other arm behind his back, hidden beneath a half-cape, and Tom shivered in recognition, hoping that no-one would make the connection between the allegorical performance in front of them and the one-armed man who stood behind the audience.

"I'm neither cold"—the urchin—"nor very old. My time's not yet, pale Dr. Death."

Making a ward sign, he slipped away, was lost among the onlookers.

Tom turned.

"My Lord." It was Xyenquil, smiling with chagrin. "I'm the district coroner, among other duties. Hence the young lad's—"

"I understand." Tom spoke quickly, to distract him from the mummers' performance. "You're here on business, Doctor?"

Xyenquil ran a hand through his curly red hair.

"Not, ah . . . No. I was hoping to talk to you."

But not, Tom realized, on official premises.

"Talk about what?" Then he remembered the interrogation he had undergone, and everything they had said about Elva. "The neurosurgery. Elva's implants. What exactly was done to her?"

Xyenquil's blue eyes held an unreadable expression, and he replied with a question of his own which at first seemed neither interesting nor relevant.

"Is it true that Lords study *all* the logosophical disciplines?"

Quietly: "Yes. It's true."

"Ah. If only . . . Well, you'll know then, sir, of quantum entanglement. Pairs of particles prepared so that one will always be in some way the duplicate or the exact inverse of the other: paired spins, polarity, whatever."

"Ancient observations, Doctor. A thousand SY old. More."

"But it's ancient knowledge," said Xyenquil, "which has never lost its mystery. Not to me, at least."

It is one of the key indicators that the universe is stranger than it looks: some outcomes are determined by the nature of the experiment—a particle's properties are partially determined by the way a human observer chooses to measure it. When particles are paired, then separated by vast distances . . . whenever one particle is observed, the partner *instantaneously* changes, to remain its partner's duplicate or inverse.

It was fundamental to the Oracles' existence: since information cannot travel faster than light, the entanglement-relationship travels *backwards* through time.

"So why exactly," asked Xyenquil, "would an extended femtarray, an *entangled* femtarray, be threaded throughout Elva Strelsthorm's nervous system?"

Tom stared at him.

"I'm risking a great deal to tell you this, my Lord." Xyenquil swallowed. "But there are things happening in government departments right now which make me feel, well, uncomfortable. I just thought you should know."

It was the first indication Tom had received that the medical centre was more than just a private concern. And a hint of strange occurrences among official organizations . . .

Was that the source of the fear he had sensed, among those who were questioning him? A burgeoning coup d'état, or some other great internal change about to come over this realm's administration?

But whatever was going on, it was obvious that there were individuals with a sense of decency and honour which overrode considerations of protocol and regulations, even in a dangerous political climate.

"Thank you, Doctor."

Tom's interrogators had mentioned tanglethreads. But he had thought it was to do with encrypted comms, not the entire basis of Elva's identity . . .

And then the enormous implication of what Xyenquil was saying hit him like a sledgehammer, and he dropped to his knees on the flagstones, and vomited profusely even as the medic took hold of him.

"The duplicate . . ." Tom spoke thickly, wiping his lips with the back of his hand.

"Can't possibly be a machine," said Xyenquil. "I'm sure it can't be."

"A person?"

"I'd say so." Xyenquil's grasp, supporting Tom, was stronger than Tom would have expected. "I can't see how else it could be done."

"You're saying she . . ." Tom forced himself to stand upright, and take a step away from Xyenquil. "That there's someone else, somewhere in this world, whose mind is a duplicate of Elva's."

"I'm not sure that *duplicate* is the correct term."

Chaos . . .

"Tell me. Please."

"I'm not—" Xyenquil stopped, continued. "I believe that Captain Strelsthorm's nervous system was intimately interwoven with sensors, quantum-entangled to a similar array in some other person's body. At the moment of death—"

Tom swallowed, but could not look away from him.

"—the entangled pairs collapsed, and a one-off information transfer—a *total* information transfer—pulsed through the link as it was destroyed."

"I daren't believe it."

"But, my Lord . . ." Xyenquil blinked. "I'm sure of it. Her mind effectively over-wrote the other body's personality in that instant. The link was designed that way."

A two-way link: had the other person died first, it would have been Elva who . . .

Elva lives?

Tom closed his eyes, shuddering beneath the impact of an idea whose implications were too big to comprehend.

For if Xyenquil was right, somewhere in this world of ten billion souls there walked a person of unknown appearance and even gender whose thoughts and emotions and memories were those of Elva Strelsthorm, the embodiment of everything that was good and decent and joyful in his life: Elva, whose body had been buried and dissolved within an icy lake, but whose essential beautiful being, whose *soul* might yet survive, close at hand or forever beyond his reach.

9
TERRA AD 2142
<<Ro's Story>>
[2]

Red desert—a startling Martian red: as though this were no longer Terra—to her left, and the distant purple mesa. Above, the clearest deepest sapphire sky she had ever seen: endless and cloudless and pure, beating down with wave after burning wave of heat.

Sand crunched rhythmically beneath her combat boots; her running pace was steady, metronomic.

Last lap.

Rainbow shimmering to her right: the mistfield, surrounding the complex; inside, emerald grass of an almost Irish lustre.

Come on.

Salt taste of sweat. Keeping the pace, Ro undid the bandanna from around her neck, and wiped her forehead. And began to run faster.

Movement. A light-tan ground squirrel stood bolt upright, staring at her.

"Good morning to you," Ro murmured.

Inside the mistfield lay DistribOne: salmon-pink block-shaped buildings, a satellite of PhoenixCentral. Otherwise, the red desert stretched endlessly, flatness relieved only by tall saguaro cacti like green capital *psi*s. Like men with hands upraised.

A Mexican groundsman with sun-darkened skin, hatless, crouched on the sand, was tinkering with a battered grey maint-bot.

"Hi." Ro gave a breathless greeting, continuing to run.

He looked at her with the same expression as the ground squirrel.
They both think I'm mad.

It was early—06:52, the refectory not yet open for breakfast—but the temperature was already 27.4 Celsius. She knew both these facts without any tech devices.

Last two hundred metres, and she poured on the speed.

Pounding past the main path, she slowed to walking pace, jogged back to the white flagstones, and lowered herself into a hamstring stretch. The stone's heat seeped into her muscles, relaxing them. A far cry from Swiss winter training—

"Jesus Christ."

A tiny scorpion scuttled across the path, was gone.

She stopped in the corridor outside her room, skin prickling.

Someone's inside.

Ro did not question her intuition; it had proved accurate too often in the past.

Outside the door, a small holo hung:

*** DOROTHY McNAMARA ***
FlightSciences Dept V
*** ANNE-LOUISE ST CLAIRE ***
PRDiv Sect Gamma3

There was every chance that the "intruder" was in fact the room-mate Ro had not yet met.

She stood there for a moment, regarding the southwestern pastels of her surroundings—burnt orange, pale blue—and considered. It was almost certainly this Anne-Louise; no reason to suspect otherwise. Anne-Louise was due back from her field trip today, though this seemed awfully early.

The door concertinaed open at Ro's gesture.

"Howdy, ma'am." A tall, rangy man tipped his stetson. "Mighty pleased to meet ya."

Deep desert tan. White shirt, narrow black jeans.

Gunbelt.

Ro stared, very closely. Vision told her that a person was standing there. But as for her other senses . . .

"I really don't think so."

Silver badge, glinting. Arizona Ranger.

"Well now, purty—"

But Ro walked straight *through* the cowboy figure, which dissolved into sparkling needles, and slowly disappeared from existence.

From the floor where she sat cross-legged, an elegant dark-haired young woman—she appeared slight, but not fragile—looked up, smiling, and said:

"However did you know?"

"Anne-Louise?" Ro held out her hand. "*Vous êtes Québecoise, n'est-ce pas?*"

"*Ouais.*" She held up her hand and they shook. "*Tu peux me tutoyer, tu sais.* But I'm supposed to be practising my English."

"Me too."

"So how did you know"—Anne-Louise ejected a cassette wafer from her holopad, and rose easily to her feet—"that Clint was a holo?" She threw the wafer.

"Clint?" Ro snatched it from the air: an old-fashioned layered-crystal cassette, the type of lattice wafer that Gramps still preferred to use. "You did say Clint?"

"Clint Shade, Arizona Ranger. My hero."

They sat on their respective beds, facing each other. At the foot of each bed was a desk. Anne-Louise pointed: on her desktop stood Ranger Shade, now just a few centimetres tall, and frozen.

"The hero of *Black Devil Mesa*. My new story."

"Right, they told me." Ro handed back the cassette wafer. "You're a storyfactor."

A Gallic shrug. "An *unpublished* storyfactor."

"Still . . ."

Animated now: "My project's a new character-template shell-language."

"Er, that sounds good." There was a squeeze-bulb of electrolyte replacement fluid on the bedside table. Ro had placed it there before going out to run; she took a gulp now, and it felt good. "Very . . . interesting."

"I suppose." Anne-Louise shrugged again. "My tutor says the primary AIs are too jokey, and the secondary characters are too 'predictably unpredictable.' I mean, what's a hack to do, eh?"

"Too bad." Ro wound her infostrand bracelet-wise round her wrist. "Um . . . I need to take a shower."

"After which, the refectory will be open. Good plan?"

"I reckon so."

Despite the holo graffito in the physics lab washroom—*Flush twice, it's a long way to the refectory*—the food was in fact delicious. Ro spooned more huevos rancheros into her mouth, swallowed, leaned back and sighed.

"Not bad."

"Apart from the coffee." Anne-Louise nevertheless drained her cup.

"You were on an archaeological field trip?"

"Right. A new find. Petroglyphs, my speciality."

The refectory was bright, with floor-to-ceiling windows, and still mostly empty. There were glass-framed sand paintings and Navajo rugs on the orange walls.

"Archaeology, anthro, storytelling. Interesting combination."

A modest shrug. "My mother calls me *le terrassier*. The digger."

"Charming. How come you've an UNSA internship?"

"Apparently '*to stimulate interdisciplinary serendipity, and present a positive image to the academe-nets.*' That's what it said on my application."

"Oh, God."

"*C'est ça.* Actually, it's just money. I do PR, and UNSA gets grant money from a humanities foundation."

"That's . . ." Ro's attention was distracted ". . . not bad."

Anne-Louise looked over her shoulder, to where a lean twentyish man—bronze skin, narrow waist encircled by a silver concho belt, wide athlete's shoulders—was making his way, tray in hand, towards them.

"That," said Anne-Louise, "is Luís."

Definitely not bad.

He stopped by their table.

"Hey." Anne-Louise raised her hand. "*Yá'át'ééh abíní.*"

"And *bonjour* to you." He sat down, and held out his hand to Ro. "I'm Luís Starhome."

"This is Ro," said Anne-Louise. "Cool contacts, don't you think?"

Ro's skin tingled as she shook hands, scarcely noticing the remark about her eyes, which were their natural all-black obsidian.

"Definitely." His attention was all upon her. "She hasn't challenged you to chess yet, Ro?"

"No . . ."

"Don't let her. She's a demon."

"Thanks"—Ro did not even glance in Anne-Louise's direction—"for the warning."

Anne-Louise stood up. "Sorry, guys. I have to finish unpacking. Um, that ceremony at your uncle's hogan, Luís . . ."

"The Skyway?"

"I won't be able to make it. Perhaps Ro would be interested?" She picked up her tray. "Later, guys."

They watched her go, then Luís said formally, "I'm Luís Starhome, as I said, born for the *K'aahanáanii*, the Living Arrow Clan, born into the Tangle People, *Ta'neezahnii*."

Ro nodded, her expression serious, acknowledging the importance of his words. She would have to get Anne-Louise to explain Navajo kinship relations.

"I'm Dorothy," she said, "known as Ro, of the clan McNamara."

Luís's face was a bronze warrior's mask.

"I'd say today"—with a sudden, startling smile—"is a day of bright beginnings."

The morning was given over to a seminar. Old Professor Davenport and his partner, an AI doppelgänger, were entertaining enough, but the fractal calculus was too easy for Ro and she sat quietly, visualizing unblemished bronze skin rather than equations. Dark eyes. A turquoise and silver necklet—

Davenport was asking a question, but the woman beside Ro answered.

Ro let her attention drift again.

The sky was one huge sapphire, still devoid of cloud. At the end of the afternoon, Ro used the outdoor walkway to the dorm block, breathing in the pure still-hot air. Flowering plants were draped across the overhead trellis; a tiny hummingbird darted, insect-quick, among the blooms.

Ro opened the door to her room.

No . . .

A Navajo rug—half beneath, half covering the thing.

Off to one side, a holo floating: a chess game, one piece remaining . . .

Sweet Jesus, no.

Diamond-and-cross pattern, in brick red, earth brown, violet, white. Ro wanted to see only the rug. Outstretched hand upon the floor . . .

Look at the chessboard.

It was a king, just the one piece on the floating holo-board. Blurred . . . but that was her vision failing, not the image's resolution. Staring at the chesspiece.

A distraction . . .

Ro squatted down.

This is not happening.

But she reached out nonetheless.

And, hand trembling, she turned back the rug by one tasselled corner.

Anne-Louise.

The thing's dark tongue protruded, filmed-over eyes staring at opaque infinity, a livid crease encircling the swollen throat. Clothes slashed to shreds. Ankles bound.

Ro cried aloud, like an animal.

But there was no reaction—and never would be—from Anne-Louise's pitiful, desecrated remains.

<<MODULE ENDS>>

10

NULAPEIRON AD 3418

From underneath, it looked powerful and mean: teardrop body flaring backwards, coloured a lustrous butter-yellow, from which its long black tendrils extended.

"Fate." Tom craned back his head, staring upwards. "It's not exactly inconspicuous."

"Double bluff. No-one would expect secretive types, like us, to be riding inside." The amber ovoid, inset in Velsivith's cheek, was warm with reflected yellow light. "That's my theory."

The arachnargos's lower thorax rippled open, and narrow threads extruded down to them, fastened on, then slowly lifted Tom and Velsivith inside.

The crew dropped them off in a red-tiled hall. Tom watched the arachnargos move swiftly away, its tendrils whipping ever faster as it took a tunnel corner at speed and was gone.

"Follow me."

Velsivith led Tom through a short corridor and out onto a threadway.

That same immense shaft. The great sphere, where the Seer dwelt, still floated at the centre. But the shaft itself looked darker, more ominous, and the walls . . .

They rippled with movement.

For a moment Tom had to clutch the safety rail, stricken with vertigo, as the shaft itself seemed momentarily to come alive. But it was an illusion, though the walls were covered with movement, stippled with shapes which seemed small only from this height.

Arachnabugs were crawling up and down the walls, everywhere. Hundreds, maybe thousands, of the one-man military-grade 'bugs, on constant defensive patrol.

"Are you expecting trouble?"

Velsivith answered indirectly. "This is about as safe as anywhere can get."

They made their way down through the swaying threadway—the previous time Tom had come this way, Elva had been with him—with a squadron of Dragoons following. Their marching steps, in time, caused a resonant oscillation in the long transparent tube, and Tom was feeling sickened by the time they reached the huge sphere's entrance.

Velsivith stopped before the door-membrane.

"Go on through, my Lord. You're expected."

Why did the Seer send for me? No matter . . .

Tom stepped inside.

This time, I'll get the answers I require.

Lev-throne, hovering, in the great round chamber.

ORACLE KILLER. The wizened young/old Seer bowed his head forward. **DO YOU SENSE DEATH?**

Tom, not knowing what to make of this, turned sideways on, crouching slightly on the floating step.

YOU THINK—an electric glimmer in the Seer's eyes—**I'M THREATENING YOU?**

"You mean you're not?"

The skull-like throne dropped lower.

YOUR GIFT TO ORACLE D'OVRAISON . . . WAS AN UNEXPECTED SURPRISE. IF YOU'LL FORGIVE THE TAU-TOLOGY.

In fact Tom had simulated an entire personal reality for Gérard d'Ovraison. From a certain moment onwards, the Oracle's foreseen future—which he had been reporting as truecasts all his life until that

time—was a fake, a world of rich, deeply interwoven, implanted perceptions generated by Tom's modelling 'ware, using algorithms which
could never be reified, fulfilled, in the realspace universe.

But in mu-space's fractal dimensions, logic as well as physics grew
more subtle and capable, and the limitations of this reality's mathe-
matics, as outlined by Gödel's Theorem, faded into insignificance.

"I gave the Oracle what he deserved."

Redmetal poignard, sinking in to the hilt.

Tom controlled his breathing: proven logosophically to be the one
natural process which links the unconscious to the conscious mind, a
bridge between autonomic and central nervous systems, the only func
tion where thought and non-thought can share equal control. Since
antiquity, both mystic and fighting disciplines have used breathing
techniques to combat uncertainty and fear, but only a logosopher could
fully understand the reasons why that worked.

He waited.

ENTANGLEMENT—the lev-throne spun a full circle—IS THE
ROOT SYSTEM BENEATH THE COSMOS.

Tom's leg was not healed yet. But adrenaline would power the
attack, if that became necessary: three lev-steps, jump into space,
knife-hand to the throat as he reached the Seer.

YOU WON'T BELIEVE—tricons tinged with ironic blue, as the
helm-throne retreated once more—UNTIL YOU SEE.

"See what?"

Sapphire lightning curled and spat.

The air pulled apart.

Molecules, growing into great glowing shapes, rushed past as he
fell *into* reality. Deeper, inwards . . . until spacetime's fabric unravelled,
and Tom slipped inside the weave.

Twisted spheres of Calabi-Yau geometry.

Illusion.

The sometimes compactified, sometimes limitless extra dimensions of realspace: at ultra-magnification, each geometric point—formerly a tiny, infinitesimal sphere—became a twisted, curlicued complex knot which Tom perceived with a sense beyond sight. He was becoming aware of the world's hidden aspects, the hyperdimensions whose existence human beings can infer but never truly experience.

And then a vision:

Her features are a little softer; her hair is long. An old, old ribbon of scar on her left hand which was never there before.

She is wearing a military uniform of unknown allegiance.

"I would like," she says, to a committee of senior officers, "to make a full report—"

Twist, plunge.

Elva!

He might have screamed.

Again:

Elva spins round, graser pistol in hand, just as the chamber door-membrane denatures and falls apart. Uniformed figures burst in upon her, and she struggles but they are overwhelming her, as five more enter, reinforcements, holding back to train their weapons upon her—

No!

—until a one-armed black-clad figure leaps through an archway, kicks low, hits a second trooper three times before anyone perceives his presence, takes out a third trooper with a high spinning kick—

"Elva. Didn't you know I'd come back for you?"

—and laughs, mad and triumphal, as the others come for him.

And spin.

Twist.

Elva! The new Elva, the one who lives . . .

There was a sense of being torn apart—no, being torn *away* . . . from Elva, from everything, and he reached out yelling but it was too late because the world was rushing past, a great flood of implacable geometry, her image dwindling, slipping away, as atoms shrunk to normal size and reality shivered into being all around him . . .

The Seer's chamber.

"Come back—"

And then he was sprawled face down on the hard lev-stone, arm outstretched towards the illusion of Elva, the future-vision—in which his love still lived—vivid in his mind, while the floating lev-step on which he lay seemed a cold, hard illusion scarcely worthy of consideration.

His entire body trembled once, shuddering uncontrollably.

Tears tracked down the Seer's cheeks.

Tom, sitting up as the shock symptoms eased, stared at him.

"Seer? Why are *you* so . . . ?"

Young/old features, bathed in blue light as lightning continued to crackle and jump around the chamber's flanged walls.

YOU THINK LIFE MEANS SO LITTLE, TO ONE WHO CAN SEE?

Tom shook his head, not understanding.

"I don't—"

GO WELL, MY LORD.

That was when the ceiling fell in.

It enveloped him. From among the panels, a glassine section dropped, instantly forming a block which imprisoned Tom, yet allowed him to breathe.

He raged, but could not move inside a cocoon which was soft and translucent but absolutely massive. Like an amber-trapped insect, he was totally without power or control over his situation, and it stripped him of dignity and purpose, leaving only fear.

Elva!

Trapped, he could just make out the Seer—

Then Tom stopped, and shivered. He ceased his struggles.

Outside, something strange was happening.

A ripple at first, a disturbance in the air which became substantial, a flickering of *black flames* pushing reality apart, and everything seemed very odd and distant but Tom knew that this was not a dream.

Dark Fire . . .

And then it began to grow, that light-sucking conflagration, those flames without heat which seemed the inverse of every fire Tom had ever seen. To grow, to spin . . . to advance towards the Seer, whose helm-throne hung unmoving at the great chamber's centre, heavy with acceptance of his Fate.

Thunderstorm-black, space-black, the disturbance spun faster, accelerated beyond tornado speed, with flickering hints of impossible twistings, mind-bending geometric transformations beyond human comprehension, strange hints of bright scarlet amid black flames whose appearance denied any understanding of the Chaos-driven processes which had given them birth.

The very air shivered apart.

Get out of there, Seer!

But there was nothing the Dark Fire's poor intended victim could do to save himself.

Spacetime itself became fractured, and for a moment Tom thought he glimpsed scarlet-clad human figures within the impossible maelstrom . . . then something reached out, enveloping, and the Seer's scream pierced even the thick imprisoning smartglass: a voice finally made real, in the moment of his final agony. And then the blackness grew absolute, spinning faster but shrinking now . . .

Sweet Fate, Seer.

. . . dwindling to a point . . .

You saw it coming.

. . . flickered . . .

Why didn't you get out of here?

. . . and was gone.

But Tom knew better than anyone how Fate could envelop the most driven of people, and he pressed his hand uselessly against the glassine prison, knowing that he would have to wait for release, and that there was no good he could do for anyone right now.

Outside, the helm-throne floated intact, but the torn red meat scattered around its interior, glistening wet and steaming with diminishing heat, was long past bearing any resemblance to humanity or to life.

11

NULAPEIRON AD 3418

Silver bubbles floated past him as he dreamed.

My Lord . . . Resonance of almost-words, beyond the emerald sea. Warm languor. Friendly femtocytes, gentle as kisses, within his wounds.

"Lord Corcorigan." Slipping away. Chill air, waking him. "Welcome back."

Tom coughed, sat upright in the tank as green gel sloughed off.

Xyenquil held out a robe for him.

"I'm afraid," he said, "that they'll be questioning you again."

As he helped Tom on with the robe, he clucked his tongue and added: "The new limb, my Lord, is growing nicely."

On a smartnacre chair sat Feldrif, thin and dark. Behind him stood Ralkin Velsivith, thoughtfully rubbing the amber below his left cheekbone. The ovoid jewel was the exact same hue as Feldrif's eyes.

The doorshimmer was guarded by two big men, muscles swollen with testosterone and growth-factor implants, who stared ahead and said nothing.

"It just . . . engulfed him," Tom was saying. "The Seer, I mean."

Velsivith remained silent.

"Where did it come from?" Feldrif's tone was sceptical. "Through the chamber wall? Or did it simply appear?"

"It just—I don't know."

Velsivith: "And could you describe this, ah, phenomenon again, please?"

"Like a vortex. But strange perspectives . . . What do your holologs show?"

Feldrif leaned forward. "Why do you ask that?"

In the previous interrogation, Feldrif had been the polite one. But this time the others were absent, and Tom had all along thought that his civility had been a role, ready to be discarded when the situation called for more direct means of questioning.

"Because . . . Your deepscan must keep an archive."

"And how do you know so much about our security?"

Tom shook his head, saying nothing. A pain was beginning to throb over his left eye.

They had already admitted they had deepscans in the Seer's chambers, when they had talked to him after Elva's death.

Elva, my love . . .

"Look." Feldrif crossed his arms. "You're in a great deal of trouble, Lord Corcorigan, so I suggest—"

"Yeah?" Tom's near-patrician accent dropped away, revealing the harsher tones of his childhood in Salis Core. "Or maybe you are, for losing the *resource* you were supposed to be protecting."

"You *dare*—"

"Great idea." Velsivith brought his hands together in a loud clap. "You two fight it out in here, while I try to find the killers. OK?"

"Fate." Feldrif leaned back in his chair, amber eyes glaring.

To Tom, Velsivith said: "The security logs show nothing. I mean, completely blank. And that's no mean trick."

"If the prisoner"—Feldrif indicated Tom—"was harmless, why did the defence system trap him?"

"The Seer triggered it to save me. Kept me out of harm's way."

"Chaos." Velsivith cursed.

"You don't agree?" Feldrif looked almost gleeful.

"No, I do." Velsivith clacked a fingernail against the amber ovoid in his cheek. "That's the problem."

Feldrif stared hard at Tom.

Was the Seer an Oracle?

The question ran through Tom's mind, over and over, as his escort—twelve armed troopers—took him back to his apartments. They left without saying a word.

Were his visions truecasts?

Or merely possibilities?

Elva said: "*Boo!*"

Tom stumbled backwards, and he gasped.

"*Did I scare you?*" She gave a wicked grin. "*Well, I'm a ghost, so I probably did.*"

Tom blinked, trying to focus on the image.

Oh, Elva.

His heart beat wildly inside his chest, like a trapped animal fighting to get free.

"*If you've managed to open this, it means I'm legally dead, according to the local security nets.*" She drifted above the half-opened black case. "*. . . And I know it's you, Tom.*" A shrug. "*Otherwise, this would be a different sequence, with a less friendly message. Your biosigns have registered. The less obvious compartments will open for you.*"

Tom opened his mouth to speak, then shut it.

It's just a recording. No interaction.

But it seemed he could reach out and touch her, feel her warm skin—

"*Good luck, my Lord. You've always been the best.*"

The holo-Elva winked out of existence, and Tom turned away with a stifled sob.

It was a hoplophile's dream.

Laid out on the bed—on Elva's bed—were the contents of her intricate bag.

No smartweapons, which was good: defensive femtotech would always detect, and usually counteract, anything which was too clever. Instead, there were spin-darts and throw-chains; sticky razor-burrs; toxin-coated spit-needles and snap-blades. A matching pair of nacre-handled monowhips.

"Which army were you going to take on, Elva?"

Tiny ping-bows, currently disassembled, with exothermic bolts. Shiver-crystals—plus timers—with hydrofluoric acid cores.

And more.

Spikes: fast-dissolve toxic, and armour-piercing vibro. Explosive flakes. A nozzle-spray with unknown contents. A titanium-handled vibroblade. Extensible finger-claws—

"That one will do."

Tom picked up the lightweight vibroblade.

He walked out of Elva's chamber without looking back.

Naked, covered with slick sweat, he knelt, sat back on his heels, eyes squeezed shut as he prepared himself, tightened his nerves to the highest tension they were capable of. Remembering the Seer-induced vision, focusing on that future which must come true:

Elva spinning to face the troopers who burst in upon her.

The vibroblade was slippery in his grasp.

Dark-clad figure, spinning kick, laughing as he saves her.

Breathing fast and heavy, as though he were sprinting, close to the finish.

The *one-armed* man who saves her.

Crying inside, knowing he had to do it, to fulfil the Fate he had seen, which he so desperately wanted to make real.

The one-armed man who is Tom Corcorigan.

Now.

Fear, making him hesitate.

Do it now.

The vibroblade spat into life.

Smoke, acrid yellow/grey, and the burning pain.

Tom screamed.

Cutting high, so the growth-control implant was removed along with the flesh and soft, growing bones.

Screamed louder.

The thump as dead meat hit the floor, smoking. Roasting stench . . .

Elva!

Wave after black cascading wave of pain crashed down upon him, pounded him, buried him, smashed him. And scattered the pieces to dark oblivion.

12

TERRA AD 2142

<<Ro's Story>>

[3]

They danced.

Diminutive brown bodies, startling mask-faces of turquoise and brilliant white, of black and red, with fierce eyes and whiskers . . . But they were tiny, dancing around the bonsai atop the credenza, waving their minuscule spears and chanting, with the volume turned low.

"Kachinautons." Sergeant Arrowsmith waved them to silent stillness. "Traditional."

"I'm sorry." Ro hugged herself. "I don't feel too good."

Arrowsmith settled back in his chair, shifting his sidearm's weight. The belt dug in below his rounded belly. But his shoulders were wide and athletic, his bronzed face strong. He had pulled his chair round to face Ro's, so there was no desk between them.

The air in his office was very cool.

And quiet.

It struck Ro that this was a Navajo thing, not needing to fill a void with words. With Anglos it would be an effective interrogation method.

"She was very sweet," Ro said. "Even though I'd just met her . . ."

Arrowsmith nodded. "In your statement, you said it wasn't just a random intruder."

"There's a sensor array just inside the mistfield. Teardrop sniff-cameras floating at random . . ." She saw the intense concentration growing in his dark eyes. "My home is a UNSA training school in Switzerland, run by my mother. I know about security protocols."

"And the logs show . . . ?"

"I don't have security officer access." Ro shrugged. "Not in Distri-bOne."

She wondered if the question had been deliberate, a trick.

"Perhaps you'd like to wait outside, Ms. McNamara."

"Something to eat?" asked a chunky uniformed woman, pausing in the cool, glassy atrium.

"You bet," said her colleague, a lean, tanned deputy.

Not talking to me.

Ro's stomach growled.

She had not eaten, had not even thought about it, since discovering Anne-Louise's body. An entire day without food.

There were Tribal Police and Rangers, and many people in civilian clothes, wandering around Police HQ. But the smells of food came from beyond a glass door decorated with a virtual-image holo:

** STAFF AND AUTHORIZED VISITORS ONLY **

Ro was sitting on a bench in the foyer, and beginning to feel faint. It seemed shameful, almost blasphemous, but she had to eat. Anne-Louise would not have wanted her to starve.

The two officers stared into red wall lenses for ID-scan, then the door slid open—aromas of hot food escaping—and they stepped inside. Ro watched the door seal shut.

A simple recognition: *I'm hungry.*

She cast a glance around the busy foyer: no-one was looking at her.

"OK," she murmured. "Let's try it."

She got up, walked unobtrusively to the nearest lens, and stared into it. Beyond normal perception, buried circuitry felt like a distant stream in which tiny fish darted, the flows obvious to one who was familiar with their ways, like a woodsman who can see and feel what city folk cannot. It was nothing she could have explained to another human being.

If I am human.

In the depths of Ro's black-on-black eyes, a tiny golden spark of fire glimmered . . .

It worked.

. . . and was gone.

The door slid open.

". . . the stiffest stiff I've ever seen"—the speaker was a white-haired woman wearing a lab coat—"and the deceased's name was Woody!"

Laughter from the others at her table.

Anne-Louise's dead protruding eyes . . .

Ro forced the image away.

". . . ergot victim," a big-bellied man was saying, "when I was in Tunisia. Kept seeing spirits, like *chindhí*"—he glanced around: no Navajo officers were nearby—"and did himself in, inside the very granary the fungus started from."

The other forensic staff continued eating, not bothered by the imagery.

"Yeah, so what?" asked one of them, munching an open sandwich.

"So first he placed his head between the grinding wheel and the stone . . ."

The white-haired woman looked over at Ro, who was sitting by herself next to the window.

"I'm Hannah," the woman said. "You can join us if you like."

It was a tentative invitation: there was a noticeable gap between their table and the others. Even hardened police officers had other things to talk about over lunch besides the ironic and often undignified ways in which ordinary human beings meet their end.

"Sure." Ro carried her tray over, and took a vacant chair between Hannah and the large man who'd been describing his Tunisian trip. "Is that fried manta you're eating?" Determined to put her grief aside.

"Yep." The man patted his belly. "Lots of locals won't eat seafood, but I love it."

"You know that rays, if they don't feel too good," said Ro, "regurgitate their own stomachs."

"What?"

"Sure. Their stomachs, turned inside out, dangle from their mouths, and they rinse them off. Then they suck 'em back in."

"Gross." One of the other techs nodded in approval. "I like it."

"And more efficient than simply vom—"

Sergeant Arrowsmith was standing by the table: a looming, bulky figure. He stared down, with neither comment nor judgement in his gaze.

"I see that you've made some friends."

<<MODULE ENDS>>

13

NULAPEIRON AD 3418

It burned: the missing left arm. Fire traced the nonexistent nerves, delivered sensations of cramp-knotted muscles. An acidic itching of skin which could never be scratched.

Elva.

Wrapped in a heavy cape and leaning on a cane, he stood at the black lake's edge. Stared into its night-dark depths. Fragments of her corpse would have settled on the bottom: the parts which had escaped digestion by teloworms. Microscopic life would already have gone to work on those tiny remains; one way or another, she was wholly absorbed into the local ecosystem.

And yet he had seen a future in which he rescued her. In which a one-armed Tom Corcorigan saved the woman he loved; and he believed in that vision strongly enough to have shorn off his regrowing left arm.

Giggling, high voices.

Tom looked up. A small group of adults and children, maybe two families on an outing, settled further along by the lake, placed unopened picnic parcels on the broken grey stones.

So what do I do now?

Black-clad figure, leaping into the chamber, where soldiers threaten Elva . . .

In the vision which the Seer had granted him, there were tiny differences in Elva's appearance, but she looked like the woman he had grown to love. If that body had belonged to a twin or to a clone, then life experiences would account for the changes; and the physical duplication would mean that her personality would be less altered by the transfer.

Though what effect the experience of deliberate suicide might have upon a person, before awakening in a sister's body, knowing that you had caused the sudden and permanent erasure of that body's original personality . . . Tom blinked, aware of his ignorance, his only certainty an absolute determination to find her.

But the vision's remembered sequence gave no hint as to her location in space, or the time when those events occurred.

He turned away from the lake, a strange sound catching in his throat, and the playing children froze, then looked to their parents for support, knowing that their mothers and fathers were omniscient and strong, ensuring their security, defining their entire childhood worlds forever.

A vassal, barefoot and carrying a small bundle, entered the cavern. She descended the scree slope, stopped at the water's edge and genuflected.

"What do you want?" Tom gestured for her to stand.

"My Lord."

She placed the fabric-wrapped bundle on the stones.

"What—?"

But she was already leaving. Stones scrunched beneath her bare feet as she made her way upslope.

Tom used his cane's tip carefully to pull back the fabric. Inside lay a bluemetal poignard.

Fate . . .

Awkwardly, he picked it up between thumb and forefinger while keeping hold of the cane. At the hilt's end, an archaic flatscript insignia which he recognized: kappa and alpha entwined, sign of the strange vanished weapons suppliers known as Kilware Associates.

Its balance was perfect. Save for the colour, and the hallmark, the poignard was twin to one Tom had once owned.

Scarlet blood across a blue/white floor . . .

The one he had used to kill the Oracle Gérard d'Ovraison.

✧ ✧ ✧

His fitness increased by geometric progression.

There was a long gallery with angular, intricately carved pillars set every ten metres, and he used them as markers. Early in the morning, with the gallery almost deserted, eerily lit by floating half-power glow-clusters, he jogged slowly along the central blue-carpeted aisle, from the beginning to the second set of pillars, and retraced his steps, ignoring the pain.

He was puffing, totally winded.

But the next day he jogged faster, and pushed himself all the way to the fourth pillar. On the third day, he made it to the eighth and back.

He spent most of his time studying—across a range of subjects whose choice seemed random—inside his expensive apartment. Soon, he would have to move out, or start earning credit.

But Elva had dealt with the finances, and he wanted to put off that particular pain as long as possible.

Outside, though, when he walked the boulevards, he noticed a new tension in the air. Occasionally, random brittle laughter rang out from a daistral house, before dying abruptly, cut off too soon. While here and there, among the crowds, Tom saw teams of scarlet-caped men and women in unfamiliar grey uniforms, all with an odd intensity of gaze.

And their capes' hue was familiar: the same shade as the cravats of the unnaturally synchronized team who had caught the thief, and the clothing of the mysterious children by the black lake in which Elva had been buried.

Once, a passing age-bent woman muttered something about "*Chaos-damned Blight*," but she broke off when she noticed Tom's regard, tugging her shawl up around her straggling white locks, and shuffled away into a side tunnel. By the time he had decided to follow and question her, she was gone.

There were news pillars, whose intricate embellished tricons were on display at major intersections, and according to them the Aurineate

Grand'aume's prosperity was at an all-time high, while social events were flourishing and the normally low crime rate had dropped to zero.

During one of those walks, he thought he saw a black-cowled figure watching him. But when he approached, Nirilya turned away, and left.

He could have run after her, or made his way to her home, but instead he returned to his own apartment, and resumed his logosophical studies. Looking for any hint or clue which might lead him to the location of that vision which he hoped was not a dream.

On the eighth morning he jogged—slowly, wheezing—a little over five klicks. His gait was awkward, almost stumbling, and his diaphragm was tight with pain.

Ninth day. Keeping the same distance, Tom tried for a smoother motion, with controlled breathing. Over short stretches, it almost came together.

It was very early, before dawnshift, and the gallery was empty. The day before, there had been stares from the few passers-by, and he wanted to remain anonymous. Whatever the reasons for the realm's change in atmosphere, Tom took a new accessory with him on his workout: the bluemetal poignard, tagged to his waist.

As a message, its meaning was one he could not decipher: he did not know who had sent it, and had no idea of its significance unless its near duplication of a weapon he had lost was some comment upon his current quest for the new, living Elva.

And if someone knew that much, they ought to show themselves and help him. But it seemed that was not going to happen.

In the evening, slowly, for the first time in many days, he worked through a phi2dao fighting set, a beginner's form.

There was an old woman who sold minrastic cakes and broth from a stall. Tom got into the habit of buying a cake, mid-morning, as he strolled the busy length of Arkinol Boulevard. One day, as Tom walked away munching, a man sidled up to him, crystal in hand, and whispered: "Want to see the news?"

But there was something about his expression which Tom did not like.

He moved away, close to a female astymonia trooper who was standing beside a pillar. When he saw her uniform, the furtive man started, then turned and slipped away into the crowd, leaving Tom puzzled and uncertain.

Is the news a black-market commodity now?

At the minrasta stall, the old woman was determinedly staring the other way. It told Tom all that he needed to know. The Aurineate Grand'aume was changing, undergoing one of those societal phase transitions which happen seldom, but he was here to see it happen. He could investigate . . . Yet soon he would be moving on, and the political affairs of one small though prosperous realm within the whole of Nulapeiron were hardly his concern.

Day forty.

"Sir, can you . . ." A freedman, asking for directions.

But Tom was hurtling past, legs pumping, thrill-adrenaline coursing through his veins.

Sorry.

He hit the arched footbridge at top acceleration, sprinted over the top, turned left and pushed down hard. He raced along the redbrick footpath, black canal to his left, dark rounded ceiling overhead.

Digging deep, he ran.

Laughter inside, the pure joy of free athletic movement, once lost but now regained.

Bright silvery cargo bubbles drifted past on the canal, a chain of them heading back the way Tom had come, and he wondered what might be inside. Then he was past them, entering a three-dimensional maze of deserted but clean ramps and stairways, arches and spirals, and he took the obstacles as fast as he could, vaulting a banister—to his own surprise—and dropping onto another pathway.

The path was tiled in ochre and green. On a whim, he followed it, running easily, as it led into a side tunnel, a tributary of the main canal. His footsteps echoed strangely, almost musically, as he ran, enjoying the physicality, deep into kinaesthetic Zen.

And then he heard a scream.

The gunman was a large square-faced man, shining graser pistol in hand, trained upon the small elfin woman. She stared at him defiantly.

"Bitch! I'm going—"

Tom kicked the back of his right knee, smashing it downwards into stone, hooked the sleeve and stamped on the man's exposed ankle, splitting the achilles tendon. Smiling as he wrist-locked the arm, straightened it, and broke the elbow across his knee.

The graser pistol clattered on the tiles.

"Nasty," said the woman he had rescued.

The disarmed gunman lay in silent frightened shock, staring up at Tom.

"Thanks. Really," she added. Her voice was high, almost fluting, but it was the rainbow shimmer which held Tom's attention. "I'm very grateful."

Pretty diffraction patterns played across the transmission end of the graser. He had not seen her pick it up.

"And you gave me back my pistol, too."

Chaos. I'm a bifurcating fool . . .

She backed slowly away. Reaching a narrow exit, she slipped inside, was gone.

"My . . . Lord. You have to leave this realm." The injured gunman was panting now. "She stole . . . crystal. Thief."

"Who are you? A courier?"

For a moment, the man could not speak.

Then, "Sentinel . . ."

He passed out.

The journey back was nightmare and farce combined.

A dead weight across Tom's shoulders, the near comatose man—a courier, despatched by Sentinel to deliver information to Tom, not get half-killed by him—stirred and muttered from time to time, throwing Tom off balance. Then came the convoluted conjunction of ramps and stairs, where Tom had to climb, thighs burning, pain clawing his lower back, struggling to keep upright.

"Bifurcatin' . . . Chaos."

Downwards. He looked for a ramp, found none, used the steps. But it was hard, descending but unable to look down at his feet. Towards the bottom the open staircase spiralled and the wide steps themselves were curved and that was where he lost it.

Black waters coming towards his face.

There was a heavy splash—the injured courier falling in—and then cold water enveloped Tom, before his conscious mind had even noticed that his foot had slipped.

Fate damn it!

He had never learned to swim.

Struggling at first, but thirteen Standard Years of physical training told him to relax, and he did. Floating to the surface, striking out, but the courier was drowning—

Cargo bubbles.

It was another string of the big floating bubbles and Tom jerked his head out of the way just in time, as the leading bubble slid past. There was a protruding rim around each one, just above the surface; Tom grabbed the nearest, jack-knifed upwards, kicked through the membranous top, and was in.

"Help . . ."

Cold water had revived the courier and that helped: he reached out and Tom grabbed then hauled him bodily over the edge before his strength gave out. The man's legs were still dragging in the water but Tom lay back on broken cargo boxes, too tired to care.

Something small and black sprang into the air, dropped into the water with a tiny *plop*.

"Catch it!"

Black, the size of a child's fist, they bounded all over the loading dock.

"I've got one."

Laughter, as it slipped from the stevedore's grasp and bounced out of reach.

It was the cargo Tom had disturbed, coming to life now where the warmth was greater: hundreds of frogglies, each one black and round with a single yellow eye, a pair of springy legs—and a dislike of being roughly handled.

Off to one side, two medics were working on the injured courier. He lay on a blue emergency pallet, eyes closed as they fitted an amber cast to his shattered arm.

"Friggin' stokhastikos!"

One of the men tripped, caught off balance by a froggly underfoot. He fell heavily onto the flagstones, and the two frogglies he had been holding bounced free.

"This is your fault," the foreman said, trying to hold in his laughter. His big shoulders shook.

"Sorry." Tom could not help grinning.

Two more men entered the dock, and Tom recognized them both.

What are you doing here?

It made reasonable sense that Xyenquil should be involved in a medical case, come to see the injured courier. But he was accompanied by a blond man wearing a violet tunic and burgundy cloak, with an amber ovoid inset on his left cheek: Ralkin Velsivith. News travelled fast.

A froggly bounded across Tom's path as he made his way towards them.

"My Lord." Velsivith gave an abbreviated bow. "Exactly what happened to him?"

"I'm not *exactly* sure," said Tom.

The words roused the courier, who looked up from the pallet. Half a dozen frogglies were sitting on his chest. But he stared at Velsivith, taking in the twin daggers at his hips, the unmistakable security officer demeanour—

"No!" Xyenquil dropped to the man's side, fumbling for a medi-strip.

The courier's eyes rolled up in their sockets—

Sweet Fate.

—and his body gave one great spasmodic twitch, then lay still.

"Destiny!"

Thanatotrope.

"Another suicide."

Velsivith stared at Tom.

"I don't—"

But Xyenquil was running a scan over the courier's corpse, and when he looked up it was almost with relief.

"An ordinary thanatotrope, if that makes sense." He shrugged. "Just a suicide implant. No additional features, I'd say, unlike Captain Strelsthorm's . . . Well. But whoever he was"—nodding towards Velsivith—"he chose death rather than your custody, Lieutenant."

Velsivith turned away then, but for one extraordinary moment Tom could have sworn that it was tears that caused the lieutenant's eyes to glisten: a strange liquid regret which was totally incongruous on a hardened intelligence officer.

Particularly one who worked for an organization which had the safety of the wealthy Aurineate Grand'aume as its prime remit, and the implicit authority, Tom was sure, to carry out its work in any fashion necessary.

14
NULAPEIRON AD 3418

Creamy jade, carved opalescent panels which cast their own diffuse light—for an interrogation chamber, it showed a great deal of style.

"If I'd wanted to kill him"—Tom sat down on a low jade bench, facing Velsivith—"I wouldn't have carried him to safety. I could've drowned."

"So you were friends." With a fingernail Velsivith tapped the ovoid in his cheek. "Or merely colleagues?"

"I'd never seen him before."

"So you said."

Tom tried to keep calm. This was standard technique, nothing more. Nothing personal.

But Velsivith's attitude had changed, covering any evidence of regret and replacing it with impersonal efficiency, as though he were under scrutiny as much as Tom.

"I've nothing to hide." Tom shrugged.

Velsivith reached inside his cloak, pulled out something.

A bluemetal poignard, sheathed.

Searched my quarters. Bad sign.

"Somebody gave it to me." Tom shook his head, exasperated. "A vassal. With no message."

"And?"

"And nothing."

Did the Kilware Associates hallmark mean anything to Velsivith? Tom suspected the shadowy weapons suppliers of a great deal, but this was the first sign of them he had come across in years. And there were more pressing concerns, which made Tom question the wisdom of meekly following Velsivith to this place.

"You have to leave this realm," the courier had said.

Perhaps he should have taken more notice, treated it with urgency.

Sentinel. You tried to warn me.

Risking a courier. But why commit suicide?

There's more going on than I know about. Far more.

"I'm sorry." Velsivith looked down at the floor. "I'd like to believe you, Lord Corcorigan. I really would."

"So why don't you—"

But then a platoon of soldiers burst in.

Move. Now.

The most propitious time for escape from capture is the first few seconds. Tom launched himself, leaping from the bench, crescent kick deflecting the first soldier's graser rifle, straight-arming him into another's field of fire, a clear path to the doorway but—

Flash of white.

A stunburst exploded and he fell.

Darkness.

Came to, retching.

Cold, naked, fastened somehow in a standing position.

Destiny—

He coughed, spat. But the phlegm landed on a floor which was liquid red and glistening, like flayed flesh, and his spittle was absorbed quickly, greedily.

Where am I?

Pink/red gelatinous tendrils encircled his upper arm, his ankles and his throat. Merging with the floor, the walls. The entire chamber was of warm, wet flesh-like stuff. As he watched, it pulsed once then lay quiescent, gently quivering. It was like the interior of a great stomach, and he the food morsel about to be dissolved in acid and digested: tiny and of no significance beyond his constituent minerals and macromolecules.

Tom's stallion talisman no longer hung round his neck.

Father . . .

Carved by his father, enhanced by the Pilot . . . he never, ever removed it. Anxiety made him suck in a breath: instant cold pain flared in his mouth, rousing him.

Evaluate.

They had broken several of his teeth. His right eye was swollen shut, thick with fluid pain, and his left thigh throbbed. When he swallowed, a tight dry band of agony tightened his throat: someone had struck him across the larynx with fatal intent, and he knew that he was lucky to be alive.

Some luck. Should've known . . .

His diaphragm was cramped with tension, and his ribs—broken, for sure—lanced sharply with every breath.

"Well, well."

A stocky figure clothed in grey, with hood and heavy gauntlets, came through the red flesh-wall—it *slurped*, liquid and obscene, as he slipped inside—and he stopped, pulling off the hood. The man was grizzled and scarred, and grinning broadly.

"Neural interrogation," he said. "Heard of it? Does no real damage, just hurts like heisenberg."

Tom stared at him.

"Thing is"—the man spat—"clever folks know that. Override the pain, like. So we doesn't waste our precious bleedin' time with it."

"What . . . do you want to know?"

A shrug of heavy shoulders. "Not a soddin' thing, me darling boy."

Then his gauntlet-clad big hand slowly encircled Tom's soft defenceless testicles, rough against flaccid skin, and tightly squeezed. Molten pain exploded, pulsed in sickening waves, even when the iron grip relinquished its agonizing and degrading hold.

Smiling, the grizzled man swiped his hand, stiff-fingered, across Tom's stomach. For a moment nothing happened, then Tom's abdominal skin split apart, red and glistening, revealing greyish balls of fat bathed in warm blood, with layered fibrous muscle.

"Looks like you got guts, boy." His face was mere centimetres from Tom's, and his breath stank of something foul and rotted, even through the waves of agony rolling over Tom. "Who'd'a thought?"

And then, with a grey-toothed smile which knew nothing of decency or compassion, alive with its own twisted fires and desire, he bent down over Tom and got to work.

". . . you know about the Grey Shadows?" Woman's voice.

Shadows . . . Blood-red, and hazy.

Steel whip, singing.

"No—"

Cracked against the backs of Tom's bare thighs.

Hood pulled halfway up, the grey-clad man grinned, halted, waiting for relief to pulse through Tom, then the realization of false hope . . . A feint, to break the rhythm, before it sang its hymn of blood and steel once more.

Crack.

"The courier?" Her elegant tones swam in and out of Tom's awareness. "Well?"

He shook his head, tried to speak through swollen lips.

Don't know.

"Did it? Why?" Insistent now.

"Wha—?"

"Strelsthorm killed herself. What happened?"

Shook his head.

Tendril, tightening round his throat.

"Enough." And with exquisite insouciance: "I'm bored."

Squinting, he followed her motion: heading for the fleshy wall . . . and it opened at her approach. She walked through—glimpse of plain tunnel beyond—and then it sealed shut.

She wore grey, was hooded like the torturer.

Toxin.

This was important and he must remember it. Protective clothing, and wet glistening walls which were surely pregnant with deadly neurotoxic fluids. There was more than heavy raw-flesh membrane holding him trapped and helpless.

"Hey, you know," the torturer clapped Tom's bare shoulder, "*I'm not bored. Not yet.*"

He pulled open his tunic a little, to show the stallion talisman hanging amid a forest of black wiry curls. Then leaned close as a lover, displaying his twisted grin, his rotten breath.

"Thanks for the pretty present, boy."

And began to explore new avenues of inventiveness.

Plotting escape vectors: squinting, using the part of his mind which, after the Sorites School's relentless drilling, never stopped its rational analysis. He modelled the wet toxic membrane as overlaid scalars of viscosity and toxicity, as a first draft; then shifted it into a seven-dimensional phase-space of his own imagining, searching for the minimax flaws which would allow him to—

A crack of pain.

Tom screamed, high-pitched, a sound that was scarcely human, as a great tsunami wave of black awful suffering crashed through his being, splitting his logosophical constructs apart. Rational thoughts spun away, torn in fragments, twisting in the flood like useless flotsam, never to be recovered or even glimpsed again.

He tried to hold his bladder, but at some point he had to let go. Sudden urine spattered off the floor, trickled down his bare legs, wet as blood and hot as shame.

The torturer laughed, knowing a psychological barrier had shattered beneath the stress.

"Now I can use the brass needle," he said, "up into the urethra. Without getting pissed on, I mean."

Throat restraint. Tom could not speak.

Some of the wet oily exudate, leaking from the walls and dribbling thickly along the restraining tendrils, finally reached Tom's skin. Torched it, with a deep acidic burn.

"No—"

It began again.

They used their whips and needles: for hours, perhaps for days. *Thirty-six hours*, whispered some fragment of Tom's disintegrating mind: a rational cog in a shattered machine.

Dehydrated, weak, but no longer aware of hunger or thirst: he—it—had become an organism overwhelmed by its most basic chemical perception, an immense and pressing tropic need made worse by the impossibility of movement.

Pain.

Immense pain. The need to escape; the trapped despair.

And finally the moment which had to come, when relentless pressure and implacable dissolution became too much to bear.

"*Stop . . .*"

Whip, song, blood.

"*I'll . . .*"

The soiled and stinking animal which had once been Tom Corcorigan whimpered. It moaned, it mewled, and cried at last:

"*I'll tell . . .*"

Woman, bending close. Intimate yet impersonal, sure of her control over the cringing mess before her.

Muldavika. He recognized her now, despite the hood. One of his first questioners, when he had been Tom Corcorigan, and life was wonderful had he but known it.

Coughing, almost choking, he could not speak.

Ring.

"Damn it." She turned to the torturer: "Relax the throat restraint. This *thing* is going nowhere."

Silver ring, glinting, and then he got it: the control locus of the flesh-wall's unfurling motion. It was big, the control ring, fitting over the gauntlet, round her forefinger. That was what kept her safe, granted her passage through the wet raw-flesh barrier, unharmed by acid exudates or dripping neurotoxins designed to kill.

It moved towards him, that hand, towards the fleshy restraint which burned his throat, and the ring's proximity caused the tendril to loosen: just a fraction, but that was all he needed.

Now.

She was close and his limbs were enclosed but her face was centimetres from his, hood pushed back a little to hear his words, and he snapped forwards and sank his teeth into her nose.

Bite.

It was animal desperation, and it worked.

"Ah! Get him—"

Bite hard.

Teeth clenched, he hung on.

A civilized human might have found humour in the situation, but the half-sentient organism once called Corcorigan was fighting for pure survival. He pinned his victim, sending every last fraction of his strength into his jaws—*predator's jaws*—and she yelled for help, arms flailing.

Bite, and don't let go.

Bright hot copper taste.

Then her flailing ring hand struck the tendril which held Tom's wrist. A loosening . . .

Yes!

His hand slipped free.

Half-fist to the larynx, grab her gauntlet—he twisted, felt the small bones snap, pushed her hand against the remaining tendrils, and gave an incoherent grunt of triumph as they dropped away beneath the control ring's influence.

Danger . . .

The woman was on the floor, one hand between her thighs and the other clutching her face, crimson blood trickling through her fingers. But the torturer crouched before him, raising his steel whip—then hesitated at the final moment, as though seeing something in the creature which confronted him that gave life and substance to childhood tales of Chaos demons, the eternal burning afterlife: pitiful attempts to instil restraint and sympathy in the uncontrollable boy who became a man of pain and power and degradation.

The unthinking Corcorigan-thing was on him then, animal-fast and without restraint, raking the face—darkness blossoming in eyes which had seen everything—then collapsing the throat, and the torturer's twisted life was done.

It burns.

Every barefooted step Tom took upon the red flesh-floor coated his feet with hot stinging acid. A thinking being would have howled, but he was something primeval now: crouched prey, fleeing from the hunt, with death so close he could taste it.

He— it—took the control ring from the mewling woman's finger, squinted, saw something else—metal, pretty: *horse*—and tugged it off the bad man's corpse. Slipped the bauble over his, its, own neck.

Good . . .

Ten burning paces.

Move.

Held up the ring, and the flesh wall folded back.

Then, hunched over with cramps and pain, naked body coated with slick warm blood, the half-conscious primate stumbled through the acid-coated opening, into the cold stone corridor beyond.

Move now.

15

NULAPEIRON AD 3418

Naked, trembling, the wounded unthinking being called Tom Corcorigan moved, hid shivering in an alcove at the sound of voices, stumbled out when they had gone. The conscious rational being could not
have moved with such desperate, effective awareness; but the Corcorigan-thing sensed knots of humanity ahead—from subtle cues only
the deep reptilian senses could work with—and avoided them.

Jade corridors, marble halls.

Move.

Uniforms, voices and . . .

Go.

. . . vibration.

Spiral staircase all of stone: cold relief beneath his bare acid-burned
feet as he ran downwards.

And then a roar which filled the air.

It was huge and bronze: a vast cargo train which, stationary, stretched
the length of the great loading platform and still reached invisibly into
the dark tunnel fore and aft.

Wordless fear. An unreasoning desire to escape—deeper than emotion: a primitive drive at the organism's cellular level. Crouched naked
behind a pillar, shuddering now.

Pain.

Ignore.

Rolling spheres of raw, stinging flesh.

See them now.

Hundreds of stevedores were at work, marshalling the things with wicked stun staves, keeping their distance. A dozen, two dozen great flesh-spheres—red and glistening wet with exuded toxins—rolled down brass-coloured ramps, lined up in formation upon the platform.

Brought here by bronze cargo train, destined to line more torture chambers. Inserted in place, they would expand to cover any chamber's walls, pulsing in hunger for the prisoner-morsels which would be fed to them.

Perhaps some rational fragment in the escaped creature's mind wondered what was happening here, deep in the prosperous Aurineate Grand'aume; but non-rational awareness was filled with a more immediate knowledge so deep it defined reality: time to leave or die.

A flesh-sphere rolled past, with a soft, liquid sucking motion, followed by white-faced stevedores who looked as though they would rather be anywhere else but here.

Shining. Silver.

He frowned, grasping after the thought.

Then it came—*ring*—and the near-mindless thing which had been Tom Corcorigan held up the captured control ring, clenched in his hand. And the flesh-sphere veered in its path, away from the hidden ring-holder, and the stevedores jumped but too late.

One of them screamed, but it was his mate who fell back, face already half-digested by pungent acid.

Escape vector: clear.

Time to run.

He crossed the platform, sprinting fast, then threw himself forward, tucking into a ball at the last moment and rolling clear. He dropped into darkness, fell, rolled once more.

Sharp stones, darkness. Distant shouts—cries for medics, not for soldiers.

Ignore.

He was underneath the platform's edge, and he moved quickly

now, towards the front of the train, moving by instinct. Into the black tunnel, where the long leading cars had already been unloaded.

Membrane . . .

He clawed his way through, hoisting himself inside the cold empty car where the air lay flat and dead. Hard, the floor. Chilling to the bone.

Relief, after acid burns.

Then a howling, a lurch forwards, and inertia tipped his naked form across the lightless car's interior, then nothing.

The comatose organism whimpered once as the train picked up speed, a rocking motion as the long cars rode their massive sound wave through passageways in solid rock. The naked, frail, injured being hunched itself into a foetal curve, sliding ever deeper into shock, bringing the life process shutdown which can save the body or destroy, and remained that way until the silence came.

16

NULAPEIRON AD 3418

Rasping wounded-animal sounds. Pitiful, crawling . . .

The noise came from Tom's own throat; he was the wounded creature, crawling in darkness. Trembling, unsure where he might be.

Get out.

Something in his grip, a stanchion, and he hauled himself upright. Taking cautious steps forward—his acid-stripped soles, raw and weeping fluid, adhered to the freezing metallic floor; gritting his broken teeth, he tugged them free—then stumbled forward, door-membrane sliding across his naked skin. Cool liquid draughts swirled around him, and an involuntary sneeze convulsed him, pain clawing his stomach and fresh blood-flow starting.

The stone platform was grey and dingy, and quite deserted. Areas of blue-tinged light slid at random, from cracked glowglobes slowly moving through the air.

He fell.

Yellow fluorescence burst in his eyes, disintegrating the Tom-awareness. But still he crawled . . . and this time the thought pieces coalesced, re-forming, and though it was reflex which caused him to grab a rust-streaked pillar and haul himself upright, it was Tom Corcorigan again who stood there, swaying on his torn, painful feet.

Pain.

Narrow maintenance tunnel: round entrance at waist height, wide enough to crawl through.

Use the pain.

Forced himself inside.

He moved on hand and knees, head rocking with every push forward, trying not to think of the grime infecting his sticky wounds. Just pushing—

Stop.

Almost toppled into space.

Hand clawing into a gap between blackened stones, he hung on at the tunnel's end, leaned forward. A transverse tunnel, wide but ill-lit, ran past below.

Orange glowglobes circled over cracked plinths on which the remains of shattered statues stood. The women who waited there were resigned or sad, anger and resentment buried by fatigue and pragmatism: the need to attract business. Scant rags, barely concealing too-thin bodies. Narrow shoulders hunched against the cold.

Three men in rough surcoats walked past, but it was nearly dawnshift and they did not even glance at the women who offered themselves.

"Time"—an older woman with a scarred face—"we gave it up for the night."

"I only give it up for credit, dearie."

The other women were too tired to laugh. One tugged off her earrings, cheap imitation amber which for a moment brought Ralkin Velsivith to mind.

Just how bright is he?

They would have sealed off the interrogation levels, and there were so few ways out—could they follow him here?

Perhaps it was that thought which cost him his balance, as he leaned too far over the edge and tried to crimp his fingers on a worn gargoyle's head, but too late.

Falling, surrendering at last to gravity, to Fate . . .

Flagstones rose up to smash him.

Swaying, the ceiling, where the fluorofungus sprawled, diseased and sickly looking.

Women. Carrying him.

Gentle hands.

"My place . . ." Her voice came from a vast distance, though she spoke right by his ear.

Laid him down, on a rough sacking bed.

". . . to the Coders."

"Later."

He lay back, gasping, sliding in and out of consciousness, while rake-thin women with bitter faces and foul mouths and roughened skin and every reason to hate and despise the male gender tended him as carefully as they might a precious newborn child.

". . . with us, don't worry."

"He was in a bad way."

"Doesn't look too . . . Is he awake?"

Sliding away from the world as they lifted him, gently, and laid him down onto something soft. Grey stone ceiling, drifting past above.

"Here, by the autodoc."

"And lift . . ."

Awoke naked on a pallet. A—thing—was sitting on his bare chest.

"Ah—get off!"

Black, fist-sized. Its two feet felt like wet rubber; its single yellow eye blinked slowly, once, then stared. Tom raised his hand to swipe it away.

"Don't harm them." A woman's voice, from an archway to his right.

Them?

He raised himself up—the froggly on his chest hopped lower down his stomach, eye wide open—and saw four more of the little things huddled together between his feet.

"You frightened them." The woman—white skin, grey dread-locks—kept her voice low. "They were helping you."

A pink sheet covered the lower half of Tom's body, preserving his modesty.

"Sorry, fellows." Tom reached out his hand. "Hey . . ."

The nearest froggly jumped into reach.

Tom stroked its round head/body, and the yellow eye squeezed shut with pleasure.

"Look at your stomach." The woman, dressed in a pale grey tabard, pointed.

Glistening, the skin.

"What the Chaos?" Then, as the froggly's eye snapped open: "OK, little fellow. It's all right."

"Their exudate," said the woman, "has healed your wound."

Tom shook his head, looking down at the other four frogglies watching from the bottom of the pallet.

"Not bad, little ones. I didn't realize you work for a living."

"They like you. And the healing's proceeded fast, too. Somehow"—with a brief smile—"the two usually go together."

"Oh." Tom did not know how to answer that. "Er, thank you."

"It's our duty."

Her grey tabard was more sumptuous than it first appeared: gloss and matt cells, laid grid-wise, shifting colour as Tom watched. A second later, the pattern shifted once more: an ecology of cellular automata playing out their lifecycles within the woman's garment.

A row of tiny ruby stars across her forehead.

"You're a—"

"Holy Coder, yes." A wry upturned grin, and she shook her dreadlocks: tiny woven-in silver skeletons jangled. "That's what they call us."

Church of the Incompressible Algorithm.

Like his interrogator, Muldavika, in the Aurineate Grand'aume.

But this one was armed with no more than a medical delta-inducer, and she was pointing it at him.

"Sleep," she said, and the world went away.

"Looks fit enough, beneath the injuries."

"There's only one muscle"—a man's voice, somewhat high-pitched; educated but not patrician—"you need to worry about keeping active."

"That's not muscle, that's blood-flow. Oh . . . you mean the heart."

"I'll say."

"Ha! As though you were interested."

In his sleep, Tom smiled.

How bright is Velsivith?

Would he have connected the flesh-sphere incident on the loading platform with Tom's escape?

Tom jerked awake. He was on the pallet, but clothed in grey: trews and jerkin, the empty left sleeve tucked in. And his stallion talisman formed a small comforting lump on his chest. He touched it through the cloth.

But it was not Father's memory which sprang to mind.

Velsivith.

Would Grand'aume Security track him to this place? He was surely out of their realm.

Tom looked around the bare chamber, the autodoc folded up by the wall. A narrow-shouldered, shaven-headed man was by the doorway, watching him.

"How are you feeling?"

Tom clenched his teeth, fighting down a wave of sickness.

"Never better," he said finally.

"That will be a white lie, I hope."

"Maybe. But I *have* felt worse."

The thin man, whose name was Zel, led Tom into the next chamber. It was a simple hall with plain bench seats facing a low altar, where the woman with grey dreadlocks was polishing a brass thurible which reeked of burnt incense.

"I'm Fashoma."

Tom hesitated, then: "Call me Nemo."

Beside Tom, Zel made a low noise which might have been concealed laughter, and Tom was impressed: a man who knew at least a smattering of archaic tongues.

"Why don't I"—Zel took hold of Tom's arm—"show our new friend around."

There was an alms residence, the Hostel Réfacto naBrethren, in which indigent men temporarily lived. Attendance at evening service meant one could receive free dinner afterwards; to sleep in the residence, one had to work during the day.

The sporegardens were an intricate network of miniature tunnels branching out like capillaries from a central chamber, splashed with yellow and purple dendritic growths. Tiny airplants floated along the channels, their fragile roots dangling, their low-pressure sacs swollen and glistening, trailing exotic scents along the gentle air currents.

Tom spent the morning in the company of a thin youth called Prax, helping him to load small harvested sporefruits into a basket. After a couple of hours, though, an extended wave of dizziness washed through him, and drops of sweat sprang out across his clammy skin.

"You don't look so good," said Prax.

"I think I agree with you."

So he went back, nodded to Zel at the hostel entrance, and made his way to the autodoc chamber. There he lowered himself stiffly onto a bier, then slid swiftly into sleep, not awakening until the evening.

Then he walked through the clean, plain corridors, pausing before a tiny holo which told him for the first time exactly where he was— Drelario District, Kuig na'Balizhakh, Shichi no Planum: in the Seventh Stratum of Count Yvyel-ir-Balizhakh's demesne.

There were two other realms between here and the Aurineate Grand'aume, but they were all part of the same sector, and Tom could not help wondering whether he had placed enough distance between himself and the strange malignant forces that had reached out and demonstrated how tiny individual lives can be washed away by the tidal forces of violence and self-serving legality.

Perhaps these were strange thoughts for a former member of LudusVitae's revolutionary movement to be having. Tom rubbed his face hard with the heel of his palm, and walked deeper into the hostel.

At the rear, Zel and Fashoma were working in the kitchen, making occasional smart remarks—maybe not all religious types had their senses of humour excised at birth, after all—and at ease in each other's presence. A matter of long-standing camaraderie, nothing more.

Tom realized then that the peace and harmony which visitors and residents seemed to breathe in with the air were created by these two people, from a spirit of love and charity which transcended rage and jealousy and vengeance.

And he felt like someone tracking dirt and muck across a newly washed floor; and knew then that he would have to leave before he dragged his violent past and future into their carefully managed lives.

Not everyone who stayed at the Hostel Réfacto naBrethren shared that same spirit. Later that night, as they dined from plain ceramic tables in the whitewashed refectory, Tom noticed a large grimy man with bloodshot eyes stealing Prax's dessert. Evidently Zel was on the lookout for such events, because he replaced Prax's dessert, and spoke in calming tones to both of them.

But afterwards, when Zel had returned to his own seat, Tom heard part of the cold promise which the large man muttered to Prax. And, as young Prax blanched in sudden realization of his own vulnerability in a hostel with communal dorms, Tom could guess at the promise's full import.

Then the large man caught Tom staring, and winked.

Later, as they filed out of the refectory chamber, Tom felt a light touch on his forearm.

"Hey, one-arm. I'm Grax, and I ain't never had no cripple."

And the wide square hand was trying to grab him but Tom moved faster, an inner wrist block with perfect torque, power from the tension in fist and abdomen, and the large man had spun in a half-circle before he realized what was happening.

Tom whipped forwards, palm-heel to forehead, and Grax's large head bounced off the white stone wall with a dull thud, and the angry light faded from his eyes as he slumped slowly to the floor.

"Sorry," said Tom.

Zel and Fashoma were watching open-mouthed, with mingled fear and sorrow, but when Tom thought about what had just happened he felt no true regret.

Basic logosophy included a neurocognitive model of human behaviour, which lay at the heart of logotropical design: those tailored molecules built from pseudatoms designed to educate anyone who had been through the disciplines. Because consciousness is a thin layer upon the thousand-personality community which resides in every human brain: a strange illusion which seems to initiate action, but results from electrical changes which take place a third of a second *before* volition.

Tom had experienced Zen Neuronal Coding before he had ever dreamed of attending the Sorites School.

It was the hand which blocked.

The fighting technique had been automatic, astounding in its remembered clarity purely because conscious thought had no involvement in the action.

Paradox, duality—because sometimes it is the mind which defines the body.

Even in archaic cultures, there were individuals with fully developed multiple personalities. Depending on which daemon was momentarily in charge, the individual's body could change dramatically: shifting eye colour, banishing or resurrecting serious diseases.

And, as he stepped over Grax's slumbering body—the big man now emitting stentorian snores, as though gentle sleep instead of sudden knockout had fallen upon him—Tom wondered just how much of his own life was illusion.

Elva.

"Nemo." It was Fashoma's voice, but he ignored it.

You still live, inside the Seer's vision . . .

Somehow, this was a defining moment.

As Tom walked away, blinking, he knew that there was only one chance of retaining sanity and meaning in his life, and that was to focus purely on a single goal amid the whirling possibilities and complexities woven through the world, yet with no hint or inkling as to how he could possibly find her.

17

NULAPEIRON AD 3418

Fashoma had been quiet all morning, and was nowhere to be seen now. Zel clasped Tom's wrist in farewell, before handing over a small satchel of supplies.

"Someday, perhaps," said Tom, "I'll be able to help someone else, the way you've helped me."

He was echoing a promise he'd once made to Vosie: another woman who had saved him. It was a debt he had not yet repaid.

"That's the only kind of recompense I'd consider." Zel smiled. "You'd be a natural, should you ever decide to join the Church."

Multi-threaded mantras sounded intriguing—one of their core practices—but Tom knew that was not enough.

"Take care of yourselves."

He hitched the satchel over his right shoulder, and set off along a plain-walled tunnel.

For twenty-three days he walked, making better progress as the last of his injuries healed, until he was trekking thirty kilometres daily between dawnshift and darkfall. Through crystal caverns with spilling waterfalls, foaming white into bottomless black pools; along ghostly, empty boulevards and gallerias where his footsteps sounded hollow, in long-deserted realms—though Nulapeiron held ten billion souls (and even that was not common knowledge among the plebeian classes), in previous centuries there had been many more—and among the crowded thoroughfares and busy markets of three different demesnes, Tom made his solitary way.

But there were not always public water pools or Aqua Halls to drink from, and his dwindling supply of low-denomination cred-needles meant he could not continue travelling this way. Too many residential tunnels required loyal-subject earstud IDs before allowing people entrance to eateries and hostels.

He could sleep wrapped up in his plain travelling cloak, but there was no avoiding the need for food and water.

He found himself standing one day in a darkened rocky place where reality shifted, a tunnel exit before him suddenly plunging out of existence, while two narrow clefts sprang into being. Tom stumbled, falling painfully onto one knee, wondering whether he had finally lost his mind.

Then everything around him flickered into a third, new configuration.

Holo illusion?

But he snapped his fingers, and although his hearing was not astute enough for echo location, the rocks before him seemed solid. He picked up a tiny pebble, threw it, and it bounced from hard, gnarled rockface and clattered to the ground.

Then light and shadow flickered again, and when Tom had re-oriented his perceptions he was surrounded by tall, bulky housecarls: muscular warriors helmed in polished bronze, allegiance cords knotted round short tunic sleeves.

Their morphospears seemed to gleam with an inner creamy light, sharp cutting blades positioned centimetres from Tom's unguarded throat.

"Do you have business"—gravelly voice, invisible helm-wrapped expression—"within the Bronlah Hong?"

"I don't know," said Tom.

His missing arm was the mark of a thief, but there were other ways to lose a limb and these were warriors. The carls made no attempt to insult or brutalize Tom as they led him through a series of confusing tunnels—"Maze of Light and Dark," someone muttered—as the source of reality shifting became clear.

It was simple but effective: strong light sources which flicked off and on at random. Contrast produced black shadows, hiding all detail; immediate change created the illusion of total reconfiguration.

The housecarls marched steadily, surrounding Tom, unaffected by the dizziness which threatened to pitch him forward every time the illumination changed.

In an interview chamber, they left him with a wizened man called Shihol Grenshin, whose skullcap incorporated woven aphorisms in a dozen languages. The Bronlah Hong, he explained, was a trading house with long-distance commercial relationships stretching across three sectors, and they were always—when Tom asked about recruitment—looking for experienced merchanalysts with good linguistic skills.

"*Sukhazhitne na'Noighlín?*" he asked casually, in a thick buzz of Noileenski consonants, and seemed satisfied with Tom's reply: "*Nique parovihm.*" Just a little.

There was an aptitude test, which consisted of holomapping cargo distribution and transport requests into complex labyrinths of tesseract-labelled arcs and nodes. To someone of Tom's background it was too easy, and he deliberately introduced errors into his model.

It would not do to advertise his logosophical training.

"Hmm." Master Grenshin walked around the model, fingering his chin, sunk deep in thought. "Interesting perspective here"—he pointed—"and that minimax could save us money right now. Real credit, I mean."

Then he turned and shuffled away, long robe scuffing the dusty floor, and it took Tom a moment to realize that he had got the job.

That evening he accepted a towel and a blanket from a square-faced woman, who pushed them across her pale blue counter top, then directed him towards the male workers' tunnel.

"Third sleeping alcove on the left," she said. "Meals are paid for directly from your tendaily credit, in case they didn't tell you. And what"—turning to her small holopad and gesturing for dictation mode—"is your name, young man?"

"Gazhe, er . . ." Tom coughed, throat dry and head pounding with dehydration. "Gazhe Fernah, ma'am."

Something in his tone softened her expression.

"There's an aqua chamber to your right." She pointed. "Use as much as you like."

That first night, alone in his alcove behind heavy drapes, he opened up the stallion talisman, revealing the mu-space crystal secreted inside, but did not dare to operate it. He had no idea what emissions it might produce in its damaged state, or what kind of surveillance the Bronlah Hong's internal security teams had in place.

But he fell asleep with the talisman clutched in his fist, and dreamed he walked beneath Terra's wide blue open skies, on Alpine slopes with sweet green grass brushing against his ankles, and woke tense with disappointment in the real world next morning.

His new colleagues were pleasant enough: self-effacing Mivkin, who spoke with a slight lisp and showed Tom around; Jasirah, small and dark-skinned, her smile bright but infrequent, who told Tom after a few days that he should not chat with the carls who were on security duty.

"Not the done thing." She half-whispered, as if she were sharing a valuable confidence. "A matter of status, you know."

Then she nodded as though accepting grateful thanks he had not in fact offered.

Later that afternoon, having strung together a sequence of shipment plans in a profit-optimizing fashion which owed nothing to the Hong's usual algorithms, Tom walked out into the unsettling tunnels which formed the Maze of Light and Dark, and watched the shifting colours and sliding darkness.

"Makes me sick just looking at it." The amused voice came from behind him.

"Hi, Horush." Tom nodded at the young housecarl. "I know what you mean."

"Old Lafti"—Horush was referring to the carls' master-at-arms—"said you've requested permission to go running here."

So much for secrecy.

"I know it sounds crazy—"

"He reckons you might be a mad bastard." Horush removed his helmet, revealing creamy brown features, and rubbed his hand through his black cropped hair. "Which is a bit rich, coming from him."

Horush was gangly, hard-working, twenty SY old but with the appearance of someone younger, with a strangely vulnerable, almost girlish smile. If there was anyone less likely to develop the berserker rage which carls held in such reverential esteem, Tom had yet to meet them.

"I'll take Lafti's remark," he said, "as a compliment."

It was five tendays later, of uninspiring work days but increasing vitality in his physical training, that Tom was finally invited to lunch: formal luncheon with Master Trader Bronlah. As Tom left the work chamber in Master Grenshin's company, Jasirah's gaze followed him, swollen with jealousy. For three Standard Years she had been indentured here, her contract annually renewed, yet this honour had never come her way.

It was a privilege Tom could have done without.

The merchant was pot-bellied, a white goatee framing his small red mouth, and he sat cross-legged on a floating lev-cushion at the head of the low table, while his employee vassals, Tom among them, knelt in twin rows facing each other, sitting back on their heels on the rough matting which covered the greystone floor.

Rich burgundy tapestries decorated the walls, and golden glow-globes floated everywhere. The food bowls were of deep red and blue, so dark they appeared black except when direct light revealed their true lustre; the food itself was varied and multicoloured (indicating a nutritious range of bioflavins) and superb in quality.

There was no idle conversation beneath Harson Bronlah's impassive stare. When Tom attempted to make a remark about the coming Anzhafest holiday, and the airblooms decorating the corridors, Bronlah looked at him in near-autistic silence, killing the pleasantries stone dead.

Miserable bastard.

But later, during the meal, when Tom mentioned the new reoptimization algorithm which balanced content versus context in a time-dependent fashion, working with many-dimensioned manifolds, Bronlah asked several penetrating questions. Afterwards, though, with that topic exhausted, Bronlah fell back into his emotionless, unspeaking state.

Then, as dessert was served, the man next to Tom leaned over and whispered: "Senior staff only, for the next part."

Opposite Tom, a young (though silver-haired) woman called Draquelle was already rising to her feet. She nodded to Tom, causing the long white scars along her face to ripple with reflected light.

He rose and followed her.

As they were halfway down the exit passage, a slim hand beckoned from a shadowed side entrance.

"Could you attend to that?" asked Draquelle. "I really need to get back to work."

"All right."

It was a vassal who had signalled, a slim Zhongguo Ren woman, and she smiled without warmth and led the way past dark alcoves, through velvet drapes into a wide low-ceilinged round chamber, artfully lit by glowclusters, where an old man was reclining nude on a couch at the chamber's centre.

Tom was taken aback, until he noticed another woman with pale oriental features, robed in elegant gold-chased silk, constructing a holosculpture of the old man, with deft scoops and caresses of her fingertips in empty air.

"The secret of truly mastering a thing," she said without looking away from her subject, "is to teach that thing to another."

Long years of servitude taught Tom to hide his smile.

I'm here for an art lesson?

The vassal touched his arm, and whispered: "Madam Bronlah has another sensor field initialized over here."

"Thank you."

"There, and there." She guided Tom's wrist. "Oh, that's marvellous."

Immersed in the moment, Tom watched—it was all about seeing, he realized: focusing attention on the old man rather than his own movements—wiped a final control gesture, and stepped back from the sensor-field.

It was minimalist and ghostly, but it captured a certain feel, and Madam Bronlah was as pleased as he was.

"You have real talent," she said, though her own work was exquisite, more than Tom could ever hope to achieve.

"My thanks." Tom gave a courtly bow.

But her breath hissed inwards at his gesture, and he knew he had revealed a nicety of noble protocol which a lowly merchanalyst should know nothing of.

She was much younger than her husband, and very beautiful, but those dark eyes which had been so beguiling now masked her thoughts, as he backed out and took the nearest exit.

In his hurry to get out, he had taken a different passageway, but it curved in the right general direction.

When he stepped out of the passage, he was back where he had started from; but the dining chamber was now in semi-darkness, almost deserted. Two men were frozen in a tableau of unspoken tension, while a lacquered shellac box floated in the air between them.

Master Trader Bronlah still sat upon his lev-cushion. Facing him, cross-legged on the floor where the low table had stood before, was a Zhongguo Ren man wearing a heavy surcoat and a round pointed hat with long ear flaps. His hands rested upon his knees, and small carved steel plates were set into his knuckles: art and weaponry combined.

"Pardon me." Tom bowed. *"Nǐmen hǎo."*

The oriental man—surely a representative of a secret society—stared at Tom without speaking.

"Are you still here?" The master trader scowled.

"I was asked to assist, sir . . ."

Tom backed away, but not before he had seen the Zhongguo Ren adjust his tunic, caught the sight of flashing sapphire at his throat.

I've seen that colour before.

The blue fluid in which his boyhood friend Kreevil had been imprisoned, with other criminals. His friend Zhao-Ji, too, in later years . . . And the lightning in the Seer's chamber. It had something to do with Oracles, though in what regard he had no idea.

Tom left, knowing that he had learned nothing which should put him in jeopardy—many trading houses dealt with Zhongguo Ren secret societies, after all—but feeling an unsettled emptiness, which disturbed him on several levels.

Perhaps it was just the reminder that there was more to life than mundane work, that true magic has always lain at reality's heart while social convention is both as real and illusory as the chemical imperatives which rule ants in a nest—the queen's pheromones creating commands which are absolute but only in that context—and that while he was wasting time in obscurity, there were Oracles and Seers and strange powers following their own intangible and complex purposes.

And the only woman who could bring meaning to his life was somewhere in the world, possibly in danger, waiting to be found.

18

TERRA AD 2142

<<Ro's Story>>

[4]

PhoenixCentral.

Blue glass pyramids, in which hundreds of personnel worked. Other buildings were black and silver, tensegrity-framed polyhedra larger than cathedrals, their dark window facets concealing complex inner architecture from the blazing sun. In front of them ran a yellow runway, around which air-cars hovered.

Beyond, sere red desert lay baking beneath a cloudless sapphire sky.

And it was hot.

Ro shaded her eyes against the light: high above the horizon, a small dot was growing steadily larger.

"Are sure you—?" The voice behind her was cut off.

I don't need a bodyguard.

Sound of a gull door descending. Ro continued to watch.

Speck, glinting as it adjusted yaw, then pitch.

White, glimmering.

And then it was very fast, reflected sun blazing and its delta wings clearly visible, and the mu-space ship was hurtling down towards the yellow strip. Faster, and faster, then suddenly it was hanging raptor-like before the swoop, talon-skids extended as it glided in to land.

My God.

Smoke billowed and a screaming filled the air as friction-deceleration slowed the huge ship. As it passed Ro's position—and she appreciated for the first time how big it really was—a hot pungent shockwave buffeted her exposed skin.

Nicely handled, Pilot.

It came to a halt beside the extended passenger complex.

Behind her, a dull tapping: her assigned escort, Flight Officer Neil, was trying to attract her attention from inside the air-taxi. She ignored him.

Ground vehicles, like attendant insects, swarmed around the big delta-winged ship. Scorpion-tailed grab-cranes shifted passenger crates onto fluorescent orange flatbed TDVs. Thermoacoustic drives whispered into life, and the flatbeds slowly bore the encased, comatose travellers to the complex's Awakening wing.

Full med facilities awaited them, just in case, as did UNSA's *LitIg8* AI: ready to offer an out-of-court settlement (via any injured passenger's EveryWare proxy) at the first hint of neural damage.

Small white TDV, with a silver scorpion tail.

Ro swallowed.

She watched as the tail extended, daintily dipped over the ship, and rose again with a dark blue ovoid clutched within its pincers.

The Pilot's cocoon.

The vehicle drew closer, and stopped only two hundred metres from Ro, by the nearest pyramid complex: a rearing construct of dark blue, almost purple glass. The cocoon, lowered to the ground, split open. A slender, near-emaciated Pilot stumbled onto grey tarmac as attendants rushed to help.

Twin sparks of sunlight where his eye sockets should have been.

Mother—

Like her, like all Pilots, this man's eyes—rendered useless by the neuroviral rewiring of his visual cortex—had been surgically removed, replaced by high-bandwidth I/O-buses: the main interface to his ship's sensors.

But in mu-space he could see, know the joys of that fractal continuum in ways unaltered humans could not dream of.

It was the first time Ro had watched a mu-space ship in action, and suddenly the magnitude of the Pilots' suffering, of Mother's sacrifice and that of the father she had never known grew massively clear, overwhelming her. And the unfairness, for she could not understand how society—how anyone—could allow this to happen, without searching for another way.

But the loss of a few individuals' realspace eyesight was insignificant compared to the economic benefit of travel to the stars.

Dart, my father. If only you had lived . . .

Then she was stumbling, half-running along the tarmac, away from the landed Pilot and his helpers, away from everything, away from the air-taxi she could hear coming to life behind her, rising in pursuit.

It was cool inside the air-taxi, and she leaned back on the soft bench, while Flight Officer Neil held out a chilled glass of water. Ro took it, gulped the water down.

"I don't need a bodyguard," she said.

"I'm sorry?"

"Ah . . . I beg your pardon. I didn't realize how stressed I was."

"With good reason." He leaned forward, and tapped the control panel unnecessarily. "Command: resume journey."

"Acknowledged."

As the air-taxi rose to hovering height, Ro noticed for the first time that FO Neil was about her own age, in full dress blues with platinum award strips. Perhaps just a little too clean-cut, the chin with a hint of fragility . . . But she was staring at him, and he blushed minutely before looking away. His profile was about perfect.

Was my escort selected for his looks?

But she could think of no reason why the UNSA authorities should pay that much attention to the visit of one lowly intern. Unless they were worried about undue publicity following Anne-Louise's death. Certainly no-one other than the police had attempted to interview her.

"My mother," she said suddenly, "was a Pilot too."

"Really?" A tone of polite interest. "Oh, yes. I believe I knew that."

Something . . .

Bringing her senses to bear: on pupil dilation, skin lividity, respiratory rhythm. And the conclusion was obvious: he knew something of her past, had *intended* her to see the returning Pilot.

As a test of her reactions? But what relevance could that possibly have to anyone at UNSA?

Slowly blinking her jet-black eyes, she wondered if they had any idea how different she was from other people, and a wave of coldness which had nothing to do with the taxi's air-conditioning shivered across her spine.

Mother. I wish you were here.

She was out of her depth.

Flight Officer Neil stalked back and forth in the reception room, and Ro needed no special perception to see that his anger was real.

"For God's sake!"

They were in a small reception room, with a young junior administrator—a civilian—behind the main desk, trying to look busy, constructing a FourSpeak report amid a sheaf of holoplanes, while avoiding Neil's gaze. Ro clasped her arms around herself and looked outside. On the tarmac, despite the late morning heat, fit-looking men and women in white jumpsuits were running past in cadence.

Pilot Candidates.

She turned away.

In the grey-walled corridor beyond Reception, a white-haired woman with a deep tan was walking briskly past. She was dressed in a pale blue suit: business-conservative cut, but expensive shot-silk fabric. Two nervous-looking aides stumbled along behind her, trying to keep up.

"I'm sorry." Neil was at Ro's shoulder. "I can't believe they brought you all the way out here for this."

Behind the desk, the young administrator swallowed and said, "I think the, er, Mrs. Haverley's condition changed suddenly."

"A medical emergency?" asked Ro.

Neil frowned, and Ro heard his subliminal repressed remark as though he had shouted it aloud: *There will be if someone's not careful.*

"The person you were about to see"—Neil glared at the receptionist—"is off home because his wife's giving birth. I don't know—" He stopped, then added: "I'm not fully briefed on this. You were here for counselling?"

"Not as far as I know."

Which begged the question, why was he here to escort her?

To observe me. She was suddenly sure of that. *But why?*

"My God. It was your roommate who was killed in DistribOne, wasn't it?"

"Her name was Anne-Louise."

"I'm sorry . . . Ah, they probably had you seeing Dr. Haverley to check you're OK."

"Concerned about me?"

"Or avoiding a lawsuit. I—Were you close, you and Anne-Louise?"

"I'd only just met her that morning."

But I saw her there, bruised corpse with a dark swollen tongue . . .

Neil's hand was guiding her to a seat, and she held a comforting certainty that his concern at least was real.

"You should go home," he said, "to DistribOne."

"No." Ro felt suddenly calm. "There's something I'd like to see."

Open to the sky: blue mats, broken white walls. Perhaps it was a mistake to come here.

It felt like sacrilege, wearing her boots, but Ro walked to the mat's centre, knelt down and sat back on her heels. *Seiza* position. She could feel the echoes of warrior training: so many hours—hundreds of thousands of hours—filled with effort and energy. Ancient fear pheromones still lingered: faded scents of sweat, of occasional spilled blood.

Mother had trained here, and Gramps had been her sensei.

Ro clapped her hands in the traditional manner, and bowed to the dojo-spirit.

Some of UNSA's own military police had kicked down one of the walls, according to Neil, after demolition cranes had pulled the roof away. No-one trained here any more.

Fifteen years earlier, aikido/Feldenkrais—spatial awareness training—had been in vogue for all serious athletes. Now, although Zürich Flight School still sent its most promising Pilot Candidates to be taught by Karyn McNamara, most UNSA centres were phasing out the practice.

Ro bowed once more, palms on the ripped blue mat, then stood up.

She walked away without looking back.

Neil was waiting for her, on a vacant red-sand lot between two dark glass buildings. Sweat patches showed on his uniform.

"Sorry," said Ro. "You should've gone inside."

"No problem. Actually, I have heard about your mother. Something of a legend around here."

Ro smiled.

"And," Neil added, "in the aikido world too, is that right?"

"Ranked *judan* by the Kyo¯to Honbu."

Neil whistled, and Ro was impressed that he understood. Where other arts had abandoned the old belt rankings—after so many self-awarded high grades had rendered the whole concept laughable—aikido had reverted to traditional practices, and typically it now took a decade of hard work to earn a first dan. As for tenth dan, there were three tenth-degree black belts in the world, and Mother was one of them.

"UNSA service"—Neil gave a self-effacing grimace—"is a family tradition for me, too."

Ro just looked at him.

"My brother Neal," he said, "was a fighter-shuttle pilot."

Ro smothered her reaction with a tight cough: easy enough in the hot dry air.

"Neal Neil?" she asked.

"Yeah. Did I mention my first name's Armstrong?"

"Oh, God."

"Exactly. Come on, let's get inside."

As they walked together, boots scrunching softly on the sand, he added: "I had a Puritan ancestor called Punishment. Joined the militia, never got promoted beyond two stripes."

Ro gave a small groan.

"And his cousin Trauma, got as far as maj—"

"Thanks," said Ro. "I think I've got that one." She stopped before the glistening black glass door. "So you were kidding about your brother."

Their two reflections, distorted, stood together in the glass.

"Oh, no." Shading his eyes, Neil looked back towards the dojo's broken shell. "That's all true."

"You said he *was* a pilot." Something in Neil's tone made Ro ask the question: "What happened?"

"His name"—Neil's smile switched on, then off—"made him fast with his fists . . . and his brain. Excellence-grade honours from VirtU, then a masters from Jakarta. But he wanted to be a top gun."

Ro held her breath.

"It was a training run." Neil stared into the distance, but his thoughts were focused inwards. "Mach nine, and he ploughed into the Tibetan Alps, for no good reason that I ever learned. End of story."

"I'm sorry."

Neil held up his hand, and the black glass door slid open.

"He was twenty-six years old."

They went inside, into cold air. Ro shivered as the door slid shut behind them.

In the high-ceilinged museum complex, a space capsule hung, the exact colour of an old copper coin, protected by its covering of clear laminate. It was an Apollo craft, rescued from the Smithsonian's ruins—three decades before, during the Week DC Burned—and Ro could not imagine the bravery of the men who had flown inside.

Beyond another display, Ro saw the woman she had spotted before: tanned, white-haired, with a pale blue suit of understated elegance, undoubtedly expensive.

"Your mother"—beside Ro, Neil pointed to another exhibit— "went up in something like that."

Dear God.

It was not the full ship: just the Pilot's cabin, cut open to the public gaze. Freed of the foamy cocoon material, its revealed interior was cold and spartan. The I/O ports were two plain sockets in the turquoise ceramic bulkhead—and the Pilot would have been plugged in via high-bandwidth fibres attached in place of her eyes.

The tanned woman was walking towards her, but Ro's attention was riveted by the display.

I was born in one of these.

Ro shivered.

Slender robot arms, like praying mantis forelimbs, were angled against the cold bulkhead. For no good reason, the sight unsettled Ro.

"Myosin-activation strips." The woman's hand was elegantly man-icured, though her fingers' knuckles, as she pointed at the loose-hanging strips, were swollen with age. "In lieu of exercise. Not too different from today's setup."

Her voice was crystal clear, devoid of accent.

"It looks," said Ro, "like a medieval torture chamber."

"I suppose so."

The woman emanated a sense of presence, and when she laughed Ro found herself smiling in response.

"My name"—the woman held out her hand for Ro to shake—"is Ilse Schwenger. I worked with your mother."

Neil, behind Ilse Schwenger, was standing almost to attention.

"Not a Pilot, then," said Ro.

Neil winced. Whoever this Schwenger was, he knew her. Was aware of her importance.

"Ach, no. Just an administrator, who was able to help Karyn at . . . an opportune moment."

It was you.

Ro knew who this woman was.

You got Mother her ship.

When Dart Mulligan had been lost in mu-space, Pilot Candidate Karyn McNamara—his lover—had undergone the viral rewiring, and persuaded Ilse Schwenger, then a divisional director, to upgrade a newly commissioned ship: a solo search and rescue mission. The designated Pilot had been bumped off the schedule, and Karyn—Mother— had taken his place.

And she was already pregnant with Ro.

Mother had never said exactly what occurred, but there had been blackmail involved, and Machiavellian intra-UNSA politics. Mother and Gramps furnished material which Schwenger utilized to destroy her enemies' careers, while advancing her own.

And Mother had gained the ship she needed.

"Walk with me." Schwenger took Ro's arm.

"All right."

They strolled past a Long March rocket. Neil followed.

"You look," said Schwenger, "a great deal like your mother."

Several years younger, Ro realized, *than when you met her.*

Less experienced, more easily manipulated.

"But I don't have my mother's eyes."

The Pilot, three inches high, stood up in the tiny open-topped ship and said: "*Entering mu-space now!*"

Shaking her head, Schwenger replaced the toy on the glass-topped counter.

"Tasteless. But what the visitors want."

There was a single attendant, a superfluous youth: the souvenir shop's AI could handle everything.

"Uncle Cho might find it amusing." Ro tapped her golden strand, and placed the order. "When will it be delivered?"

"Um, right away," said the youth.

Since Chojun Akazawa was in Jakarta, that meant a local replica would be created and delivered, but that was OK.

Ro took a last look around. Candies—amber "mu-space" jelly strips with embedded liquorice stars; chocolates shaped like the UNSA logo—and child-sized uniforms. Infocrystals which she would have liked to browse through, if she had been on her own.

"I remember Chojun. He helped your mother." Schwenger bent close to Ro as they left the shop, as though sharing an intimacy. "Furnished the technical data for the field generators."

They were in a carpeted corridor. Like the rest of the complex, it was nearly empty: just a few uniformed staff in the atrium at the corridor's end.

"It didn't work, though."

Ro knew that Mother had tried everything to free Dart, Father, from the mu-space energy pattern which held his ship. But it had threatened to engulf them both, and Dart had deliberately collapsed his protective event-membrane when he realized that Karyn was in danger. Even as his bronze ship imploded, disappearing in a myriad glowing shards, Mother had escaped, and broken through to realspace.

In stress-induced, agonizing labour.

"Pilot Dart Mulligan," said Schwenger, "learned that Karyn was pregnant. Did you know that? He interfaced to your mother's internal systems. He knew."

"No-one told me."

Father. You killed yourself for me?

"And the breach birth must have been terrible."

Ro looked at her.

"I'm sorry?"

"Ah . . . Well, I'm sure you're old enough to know. There were . . . complications. When your mother returned to realspace—to random coordinates—she was already in labour, and only a caesarean would do. She used the internal robot arms on herself."

"How?" Ro's voice sounded small to her own ears.

"They have laser cutters, you know. And internal pre-processors, to keep on going even when the Pilot has lost consciousness . . ."

There was a bench by the wall, and Ro crossed to it and sat down, feeling shaky.

She cut herself open.

Drifting, alone and in pain, in dark endless space.

Sliced herself. To produce me.

Afterwards, as Neil saw her to a waiting air-taxi, she took hold of his sleeve.

"Armstrong?" She used his forename for the first time. "Why was I brought here?"

Ilse Schwenger had left her sitting on that bench, after a polite farewell.

Neil shook his head. "I've no idea."

It was written throughout his being, in unmistakable body language: he liked her, disliked his task—to report back on what he had observed—and knew nothing of the political machinations which lay behind her being here. He was complicit, but only to the extent of following orders whose purpose he did not understand. And both of them knew her meeting with Ilse Schwenger was no accident.

Just what did I learn here today?

She felt the pressure of Neil's gaze, intent upon her, as she slid into the air-taxi's cool interior and the gull door lowered into place. She waved, sat back. But in her mind was the holo image of a single chesspiece on a floating board, and the grotesque thing which lay on the floor beneath it.

Anne-Louise. Did someone kill you for a reason?

Then the ground dropped away, and the taxi was high above the long yellow runway. It arced over the glass buildings, acceleration kicking in, and zoomed upwards, leaving PhoenixCentral far below.

<<MODULE ENDS>>

19

NULAPEIRON AD 3418-3419

Tom, cross-legged upon his sleeping cot's rough ochre covering, shut down the bulky holoterminal beside him. Reckless, perhaps, to have borrowed the terminal from the merchanalysis hall, not to mention invoking the crystal's functions, but suddenly he did not care if they threw him out of the Bronlah Hong, or worse.

He sealed the crystal inside the stallion talisman once more, and looped it round his neck. Looked down at the cot, and knew he could not sleep just yet. Returning the holoterminal could wait until morning.

Slipping through the faded drape, he walked silently along cold grey flagstones—there were mutterings and other sounds from the alcoves he passed, but most of the men would be asleep already, worn out from a long working day—until he reached a cross-tunnel, and headed towards the nearest security station, looking for someone to talk to.

Behind the granite desk, a huge black-skinned, square-bearded housecarl stood chuckling. His copper helm hung from his belt like some grisly warrior's trophy, and sweat was trickling down his forehead. His hand, as he wiped away the drops, was twice the size of Tom's, maybe more, and his shoulders were massive.

"What's up?" said Tom.

"Caught what you might call an interloper"—shaking his head, grinning—"from the freewomen's washchamber."

"Sweet Chaos."

"Heard the loudest scream you could imagine. One of the women had gone in, found this bedraggled flashdust addict washing himself from a drinking flagon."

Tom could not quite share the amusement.

Cold flagstones beneath his stinking, shivering body. The feet of passers-by, disturbing his dayshift sleep—too dangerous to close his eyes at night. Dark extended memory gaps. Scratching his ever-itchy scab-encrusted skin. The hunt, always, for more booze, for the sweet hot liquid dragon which could make him feel alive . . .

Lost years.

"Poor guy."

"I guess." The big carl's expression grew kinder. "He was dressed again in his rags by the time I got there. Smelled bad . . . But he'd been beaten, and cut. You could tell. I told the proctors, when I handed him over."

The addict must have wandered in from the enclosing realm, Bilyarck Gébeet; perhaps it made sense to hand him back over to the Gébeet's proctors.

"You know how it feels," said Tom.

"To be beaten?" A heavy shrug. Beneath his tunic, the big carl's trapezius muscles bunched up like coiled cables, relaxed. "It's been a while."

"But you don't forget."

"No." Looking directly at Tom. "My name's Kraiv." Holding out his massive hand.

"I'm—Tom. They call me Gazhe round here, but it's not my true name."

They clasped wrists. For all Tom's wiry strength, he knew the other man could crush his bones with little effort, if he chose.

"Well met, my friend."

The next night Tom ran eight klicks along the Light Maze tunnels, worked flow/focus fighting forms over and over on the uneven stone, among shifting shadows: striving against imaginary opponents, kicking and gouging, throwing and striking, until he finally stopped, chest heaving, his body hot and slick with sweat. Not yet at peak, but finally recovered from the ordeal in the Grand'aume's dungeons, smiling to himself in the quiet knowledge that cleansing adrenaline and pouring sweat had once more excised the childhood demons from his mind.

For a time.

The day after that, Yim Roken, Master Grenshin's dour deputy, put adhesive scan-tags on every terminal: a coincidence, Tom assumed, because Yim Roken said nothing throughout the procedure, and he would never miss an opportunity of accusing a subordinate caught in wrongdoing. But it prevented Tom from borrowing a holoterminal again.

Yet that evening, as though in validation of those mystics who teach that overwhelming belief creates reality, Draquelle came into the men's residence tunnel with a gift. It was a small holopad, delivered at Madam Bronlah's orders. At insignificant cost to the Master Trader's wife—but to Tom it would make all the difference.

"Thank you," he said, and bowed to Draquelle formally, as if she were a Lady.

For the holopad could be used for more than amateur art.

Over the coming Standard Year he worked hard: running and logo-sophical work—exploring new theorems, mapping out new simula-tions—early in the mornings; a long day in the merchanalysis hall; then studying and reading, followed by strength training and phi2dao at night.

Each night he slept without dreaming.

His research proceeded incrementally, while his physical training worked through phases: increasing intensity through a tenday, then dropping back to easier levels, before building up again. But each beginning was a little higher than the previous; each peak a new achievement.

The merchanalysis work was purely to keep him alive, but there were some snippets which would remain with him.

Such as the time Yim Roken slammed a fist on Mivkin's desk, saying: "If there's an eduthread that can teach you not to be a moron,

I'll pay for it myself." And Mivkin's remark, later, to Tom: "I thought I'd left schoolyard bullies behind, but I was wrong."

But Mivkin had no interest in learning the disciplines of self-defence which would protect him—psychologically, physically—from such overbearing gas-bags, though Tom quietly offered to teach him.

In the kitchens, old Xalya would try to give Tom extra helpings—he was the only temporary-indenture merchanalyst who ate with vassals—while complaining about her corns and blisters. In the workplace, Jasirah's petty jealousies, and her colleagues' exasperation with her, afforded Tom some amusement.

And sometimes, the housecarls would allow him into their barracks, where he could watch them training, empty-handed and with weapons. They used tsatsoulination breathing and control techniques, beyond anything Tom had learned in phi2dao flow/focus training.

No-one, at least verbally, invited him to join in; he was happy to observe.

Tom was not there the night young Horush was injured, far more seriously than anyone realized at the time. The various accounts provided to him by his friends among the carls enabled him to piece together what had occurred.

One of the spectators was a lean housecarl called Harald, sitting on a bench at the side, his arm encased in amber gel: an injury gained from groundfighting with Kraiv five days earlier.

"He was on top form that night," Harald told Tom later. "Never seen Kraiv looking so good."

Every warrior in the platoon was already breathing hard, tunics dark with sweat, muscular bare limbs glistening, when the drillmaster sergeant, his long face rippling with old scars, called the carls out in groups of six, for synchronized spear work, using forms that were normally performed solo.

With heavy morphospears, each weapon tuned to basic halberd

configuration, the six men stamped and spun in unison across the battered, padded mats stained brown with old blood, avoiding the mattress-wrapped pillars, venting their berserker roar as they hacked and killed enemies of their own imagining. Kraiv fought hard, eyes crazed, white dry spittle encrusting his mouth: a big gentle man transformed into a rabid, vicious beast.

"And fast," said Harald. "For a man that size."

Behind his back, the big carl was called Killer Kraiv, partly from the insane berserker stare which clicked into place behind his eyes whenever he got deeply into solo practice. But partly, too, it was in contrast to his normal nature: easygoing, always concerned with other people's troubles and willing to help.

"Next group," called the drillmaster sergeant.

When the entire platoon of thirty men had demonstrated their skill, he called back the first group and gave the command: "Partner up!"

It was unarmed close-quarter combat, a sparring session, and young Horush was the third opponent Kraiv faced.

They moved fast, Horush trying to use his lanky speed in avoidance, but Kraiv's huge muscular form whirled and leaped across the mats in unpredictable ways, and just as Horush leaped to attack, a flashing backfist, light and whippy and totally unseen, struck him on the temple and he fell.

Horush was back on his feet almost immediately, while Kraiv apologized as the berserker stare dropped from his eyes. Just one word: "Sorry."

No serious fighting school, if it is of any worth, permits more than a single word of abbreviated apology; some allow none at all. It is to do with attitude of mind, concerns of life and death.

But Tom wondered, as he heard the tale, whether there was any sense in a system which pitted lightweight youths against massive, seasoned warriors in a sparring situation, and expected no-one to get hurt.

The training session ended in good order, and the carls went to wash and change, then meet up with the womenfolk who would have undergone their own training during the day. En masse, they would retire to the great dining chamber where circular bronze shields glimmered upon dark walls, to eat their one true meal of the day. It would be a big one, a warriors' dinner, consisting of at least four courses, during which they would flirt and laugh and boast: taking the opportunity to relate tall, outrageous tales or spin convoluted, often surreal riddles—always friendly, always competitive.

And it was afterwards, when Horush was walking back towards the barracks' sleeping chambers, that his eyes rolled up in their sockets and he crashed heavily to the flagstones. Harald was the first to drop to one knee, put his fingertips to Horush's throat, and discover there was no pulse to be felt: none at all.

But Horush was sitting up in the autodoc and talking when Tom arrived at the barracks' med complex. Tom broke off a glucose-bulb from a copper syrup-tree, and handed it to Horush.

"They revived you, then," he said.

"Thanks." Horush sipped, then leaned back, closing his eyes. "Good. I—"

His eyelids fluttered.

Tom looked away, thinking only of *Elva as the thanatotrope took hold, flooding her nervous system with fast-acting toxins, while the implanted femtarrays spun her soul across spacetime to the waiting duplicate and her true body died—*

". . . not too long." The on-duty medic, a carl with a white-edged tunic, was leaning over the display's phase-spaces. "In fact, I think he should sleep now."

"Will he be all right?"

"I'd say so. But don't, um . . . Don't say anything to Kraiv, OK?"

Tom blinked. "He doesn't know?"

"Not that it's his fault. I'd rather not worry him."

"Right. I can see that."

Tom shook his head, sure that he was missing something, but the medic was already leaving to check another patient.

The next morning was strange: the start of the annual holiday, after which the relaxed and revitalized merchanalysts would be expected to renew their indentures.

And Tom had agreed to go with the others downstratum for three days—a decision which no longer made sense to him. But he knew only that he was ready for a change, in a way that meant more than a brief time away from the mundane work which was killing him with boredom.

He was getting no closer to Elva while he remained here.

On the way out, he could not help but look inside the dusty merchanalyst hall—Master Grenshin was there, bent over a solitary workstation; Tom backed out quietly—before meeting the rest of the little party. They were waiting beyond the Light Maze, at an octagonal archway which led through to the realm of Bilyarck Gébeet.

"Hi, Gazhe." Mivkin's lisp seemed more pronounced, and he grinned like a schoolboy. "Time off at last, eh?"

"Finally."

Mivkin was cloaked in plain grey, not unlike Tom, but Jasirah was decked out in bright joyful scarlet. Dour Quilvox had threaded tiny coloured beads into his long beard, and his quilted surcoat was embroidered with intricate patterns. Ryban, shifty-eyed, wore a tattered brown cloak which might have been made from sacking, perhaps stolen from a godown storage chamber.

"This way." Jasirah pointed, taking charge.

Mivkin winked at Tom.

Their travel-tags authorized them to descend at one point only, so they followed a festive penrose-tiled corridor—red, green and cream predominating—through to a wide piazza in which long silk streamers floated, and exotic scents moved upon the air.

There were grim expressions among the people who thronged the piazza, despite their brightly coloured tunics and soft, floppy caps: standard costume for local holidays. Still, Jasirah pushed her way through the crowd in a straight line, without deviation, for all her lack of height. Tom followed with the others, smiling slightly as they made mock salutes behind Jasirah's back.

Off to one side, a musical mendicant group was playing the Grilvin Fantasia on pipes and aerolutes. It was an ode to their order's founding martyr, and their robes bore woven representations of the active macro-molecule in the poison St Grilvin had been forced to drink. Their clothes and skin were impregnated with doses of the actual toxin, steadily increasing as their immunity built.

Which was why ordinary passers-by kept clear of them, giving Tom a glimpse along a grey colonnade. At its far end was a piazzetta whose floor was tiled in metre-wide squares: white silver-shot marble alternating with black obsidian.

Men were standing on the squares, but it was the two others, seated on opposite lev-chairs overhead—opponents, facing each other across the piazzetta's width—who caught Tom's attention. One was an ordinary merchant, he guessed, with a flushed face and worried eyes. But the other . . .

Clad in black, with white lace at throat and cuffs, the elegant man sat with chin on fist, regarding the thirty-two people who stood below: his liveried servitors, face to face with the merchant's barefoot vassals.

Schachmati game, Tom realized. *With people as the pieces.*

And yet none of it made sense.

There was none of the celebratory atmosphere one would expect, given such an unusual event. And it *was* remarkable that a Lord should visit this far down, in Bilyarck Gébeet's Seventh Stratum. Yet there was no mistaking the man's noble origins, from the cut of his clothes to the studied arrogance and ennui as he floated above his plebeian inferiors.

There was a scent pedlar nearby, carrying a tray of small stoppered bottles. Above the tray, cheerfully bright hololabels advertised exotic fragrant oils at reasonable prices. But the pedlar's expression was grim.

"Who is that, over there?" Tom stepped closer, keeping his voice low. "A Lord?"

"Viscount Trevalkin."

"And the game they're playing?"

"With people's lives." The pedlar spoke in a sour whisper. "That trader boss may be a traitor, but there's no need to draw things out."

"Traitor?"

There were spearmen standing at watchful attention along the colonnade, and while their ceremonial weapons and dress uniforms were in keeping with a noble visitation, the graser pistols tagged to their hips were purely functional. Every one of them looked lean and fit. And two officers, off to one side, were blatantly watching the piazza's crowd.

Looking this way.

Tom turned quickly away from the pedlar. Behind him, he could hear the man taking the hint, his scuffling footsteps disappearing as he faded into the throng. If he had any sense, the pedlar would extinguish the hololabels and get rid of the tray.

Jasirah and the others were already beyond the piazza, walking along a grey corridor lined with golden glowclusters. Tom followed, tugging off his grey cloak as he moved among the crowd—a simple change in appearance—and bundled it under his arm. Then he was in clear space, into the corridor, and lengthening his stride.

Around a bend, and no sign of anyone following. So he had not alarmed the soldiers that much.

"Gazhe? Are you coming?"

Some holiday.

Tom smiled then, to reassure his friends who were in need of this break as much as he was. And he wondered, as he walked faster to catch up, whether he should have learned something from the carls' custom of total relaxation: each evening a celebration of the day that had passed. For Tom allowed himself no opportunity simply to relax and do nothing: every moment was a time for preparation or for action, born from the knowledge that life is too short and fragile to waste, and that if Destiny deals a hand, there is no choice but to play the game and play it hard, doing everything to win.

In his case, failure would mean despair, an end to driven purpose; and victory would be defined by seeing Elva once again.

20

TERRA AD 2142

<<Ro's Story>>

[5]

In one corner of the dimly lit gym, a narrow-shouldered black man was working a solo fighting form: sudden shifts of motion, dropping to the floor, striking in odd directions; nothing acrobatic or overtly violent about it.

"Most people," said Lily Degas, "don't rate pentjak silat too much."

"In which case"—Ro regarded the strange techniques, the subtle oblique attack angles—"most people don't know shit."

"Girlfriend, you got that right."

Degas was the owner: thick-waisted, with grey-flecked hair, but hard-looking, a little scarred around the eyes. Even without the holo in the foyer—Degas with championship belt held aloft—Ro would have known that she had fought in the ring.

"Come on," Degas added. "I'll show you the locker rooms."

No frills. Sweat and effort. Ro pounded on air pads and electromag shields, then sparred with an older woman, and finally a young hispanic guy with loads of spirit but none of Ro's tactical awareness. Afterwards, Ro touched gloves with her sparring partners, and limped off towards the showers, stripping off helmet and chest pad as she walked.

Later, heading out into the warm night and feeling good, her hair still damp, Ro retrieved her new bicycle. She thumbed the handgrip, releasing the security locks, then mounted the saddle. Breathed in the clean air, then glanced back at the floating holo sign—**LILY'S KICKBOX**: *Kick-Ass Good, but Humble*—and grinned. It was a far cry from Mother's clean, tranquil dojo: different path, same goal.

She placed her right foot upon the pedal—

"Ro?" It was Degas herself, standing in the doorway.

"Yeah? I mean—"

"Can you come back inside for a moment?"

Puzzled, Ro dismounted, and walked back to the gym's blue-painted door, not bothering to re-lock her bike's safeties—it was a hassle. She positioned herself so that she could keep the bike in sight but Degas swung the door firmly shut, blocking off the outside world.

"The thing is . . ." Degas paused, then: "I was a cop's wife for fifteen years, y'know?"

Ro did not want to ask what had happened to him. She remained silent.

"Are you in some kind of trouble, girl?"

Ro shook her head. "Not that I'm aware of."

Degas frowned.

"Look . . ." Ro, feeling uneasy, stepped past Degas and pushed the door open.

Her new bicycle was gone.

"Shit!" She crouched, ready to run in pursuit—she could hear the thief, already out of sight around the corner and pedalling hard—but a firm grip caught her sleeve and swung her back inside.

Ro's fists clenched . . . but she did not intend to fight Degas.

"Cool it." The warning was unnecessary. "If the bike's been pinched, you might be better off."

"What . . . do you mean?"

"Someone—a Mexican, no-one I know—brushed by the bike earlier."

Ro stared at her.

"So?"

"So if he wasn't dropping a bug on you, I'm your maiden aunt." A quick smile. "And I ain't no maiden."

Bugged? Ro did not know what to make of that. She took a taxi— ground-TDV—back to DistribOne. In the morning, clear-minded, she would decide whether to report the bike stolen.

Professional surveillance . . .

Something to do with Anne-Louise? The notion made her shiver.

She tapped her strand to pay the taxi, then slid out into the pleasant warm night air. Above, the black sky hung over the desert, studded with silver stars. Before her, inviting, DistribOne was a fairytale oasis in the wilderness, bedecked with orange-white lights.

In the refectory, Ro ordered decaf coffee from the AI. Gradually, she became aware of a low buzz of excitement. In one corner, several students were gathered around a holodisplay, watching a news bulletin. And two carafes of wine, one almost empty, stood beside it: an impromptu party.

"What's up?" she asked.

A teaching assistant called Zoë—Ro had seen her around, was envious of her clear, creamy complexion and lustrous grey eyes— looked up from an armchair and giggled.

"Illegal aliens," she said. "Well, one of them, at least."

The others, ignoring Ro, huddled closer to the holo.

"What do you mean?"

"Got loose. Not sure it was even supposed to be"—Zoë hic- coughed—"here on Terra. Zajinet embassy's getting a roasting."

In the image, an anti-xeno demonstration was in progress. The protesters' holo banners flickered and broke up. Accidental beat-fre- quency effects, with the camera-scan cycling out of synch? Or a subtle form of censorship?

But it was still possible to infer what they read, and few of the slo- gans would win prizes for originality: *Aliens go home,* or *Earth for Earthers, space the Xenoes.* Even *The Only Good Alien Is A Dead One,* and the nearly humorous: *I love Xenoes . . . curried and hot, with rice on the side.*

"Xenophobes" once referred simply to those who fear strangers. Now it was a polite term for wrongthinking bigots who blamed beings of different appearance and mentality for the inadequacies and failures of their own pitiful, misery-drenched lives.

The only thing Ro could not understand was why this particular demonstration was occurring, and why the news was so important.

"What," she asked slowly, "is a Zajinet?"

"Huh?" Zoë leaned closer, peering, and Ro could smell alcohol vapour upon her breath. "Just got here, yes? Well"—Zoë half-stumbled from the armchair, but caught her balance before Ro could grab her—"you'd better come with me."

"I don't think—"

"Ah . . . Right. New girl. Not authorized."

Ro stared at her. "Why don't you show me anyway?"

"No bilateral symmetry even." Zoë spoke with alcoholic over-careful enunciation. "It's not that common, on life-supporting worlds."

Around them, the lab was blanketed in gloomy shadows.

"Surprising."

Ro did not have access to UNSA xenofiles, and xeno visitors were generally kept out of the public eye. Of the thirty biocapable worlds, only a handful had sentient species. Two had interplanetary space-flight; it was rumoured that the Zajinets might be a third spacefaring species, but no-one knew for sure.

A holo grew into being.

"They don't look like much," said Ro.

Red network, fractally branching. A pattern in light.

"That's their core form. Internal." Zoë's diction was improving. "They usually look more like this . . ."

The image flickered.

It might have been a garden decoration, an impromptu sculpture of heaped boulders and stones, save that it was the size of an elephant, and it moved. Somehow the separate inorganic clumps held together as the whole ensemble stumped about, then glided along a shining path formed of metal, or perhaps of ice.

"Kind of a shell they build around themselves."

"Ugly-looking." Ro gestured for explanatory text-tesseracts, but the display did not respond: she really was not authorized.

"Well, they all look like that. They've got ambassadors in Moscow and Tehran. What do you think?"

"About what?"

"Interesting enough for project work? We need good researchers."

"I guess," said Ro.

A chance to work with aliens?

But she was an intern, still a student.

No way they'll give that work to me.

"Le . . . less . . . Uh, let's go join the party."

Ro muttered to herself. Aware that she was sleeping, face down on the bed. And then the muted chaos of overlaid whispers in the dark:

<< . . . arcs joining: and entropic diffusion extends . . . >>

<< . . . white, she survives the pearly nascent . . . >>

<< . . . burgeons the nexus: sweetening death . . . >>

<< . . . yet cold as matrix overdrives her future . . . >>

Ro jerked awake. An unsettling dream?

But neither the whispered sounds nor the half-sensed images faded as she sat bolt upright in the darkness.

<< . . . she sees! . . . >>

<< . . . sensitive, this one . . . >>

<< . . . affirm! confirm! . . . >>

<< . . . aware: beware . . . >>

Emerald fire, incandescent in the night shadows: a twisted dendritic network of glowing, burning lines. It was a nightmare, fiery in the darkened room, hovering over Anne-Louise's empty bed.

"Ah!" Ro threw her sheet from the bed. "Get back!"

She rolled sideways, moving fast, head pounding—

It disappeared.

—then stopped, almost falling over.

It's gone.

Trembling, she sat back on her bed. Sweat covered her. Scalp prickling, stomach heaving . . . but there was nothing here. The shadowed bedroom was empty now, save for a dead person's bed, a quietness which seemed more empty than the void, and the burning afterimage in her memory of an eerie inhuman ghost which surely could not exist.

<<MODULE ENDS>>

21

NULAPEIRON AD 3419

Ninth stratum, in Bilyarck Gébeet: the vacation's second day, and its true beginning. But it started with a disconcerting, overheard conversation.

Breakfast was interesting; they dined in a low-lit eatery at whose centre lay a pit in which orange-hot liquid magma flowed. The place was warm despite the insulating clearshell, and in the lava small hexagonal flukes bobbed occasionally into sight.

Jasirah had excused herself for the moment, and Quilvox was muttering that perhaps they should have left her—he referred to Jasirah as "Old Misery"—in the Bronlah Hong. Tom was just opening his mouth to say she was not that bad, when a fragment of speech drifted from a neighbouring table, as the background chatter briefly faded.

". . . best one, I thought, was 'Mincing Minnie Mixes Metalinguistic Metaphors.'"

Tom froze in his seat.

"The best from *Playing the Paradox*, maybe. But the second collection was a lot funnier overall: *Auntie Antinomy Dances the Fractal Fantastic*. What a laugh."

"Subtle, too," he heard a woman say. And something told Tom that they were a group of school magisters, even before she added: "I'd like to try it out on my students, but I'm not sure they'll understand it completely."

"I'm not even sure that I do," said one of her colleagues.

Tom was holding his breath. Slowly, he released it.

"I wonder if he'll ever write a third . . . ?"

And then Tom was walking away, having tossed too many cred-spindles upon the table, just needing to escape. Jasirah was returning, but he brushed past her without a word, into the spiralling tunnel beyond.

They're talking about my poetry.

His tutor, Mistress eh'Nalephi, had caused the first volume to be published, and had presented him with the crystal-shard on the day he turned twenty-three. At the time, he had been filled with a nameless joy which turned the world into magic and for a while brought perfection into his life.

But that was before he became a Lord, killed an Oracle, joined and subsequently abandoned a revolutionary movement, spent years wandering in a fractured, alcohol-deranged daze before fighting his way back to recovery, only to watch the single living person who truly mattered to him invoke thanatotropic toxin implants, for her own tangled and indecipherable purposes, and die before his eyes.

It was Jasirah, despite her reputation for hostility and jealousy, who sought Tom out. She found him standing by a long transparent water pipe which ran past a cloister at shoulder height, watching the silver bubbles and small bright-yellow cleansing fish, but seeing nothing.

"Come on," she said.

And led him back towards the eatery, while Tom apologized for his actions without explaining them. But when they reached the magma-pit chamber, the others had already left.

"Sorry." Tom looked at Jasirah and shrugged his shoulders. "I guess it's just you and me."

The colour heightened in Jasirah's round cheeks, suffusing her already dark skin. Then she cleared her throat and told him that she would like to go shopping.

Later, after several hours spent in fabric emporiums where Tom struggled hard to conceal his overwhelming boredom, they had lunch together in a tiny piazzetta where quickglass automaton-birds glided and whistled among the trellises and airplants, dipping and soaring without ever stopping to re-energize.

Tom listened while Jasirah talked of her childhood in the Garujahn

Protectorate, of her overbearing mother and often absent father. Then, in a sudden shift of subject which Jasirah seemed to think was entirely natural, she declared: "I really need to get my fortune told."

"I don't think"—Tom tried to keep the laughter from his voice—"you'll find an Oracle round here."

She gave him a small, quizzical look.

"We passed a scryer's booth," she said, "when we walked through the market."

The tent's interior was dark, lit only by a row of fluorescent bell jars and Klein bottles in which strange albino serpents with flat crested heads flexed and coiled, regarding the human interlopers with eyes like blood-red stones. On a small stool before a triangular table, the scryer sat hunched, a grey shawl pulled hood-like over her head, hiding her features.

Her voice was ancient, quavering, and her hand shook as she accepted Jasirah's proffered fee. Then a young beefy man came inside the tent, though the scryer had given no signal.

Tom watched as the assistant drew on heavy gauntlets, then removed the nearest serpent, looped round his wrists. He held the flat triangular head, pried open the jaws, and pressed the serpent's narrow, curved fangs into the old woman's scarred and bony forearm. The reptile remained expressionless, unblinking, as venom pumped into withered, punctured flesh.

Nor did it offer more than token resistance as it was forced back inside its glowing glass prison. Then the young man sealed the jar, shed his protective gauntlets and left, having uttered no word to either his employer or her clients.

Tom looked at Jasirah for her reaction, but she was intent upon the scryer's hooded features.

From the three-sided tabletop, a small collection of crystal dice rose into the air.

Am I supposed to be impressed?

The dice dropped and rolled. Then the scryer produced a deck of cards, and spread them face down across the table, and motioned for Jasirah to pick one.

"Seven of Ships." Jasirah looked up at Tom. "But what about its conjunction?"

It was the scryer who turned over the second card—Ace of Wands—and at the sight of it Jasirah turned away, shoulders drooping with disappointment. When she picked the final card, it was the Swordsman—armed nobleman in profile, en garde, foot upon a vanquished opponent—and it seemed to confirm Jasirah's expectations.

"Thwarted," said the scryer, "in love."

Then she pulled back her shawl, revealing the brass-coloured threads woven across her eye-sockets. And, turning her lined face towards Tom:

"Your turn, my Lord."

Jasirah tried a brave smile, as though the scryer's words were a joke.

"I'm not a noble," Tom said.

But deep lines etched curves to bracket the old woman's mouth, an expression which managed to combine both amusement and disapproval. He felt like a miscreant schoolboy, caught misbehaving by a senior praefectus, trying to hide his guilt before a magister with lies and indirection, with no hope of success.

Four of Serpents.

"A beginning," the old woman said, "born of adversity."

That, to a one-armed client: anyone could have guessed as much. At least, if she were not truly blind—

But she called me Lord.

"And"—with a nod towards the crystals which had rolled once more—"I see a red-haired woman in your early life, my Lord."

Tom's skin crawled.

Mother.

Giddily, he watched as the old scryer drew another card from the spread, and then a third.

"The Sorcerer," murmured Jasirah, "and the Fool."

Tom laughed shortly, without humour, but Jasirah shivered, her round face pinched with concern.

"We need," rasped the scryer, "a five-spread."

The Nine of Ships.

"Last card."

Benoited Chaos! he cursed. *Irrational nonsense.*

But fine hairs stood up on the back of his neck as she turned the card over: glossy, baroque patterns surrounding a central dark-haired figure whose eyes were obsidian, black upon black, and he did not need Jasirah's startled exclamation to tell him the card's designation.

The Pilot.

"Gazhe . . ." Jasirah's brown eyes were bright with tears, imploring.

But Tom was already on his feet.

"This day . . ." The old woman paused, then: "You will learn a thing, my Lord."

I've learned something already.

Confused, suddenly afraid, he plunged out of the tent and into the light, the bright busy marketplace, and stumbled towards the nearest exit. It was raw, this tunnel, but he moved on quickly, almost running, hurrying along the tunnel's length until he came out into a wide natural cavern.

He stopped, catching his breath, and then the true nature of his surroundings became clear. For everywhere the stone was patched with sickly, moribund fluorofungus, stippled with liquid infection and glowing deathly green. While up above, near the dripping ceiling, dying blindmoths, feasting upon disease, fluttered in vain, unaware that extinction was almost upon them.

And yet, and yet . . .

It was the evening's events, not the scryer's unsettling words, which brought the message home to Tom: that things had changed in the world, had perhaps started to change sometime during his four Standard Years in exile. And that these changes were unrelated to LudusVitae and affiliated movements, who had coordinated uprisings throughout Nulapeiron in the event known as Flashpoint. Its results had turned out to be Chaos-damned and paradoxically unpredictable, as revolutionaries suborned so many Oracles that neither the ruling powers nor their opponents knew any longer which truecasts were trustworthy and which were merely simulated dreams of a future that would never occur.

He did not know how many Oracles remained alive. Surely there were thousands of them, still. But whether people would ever again blindly accept the validity of their truecasts, that was another matter.

Am I that insane? In his alcove at the travellers' hostel, Tom stared at the blank whitewashed wall. *Am I ready to believe an old woman who's injected serpent venom so often she's probably psychotic?*

Or perhaps it was the fact that she had made no mention of Elva which was upsetting him. And that was foolish, since he could not rationally believe the scryer had any kind of true ability.

Though he had already run long and hard today—just before dawnshift, in shadow-shrouded empty tunnels—he was trembling with the need to burn more adrenaline. He changed into his cheap, one-piece training suit, and pulled on the soft, battered climbing slippers he had bought from a pawnshop. Then he walked out to the nearest natural caverns and, without warm-up, began to climb.

For an hour he worked problems, traversing his way from one cavern to another. Close to ground level, he threw himself upwards in a series of power moves: from knees turned out in the frog position, launching himself up to grab a ledge or crack, crimping his fingers and smearing his inner soles against the rock.

Then he went for the heights, concentrating on soft limberness and precise technique, the rhythm of counter-tension versus relaxation, and passed over a narrow abyssal rift by spidering his way across the ceiling.

Finally, he found himself near the apex of a long, cathedral-like space, at whose far end the rockface sloped inwards, smoothly, to a great gargoyle figure: spread-winged and leering, it must have been a hundred metres or more in width.

Smiling, Tom worked his way along and down. On the slope, he walked across upright, relying on friction without using his hand, then reached the vertical rock, hooked into a fingerhold and leaned back, so that torque pressed his feet into stone.

Something . . . ?

A distant clatter of sound. Tom remained still, his breathing shallow, but there was only silence now.

Come on.

He laughed softly to himself as he clambered up the final portion, swung across to the gargoyle's giant stone wingtip. Hooking one heel, Tom pointed the other foot into a narrow gap, spreading his hips, maybe a hundred and fifty metres above the great cavern's chopped and fractured floor.

Then, controlling abdominal tension, he released his finger crimp and slowly tilted backwards, until he was hanging head down—feet spread in forward splits between two stable holds—hand dangling down into the void, arm relaxed.

Finally . . .

All fear was gone, as though the world itself had settled back into place.

Thank Fate.

It was one of those moments when life was precious, filled with wonder, as he stared at the distant floor above/below his head.

And then there was movement.

They danced and flowed: from everywhere they came, like boiling swarms of termites, into the cavern beneath him. Long, sinuous myriapedes, their rounded segments looking hard, armoured. Dark lev-cars. And soldiers on foot: seen from above, their helmets were like small round pellets; but their sense of purpose was manifest.

And, as Tom hung there watching, the first myriapedes halted, segments splitting open, disgorging troops and equipment.

For a moment, he thought he was seeing an invasion. But then he realized that the dun colours were those of the Bilyarck Gébeet's own forces, and that they were inflating bivouacs behind defensive emplacements, and posting sentinels.

Manoeuvres?

Every demesne's armed forces needed training. But it seemed to Tom—as he swung himself back upright—that the platoons and companies now entering the cavern moved less fluidly than their comrades in the vanguard, needed officers to tell them how to order themselves and set up camp. They might be newer recruits in training—or they might be conscripted troops who had none of the experience and spirit of men and women who had devoted their lives to military service.

Tom began to move, swinging from hold to hold, going for speed and momentum now, wanting to make himself scarce before sensor-fields were put into place and someone with an itchy finger mistook Tom's intentions and depressed the firing stud for that high moment of spurting orgasmic joy when graser fire splits the air and a human body falls.

But, whatever the truth of the events occurring below, it seemed certain—or so Tom thought, as he climbed dangerously fast—that Bilyarck Gébeet was a realm preparing itself for war.

22

TERRA AD 2142

<<Ro's Story>>

[6]

Aching blue sky. Sere red. Desert heat.

"Message sender is Albrecht. Subject is: How are you doing?"

So hot, it melted through to her very bones.

"No-read del," said Ro, and the teardrop icon winked out of existence.

A broken shadow crossed the dusty ground behind her.

"You ready?" Luís Starhome's voice.

Ro turned. His face was bronze in the desert dawn, untouched by sweat.

"Sure. Mrs. Bridcombe"—Ro tapped her infostrand, powering it down—"already saddled Quarrel for me."

She walked back to the corral, half expecting Luís to ride Bolt—Quarrel's half-sister: same dam, different stallion—bareback. But Luís threw a light saddle across the strong-looking mare, cinched the magstrap with practised ease.

Ro mounted as best she could.

They waved towards the low pueblo-style ranch house. Behind the polarized windows, the tall figure of Alice Bridcombe waved back.

Slowly, Ro and Luís urged their mounts into motion. There was a reassuring gurgle from the saddlebags: full water bottles. Strands and EveryWare notwithstanding, this was still a desert they were riding into. A place of danger.

And death was no abstraction. Anne-Louise's murder had taught her that.

As she rode, she thought about Flight Officer Armstrong Neil, and the meeting with Ilse Schwenger which was surely prearranged, but whose purpose remained a mystery. It was the next morning that she had learned of the field trip to IllinoisCentral, the second-busiest spaceport on the continent: an unexpected bonus for an intern who was new to DistribOne.

Frau Doktor Schwenger, pulling strings?

And this was what Ro had seen, as she sat with her strand's analysis displays pulsing and scrolling, and watched the departure lounge:

An old woman, bent with care and paranoid mistrust, carrying her own baggage while an empty smartcart trailed almost plaintively behind her; a newly married triple, voluptuous fem-bi linking arms with her blushing partners, wedding-glitter sparkling on their slash-cut suits; a large family, farewell tears tracking down their cheeks, followed by a small convoy of heaped smartcarts—emigrating offworld; a teenage boy, wired with excitement, his wide-eyed stare brightening when he saw Ro.

Behind the swirling crowd, the vendors: faint warm scents of toffee-ants—nouveau africain vite-cuisine—and butter-fried cicada-chews; of beer (inadvisable before a mu-space voyage's delta-coma) and fresh-fruit shakes; of dark rich coffee.

Later, Ro had been the last one into the small private lounge, where the other researchers were already breaking off chunks of caramel doughnut, sipping espressos.

". . . got Jim bumped off the list," one of them was saying.

"Must be someone's little flooz—"

Their voices died as Ro stepped inside.

"So . . . 'He went to town.'" Ro shifted in her saddle, trying to ignore the chafing. "How would I say that? 'He went.'"

They were a world away from UNSA and its bureaucratic machinations, in a desert which stretched to the horizon in every direction, looking stark and eternal—except that once, in its geological past, the wide sands had formed a sea floor, while strange forms, few of which would leave any traces for the curious hairless primates to follow, swam in the warm, salty waters which covered it, thinking mysterious thoughts, hunting their exotic prey.

"That depends." A tight smile. "The verb expresses the method of locomotion. *Kintahǵóó 'o'ooldloozh* if he travelled on horseback, *kintahǵóó bił 'o'oot'a'* if he flew."

Ro blinked. The hot dry air was making her sleepy.

"You mean, 'rides' and 'flies.' But what is the simple verb: 'to go'?"

Luís shook his head. "The verb is bound up with context, always. There are different words for travel on foot, or mounted, by ground vehicle, or by air." Luís made a gesture with his mouth which Ro could not interpret. "And, for the same mode, different terms depending on speed."

"But—"

"Also, if there are several possible consequences, the verb choice reflects the result. Or the frequency: to do a thing once, to do it many times on one occasion, to repeat it on many separate occasions . . . They're different words. Different *ideas*."

"My God." A linguistic timelessness? An alternative concept of cause and effect? "That's amazing."

What difference might it make to her worldview if she were fluent enough to think in Navajo?

And when the People, the *dine'é*, feared evil *chindhí* spirits, did they sense something real and tangible which poor non-Navajos, bound by their limited ways of perception, simply could not see?

Superstitious nonsense.

Ro touched her heels to Quarrel's flanks, increasing the pace.

In the sweaty darkness, the Singer's—Luís's uncle's—lined face was a graven ancient mask, whose eyes had looked on sights no man should experience. The hogan's interior was not small, but the dark air seemed to draw in, to vibrate with resonance as the chant continued.

It was a Far Voyage Way, a family Sing, and it gradually dawned on Ro that the ceremony was focused on Luís.

There were six Navajo men and two women, besides the Singer and Luís. All were family members, though clan kinship was another complex relationship Ro had not deciphered: in some sense, everyone belonged to two tribes—born *into* the maternal clan, and *for* the father's.

As the ceremony drew on, the mundane world—that manufactured illusion of consensual reality—slowly receded, and the hogan defined the cosmos, where Luís, like a bronze warrior from olden times, was bright in its firmament. Ro felt herself swaying, lost in the rhythms of the Sing, enchanted by the gestures, entranced by the repeated elaborate giving of turquoise and bright shells: always the same four colours (white, yellow, blue, black); always the fourfold repetition in the chants.

One of the women, leaning close to Ro so she could whisper, translated part of a story: of Coyote, the Trickster, gambling all in an eating contest. Using his supernatural abilities to eat not just the food, but the plates and even the tabletop as well.

But Ro, brought up on Norse legends, already knew the tale, except there the Trickster was Loki. And eating contests were a fantasy of starving folk, like 1930s Depression-struck America.

"*I am the Trickster, and I dance upon the boundary between Chaos and Order, the Dark and the Light.*" The woman's whisper, in counterpoint to the Singer's octave-wide range of chants, became hypnotic. "*For the Holy People know the Four Houses: Dark Wave to the north, Gravity to the south, Strong Nuclear to the east and Electroweak to the west. And I move among them . . .*"

Luís had said that ceremonies continued to evolve: he had not mentioned they included unified matrix theory, the Fourfold Way.

Ro watched him now: face bronze, then gold, in the flickering firelight.

You're the one.

They hadn't even kissed, but she was sure.

Around them, the chanting, the flames and the dancing shadows:
but she was aware only of Luís, and the tangible bond coalescing
between them.

*"And the locusts broke through the sky's blue shell, into the world above
where the Yellow Grasshopper People lived . . ."*

Different races, ascending through stratified worlds until finally,
the *dine'é,* the People, were born of First Man and First Woman.

Hours passed.

Or centuries. Stars tumbled, nova heat burned, and pulsating darkness took hold.

Sharp scent of mesquite.

I'm having a vision.

But that was a metathought, soon discarded.

The world faded.

A chesspiece upon an infinite board. A solitary king—

The piece. Why was it important?

Anne-Louise. It floated, above her body.

Board shrinking, rotating. It was eight-squared now, in normal
planar dimensions, and the piece occupied the seventh rank upon the
fifth file. The realization came to her: it was not the piece, but its *position* which held import.

Keep that thought . . .

Fighting to hold the vision: but that was a bagatelle, a surface illusion, before the deeper dream which was to come.

No—

But her strength was insufficient to hold the chessboard or
reality—the smoke-filled hogan—in her mind.

And then it was upon her.

Adrift in a golden sea.

The universe she had always dreamed of.

Golden amber, and the floating stars: fractal, black. Spongiform absences of light.

Her birthplace.

And the drifting crimson streamers, like nebulae, of vast dimensions. Where place and time vary according to scale, not velocity.

Where logic was complete, and all that was true could be deduced.

Home.

Where self reflexive recursion, and infinite paradox, might be resolved.

It called, it called, to the aching void inside her.

Mu-space.

Infinite and infinitely complex, it sang.

It beckoned.

Home.

For three nights, they performed the Sing, and Ro's spirit soared free.

At the third night's end, they carried her outside, and laid her down on the supportive ground. Cold air washed over her, as she stared up into the still-dark sky where silver stars shone. Only a touch of lime in the eastern skies bespoke the coming dawn.

"You saw deeply." One of the men, his voice serious.

"That I did." She looked up at him without smiling.

He nodded, and walked away.

Luís reached out his hand—the touch of his smooth skin was like fire: a burst of pleasure, intense and prolonged—and helped her to stand.

Breakfast—eggs and beans cooked over a real fire—tasted heavenly. They sat cross-legged on the reddish sand, eating in easy silence. Behind them, the horses, saddled up, patiently waited.

She watched him: the controlled gestures, the centred calm.

Some fine day, I'll make you lose control.

Inwardly smiling, she poured him coffee from the self-heating chemoflask.

Afterwards, mounted, they took Quarrel and Bolt to the sandstone mesa's edge and looked down upon the wide, flat desert below. DistribOne was a tiny distant cluster.

Leaning against her saddle's pommel, Ro said: "The *bilagáana* world." She used the Navajo term for Anglos, not knowing whether it was value-neutral or derogatory.

"And mine."

There was a Teutonic exactness to his speech. Ro assumed he meant it was *one* of the cultural worlds in which he lived.

Luís slid down from his saddle. Reins in hand, he walked—lean and athletic, his every movement, magnet-like, drawing Ro's gaze—to the mesa's edge. The sheer drop seemed not to bother him.

From his saddlepack, Luís drew a silver/turquoise bracelet, and fastened it round his wrist. Infostrand: like Ro, he had been offline for three days.

He tapped a silver conch on the bracelet, stared intensely—a lased-in display, invisible to Ro—and nodded once as he tapped the bracelet off.

"Bad news?" asked Ro.

Luís looked at her with dark unreadable eyes.

"Not for me."

"I'm sorry?" Ro swung her leg back and dropped from the saddle. "What do you mean?"

She walked up to him.

God, I want you.

Standing centimetres apart. Proximity: she was aware only of him, of his strength and presence and sheer desirability.

"I'm going to Tehran," he said. "That message confirmed what the Sing told me."

For a moment, Ro could only stare.

Then, "What's in Tehran?"

But, spirit sinking, she knew the answer before he spoke:

"The stars."

<<MODULE ENDS>>

23

NULAPEIRON AD 3419

They ended their holiday a day early.

Some homecoming.

It hung there, in a man-shaped basket floating vertically in the gloom: blackened, roasted flesh. Hanging above the piazzetta's black and white squares; once a human being, now flensed and burned, with the cooked-meat stench pervading the still air.

Behind Tom, Mivkin turned away, retching. Jasirah was stumbling back into the tunnel from which they had come.

Abomination.

There were others, floating in two rows. Sixteen black/red forms, some with viscerae spilled forth and burst, glistening like liquid pain where pale beams of light filtered through from the larger piazza. And then *one of them moved* and Tom, too, dropped to his knees and vomited clear bile.

Tom cast aside his cloak, stared upwards into the gloom.

"What are you—?" Quilvox stopped.

But it was Ryban, the quiet sneaky one, who surprised Tom. From within his broad sash, he brought out a long narrow blade, and proffered it hilt first.

"I'd be honoured, my Lord." His voice was a low whisper, but it charged the air.

"You know."

"Looking at you now"—with an ironic half-smile—"I recognize you, at last."

"My thanks."

Tom took the stiletto, slid it inside his tunic, and ran lightly to the nearest wall and jumped, reaching up to grab. There were shallow grooves cut into the polished rock, and he used them, moving quickly. Reaching the ceiling, he stepped out onto a glowcluster—it bobbed once, beneath his weight—then vaulted onto the first floating lev-cage.

Its occupant was truly dead, teeth bared in a death rictus where the face was burned away. Denatured white slime nestled in the cooked eye sockets.

Tom leaped to the next cage.

No life inside here, either. But this one had torn the flesh from his fingers against the wire-thin bars, scraped down to the gleaming bone, before death claimed him. Tom could not imagine pain so great that he would rip himself apart in the effort to escape.

And then the next.

Seventeen cages in all. Tom remembered the schachmati-playing merchant, and the living men who had been his game pieces, facing the noble Viscount Trevalkin. And in the piazza, instead of holiday atmosphere, the grim mood of spectators who had sensed that something beyond their ordinary experience was about to happen.

". . . *traitor*," the pedlar had told Tom, "*but there's no need to draw things out . . .*"

If he had stayed, could he have prevented this?

Another twitch of movement, from the same cage as before.

There were glittering flecks in charcoal-encrusted flesh which had bubbled as it roasted. Perched atop the cage and peering down inside, Tom wondered whether the torturers had used femtocytic healing insertions to keep their victims alive longer than any human should endure.

". . . *er* . . ."

Tried to speak, but its tongue had been slit in two, and half of it was blackened.

"Don't talk."

Tom held on to the cage, steadying himself. Inside, the roasted remnant moved, and groaned.

"... *er* ... *ire* ..."

There was only one thing Tom could do for the man.

"... *ware* ... *erk-ire* ..."

Braced with his feet, reached inside his tunic.

"... *ess* ..." Acknowledging Tom's intent.

Blade, shining where it caught the light.

"... *ah* ..."

Entered, and did its work.

No-one talked to him as they returned through deserted tunnels to the Bronlah Hong.

While the others went to the communal chambers, looking for company, Tom went alone to his sleeping alcove, pulled the drape across, and lay down on his pallet, knowing there would be little sleep tonight.

He remained unmoving, aware of the hard mattress beneath his back, eyes open and controlling his breathing, while the long hours passed.

But sometimes the curtain which separates dreams, thoughts and passions tears a little, rips just enough, and at some point in the grey pre-dawn hours, slipping among those reality-states which are neither consciousness nor sleep, a true memory visited him.

He is fourteen SY old, sitting alone in a quiet tunnel near the marketplace, closing his eyes and holding the stallion talisman, remembering the day of its creation, his poetry-in-progress floating still above his holopad.

And a woman's voice says: "Don't get up on my account."

Her chin is elegant, her complexion olive and flawless, dark hair hidden beneath her burgundy cloak's hood.

"May I?" And then she is holding the silver talisman. "Quite beautiful."

"It—it's a stallion. A mythical beast."

He can't believe he is talking to this woman.

"And this poetry?"

"Mine. I write—"

"Competently." The display rotates at her gesture, though it is access-keyed only to him. "A nice sense of space, for someone who has never seen the sky."

Shortly afterwards, she is inserting a small black ovoid capsule inside the stallion talisman, which has somehow split in half for her. She shows him how to seal it shut, how to open it again with a gesture.

Then, grimacing: "If only I had more—well, I don't." Glancing along the corridor. "Life is a mortal pilgrimage, my friend."

She places the talisman in Tom's grasp, clasps her own hand over his fist.

"When the dark fire falls, seek salvation where you—"

But then she is standing.

"I won't tell anyone," he says.

Fingertips brush his cheek.

"Good luck."

And then she breaks into a silent run, is gone.

Tom stares into grey twilit shadows, and swallows once, remembering.

The next morning, in the crowded marketplace, a sudden hush descends, and he sees her being led to the round chamber's centre, manacled, head bowed in defeat, surrounded by armed militiamen.

Then an officer raises his baton, and the ceiling-disk rotates, and a stairway to the stratum above spirals downwards and slats click into place.

And this is her moment.

She dabs at her eyes, as though the manacle bar weighs nothing, and flicks something aside. And when she looks back at her captors, everyone can see that her eyes are pure obsidian, black upon black with no surrounding whites, and it is Father who whispers the shocked recognition, a memory of ancient tales: "A Pilot!"

In those eyes, a golden glimmer.

And Tom looks away, before a blinding flash fills the marketplace and people fall screaming, clutching at their eyes.

Her cape flies at a trooper, then she whirls into action, ducking low, leaping high, kicking and striking, thrusting troopers into each other's line of fire, before breaking free and sprinting for the stairs.

Tom's two fists are clenched as he screams silently for her to run.

Her foot lands on the fifth rung, flying upwards fast, and it looks as though she's reaching freedom but then the spitting, lancing beams impale her, and it is a broken, lifeless body which topples to the flagstones, and lies twisted and angular, forever still.

Sweat coated his body.

It was the time he met a legend, and knew that she was real. It was the moment that changed his life. But more: she had given him a warning, fifteen Standard Years before, which he had not recognized until this second.

For the roast-meat stench of her half-burned face brought back a more recent waking memory, of the poor wretch whose suffering he had ended with a borrowed blade today, and the half-formed words of warning which the dying man had tried to utter.

"*. . . ware . . . erk-ire . . .*"

And perhaps Tom did sleep then, and maybe dream, but when he awoke it was with a vision fading before his eyes, of eerie red-clad children who moved in silent synchrony beside an icy lake, of the edelace which had attacked one of their number, and the old man who had used his cane upon it. A cane from whose point black flames had sprouted. As black as those within the spacetime maelstrom which had whirled and roared inside the Seer's chamber, and bloodily snuffed out his life.

Dark fire.

There was an enemy, whose nature or purpose Tom could not know, but of whose existence he was suddenly certain. And for sure, he knew one of its names.

Dark Fire.

24

NULAPEIRON AD 3419

An icy atmosphere had settled in the merchanalysis hall, where dim glowglobes slowly orbited in the dusty gloom. Master Grenshin sat hunched before his narrow desk.

"I'm not getting any younger," he said finally. "I'd hoped . . ."

"Sorry."

"An you need references, Gazhe—if that's your name—"

"It isn't."

"I'll provide the references anyway. Call by later."

"Thank you, sir. The others . . . I think they're all renewing, though I'm not sure."

"I know. They think things might be safer elsewhere." Shaking his head: "Dark times, my young friend."

"I fear so." Tom stood, pulled his new dark-green travelling cloak around himself. "Sir? Do you know anything of a certain schachmati game which took place while we were on holiday?"

Master Grenshin tugged at his skullcap, adjusting it. "You mean Viscount Trevalkin. Against Trader Vulan." Then, with ancient weariness veiling his eyes: "Vulan lost."

"And so did his vassals."

"A sword?" Horush stared at Tom. "What kind of sword?"

Horush looked as bright as ever, taking his recovery for granted. He remembered nothing of his conversation with Tom in the med chamber, yet somehow knew that Tom had been to visit during the long hours in the autodoc.

"What kinds have you got?"

"The kind you slice 'em with"—a grin crossed Horush's brown-skinned narrow face—"and the kind you use to stick 'em."

"Show me."

Horush led the way to the armoury.

The piazza had been scrubbed and polished for the public meeting, and extra glowclusters (with casings of gleaming brass) floated below the ceiling. In the adjoining piazzetta, glowflitters sparking reflected highlights from the filigreed floating cages, still bearing their grim reminders of the Viscount's actions.

There were troopers everywhere: in the markets, in the residential tunnels, taking over alcoves for their own use.

And, in the piazza, a noble representative was entering—a fleshy alpha-servitor robed in purple—surrounded by a platoon of smartly dressed soldiers. They wore formal half-capes in white and blue, narrow halberds held vertically, and when they wheeled and stamped to attention, the butts of their halberds struck the flagstones with a synchronized crash.

"I give announcement," cried the servitor, "in the name of our ruler, Duke Yvyel the Great, and his esteemed cousin, Viscount Lord Trevalkin."

There was a shift of random movement in the crowd, a murmur among the gathered smalltraders and freedmen.

"For our protection, the Ducal Halberdiers, along with the Viscount's personal guard, will be locating their barracks among us."

"*Not where you sleep, I'll bet*," muttered someone near Tom.

But, as Tom began to insinuate his way through the crowd, he realized that though there were unhappy faces and a few whispers, no-one wanted to be first to show open dissent. Perhaps the scorched, ruined corpses floating in the piazzetta were an indication of noble policy in that regard.

". . . to take special precautions, show goodwill to the troops protecting us, until the current circumstances . . ."

Tom was near the front rows now, squeezing harder to force his way through the onlookers.

". . . that Viscount Trevalkin has declared will not last long. To expedite troop movement during the emergency, all floor hatches will . . ."

The servitor's voice trailed off.

Tom stepped into the open space before him. From his belt he drew a pair of new gauntlets; the movement of his cape revealed the absence of his left arm.

"The Codes of Governance"—Tom projected his voice: low-toned, but carrying—"may be ignored." He nodded towards the piazzetta, the hanging bodies. *"But les Accords d'Honneur are another matter."*

There were gasps from behind him, and the servitor's fleshy face grew pale.

"You . . . can't . . ." He turned to the soldiers for help.

But their officer shook his head, very slightly, his expression tightening. Then he stared at Tom.

"My name," called Tom, and his voice rang now throughout the piazza, "is Lord Corcorigan, of Demesne Corcorigan, Gelmethri Syektor."

Shock rippled through the crowd as he flung his gauntlets down. They slapped against the flagstones at the alpha-servitor's feet.

"And for honour's sake"—completing the legal formula—"I require the blood of Viscount Lord Trevalkin."

But no-one came.

Tom had counted on that, to some extent. It gave him time, to buy a copy of *les Accords d'Honneur* from a literary-crystal shop he frequented—with his noble status revealed, Tom now had access to the restricted portion of the inventory, including *les Accords*—and to seek out the advice of Swordmaster Firlekan, a senior weapons instructor among the housecarls.

But instead of delivering verbal wisdom, the swordmaster had invited Tom onto the practice floor.

In a whirl of blades, they stamped and spun across the chamber: to cut and stab, bind and thrust. Attack, parry—Firlekan delivered curt advice between onslaughts, as his weapon wove blistering patterns in the air.

And finally, he called a halt.

"My Fate." After the salute, Tom put his blade down, pulled the protective mask from his head—like Firlekan, his hair was plastered against his head—and loosened the padded tunic around his torso. "That was hard work."

Mask under one arm, Firlekan nodded. "You use space," he said, "magnificently, my Lord. I've never seen a weapons novice perform so well."

"Call me Tom."

"In five SY, with discipline, you could be a top-class swordsman."

"Thank you."

The qualified praise told Tom everything he needed to know about his chances of surviving an encounter with Viscount Trevalkin when there was no protective clothing and the blades were sharp, the intent behind them deadly.

"The thing is," said Firlekan, "you have to find your own—"

A carl appeared in the square entranceway at that moment. It was Harald, his lean face masked with concern.

"Young Horush . . ." He looked from Firlekan to Tom, as though disbelieving the words he was about to utter. "He's dead."

Small glowglimmers circled in the dark chapel. Pungent purple incense smoke lay heavy as grief upon the air. And Horush, in repose: his dark skin turned grey in death, despite the preserving membrane which turned his body into a glistening statue.

Watching over him, cross-legged on low meditation stools, three big housecarls loomed like graven statues, shadow-wrapped and still.

Tom bowed his head, and genuflected.

Horush laughing, eyes bright with confidence, humour—

Tom shook away the vision.

Lowering himself to the flagstones, away from the mourning trio, he sat cross-legged, cleared his mind—and saw, hanging upon the wall, three knotted whips gleaming wetly beneath the glowglimmers.

He could not see the dark stains on the mourners' tunics, across their backs, but the near-subliminal cupric tang of blood was upon the air, beneath the smoke. One of the trio was Kraiv: a massive black presence, who seemed carved from obsidian.

Don't blame yourself, my friend.

Blame: for the undetected haematoma—the result of his sparring injury—which had burst open in Horush's brain. On solo guard duty, the young carl had lain dying, alone for hours, while the blood which should have brought him life flooded through the delicate contents of his skull and extinguished every thought and memory which had once glimmered there.

Tom rose, made his genuflection once more, and quietly left, while the three chief mourners maintained their vigil, as solid and unmoving as statues mounted over a warrior's tomb.

Salamander Hour. No-one there.

Tom waited in the deserted piazza for another two hours, practising a slow-moving meditation form, trying to slow his heart's pounding. Then he took a small crystal—which he had spent hours preparing, getting the wording just right—to the Zhongguo Ren courier who was waiting for him.

Madam Bronlah had agreed to help, and made it clear—without ever being so crass as to say it—that there was a burden of debt upon him now, to be repaid should he survive. But Tom had learned—early on, in the Ragged School, from his friend Zhao-Ji—the concept of reciprocity, of *guanxi*.

The crystal contained a message which was brief by noble standards, incorporating two quotations from the Accords.

In the event that a challenge be not replied to within two Standard Days, or such period as the Aggrieved Party shall declare, then to the latter shall fall the duty nominating time and place.

And, from Article XVII:

. . . fail to meet, or to the Aggrieved Party's satisfaction and without reasonable impediment provide alternative venues, so shall Communicado ex Domensis be called upon said defaulting Challengee.

Finally, it named the time and place of Tom's choosing: exercising the right which had passed to him, since the challenged party had failed to reply with sufficient speed. And adding the threat of demotion, at the next noble Convocation, which no man as arrogant and self-assured as Viscount Trevalkin could possibly ignore.

Harald and Firlekan were on watch that night, near the Maze of Light and Dark.

". . . two more," Harald was saying. "Three nights of mourning, before the Axes and Flames."

"You were Horush's friend, Tom . . ." Firlekan began.

"But non-carls can't attend the ceremony. I know."

"And do you know of *Todgeld?*"

"Well, what it sounds like is—"

Harald turned away, shaking his head, as Firlekan explained: "It's not money, necessarily. But Kraiv will have to offer reparation to the family."

"I see."

And, unspoken, the extent of the price he had to pay. But knowing the way carls lived—and died—the cost could become serious, maybe mortal.

Then, "I need to train," said Tom.

"Do you—?"

"By myself is fine."

The two carls looked at the sword upon Tom's hip. The weapon which Horush had allowed him to borrow from their armoury.

Firlekan raised a fist, clenched hard.

"Trust blade and blood, my friend."

He trained amid the shifting, blinding light and shadows, danced his warrior's dance of life and death against imaginary opponents, laughing strangely to himself—

A matter of topos-logic. True/false, good/bad: background-dependent, never absolute.

—as it occurred to him that he would survive beyond tomorrow only if the Seer's visions had not been subverted, his truecasts mere distorted pictures of an imagined future, constructed in simulation with techniques which he himself had devised.

Then he went back to his tiny alcove, scarcely noticing the deference which others paid him now that his rank was known, and prepared himself for another sleepless night.

And knew with absolute certainty, when he rose at dawnshift before his neighbours, that Trevalkin would come this day.

Blackness.

A sudden shift: startling, eerie blue. Raw stone wall, looking ghostly instead of solid.

Again: blood red.

Suitable, for a place of death.

Caverns, tunnels—winking into existence, then obliterated from sight as though they had never been. And the chill smell: no woody fragrance, no scents of friendly fluorofungus. It would have been a dead zone, save for the thermal draughts which brought oxygenated air flowing through from the Bronlah Hong proper.

Shifted, again.

And off to one side, where the shadows were stable, a small group of people waited. At their vanguard, slightly apart, stood a tall, straight-backed figure. Then a shaft of yellow light fell across him, revealing the man's high cheekbones and long dark hair, tied back with a platinum band: ascetic features marred by too-full lips.

Viscount Trevalkin was dressed in grey and black, lace ruffles at collar and cuffs as though he had come here on a social outing. He drew off his lined velvet cape, and handed it to one of the two Lords-Minor who were acting as his seconds.

"So, Corcorigan. What do you call this place?"

Tom cast aside his own cloak.

"Some say the Maze of Light and Dark." When he drew the copper blade, light slid like sweet boljicream along its length, and it left the scabbard with a soft metallic *snick*. "But I call it Trevalkin's Grave."

"Perhaps." And, over his shoulder: "My Lord Sumneriv, dear chap. The sooner we begin this charade, the sooner it will end."

Manoeuvring.

An eternity, manoeuvring.

Shadows . . .

Backing away, circling. Tom moved up the scree slope, slipping once but keeping the blade pointed at his adversary. Trevalkin advanced slowly, stalking, long silver sabre held before him.

Wait . . .

Among the watchers, Trevalkin's aides and seconds standing in a tight group near one wall, muttering began to rise. Their initial amusement was fading, as long minutes went by in silence, with no attack from either man. One of them said, in a carrying voice: "Finish the scoundrel quickly, my Lord Viscount."

Murmurs of agreement. But Trevalkin's expression remained unmoved, as he followed Tom's retreat.

Lord Sumneriv, who as a nominally disinterested referee had recited from the Codex Antagonist before signalling the duel's start, now called out: "With your usual flair, of course, my Lord!"

Stony, the Viscount's face. He knew Tom was no swordsman; but

he was watchful and alert, predatory, aware—with a fighter's instincts
—that Tom had other abilities beyond the blade.

Circling . . .

Trevalkin advanced—

Light shift.

The world changed as the Maze did its work once more.

—and stumbled on the loose footing, briefly opening his guard.

Now!

Tom threw his blade.

Ikken hisatsu. One chance, one kill.

The most ancient of strategies. Of the three possible timings, the
one that takes sudden, decisive courage: *sen no sen*, to seize the initia-
tive.

Tom *threw* the sword, knowing this was the moment to gamble
everything. It lanced through the air but Trevalkin beat the blade aside
by reflex, sabre clashing against copper sword, and sent it clattering to
the stones.

But Tom was already moving.

Shadows slid, light bloomed and died again.

The Viscount was fast, adapting to the perspective shifts.

Target—

But Tom was faster.

—and strike.

Tom's shoulder stump took Trevalkin in the sternum, knocked him
back. Spinning with the momentum, Trevalkin brought his sabre hilt-
first downwards. Hard metal struck Tom's head but it was already too
late: this was close quarters, as close as it could get, and no-one could
defeat Tom now.

He used fingers into eyeballs, raking, then clasped Trevalkin's
sword arm, hard, and somersaulted forwards, taking Trevalkin with
him, landing heavily on his back but with Trevalkin underneath.

"Ah—"

Head-butt, smashing Trevalkin's skull against the rocks.

"No!" Lord Sumneriv's voice. "Stop, barbarian!"

Palm-heel, elbow. Tom knelt on Trevalkin's chest with blood-rage filling his vision, the bloodied smoking corpses in the lev-cages and the black flames which killed the Seer and Elva falling dead—

"What is the Dark Fire?" He roared the question.

In his primordial rage, his lust for bloody death, striking hard, smashing Trevalkin over and over—

"What power do you serve, Trevalkin?"

—and again, hard, until hands fell upon him, grabbing, dragging him away.

"NO!"

Sumneriv, or another Lord, yelling in Tom's ear.

I'll kill you all.

He grabbed soft testicles, snarled at the animal yelp his victim gave, elbowed another man—

"He fights the Dark Fire, Corcorigan!"

—launched himself upwards, scattering the men apart, save for the one who clung still to Tom's sleeve, yelling desperately:

"It's Trevalkin's enemy! He *fights* the Dark Fire!"

Scarlet, fading through orange.

Tom stopped, then pushed Lord Sumneriv away.

Blood lust fading . . .

As his vision cleared, he could see Trevalkin's hunched and battered form, curled upon the broken scree like a child's discarded toy, smeared with red.

Enemy?

Tom spat, tasting blood which was not his own.

"This is over," he said.

25

TERRA AD 2142

<<Ro's Story>>

[7]

I can't lose something, Ro tried to tell herself, *that I never had.*

Digging her heels in: Quarrel leaped into a gallop, his great muscles bunching and releasing beneath her, hooves clattering across the sandstone mesa.

Not something: *someone*. Luís, leaving to become a Pilot. That was the meaning of the message he had received, the invitation to Flight School in Tehran.

By the time she reached the stables, both she and the horse were exhausted, lungs heaving. On her lips, the sweat-and-tears taste of salt. Alice Bridcombe, the owner, helped Ro dismount, then—frowning— checked out Quarrel.

"He looks all right," said Bridcombe. "No thanks to you."

"I'm sorry."

I pushed too hard.

Too late to undo that now.

Finally, someone had removed the bed on which Anne-Louise had died, leaving empty floor space with the stains cleaned away. Whether they had taken the bed to spare her feelings or for more forensic tests, Ro had no idea.

As evening fell, she sat down cross-legged on the fibrous carpeting—

forcing herself to occupy the same space as that poor bloodied corpse—then closed her eyes, bringing her focus inside herself, acknowledging her conflicting Luís-centred emotions but trying to let go.

Mu-space . . .

And there was the glory of her vision: the infinite fractal-dimensioned wonder of that other continuum which she had dreamed of, or seen for real, deep inside the dream-quest she had not known she was going to make.

But there was an intrusion, inside her mystic vision. A chesspiece upon a board. A king, standing one row removed from the edge. She tried to banish it, dispel the sight, return her mental focus to fractal infinity . . .

Then her eyes snapped open, and she knew what the vision meant.

"Not the second row. The *seventh*, counting from the other side."

Floating, above poor Anne-Louise's strangled corpse.

A message.

Perhaps Anne-Louise had been playing chess when the intruder was suddenly there, and the ligature was tightening round her throat before she even realized that her world was about to end, decades before her time. Maybe it was from a story scene she had been working on, the kind of clue a storyfact might leave for someone else to decipher, thinking that others might perceive the world the same way as she did.

Or perhaps it was just a final act of desperation by some small random-firing neural shard of a once-rational brain, already fragmenting as the end drew near. A message which could be formed with a tiny movement of the fingertips, the last gesture she would ever make.

A twitch before dying.

"Position K7. Why didn't I see it?"

Because Anne-Louise was Québecoise, and in extremis everybody, no matter how linguistically talented, counts and prays in their first—their parents'—tongue.

Not *kay-seven*, the piece's position, but *ka-sept*. Pronounced: *ca-ssette*.

Like the old-fashioned crystal-cassette on which Anne-Louise had kept all her primary work.

"Hey, purty lady. Howya doin'?"

Subtle overlay: Clint Shade, Arizona Ranger, seemed to be sitting back on Ro's easy chair and crossing his ankles. Highlights made the cushion appear to depress beneath the holo's nonexistent weight.

He was an illusion, Anne-Louise's fictional creation, and he had appeared as soon as Ro inserted the cassette into the holoscribe's waiting socket. But he looked so real, Ro felt she could almost reach out and touch him.

Which she did, slowly, and her fingertips passed through the spectral illusion of his sleeve, as she had expected. But he still looked solid.

"What," she asked softly, "are you doing out of context?"

The Ranger tipped up his hat, and his eyes were steel-grey, and gleaming.

"Ma'am," he said, "I was thinkin' you'd never ask."

For a long moment, there was nothing Ro could say.

Then, "Explain that, please."

"I have come across"—*ah have come acrawst*—"from the other side. The real world. Can't say"—with a glance around the room—"as I like this one too much."

Ro shook her head, not knowing what to say.

If she took the conversation along a route the programming could not deal with, the holo would vanish and she would almost certainly lose whatever information was hidden here.

"What," she said slowly, "can you tell—"

"The answer"—he tipped his stetson back down to hide his eyes—"is in Shadowville, fer sure. But there ain't no shortcuts, darlin'. Ya gotta see for yourself."

"I don't—"

But Ro was talking to an empty room.

Dusty street . . .

[[Partial immersion: all senses engaged, but not to full extent.]]

Dusty street, and the round movement of Querelle—a virtual Quarrel—
between her thighs.

[[Trickle-stimulus only, by cerebellar induction: she wanted to feel
the v-cological world; but reality remained her anchor.]]

There are swing doors, a dark saloon.

And the sound of honky-tonk, a badly tuned piano.

Ro smiles and [[shifting awkwardly on the floor, in reality]] *swings*
her leg back, and dismounts.

Then she stands in the dusty main street, hands upon her hips, regarding
the frontier town around her.

Lounging cowboys, forearms resting on hitching rails to which their horses
are tethered. One of them, his eyes pale and expressionless, spits liquid brown
tobacco into the dirt; his gaze never leaves Ro.

Respectable women, parasols held high, pass quickly by. Overhead, from
two half-open windows, saloon girls make conversation; occasionally, cold
interest flickers as they recognize a man walking on the boards below.

[[Ro gestured for the ongoing scenario to pause. For a moment, she
considered ending it totally.

There was only one drama on the crystal cassette, but it was
immense, branching through an incredible number of possible logic-
paths depending on the viewer's responses. If there was some clue to
Anne-Louise's killer buried in here, it was going to take a huge effort
to find it.

But already she wondered whether there was a hint, in the name of
the virtual horse she—as the story's viewpoint observer—appeared to
be riding in that nonexistent dusty town. For the horse was called
Querelle (and Ro knew that, in reality, Anne-Louise had rented

Quarrel from Alice Bridcombe's stables more than once); while the old technology on which the cassette was based had been called *queral*: quantum-neural networks threaded through a semi-organic substrate.

Or perhaps it was coincidence, and this was too early in the story-line to tell what, exactly, was going on.

She gestured.

"Resume narrative."]]

Stagecoach.

It comes to a halt before the hotel. The horses are dust-covered and panting. The driver's face is lined with anxiety.

Two young men come from the hotel, chatting cheerily. One climbs to the stagecoach roof, begins throwing luggage down to his waiting partner. Meanwhile, the stagecoach's door opens—creaking, a little unsteady—and the passengers begin to dismount.

Ro assumes that this is where the main plot thread begins.

What had the Ranger said?

"The answer's in Shadowville." With a laconic grin: "But there ain't no shortcut, darlin'. Ya gotta see for yourself."

But there is no sign of him here, in this part of the story.

A finely gowned woman steps down to the dusty ground. Next, a fleshy, well-groomed man with dark moustache and fine grey hat [[and <<**Pinkerton Agent**>> flashed a helpful text overlay, then vanished]] *exits the stagecoach, stops, and looks around. He appears unarmed, but Ro looks at the way he holds his left arm: crooked, ready to slide a hidden derringer from sleeve to hand in a split second.*

The agent tips his hat to Ro.

"Pleasure to make your acquaintance. I'm—"

[["Cut." Ro stopped the flow. "I really don't have time for this."]]

The dusty western town stands still.

No-one could possibly have the time to play out every variation. Life was way too short.

If Anne-Louise's ghost expected Ro to spend days in her fictional world, like some dumb character in a drama within a melodrama, she was going to be very disappointed.

Time for a more direct approach.

"Sorry, Ranger Shade." She opened up her lowest-level debugging displays. "I'm afraid this is going to hurt."

And later, when she realized just how complex Anne-Louise's story was, there was only one comment to add:

"Shit. This writing business is harder than it looks."

The story's framework supported evolution of the teleological kind: directed towards a specific climactic goal. The fractal-consistency milieu generators were unlike anything Ro had worked with; the allegory engine, with its quotient of real philosophical concepts to be embedded within the story, was beyond her understanding.

And as for characters: Ranger Shade was frozen, his code modules splayed open like dissected organs in Ro's analytical holovolumes.

"Three levels, drill in. Continue five clockpulses."

A hundred tesseracts flared: illuminating the Shade persona's internal state variables, tracking the operations through breakpoints.

"Stop. Compare shadow."

The system now showed two sets of holovolumes: two snapshots, taken five nanoseconds apart in the story's v-cology.

There was a cliché-satire factor tree: simple weighting coefficients could flip the obviously banal into the hundred per cent subversive. No big trick either way: a simple matter of accepting or twisting each labelled stereotype as it was instantiated.

From stupid bestseller to profound literature, with a handful of numbers. Neat.

Ro checked the settings that Anne-Louise had picked, found them ranging the intermediate values with occasional wild surprises, in accordance with some convoluted fuzzy algorithm.

Throughout the core, there lurked century-old inherited code fragments, written in the evolution-oriented objectilogical language known as Chocolate. Once globally popular, now consigned to the same historical niche as assembler programming: as out-of-date as quill and parchment writing.

Some of the Chocolate daemons were buried so deeply that they were like human mitochondria: fundamental components of every cell, which at some point in bio-evolutionary prehistory had been a separate species of bacteria. The complexity was staggering; Ro could only be thankful that the story's v-cology was standalone, devoid of links to the greater infraclusters and 'warenations of EveryWare.

Querelle. Was the horse emulation's name significant?

"The answer's in Shadowville." Maybe. *"But there ain't no shortcut."*

Parallel-trace debuggers tore through Ranger Shade's lifetime code. *Ah . . . What about this?*

She had found one strange, recurrent insertion. Recurring, but anomalous. It disobeyed some of the natural-law context/continuity rules which governed the story's other scenes, as defined in the master look-up matrix. And it occurred only when there were no other characters in Shade's virtual vicinity.

Did a clue lie in the software code which represented this one character's actions in all possible scenarios? In what would have been Ranger Shade's thoughts and memories, had he been a real, living being?

Anomalies . . .

Ro picked one scene at random.

"Let's take a look."

She flipped modes, became an invisible, passive observer.

Activated playback.

"Ah, Juanita . . ."

Clint Shade, leaning against the hitching rail outside his simple farmhouse, looks at the sparkling yet insubstantial figure of the woman beside him. The whisky tumbler in his left hand is almost empty.

"My dearest man." Outlines of distant saguaro show through her spectral figure, her wistful smile. "Are you troubled, love?"

"Yeah." He looks away. "Nothing new, huh?"

"Anything you would care to share with your wife?"

Shade laughs. A strange sound in the flat desert air.

"My dead wife, you mean. Shouldn't I let you rest in peace?"

For a moment, stillness.

Then, "There's little enough peace for me here." Her voice is almost a sigh. "You know that, my love."

"I know."

He glances back at his home, then turns to stare at the flat red horizon, layered with the mesa's purple stain.

"What's your score so far, Clint?"

"Two, since you ask."

"And the others?"

A pause.

"I'll find 'em all, don't worry." He looks at her beautiful dark eyes. "I promised you that."

"I know."

Clint sips from his whisky tumbler.

"So why are you visiting me, Juanita? It don't happen less'n there's trouble."

"Ah, my love." She tilts her head to one side. "You know, just before they pinned me down, they . . . One of them called me a wetback, you know?" She blinks. "I told him I'd never seen the Rio Grande, much less swum across it. He just looked puzzled."

[[Ro stopped the playback, used her infostrand to check the defunct racial epithet's origin—from swimming across the river from Mexico: confirmed—then resumed the story.]]

"Cruelty comes from ignorance." Shade's hand rests on the hard walnut grip of his low-slung Colt .45. "Least I know my limitations." His forefinger rests briefly on the slender trigger. "And my strengths."

"So what's really troubling you, Clint?"

Silence. Then: "There's a stranger in town, darlin'."
Overhead, a lone eagle wheels.
"And?"
"Pinkerton's are interested. And that renegade creep, Slim Thatcher. An'
he's part of Sacchi's little net of raiders, I'm sure of it."
Juanita grows strangely silent, even for a ghost.
"Mebbe Sacchi gave the orders his own self, about what happened to you,
an' maybe not . . ."
As his eyes harden, dazzling sparks begin to evanesce about Juanita's form.
"But I've some questions"—he draws so fast the Colt seems to leap into his
hand, then slowly reholsters—"that need some answers."
Sunset is upon the world, orange light dripping across the desert, as
Juanita's ghost swirls apart, fades into insubstantiality, is gone.
"They killed you, my darlin'. They won't get the stranger."
He is still leaning against the rail as sunset slides into night.

Ro flicked off the display.
Sacchi's net . . . Zajinet?
Too facile, too contrived. Wasn't it? But: *Pinkerton's . . .* Official
agencies? The police?
Perhaps she had assumed too much, thought that there was more
encrypted within the story's fabric than Anne-Louise had in fact put there.
And as for the stranger . . . Anne-Louise herself? Or someone else?
I'm the only newcomer in DistribOne.
For a long time, Ro stared at the space where Anne-Louise's body had
lain. Then she shivered, and abruptly stood up, knowing she could bear
the empty accusing room no longer, and went to look for human company.
But when she returned, much later, the crystal-cassette was gone.

<<MODULE ENDS>>

26

NULAPEIRON AD 3419

Orange fire, red-hot liquid.

It spat.

Crackled, burned.

A glowing blob of magma fell near Tom, but he did not flinch. He remained in lotus, seated atop his folded cloak on the dark blue ledge, while the lava pool below swirled and glowed, bubbled and flowed.

Thinking of nothing.

Dark Fire . . .

Thinking of everything.

"Come back tomorrow," Lord Sumneriv had told him at the med centre. "They'll let you talk to him then."

"And you?"

"Oh, my good Lord Corcorigan." Sumneriv sniffed from a tiny pomander ring upon his little finger. "There is very little I have to say to you."

"Whatever you wish."

Tom had walked past the chamber where Viscount Trevalkin lay submersed in healing aerogel. In the antechamber beyond, where relatives of other patients waited, a strangely self-congratulatory tricon was floating:

Thanks to our health awareness programmes, we are pleased to announce a significant drop in mortality rates throughout the stratum.

Tom suppressed a laugh, for those worried relatives' sake. Humankind's mortality rate had been one hundred per cent since the species began, and he foresaw no decrease any time soon.

Or perhaps not quite one hundred per cent.

Dart Mulligan. Do you survive still?

For once, during the effort which had burned out half of his talisman crystal's functions, Tom had made contact with . . . something more than human, in the mu-space continuum.

The original Dart, nearly thirteen hundred Standard Years before—though mu-space time is even more relative than its realspace counterpart—had sacrificed himself to save Karyn McNamara, and his ship had been absorbed by the ravening, quasi-sentient pattern of coruscating energies which had trapped both vessels in mu-space's endless golden sea.

Dart, who might have become a god.

But the Dart with which Tom had communicated described himself thus:

##I AM A SYSTEM-REFLECTION OF WHAT LIES BEYOND##

Which meant . . . what? A self-aware alter ego within the vast comms network which, Tom suspected, existed permanently in mu-space?

But if a mere reflection could be as powerful as the being Tom had talked to, what was the nature of the true Dart consciousness, residing within the stuff of mu-space? Subsumed within the vacuum energy of a continuum where infinite recursion is realizable, where everything that is true can eventually be proven, where every paradox has a final resolution.

And, if any of these speculations were even remotely true, he wondered what other powers might lurk within the universes, and what their capabilities and purposes might be, and whether ordinary human beings can have any influence over Destiny when such great beings decide to move upon the world.

Dayshift was ending when he heard a whisper of sound nearby, and opened his eyes to see Draquelle watching him. Her long, prematurely silver hair glimmered orange with reflected lavaflow, and the white scars upon her face seemed to glow with an inner light of their own.

"Madam Bronlah sends her greetings." Molten rock spat in counterpoint to her soft words. "And asks if you would like to make a journey on her behalf."

Tom let out a long slow breath. This was the payment he had implicitly promised to make.

"As her representative?"

"No. More"—with a tiny smile—"as my personal bodyguard."

"I see."

"Perhaps you do."

Draquelle lowered her hand to the front of her silken tunic, and undid the magseal before Tom could stop her.

"I don't think—"

But he had misread her intentions.

Across her flat stomach, a silver-scaled reptilian shape slid and curled. Then, within the layers of her skin, it slithered smoothly round her torso, out of sight.

"That's a femtautomaton," he said as she re-sealed her garment. "She's using you as a courier."

"Exactly right, my Lord. It's not urgent, but it's important: safety before promptness."

"Ah . . . Perhaps we could forget my rank, all right? Just call me Tom."

"Whatever you say . . ."

The "*my Lord*" was unspoken, but still implied.

"So tell me, where are we going?"

In answer, she held out a travel-tag, above which a tiny holo thread shone scarlet, woven among labelled outlines of the realms they would be travelling through. The itinerary meandered, in places almost looping back upon itself—but the quickest route was not always the shortest distance, when there were journey privileges to negotiate. Particularly during uncertain times.

The demesne she was headed for was unknown to him. But beyond it lay another realm, one he had visited in his youth: ruled then by Duke Boltrivar. *And may his soul dissipate in Chaos for all eternity, if he has one.*

Twenty-four days before the event—Tom remembered the exact figure, would never forget it—he had seen a truecast of the floods which would devastate the tunnels, drown thousands of Boltrivar's loyal subjects. *A small girl's pudgy fingers, disappearing beneath roiling waves.* He had tried to warn people . . .

But everyone knew that a truecast's predictions were incontrovertible; that there was no point in even trying. Instead, the authorities had allowed him to help in the rescue mission afterwards, and when Corduven d'Ovraison collapsed in a nervous breakdown, it was Tom's decisions—though he was still a servitor—which had saved so many lives, and made him someone whose progress was watched and encouraged by powerful allies.

Corduven, my friend . . .

The last that Tom had heard, the dead Duke (who "by chance" had been away from his realm when the floods struck, but had perished later during the Flashpoint uprising) had left no heirs to his ravaged realm, and Corduven had been granted that site for his new Academy. The place where Elva had threatened to go, when she asked for allegiance transfer and Tom refused.

Sweet Fate, Elva. If I'd only told you what I really felt.

And was this a sign, that he should be obligated to travel so close to his old friend's new demesne? Was this where he should go, in order to find the reborn Elva's whereabouts?

Or was it all the delusion of a driven commoner pretending to be a Lord, who had seen too much in his eventful, violent life?

"What's wrong, Gazhe? I mean . . . Tom."

"This travel-tag, Draquelle . . ."

"Yes?"

"It's for three people."

"Ah." With a brief smile: "I wondered if you'd notice that."

$$\diamond \diamond \diamond$$

It was the next dawnshift, long after Draquelle had left, when a large figure strode in to join Tom beside the boiling lava pool.

"Tom, my friend."

"Kraiv. How are you doing?"

"Horush is gone." There was a strange look of acceptance in Kraiv's eyes. "He was a warrior."

"Yes, he was."

Like firelight, orange reflections slid across Kraiv's dark skin, stretched tight over massive muscles which bunched and flexed as he sat down beside Tom, and stared into glowing lava.

"I've come to say farewell."

"That's not necessary," said Tom.

"I journey to the Manse Hetreece, where Horush's family live. The arrangements are already made, my friend."

He would be travelling with access-permissions organized by the Bronlah Hong: their obligation, under their contract with the carls. But the Manse was situated by the Dorionim Goldu, Draquelle's destination, and it was no coincidence that Draquelle and Kraiv were travelling in the same direction. The Hong's long association with the Blue Lotus Zhongguo Ren society in Goldu—and their trading front, the Blue Lotus Hong—had led to their contract with the carls, some ten SY before. And possibly to Madam Bronlah's marriage, though Tom could not be sure of that.

"I know about your travel plans." Tom held his hand out to Kraiv, the travel-tag upon his palm. "I've got the details right here."

But there was one last thing to deal with, before leaving the Bronlah Hong for good.

"Well met, my Lord Corcorigan." Lord Sumneriv, in the med centre's antechamber, gave a small nod whose nuances spoke of frosty disapproval, without going so far as to deliver an insult which might lead to confrontation. "He is on the mend."

Unspoken: *No thanks to you.*

"He's lucky," said Tom with only partial irony, "to have such good friends."

"More than one of whom"—with the tiniest of sneers—"needed treatment in this place."

"And you've checked what *les Accords d'Honneur* have to say about interference on a duellist's behalf?"

A flicker behind Lord Sumneriv's eyes told Tom that he had hit the mark.

"Don't worry, Sumneriv. I said it was over, and it is."

"I'm glad to hear that."

"Well?"

"All right, Corcorigan. You can see him now."

Vassals slipped out of sight as Tom walked along the corridor towards the treatment chamber. That was a bad sign, though not unexpected, given the nobility they had been dealing with recently.

Or perhaps they had heard about Tom's brutality, and the injuries he had inflicted upon the men who were supposed to be his peers.

You think I'm as bad as Trevalkin?

The Viscount had tortured another man's vassals, put them to horrific death. And who knew what atrocities he had committed in the past?

But while Tom had killed or injured only a handful of people, over the past half-dozen years, he had designed the simulation techniques which had led to the deaths of three thousand Oracles, and helped enable the uprisings which had cost tens, maybe hundreds of thousands of lives, without ever bringing freedom or equality to those troubled realms.

Perhaps I'm worse.

Viscount Trevalkin was sitting up in an autodoc.

"So . . . My resourceful adversary."

Tom brushed aside a memory of Horush in a similar position.

"Did you rehearse that greeting?"

"No more than you practised that duel. The choice of surroundings was exquisite. What did you call it? The Maze of Light and Dark?"

"I also referred to it as Trevalkin's Grave."

Trevalkin chuckled, though not pleasantly.

"Happily, Fate has turned that into a misnomer."

"You tortured seventeen people, Trevalkin."

"And they screamed beautifully, for such a long time."

Tom raised his hand, clenched into a half-fist.

"You wouldn't get far," Trevalkin said. "The Halberdiers would hunt you down."

"Try me."

"I didn't come down here without doing some research. You're an intriguing man, Lord Corcorigan."

"An interesting endorsement, considering the source."

"I didn't torture seventeen *people*, Corcorigan. I questioned a bunch of traitors to their species, who allied themselves with . . . something . . . whose presence is spreading, growing. And I mean throughout Nulapeiron."

Tom's skin prickled. "Explain that."

"There are realms which have fallen under some dark influence, like the Aurineate Grand'aume . . . Ah, I see that you're not totally out of touch with current events."

Tension—and the memory of pain—tightened Tom's entire body.

Then, "I was in one of their dungeons," he said.

"And escaped? You must talk to our strategic command. Anything you can tell them would help."

"I don't have anything to say."

"Pity." There was a long pause, then: "No-one knows how it begins, Corcorigan. People disappear, a realm's government becomes oddly organized, strange civil movements become coordinated, and then the repression starts. Opposition disappears. The previous rulers act as mouthpieces for something behind the scenes—or are replaced."

"Perhaps that's no bad thing."

"Given the nature of their replacements, I think it's very bad indeed."

"And the Dark Fire? What is that?"

"There are strange tales of odd phenomena . . . No-one knows, Corcorigan. But I meant it when I called it some *thing*. Whatever its nature, I don't believe it's human."

"But it's spreading?"

"Oh, yes. If you hear people talking about the Blight, they're referring to the same thing."

Tom thought of the troops massing around Bilyarck Gébeet's borders, and shook his head grimly.

"This has nothing to do," he said, "with my objectives."

"Really?"

"And they're none of your concern, Trevalkin."

"Purely selfish, then."

Elva . . .

Perhaps it was self-centred of him to search for her. Or madness. And if she existed, might she be looking for him, too? But she would know better, he hoped, than to look for him in the Aurineate Grand'aume.

Let them all go to Chaos, Elva. You're the one who's important to me.

And yet, Kraiv's and Draquelle's itinerary took them close, very close, to the former Realm Boltrivar, where General Lord Corduven d'Ovraison was forming the Academy which was more—Tom was sure of it—than a mere training school.

Elva. Is that where I need to go to find you?

For certain, they would have intelligence resources beyond anyone else that he could think of.

"Can you get me a noble-house thumb ring, Trevalkin?"

It would give him access to other realms, to resources not available to any commoner. Tom's own ring—a replacement for the one he had been given on his ascension to Lordship—lay somewhere in the Aurineate Grand'aume, its clearance signature automatically wiped clean after the long absence of contact with Tom's DNA.

"Maybe I could get you a ring." Trevalkin stared at him. "But if you're travelling, it might be better to go incognito. You'd make an interesting prisoner. Valuable, I mean."

In your own torture cells, Trevalkin?

But Tom did not utter the words which came first to mind. Instead, he said: "Then can you arrange a travel-tag, for one person? For entry to Realm Boltrivar. I don't need passes to the intermediate demesnes."

"You want my help?"

"You asked for mine."

Silence, then: "All right. I can do that for you."

"With no further questions?"

Trevalkin smiled coldly.

"Give my regards," he said, "to General Lord d'Ovraison."

But Tom did not get out of the treatment chamber that easily.

He was at the square-arched exit when Trevalkin, with deliberate timing, called out: "The Codex Ariston has some interesting entries in its most recent edition. Old noble houses dying out. Parvenu outsiders elevated to Lordship."

Tom paused, only half-expecting the words to come.

"Poet and psychopath. Logosophical killer. Not their exact words, you understand . . ."

Tom shook his head and walked, but the final barb followed him into the stark corridor beyond.

"So we're brothers under the skin after all, my fine Lord Corcorigan. Wouldn't you say?"

Tom walked faster.

27

NULAPEIRON AD 3419-3420

The scheduled duration was thirty to forty days: a long journey, mostly on foot, and with no certain knowledge of how far Draquelle could walk daily, over such a period. And the times were too uncertain to offer a closer prediction—Tom smiled at the term—than that.

But it would not be long before he came to realize there were more subtle factors at work, which would make the journey both longer and more interesting than anyone expected.

"Farewell, Ga—Tom. Er, my Lord . . ."

"Take care, Mivkin. And you, Jasirah."

She turned away, blinking rapidly.

Tom bowed to Master Grenshin.

"Thank you all."

He walked away quickly, more saddened than he had expected at leaving his fellow merchanalysts behind. And, in his satchel of supplies, was a small bundle: a fold-up cloak, lightweight but insulated. A present from his friends.

A cheerfully rude gargoyle, with long protruding stone tongue, leered above the archway before him. Tom stopped, waved once at the small knot of people standing near the old merchanalysis hall, then ducked into the tunnel.

Another journey.

The old excitement of wanderlust was upon him again. In his childhood, Tom had been surrounded by families who had lived in Salis Core for generations, and rarely travelled further than a few kilometres from the marketplace which formed the centre of their lives. But, since then, he had been in so many realms he had lost count, stood on the highest and lowest strata of them all, had seen even the planet's surface, been airborne in its creamy lemon skies . . .

I love this life.

It was an unsettled and possibly misguided way to live. But anything else would be boredom.

"Tom, my friend." Kraiv's basso profundo voice was calm, as he shrugged his big backpack in place, on top of his heavy cloak. "A new beginning."

"That it is."

Water spilled into a round black pool, in which tiny yellow fish with long fluorescent tendrils swam.

"Where's Draquelle?"

Kraiv shrugged his massive shoulders. "She's supposed—ah, there she is."

"Hey, fellows. Were you waiting for me?"

There was a bright shine in her eyes, which Tom chose to interpret as a traveller's excitement, like his own.

"You're right on time."

But there was a part of him, even then, which recognized a kindred spirit, and remembered how it could be . . . Which knew the dragon that lurked still in his mind, whenever he saw a flagon of cool amber beer, down whose side condensation seductively rolled; or he passed by a ganja-mask den, its scent as sweet as sugar, cloying as an overbearing lover's embrace; or a membrane-enclosed amphetamist chamber, where glowing vapours offered fire in the veins.

And if he did not smell the fruit-tinged alcohol upon her breath, the sweet tang of orthopeach liqueur, then why was it that he remembered now with cold clarity what eventually followed? The crashing blackness, the trembling inner hurt, the fragility and fractured drabness of the real external world when the bright joy had passed and only the nerve-racking need was left.

"Draquelle, do you want to be official holder of the travel-tag?"

"Sure. Come on, men. Let's go."

And Tom would wonder later if Kraiv sensed some of the same vulnerability in Draquelle. For when they walked in single file, it was with Tom leading and Kraiv in the rear, or vice versa; and where tunnels widened into boulevards, the trio walked side by side, always with Draquelle in the centre, as though two men could guard against the driven need inside her.

The new year arrived with a flurry of bright exclamations from Draquelle, during the fifth night of their journey, waking Tom and Kraiv from their sleep in a small hostel chamber with three oval sleeping pallets, one of them unused.

"Hey, fellows!"

Not danger . . .

"Huh?" Tom squinted painfully, his forehead throbbing. "What is it?"

In the shadows, Kraiv was already sitting up on his pallet, a short blade in each hand.

"It's time for celebrating!" Draquelle poked her head inside the chamber. "Why are you two sleeping?"

"Because," suggested Tom, "we're getting up early in the morning?"

"Ah . . . You two are boring, you know that?"

Tom looked across the chamber at Kraiv.

"It *is* the new year," Kraiv said.

"But you don't drink." Tom nodded at Kraiv's huge upper arm, where he knew the dark crossed-axes tattoo nestled, in the hollow between the great bunched biceps and triceps, though it was invisible in this gloom. "Or am I mistaken?"

"You know"—touching his tattoo with the flat of a blade—"about the Way of Rikleth?"

"I don't know much about the way you worship," said Tom. "But I'm aware that you don't use mind-altering agents."

"Well—"

"Oh, come on, fellows." Draquelle's voice, unnaturally bright and cheery, seemed to bounce off the dark stone walls. "Can't you relax long enough to see in Tiger Year? For Chaos' sake . . ."

"Go back to sleep," Kraiv told Tom, rolling off his pallet and sheathing his blades. "Let's go, Draquelle."

"Well, thank Fate for that." Draquelle was already leaving, pulling the heavy drape aside, revealing the corridor beyond. "At least one of you's got a bit of life in you . . ." Her voice trailed off as the hanging fell back into place.

"I'll look after her," rumbled Kraiv, pulling on his outer tunic and fastening his cloak.

"Good . . ."

Tom lay back and closed his eyes, and slid into a deep yet troubled sleep, populated by silver-scaled dragons who swam in his veins and ate his eyes, and a voice hissed, then whispered, *Like swallowing pearls,"* and Tom moaned without waking.

In the morning, fading dream fragments fell away before him in shards, and he sat up with a headache already forming.

But that was nothing compared to the way Draquelle looked, pale and trembling over breakfast. Beside her, Kraiv propped his elbows on the table and drank from a daistral bowl, forearm muscles sliding like thick cables beneath taut black skin.

From Kraiv's comments, Tom deduced that he had taken Draquelle back to her hostelry chamber just a few hours ago, and stood guard outside. If a night without sleep had affected him, there was no sign of it.

"We'd better get going." He addressed Tom, watching Draquelle. "Perhaps in an hour or so?"

"Sounds good to me." Tom motioned to a waitress, and handed over a copper cred-spindle. "Thank you."

"You enjoyed it?" The waitress looked down at Draquelle's untouched plate.

"My friend's got a touch of flu," said Kraiv. "But it was good."

"Well, Fate's Blessings, everyone." And, nodding at their packs: "Travel safely."

It was more like two hours before they had hitched their packs across their shoulders and were ready to continue their journey. But by the afternoon's end, Draquelle's composure had returned—a decent lunch helped—and she was chatting and pointing out the sights as they walked.

There was plenty to see and hear. Among the wrought-iron colonnades of Outer Yetrin, locals chattered not just in Cuiliano, but in High Brezhnakh from the northern provinces.

When they put down their packs to rest, Tom wandered by himself, admiring the carvings on stonework, drinking in aromas of roasting myosticks and tava-cake, watched children playing lightball, while vendors hawked cheap statuettes of Gholad the Conqueror and the Blessed Olivia.

It was different in detail, yet somehow it brought to mind the atmosphere of Salis Core, the busy marketplace in which Tom had spent his childhood, while Father had made and sold his wares upon their stall.

Madam Bronlah had given them credit sufficient for supplies throughout the journey, and Tom had his own savings. So when he found himself outside a musty crystal shop—an interlocking series of shadowed chambers, stacked with crystal racks—he could not resist.

Inside, he found everything from Balkrini epics to scrubdrone repair manuals. An outer chamber sold other gifts: small pseudautomata, in the form of flame-pixies, song-sprites and dream-fleas; an insulated miniature lavarium; armoured gauntlets; a battered board-game entitled "Vendetta for the Whole Family," with a free (ironic, but accurate) guide to common poisons.

"Can I help you, sir?"

"I'll . . . be back later."

He could spend hours here, but he had obligations.

He found his companions in a small plaza. Draquelle's eyes were very bright, and her voice was too cheerful as she said, "It's time we were getting on, don't you think?"

Kraiv shook his head: a tiny movement.

"All right," said Tom. "Let's go."

For the next two tendays they travelled, making slow progress. At lunchtime or in the evening, Draquelle would disappear to drink alone: sometimes enough to slur her speech, but not to prevent her walking on.

And then, on the evening before they were due to leave civilized tunnels, and strike out into the interstitial territory between Syektor Krafmant and Ghemprogini Sectoro, Kraiv came into Tom's hostelry sleeping alcove.

"Sit down." Tom shifted to one end of the pallet: there were no chairs. "What's up?"

"Draquelle told me a little about her childhood."

"Ah." Tom looked at him. "Was it bad?"

"Three Standard Years," said Kraiv carefully, "in the service of an Oracle."

"Chaos."

"Precisely, my friend."

Ah, Draquelle. How can anyone blame you?

Tom knew something of the Oracles' nature: neural groups within their brains experiencing time-flow in two directions. It was hard for anything like a coherent personality to form if the world appeared a kaleidoscopic mess, its patterns discernible only to an outside trained observer.

Some—perhaps most—of the Oracles required extraordinary stimulation to bring their personalities into the normal flow of time.

Or perhaps that was an excuse to realize the darkest and most twisted perversions which could lurk deep within mankind's archaic reptilian brain, hidden away by the nature of higher thought and the conventions of society.

So Oracles were given servitors, and allowed to treat them in ways the Oracles' noble patrons—Lords and Ladies of exquisite taste and superb logosophical training—cared not to learn about.

And sometimes the servitors and servitrices, if they had outlived their usefulness but survived relatively intact, were cast loose into a world which could not afford to care about their pasts, and in which they were often ill-equipped to survive.

It seemed strange that Madam Bronlah would use Draquelle as a courier.

"She keeps an eye on Draquelle, normally," Kraiv decided. "Maybe she wanted her safely away from the Bilyarck Gébeet."

There had been no news, good or bad, of the Bronlah Hong, or the realm in which it lay.

They spent the next night, and the next, in a dead realm without a name, passing through long deserted gallerias with broken alcoves and shattered pedestals, where ceilings glowed strangely purple, and rustling ciliates disappeared at their approach.

They slept wrapped up in their cloaks, packs serving as pillows, but fitfully, in grey darkness, surrendering to fatigue yet snapping into wakefulness for no good reason.

And then they were into natural caverns where the going grew tougher, and they slipped on shale, negotiated cracked and jagged slopes, rarely stopping to rest.

It puzzled Tom that Draquelle coped so well. But on their third day inside the wilderness, as he took up the rear in a low passageway where moisture dripped from bulbous stalactites into small murky pools, he found a discarded drink-bulb, and knew where her good cheer originated.

And then they were through a militia-guarded checkpoint and back into populated tunnels, where Draquelle exclaimed loudly that she was looking forward to a long cool aerogel-bath in the first hostel they came to, relief and need adding a tremble to her voice.

Her crisis came unexpectedly, after days of progress. It was only later that Tom told himself he should have recognized the pattern of self-denial followed by relapse.

For twelve more days they travelled, and three of those days were easy ones, atop soft flat cargo-slugs, sliding their steady way towards Kizhtigan Praz, a realm which Tom had thought existed only in legend.

On the fourth day, when the caravan's route diverged from theirs, Tom and his companions dismounted, waved their farewells to the hooded caravanserai, and continued on foot.

Draquelle was living cleanly.

At one point, she opened her belt pouch, and handed all her cred-spindles, and her single cred-ring, to Kraiv.

"I'd feel better," she said, "with a warrior looking after them."

Kraiv nodded solemnly. Tom looked on, smiling at them both.

It was a tenday later that they entered Verinadshi Demesne—on the ninth stratum, having descended two strata so far—and decided that they needed recuperation. They checked in to a hostel, left their baggage—security was provided by a tall lean M'gasai Lancer, his fealty brand dark upon his left cheekbone, who nodded to Kraiv as though recognizing a spiritual brother—and went to find a nice place for lunch.

Tom wondered, as they ate, where Elva was now.

Eating lunch in an officers' mess somewhere?

She had been wearing a military uniform in the Seer's vision. But

Tom had not recognized its cut or colours, and the visual background provided no clues.

Next morning, Tom walked by himself until he found a long twisted tunnel called Bahreen naBringlódi, where dreamshops, love-poets' booths, and crystal sellers did quiet trade side by side. Passing beneath a flatscript holo which read *Chrystalli Andromedae*, Tom found himself amid racks of crystals.

"Any recommendations, Roj?" he heard a freedman ask.

The proprietor hooked his thumbs into his patterned jerkin's pockets, then rapidly listed titles. Tom listened for a moment, then wandered among the racks, finally depositing a handful of crystals on the counter.

"This one's good," said the owner, picking through them. "But I wouldn't waste my time with the Rihdal. *Yortin's Temptation* is the worst thing he wrote."

"But that doesn't—"

"Listen." And, inserting the crystal in a slot, he read aloud: "'The demon was slimy, its purple tentacles covered with weeping pustules and more slime, its sharp-fanged orifices pulsating, but the mighty-thewed Duke Yortin felt himself grow strangely excited, sword hilt clammy in his—'"

"All right." Tom was laughing, despite himself. "Tell me what's good, that I probably haven't heard of."

"OK, then. Pèdd?" The proprietor called to a tall man stacking racks. "Get these for me, would you."

A short while later, Tom found himself leaving the shop with three times as many crystals as he had intended to buy, but pleased, certain each crystal would be good.

He nearly returned straight to the hostel. But something made him continue walking, and soon he was in a low rectilinear cavern of deep-blue polished stone, with rows of shining pools on floor and ceiling. The slow *drip, drip* of quicksilver droplets falling upwards, into the ceiling pools, was strangely relaxing.

Then he passed through a series of chambers where abstract shapes coalesced from floating ting-mist, and scintillated.

It draws me, this place . . .

And then beyond, into a votive tunnel where ornate shrines stood softly glowing, and ordinary lay folk came to pray or meditate.

There was an air of quiet anticipation: a gathering of onlookers including children who nudged each other, whispering, and spontaneously erupted into energetic running, chasing one another, then scampering back to their parents.

For all that, the tranquillity was stronger here by the shrines.

So long since I've known peace.

If he ever truly had . . .

Then a child cried out: "He's here!"

And, in the distance—far along the tunnel's vanishing perspective—an orange-clad figure came running this way, fast.

The man's cord-tied billowing garment was neither robe nor jumpsuit, but something in between. He slowed to a walk, and approached the shrine, his shaven head gleaming, his breathing deep and easy.

Then he prostrated himself, sat back on his heels, and slid into a meditation so profound that it brought a sense of calm fulfilment to everyone who watched.

A matronly woman, head covered with a white shawl, looked at Tom.

"He's very holy, this one."

Tom whispered back: "How far does he run?"

"This year, he'll run a hundred klicks a day, one hundred days in succession."

Sweet Fate.

If all the monks ran like this, and their spiritual development in any way matched their physical discipline . . .

"The monastery," the woman added, pointing along the dark clean tunnel, "lies ten klicks that way."

Tom watched until the monk rose, ran slowly at first—till the children who accompanied him dropped back, laughing—then accelerated into a smooth, gliding motion Tom could never hope to match.

Back at the hostel, he spread his new crystals across the sleeping pallet. There were tragicomic Hedolik epics, the entire ten crystals of the *Nazalam Chronicles*, and a couple of old favourites—Duke Caldwin's *Ode to a Sword*, and Jay's *Dark Cape*.

From the poetry section, he had chosen Zelakrin's *Twisted Cat* and *Gone Up In Smoke*, along with the infamous Kendrahl's two-century-old epic, *Tantala Dalquin*.

And some serious treatises. *Bioemergenics: An Introduction* was far beyond most scholars; its self-effacing title was a joke. Also *Conflict Calculus*, Count Carnbull's *Originatio* in the original Vektrohl, and Mel-Ynchon's classic *Space-Time Tensegrity*.

Tom picked up *Ode to a Sword*, inserted the crystal into his holopad, and settled down to read.

But he had scarcely got as far as the young hero's first encounter with the eponymous blade when there was a clap from outside, and the hanging drew back. Kraiv's muscular presence filled the archway.

"We have a problem, Tom."

And then Tom saw the bronze armlet gleaming on Kraiv's massive upper arm, and his heart sank.

Kraiv told the story in all the detail he knew, but at heart it was a simple one. Draquelle, passing an inn by herself, had been unable to resist. Inside, lacking funds—for Kraiv had them in safekeeping—she had pawned her travel-tag to the owner, funding a massive binge.

At some point, she had bought a round of drinks for every person in the crowded, raucous tavern, while zeitdeco music pulsed, and ganja fumes warmed the darkness.

This morning, the owner, a man named Lochlen, had agreed to return the travel-tag to Kraiv, in exchange for something of equal value.

And so Kraiv was indentured as a housecarl to the House Of The Golden Moth, for a period of half a Standard Year.

"Where's Draquelle now?"

Kraiv shrugged, then gestured towards the public wash chambers along the tunnel.

"Not just sick, Tom. Too embarrassed to face you."

Tom bit his lip.

"What about your debt to Manse Hetreece?"

"That remains."

Kraiv's bulging shoulder muscles looked ready to burst through his tunic. Every day, he lifted massive weights—all three laden packs, one-handed, if he could find no boulders—which Tom could not imagine raising off the ground.

His self-discipline was inspiring. And he would pay whatever price Horush's family, in the Manse Hetreece, demanded of him: even his own death.

And that severity grew more likely, surely, the longer his journey took.

"Does Draquelle deserve it?" Tom asked.

But if people had given up on me . . .

He raised his hand before Kraiv could speak.

"Forget I said that."

Later, Kraiv asked: "What about you, Tom? Do you journey on alone, or will you stay here?"

"I don't know. I . . ."

There would be difficulties, without a travel-tag, but perhaps that was not the prime consideration. For there had never been any guarantee that travelling to Corduven's Academy would bring him closer to his goals.

Suddenly, he smiled beatifically.

Why not?

"Don't worry about me," he said.

In the morning, he slung his small pack over his shoulder, adjusted his cloak, and set out. Avoiding the meditation chambers, he found a public cavern, one side of which was filled by a vast, translucent emerald block, in which complex wave patterns pulsed and propagated.

He sat down before a small open-fronted daistral house at the cavern's far end.

"It's phonon-based," said the waitress who brought Tom's breakfast. "Turing-capable, they say."

"Really?"

Tom gazed at the block, wondering what computations took place inside, and whether it was aware of the world in which it existed.

At that moment, a small tawny form leaped across Tom's table, seized a portion of krilbar, and bounded towards its fellows who had exploded from nowhere.

"Sorry." The waitress shooed them away. "Them marmies. What a nuisance."

The troop of tiny primates boiled across the ground, then leaped upwards, climbing the cavern walls faster than Tom could sprint, and he laughed at the joyful exuberance of their motion.

Smiling, the waitress went back inside.

On top of the translucent block, one chattering marmie sat. Then it began to pound the surface with a tiny, very human-looking hand. Tom could see the shivering vibrations it caused.

Do you dream? he silently asked the computation block. *Or have you got a headache now?*

It was almost in a dream-state of his own that Tom rose, placed cred-spindles on the tabletop, picked up his pack and left.

He was at the cavern's exit when the waitress's voice called him back. "You've paid far too much! It only costs—"

"That's OK." Tom's voice was gentle. "I don't need credit."

Not where I'm going.

There were two monks running, side by side. Tom did not try to run with them; but he noted the direction they went, and followed at an easy walk.

Soon, beyond a long market place, he found himself standing before a circular, membrane-protected, glistening bronze door. But the membrane dissolved and the door swung inwards at his approach, revealing the courtyard within.

Orange-clad monks and shaven-headed novitiates were practising a walking meditation.

There were guardian monks, but they stepped aside as an elder came forward, passing through the walking group without disturbing their movements, and stopped before Tom.

"Sir—"

Shedding his pack, Tom dropped to his knees.

It draws me . . .

Forehead to the gritty stone, Tom made full obeisance, then sat back on his heels, and spoke without gazing directly at the elder monk's impassive, stony features.

"I crave permission, an it be your will"—Tom spoke softly—"to study with the Order."

For a moment, he feared the guardians would strike, and turn him away.

Please . . .

But then, miraculously, the elder monk smiled.

28

TERRA AD 2142

<<Ro's Story>>

[8]

The missile silo, after two centuries in the desert sands, remained intact. The dark green nose cone, removed from the ICBM—though it still seemed pregnant with threat—sat above ground. The original launch-tube cover was open; plexiglass protected the sunken vertical shaft from the elements.

In their hired TDV, Ro and Luís scanned the horizon through the blue-tinted windows. No sign of anyone.

"He's not here yet," said Luís. "But he will be."

"Let's go inside."

The TDV's door swung downwards, forming a ramp, and Ro walked slowly out. Hot dry air pressed upon her skin.

Above an abandoned ancient helicopter, a blurred holo hung. Ro squinted against the sunshine to read it.

WELCOME TO THE
TITAN MISSILE
AND
TWENCEN PARANOIA
PAVILION

Luís headed straight for a low, white building. Doors to an empty foyer slid open at their approach.

"My uncle says it's automated. No staff."

Inside, conditioned air brought cool relief.

"Good."

Ro used an anonymous cred-ribbon, instead of her infostrand, to pay their entrance fees. Once through the inner doors, they bypassed the 1950s domestic tableaux—simple androids in period dress, preparing meals, listening to the wireless news broadcasts (all cold war tension and hysteria), stocking their fallout shelters—and the Montréal 2092 display, showing the terrorists' final minutes before they remotely took down the CommEd clean-fusion clusters (in the name of the Drowned Isles and other dirty-fuel ecotastrophes) and Detroichago disappeared forever.

Instead, they hurried downwards, into the facilities where four-person military teams (including women: surprisingly enlightened for the times) had kept constant watch, ready to launch nuclear death with the twist of a key—two keys, in fact: at least two people had to agree on Armageddon—and the touch of a button.

The control room was painted metal: no ceramics or smartmaterial in sight. Big dials, status lights and buttons decorated the control panels. There were technical manuals—the watch teams had been scientist/engineers as much as soldiers, keeping the nuclear missile's launch systems operational—but they were hardcopy: metal-bound paper books.

A disembodied voice asked: *"Would anyone care to launch a missile? Please take the two indicated controls seats."*

Holo-arrows pointed the way, but neither Ro nor Luís moved.

"In that case, let us demonstrate."

Two simple androids walked jerkily into the control room, took their seats, and made ready to twist the launch-enabling keys.

"I don't like this," said Ro.

Luís looked at her. "Don't worry. He told me that he'll be here, so he will. We're related by—"

On the other side of the room, a heavy metal hatch swung slowly open.

Countdown lights flickered: extinguished one by one . . .

Someone's here . . .

Ro spun and crouched, hands upraised.

Weapon—

The square, bronze-skinned hand was visible first, and it bore a scatterspray pistol. But then the big Navajo police officer stepped inside—Sergeant Arrowsmith—and slowly lowered his weapon, and smiled.

"I trust you." And, reholstering, he added: "Enough to come alone."

"Good." Ro relaxed, let out a shaky breath. "Because I'm not sure—"

Vibration and she crouched again.

Betrayal?

The control room shook on its suspension springs; the recorded sounds of lift-off roared in the trembling air. Slowly, slowly the imaginary launch completed, the missile's sound faded . . .

Sergeant Arrowsmith appeared unmoved.

"It seems"—his voice was deep, rhythmic—"that paranoia still survives, in the twenty-second century."

After the display had ended, Luís and Ro occupied the chairs; Sergeant Arrowsmith insisted that he remain standing.

"I didn't see the crystal myself," said Luís. "Or the debug scans. But it sounds just like Anne-Louise."

The sergeant's eyes were dark, unflinching. "But it's just a fiction, something she made up. You said that."

"Agreed. Yet there's more to it: information encoded, correlated with the story line. I think Ro's correct."

"And the chess-board . . ." Ro stopped.

"Position K7." Sergeant Arrowsmith sounded mournful.

"But pronounced *ka-sept*. In French, it used to be an acronym." Ro shrugged. "I know it seems feeble, but . . ."

"Like, if a dog had been involved"—Luís spoke seriously—"and the piece had been at K9, you know? If there were such a thing as the ninth row. And if she'd been Anglophone, instead of Québecoise."

My God, it sounds so stupid: a contrived whodunnit clue.

And the crystal-cassette had disappeared, with no traces remaining in the holopad's active memory or cache. No proof at all.

"But it's exactly," Luís added, "the way she wrote. The way she *thought*."

Sergeant Arrowsmith merely nodded.

Ro stared at him. Did he trust Luís's judgement that much?

Luís . . . How can I make you stay?

What could she offer him to replace the stars, the strange sights of the mu-space continuum?

"So what does it mean?" Arrowsmith made a slight gesture with his wide shoulders. "The story itself?"

"A stranger, in peril." Ro shook her head. "A cliché, but somehow wrong. There was a ghost in the story, which didn't fit the other background . . . It showed me where to look."

For a moment, she thought Sergeant Arrowsmith might have shivered: to a Navajo, she had learned, all *chindhí* are to be feared, regardless of how good a person had been in life. All that is fine and true perishes; only evil lives on in spirit.

"You believe us." Luís looked certain.

Sergeant Arrowsmith stared at him, then touched his own lapel.

It was a signal. Ro sensed an approaching presence, but no threat. And, as footsteps became audible, she looked out of the hatchway, along the grim metal catwalk, and recognized the slim white-haired figure walking towards her.

"Hello." The woman was elegant, taut-featured. "We met at the Police HQ, over lunch. You had some interesting facts to share about vomiting sea creatures."

"Yes . . . I'm sorry, I don't remember your name."

"Why should you? I'm Hannah. And you're Ro."

She held out her hand, and they shook.

"And I don't believe," Hannah added, "that your roommate was killed by a psychopath either. Not in the normal sense of the term."

Ro felt a momentary sense of joyless vindication.

Joyless, because the alternative was that Anne-Louise's death was the action of a professional, disguised to look like an amateur—who had somehow slipped past DistribOne's security—whose allies or employers must have Ro under observation. How else to explain the cassette's disappearance?

And, whether it was a sexual predator or a paid assassin who had erased her from existence, poor Anne-Louise was just as dead, either way.

The next morning, Ro skipped her academic classes. In the afternoon, she was physically present in the small seminar room; but the seminar was drawing to a close and she had paid little attention to anything Professor Davenport had said during the previous hour.

"*I believe Anne-Louise was assassinated,*" the white-haired woman, Hannah, had told Ro and Luís. "*And I use that term advisedly.*"

Ro jerked from reverie: the professor was talking to her.

". . . afterwards, please, Miss McNamara. There's something I'd like to discuss." Then, turning back to the student group as a whole: "In the matter of assignments, when you log on tonight you'll find . . ."

Shaking her head, Ro tried to dispel the flash images: Anne-Louise's impossibly angled body, inhuman rictus on the white/bruised face.

The last of the other interns filed out, and Prof. Davenport smiled.

"*I nearly missed it in the post-mortem.*" Hannah had looked to Sergeant Arrowsmith for reassurance, before adding: "*Microwave interference pulse. Multiple sources—too weak to leave individual traces—intersecting at the heart.*"

And Sergeant Arrowsmith had said: "*It's a pretty fancy way of killing someone. Everything else the killer did to her was misdirection.*"

What did it mean? That she was killed from the corridor or the ground outside the room? The distance from killing devices to the room could not be great, because the killer had then gone inside.

Unless there were two of them. Accomplices . . .

"Ms. McNamara?"

"Sorry, Professor. I'm coming."

But it occurred to her, as she walked, that Anne-Louise might have been murdered remotely because the assassin thought she had the means to defend herself. Then he would have forced his way into the room . . . purely to disguise the manner of Anne-Louise's death? Or because he—or she—was looking for something?

And if the killing was performed remotely . . .

What if Anne-Louise wasn't the real target? What if . . . ?

She did not want to complete that thought.

Oncimplant notwithstanding, Ro refused his offer of lemon nicotine-slivers. Davenport popped one in his mouth, and chewed.

"Dreadful habit," he said.

"What did you want to see me about, sir?"

"None of that 'sir' stuff, please. Um . . . I wanted to know, would you be comfortable talking to a UNSA official called Dr. Schwenger? She's officially semi-retired, but highly placed in the agency's hierarchy, all the same."

He picked up another lemon sliver.

"I . . . know who Dr. Schwenger is, Professor."

At least, I've met her. I don't know her at all.

"That dreadful business with Anne-Louise." Davenport shook his head, then slowly replaced the lemon sliver in the bowl. His sorrow looked genuine. "There may be an element of corporate guilt involved, I suppose, or avoiding negative publicity. Have you seen today's news? The anti-xeno riots in Tehran and Dublin?"

"More riots? Why now? No-one's protested about alien embassies for ages."

Davenport shrugged his narrow shoulders. "Who can tell? At any rate, you may be able to get some small advantage out of the situation."

From the riots?

Ro frowned.

Or profiting by Anne-Louise's murder?

"What kind of advantage?"

"A research assistant post in one of our prime study centres, in XenoMir. That's what they're offering you."

"In Moscow? But I'm just an intern."

"Nevertheless, that's the offer."

After a moment, Ro said, "It sounds very interesting."

"There are high-*g* Veraliks, who are interesting beings. Ephemerae from Limbo. And Zajinets—at least one at all times."

"What do I have to do?"

"Call Dr. Schwenger tomorrow afternoon, when you've had time to think it over. Is that fair?"

"Yes . . . Yes, it is. Thank you, Professor."

With a beneficent smile: "You're perfectly welcome."

At sunrise the next morning, she was in the Painted Desert, admiring the candy-like mineral strata—sugary-looking white, green, black— which streaked the low sandstone ridges.

At 9 a.m. she sat down—having checked for scorpions and rat-tlesnakes—by a fallen pink/red tree trunk long turned to stone: part of the Petrified Wood. Her rented TDV was parked back by the automated tourist stop, a low white building with a curved solar-panel roof.

I wonder what it's like in Moscow right now?

Certainly cold. *Moskva*, Moscow, was almost as chilly as London. And since the last century's North Sea convection-cell reversal, and the loss of the Gulf Stream, London was bitterly freezing: ice-locked for half the year.

Just when I was starting to love the desert.

Red sand, a twisted mesquite tree. And, above all, the sky: a startling blue, deeper than sapphire. Even when occasional clouds appeared, they were twisted into wispy configurations such as Ro had never seen.

Over the horizon, almost invisible against the royal blue, two tiny dots.

At last.

She thought Sergeant Arrowsmith and Hannah must have missed their own rendezvous. Although it had only been the sergeant's name tagged on the h-mail.

It's not them.

Ro could not have said exactly how she knew: minutiae in the handling of the craft. And, somehow, she could foretell a deadly intent from the flyers' attitudes, as they hurtled in her direction.

She pushed herself to her feet.

Time to run.

Reddish shards flying in all directions, clattering, slippery beneath her boots.

Run.

Dodged behind a horizontal stone trunk, knowing its shelter was not enough, pushing onwards . . .

Run faster.

<<MODULE ENDS>>

29

NULAPEIRON AD 3420

It was the thirteenth day.

Tom and his brother-in-enlightenment ran easily, side by side.

"The tunnel flows"—the elder monk, Barjo, spoke without effort as they increased speed, pounding over a footbridge—"the stream does not."

"No." Tom denied the koan, laughing.

"Just so." Accepting the response.

Water gurgling beneath them.

They ran.

Brother Barjo's prayers were set at twenty klicks a day—a moderate phase in his current seven-year cycle: this was the fifth such cycle—but for Tom's sake, he altered his devotions. Praying at a reduced sequence of shrines, so that he could run three seven-klick laps, offering up the tiny distance increase as a prayer for Tom's perseverance.

One lap was enough for Tom.

Until I perceive the Way more deeply . . .

For those with deeper devotion could run for longer than anyone Tom had ever known.

At his single lap's end, he would stand at the round bronze temple door, and watch Brother Barjo's diminishing slender figure, until he had run from sight. Then it would be time to join the other novitiates in the Outer Court, where they would walk, meditating, in approximate ellipses—each assigned his own path: a strange attractor whose image he would hold in his mind—without ever colliding.

An instructor-monk would stand at the Court's centre, his voice a soft, washing presence, as he spoke of the mundane (such as which scarlet fungi might be safely eaten) and the cosmic (the interconnected karma matrices).

The language was Lefanjin. Though Tom was not yet fluent, in these sessions it seemed that he understood every word with a clarity beyond normal speech.

And every other day he stood inside the Great Prism, its kaleidoscopic facets presenting infinite recursions, like geometric koans: translucent shards forming impossible triangles, or tangled non-Euclidean mazes which shifted parallax in unsettling ways.

Aeolian music, eerie and haunting, created by the Prism itself from the hot and cold breezes which flowed within, talked deeply to Tom's spirit, paradoxically unsettling yet reassuring.

Yet time itself seemed increasingly abstract, an artefact created by convention and the limited perceptions of too-busy human beings.

When the glamour became too much, he would drift away . . . Later, he would awaken in the Outer Court, while the watcher-priests who had carried him out would laugh as the focus returned to his gaze.

And Tom would smile back.

At peace.

At some point, it was his turn to accompany an elder—big Brother Fazner, strongly built for a monk—into the commercial tunnels of Verinadshi Demesne. Tom waited patiently outside each establishment where his brother-in-enlightenment visited.

Where families were shopping—this was rest-day—children would stop and point at Tom, standing there in his bright orange garb. When he nodded back, they would squeal with delight, tugging at their parents' tunics, begging to be allowed to talk with Tom.

The parents would duck their heads in mute apology, smiling.

But there were other tunnels, where garish holos in cobalt blue and vermilion red pushed back shadows, and customers hunched furtively as they passed by. Music whined, and scents of amphetamist and ganja grew strong.

But there is no dragon.

So even here, Tom was at peace: the dark yearning for alcoholic forgetfulness was driven into submission.

Somewhere on the border between sleazy quarters and bright market corridors lay the House Of The Golden Moth. It was classier than other taverns: well-dressed freemen entered without hesitation, accompanied by their well-washed, happy-looking children.

Perhaps they drew some security from the huge, dark-skinned figure guarding the door, copper helm upon his head, morphospear in hand. Around the carl's upper arm, the indenture armlet gleamed as brightly as his helm.

"Hello, Kraiv," said Tom.

The big warrior looked down at him.

Inside, while Kraiv remained on duty, Tom and Brother Fazner were led by a waitress to a small nook, where she motioned them to sit.

"Master Lochlen will be here shortly."

"Thank you." Brother Fazner bowed to her as she withdrew.

"Should I not wait outside, brother?"

"Perhaps not. Why don't you stand there?"

Was Kraiv that bad an influence? Tom felt saddened that he should cause Brother Fazner such concern.

He went to where his brother-in-enlightenment had pointed, and stood against the wall beneath a flickering orange holoflame which cast no heat.

"Hello? I'm Lochlen." A lean man, with tattooed cheeks and a dark goatee, came up to Tom. "Owner of this sorry joint. Are you my new—"

"Here I am, Master Lochlen," called out Brother Fazner from the nook.

"Ah, right." With a wry smile, Lochlen pulled a small purse from his belt. "Guess I nearly made a mistake, right?"

"If you would, please." Brother Fazner gestured for Lochlen to join him, which he did: sliding onto the seat opposite, placing the purse on the black tabletop between them.

"Tom? My Fate, is that you?"

"Oh." He turned round. "How are you, Draquelle?"

"I—" For a moment, it looked as though she was going to slap him. Then she made a visible effort to calm down, and shook her head. "I'm the last person to accuse you of being irresponsible. My apologies, Tom."

"Not required," he answered, puzzled by her words.

Irresponsible? In what way?

But to ask her outright would be impolite.

"So, should I call you Brother Tom? Is that what this"—gesturing at his orange garments—"is all about?"

"I don't yet have that honour."

"Destiny." Draquelle shivered, and hugged herself. "If you say so, my friend."

It was the form of address which Kraiv so often used.

"You and Kraiv are getting along well," Tom said.

"Oh, yes." With a small smile: "He's the reason my life's under control. Finally."

"I know what you mean."

Draquelle stared at him. "I thought you had other—Wasn't a woman involved, somehow?"

Elva?

A ghost ran cold, insubstantial fingers down Tom's spine . . . but then the moment was past.

"We must be going now," said Brother Fazner.

Though it was strictly too soon, Tom tried to keep up with Brother Barjo for all three laps, but his devotion-endurance failed, and he dropped back, gasping. Then the long, slow walk to the monastery, with the knowledge of failure hurting as much as the cramps which racked his legs.

When he entered the dorm that night, one of the other novitiates, young Yerwo, made Tom lie face down on his sleeping mat, while all fifteen fellow novitiates who slept here used strong fingers to massage painful healing into Tom's feet and calves and hamstrings.

"You tried until the body gave way," Yerwo told him.

"There is honour in that," said another.

"Thank you, my brothers."

Though the treatment was agony, when it finished the cessation was wonderful.

Tom slid into sleep.

Next morning, after the usual cold rice breakfast, two physiologist-monks inserted needle probes in Tom's limbs, and checked their holodisplays, nodding and smiling.

"Drink this." One of them handed Tom a bowl of orthorange juice.

"Today," said the other, "you run with Thrumik."

It was an advancement, despite yesterday's failure. But he should be humble, not consider his progress as meritorious in its own right, burdening his ego.

But the two monks, now testing Yerwo's physiometrics, were frowning.

I am no better, Tom told himself firmly, *than my brother.*

He drained his bowl of juice, then crossed to the limbering-up chapel, to prepare for the day's devotions.

It was the AdrenaGitha, the sprint-interval devotion, and it was agony. Its coda was a long-distance run—slow-paced, but a full twenty-three klicks.

Master Thrumik, aged sixty-two SY, running with an ethereal fluid motion, seemed to drift along the ground as though borne by unfelt breezes. After prostrated praying at each shrine, Thrumik would rise, face suffused with devotion's joy, and begin to run again.

Awestruck, Tom could only follow, carried along by the master's spiritual strength.

And so it continued.

Prayer-runs and walking meditation were the extended high points of every day, along with solitary sessions in the Great Prism.

Every morning, Tom awoke, strangely disconnected as though his spirit was elevated beyond his body. And he would greet his brothers-in-enlightenment with joyful bows, unable to comprehend the wonderful Fate which had brought him here.

Sometimes at night, though he was filled with calm, Tom felt beyond the need for sleep.

Then, he might walk around the Outer Court, performing his strange-attractor meditation again while the guardian-monks on night duty watched approvingly. Or he would go outside, for a second run among the shrine-dotted prayer-routes.

But sometimes another spirit would move him, and he would run silently along deserted, shadow-shrouded commercial tunnels, where the few passers-by ignored him.

And once, taking a shortcut through the Couloir d'Amori, beyond the membrane-curtained chambers where reclining half-clad women waited, he saw two elder monks, conversing cheerfully, exiting an establishment.

Moderation, Tom told himself. *Another approach to the Way.*

It did not matter that he, like every novitiate, was denied contact with the opposite sex. That was part of the austere discipline, the *shugyo*.

His life was as frugal as the diet which was so carefully prepared in the monastery's kitchen-lab.

But that night he dreamed of his first days in Palace Darinia, after the great crackling vibroblade had shorn off his arm, yet he performed his duties in a strange euphoria.

"That'll be the implant," his new friend Jak had told him.

The implant which numbed the pain, until Tom himself cut it out.

They gathered in the Outer Court for Brother Alvam's triumph. The atmosphere was a strangely expectant mix of calm and tension: monks of all ranks waited in serried rows, murmuring to each other, waiting for the great bronze door to swing open.

"Soon," whispered Yerwo.

And then indeed it opened, and guardian-monks bowed as Brother Alvam, glistening with sweat, half-ran, half-stumbled inside, finally reaching his goal. For the ninety-ninth successive day, he had completed a ninety-nine klick ultra-endurance *novadecenovena* devotion, and now he was spent.

Then every monk present, including the Abbot, bowed in unison, while Brother Alvam could only stand in acceptance, unable to return the gesture.

Senior monks began the Chant of Stepwise Triumph, ancient verses filling the air like incense smoke, while novitiates smiled in wonder.

Then medic-priests took gentle hold of Brother Alvam's stick-like arms—for he was emaciated, fat and muscle burned away to sinew and bone by the ongoing strength of his spiritual will—and guided him towards the recovery chapel.

"Did you see?" Yerwo continued to stare after Alvam was no longer in sight. "Did you?"

"Yes, my brother."

If only I could . . .

For the monk's exhausted frame had glowed with an inner light, eyes on fire, enlightenment shining like a nova in his soul.

Someday . . .

It was another night run, solo, and he passed through a grey-lit tunnel which seemed oddly familiar. Before one establishment a golden-winged holoimage fluttered virtual wings, and Tom slowed down to walking pace.

"Tom?" A big bulky figure, wrapped in a cape, stood below the holo. "Is that you?"

"Yes, my brother."

"I'm not your . . . You remember me, right? Kraiv."

"Of course."

"We . . ." The big man paused as a slender woman, prematurely silver hair visible around the edges of her cape's hood, came through the archway behind him. "Draquelle and I are leaving soon. My indenture ended two tendays ago."

"We waited, Tom," said Draquelle. "The monks wouldn't let—"

But Tom was walking past.

"Tom? It's half a Standard Year since we've seen you. Aren't you even going to—?"

Time to move.

Half a Standard Year?

He broke into a run.

But I'm so far from enlightenment.

Ran faster.

But then Tom's brother novitiate was expelled from the monastery.

It was with a genuine sorrow that two guardian-monks led Yerwo from the dorm into an isolation cell. Yerwo, shocked and bewildered, began to shake with resentment, but one of the monks applied a subtle wrist-lock and led him out.

Tom could only watch.

He was not the only one. In the cloister's shadows, Brother Thrumik stood silently, his expression invisible in the gloom.

"Sir?" Tom addressed him quietly. "Is there not some mistake?"

Thrumik shook his head.

"Poor Yerwo," he said, "is not up to the rigours of advanced devotion."

Tom remembered the physiologist-monks' frowns.

"Sadness."

"Indeed, my young brother-in-enlightenment."

It was a rare compliment, that form of address from an elder monk, and Tom bowed deeply. When he straightened, he had little memory of why he was standing here.

"You should sleep now," said Thrumik.

"Thank you, Master." Tom bowed again.

For three days Yerwo was made to fast, locked in his solitary prayer cell with only water to drink, and no food at all. Tom hoped the poor fellow was using the time well, for prayer and meditation, in preparation for a new Way.

"Tom?" Brother Fazner, whom Tom had accompanied into the commercial district several times, handed him a small bundle. "Take this to the Abbot, please."

"Of course, my brother."

Tom walked to the small, plush, private chapel, and found the blue membrane which led to the Abbot's chambers, and stepped inside.

A banquet unfolded around him. Local dignitaries were feasting upon exotic fleshbloc dishes such as Tom had not seen since his Palace days. Monks moved among them, serving. A few of the elders were dining—forcing themselves to break their normal diet—while the Abbot, in his blackstone chair, his curled hat skewed upon his shaven head, laughed uproariously at something a trader said.

"Yes?" One of the monks came up to Tom. "The Abbot cannot be disturbed. These are delicate negotiations . . ."

"Of course." Tom held out the package. "This is for him."

"I'll take it."

"Thank you, brother."

As he left, Tom caught sight of a sour face among the diners, lean and with a dark goatee: Master Lochlen, of the House Of The Golden Moth.

I've been there, haven't I?

Frowning, Tom walked on deep in thought, hardly noticing as he passed an open cell, just as Yerwo was being led out.

"Tom?"

"Ah . . . Go well, my brother."

"What do—Fate! Don't you realize? Don't eat the—"

But guardian-monks took hold of him then, and Tom watched sadly as they ejected him from the monastery, and the big bronze door swung shut, cutting off Yerwo's strange hysterical protestations.

In a narrow cloister, late in the day, Tom moved silently. Finally, he stopped before an opaque membranous door, and waited.

His mind was clear, so it was impossible to tell how much time elapsed before a tall monk stepped out, nearly bumping into Tom.

"Oh, I—I beg your pardon."

"My fault," said Tom. "I was standing here."

But as the membrane liquefied, Tom had seen the kitchen-lab's interior. A bright holo image—a twisted, complex enzyme around which femtovectors swarmed—was hidden from view as the door vitrified once more.

"What—what do you think you just saw, my brother?"

There was a great deal Tom had missed, but even so . . .

"I'm not sure." Tom shook his head. "I could barely make out the compiler."

The tall monk sucked in a breath. "You know of such things?"

"I'm not trained in logotrope design. But it looks clever."

"What does?" The tall monk fidgeted, unsure whether to call someone.

"The zentropes you're putting in the food . . ."

When Tom smiled, he was radiant.

". . . What a wonderful idea!"

I was always, he realized, *running* away *from something.*

But now, in his devotions, there was a beautiful, selfless goal to run *towards*, and that made all the difference.

"What is the thought"—the Abbot's soft voice came from Tom's left— "of one neurone firing?"

In the small plain chamber, Tom knelt facing a blank white wall: at right angles to the Abbot, unable to see the master's expression.

There is no logic here, said a small voice inside. *Thought is an emergent property of vast numbers of . . .*

Tom stilled his mind.

Waiting.

And then, without volition, his one hand rose, and clapped the air.

Beside him, the Abbot bowed deeply.

The next day, when Tom returned from prayer-run, the Outer Court's guardian-monks genuflected upon his arrival.

No-one told him, yet he knew that his place was no longer in the novitiates' dorm.

Instead, he passed along a colonnade, to the long rows of individual cells where true monks slept and prayed, and found a holoflame burning brightly in the final cell.

He entered, sank into lotus on the meditation mat, and focused on the yellow votive flame.

The chamber flickers.

It was so obvious now.

The flame is still.

30

TERRA AD 2142

<<Ro's Story>>

[9]

Armoured flyers, growing larger by the second.

Come on.

Sprinting, pushing hard, Ro headed away from her parked TDV, the automated tourist-station.

I'll die without water—

Rock shards splintering, cracking beneath her boots. Dry air, already burning her throat. Sweat evaporating.

Broken shadow: a flyer overhead.

Running—

But it's death if I stay.

Dodging around a polished stone-tree, stones spraying as she skidded. Then she moved upslope, thighs pumping, muscles beginning to burn.

Run.

Slipping, sliding in the scree. But she had to get over the top: out of sight if the flyers landed.

Run harder.

The air was a hot hand pressed against her face, covering nose and mouth. Getting harder to breathe—

Push now.

Then she was over the top, arcing through the air, but her foot caught on something and she tucked her chin against her sternum as she rolled by reflex, the clash/spray of tiny pebbles beneath her back, and then she was on her feet and running once more.

Shadow.

No.

Shadow, enveloping her.

I will not let this happen.

Then the gut-wrenching roar, and she opened her mouth to scream unheard inside the thunder, and the shock wave smashed Ro to her knees.

No.

Hot blood trickling from her nose.

Sound dying away . . .

She looked up, got to one knee, as the flyer landed perhaps twenty metres away, crushing a stunted mesquite tree to oblivion, settling upon splintered stone.

Don't give up.

Sprang to her feet, heading left, as peripheral vision registered the gull door's swinging open.

She ran.

Watch out!

Red light, a narrow beam, blasted vertically downwards in front of her. Stones exploded, cutting her face as she dodged, ran faster.

Two more vertical beams—

Second flyer.

—as she zigzagged, but then a sheet of light pulsed down before her.

Skidding to a halt.

Anne-Louise's killers. Must be . . .

Turning—

But why am I their enemy?

Behind her, eight—no, nine—mirrorvisored men jogged into position, grasers trained upon her.

I don't want to die.

Ro's breath heaved in and out of her struggling lungs, salt sweat stung her eyes, as she crouched at bay, looking for a way out.

Nothing.

They weren't just going to kill her. They were going to rape her first. Make it look as if some drunken band of gangbangers, rather than professionals, had done her in.

They have grasers.

She knew their intentions when the burliest of the men pulled off his mirrorvisor, laid it aside with his weapon, and degaussed his jumpsuit's magseam. And walked towards her.

"Who are you?" she said.

No answer.

The others kept their grasers trained upon her. Mirror-bright: white sunlight reflecting off the transmission ends. Prismatic colours.

Like stone, the big man's face.

Professionals. Anne-Louise, what were you—?

A heavy boot crashed into her stomach.

Shocked, she fell, mouth wide open like a landed fish. Struggling—

Didn't think he'd move so fast.

Fatal error.

If she could hang on while he raped her, gain the surprise advantage later—Bad thinking. The big man was sitting on her stomach, the hot weight of his muscular buttocks and thighs pressing her down, and then his fist swung down towards her face.

No!

She blocked the first punch, but the second got through, fast, and momentary blackness exploded as its power bounced her head off the rock beneath her.

Bastard . . .

And then her attacker proceeded to pummel her.

No—

Parrying what she could.

No . . .

Wordless pain.

Inferior position. Getting weaker.

A distant sound, a muffled twinge: the crunch of ribs going.

Then he switched intention, elbow to her head—*impact*—and fluorescent flashes burst before her eyes.

He's going to rape me when I'm unconscious.

Or reduced to a whimpering, brain-damaged animal—

I'm dead.

Couldn't move her hands.

Bands of steel—

Another man.

The second attacker, huge as the first, pinned her wrists against the ground—"No!"—while the first smashed her once more in the jaw—*fractured world, spinning*—and ripped her jumpsuit open. Gauntleted hand upon her breast, squeezing hard until she thought it might burst—

No!

Rough fingers inside her bikini briefs . . .

Lock.

Yes, that was it: the electronic lock. In the doorway at Police HQ. And those other odd occasions scattered through the years.

. . . tearing the delicate fabric apart.

Remember the lock.

Reaching inside circuitry with delicacy, unlike the hard, rough fingers forcing their way inside her—

No!

A different kind of flow: liquid, tiny, incredibly complex.

I will NOT!

Building inside her, a rage-crescendo.

NEVER!

And the explosion.

JUST . . . DIE!

Cacophony of blazing light; a brilliance of crashing sound.

DIE, ALL OF YOU!

Roaring, coruscating blaze.

Die . . .

And nothing.

And came awake, hurting.

Breathe . . .

Hard. Great mass, pressing down upon her.

Groaning, she pushed dead weight a fraction to one side, wriggled out from underneath. Stones scraped her back, and her torn jumpsuit tangled.

Pushed herself up to hands and knees.

And knelt there, swaying.

What happened?

Two dead men lying across broken stones: her would-be rapist murderers, now bulky lifeless corpses. And—

Pain shot through her bruised and fractured ribs.

Whimpering, still on hands and knees, Ro moved to the one who had held her wrists. He lay face upwards—

God, no.

She retched, thin bile extruding slowly to the ground.

What did I do?

Where his eyes had been, opaque white jelly now lay in sockets of burnt and blackened meat. Liquefied eyes, growing sticky in the desert heat.

The other corpse's head was twisted to one side, and a trickle, as of drying tears, had escaped down one roasted cheek. Already, scout ants had climbed the salty trail, antennae waving as they settled into their unexpected feast.

Sweet Jesus.

Crawling backwards, away from the men she had destroyed.

Danger . . . ?

No. Squinting, looking around—No sign of anyone else. No mirrormasked men, no flyers.

Fled?

Looked at the two corpses once more, and dry-sobbed as she pulled her torn jumpsuit around her bleeding torso.

I did it . . .

But suddenly her sobbing stopped, and she knew it would not occur again.

I killed both of them.

And she knew, too, that she had the power—that she had *always* had this power, though she had not felt it consciously before this moment—and that she would use it again should the necessity come to pass.

Good.

The tourist station was a smoking ruin. Her rented TDV was an abstract sculpture in melted slag.

They blasted everything in sight.

And fled. Because they didn't know where the energy-attack was coming from?

Irrelevant, for now.

Call for—

But there would be no help. Her golden infostrand was twisted, fused, and would not respond to finger tap or whispered command.

Shit.

She was trapped in the desert, maybe days from anywhere, with no water. Beneath a blazing sun: it could reach 130 degrees, on the local Fahrenheit scale.

It was the twenty-second century. But without communication, in an environment not meant for unaided human survival—

Damn them to hell.

—she was already dying.

Scorching sun. Hammer, beating down.

Siebenundneunzig.

A staggering step.

Achtundneunzig.

One more.

Neunundneunzig.

Again.

Hundert.

Stumbling, righting herself, panting open-mouthed with the effort.

Skin already blistered.

One more pace. Just counting repetitions in the gym.

Ichi.

Switching to Japanese, to *Nihongo.* A mental trick, in extremis: re-inforcing dojo discipline.

Ni.

Sand, hot against her face. Pressing . . .

Fallen again.

Get up.

It was a furnace.

Slowly, slowly, rocking from side to side, she stood once more.

And step.

San. Resuming . . .

Just . . . count.

And.

Step.

Chi.

Again.

Go.

Again.

Unrelenting. Blazing. Hell.

Dried blood caked her face.

Cracking.

There was a need for movement.

Get up.

Hell's furnace boiled her, tore skin away with its heat.

Get—

She crawled, a little.

Again.

Swollen tongue filling her mouth. A dry croak . . .

Ro tried to crawl, produced a twitch of effort. Then nothing more.

I'm dying.

Shallow, painful breathing rasped in her chest as roasting air, ultra-dry, sucked moisture from her lungs, desiccated delicate internal tissues.

It burns.

It slammed upon her: white-hot sun, intense blue sky.

A furnace.

No.

Fire, squeezing hard and powerful as the fist of God.

No . . .

Face in the sand.

Unable to rise.

. . . more.

It was an arroyo, a baked riverbed.

Ro shivered fitfully.

Shaking.

As though she were freezing, but the sand and air were oven-hot. Thirst, long gone.

Bad sign . . .

Her body's heat dissipation had been blown apart by thermal stress: the shivering mechanism, designed to warm the body, is also a symptom of heatstroke's final stages.

Dying . . .

Terminal phase.

Not long now, my father.

Hissing.

Snake . . . ?

And then the rumbling.

Flyer. Come to finish—

Neither.

The ground trembled beneath her.

Darkness beckoned.

Sleep?

Something wet pattered against her cheek.

Dreaming.

Again. The plop, plop of raindrops on baked ground.

Rain—

Impossible.

But it comes, finally, to deserts, too.

Lifegiving rain.

She lay there, mouth open. Half-turned, by an immensity of effort, to catch sweet falling raindrops in her blistered, swollen mouth.

Awakening . . .

Thunder, in the purple skies. Silver rain, falling harder.

Beating against her.

Large drops splashing, breaking apart, painfully healing, as though she could absorb the life fluid directly through her skin—

Danger.

Washing against her face. A flat stream, bubbling.

Lying in it.

Danger, still.

Floods . . .

Too weak to move.

But she had to remember the floods.

Get moving.

This was the desert, where riverbeds survive as sun-hardened channels, concrete-hard rippled ground in the baking conditions. And become a sudden home to raging flash floods when the storms finally arrive.

Get moving now.

Rain hammered strength into her, and she rose—slowly, slowly—onto hands and knees, and began to crawl. Head down, squinting from time to time through the rain, sighting her destination.

A flat rock, standing in the arroyo's centre.

But roiling water rushed around her wrists, above her knees, foaming and bubbling with a strength which could snatch back life more quickly than it had returned it to her.

Flat rock, in midstream. If the waters did not rise too far, she would be safe.

If she could reach it . . .

Sheets of rain fell.

Got it.

And fell.

Stone, slippery in the wet. Her fingers skidded off it, but she grabbed again and her grip held. And she pulled.

Climb. That's it.

Ro hauled herself on top of the flat-topped rock and knelt there, gasping, while wind and rain washed all around, and in the black and purple sky, white lightning cracked and thunder bellowed.

It's time . . .

And then it happened.

This is my time.

Happened, as perhaps some part of her had always known it would.

Time.

Floodwaters rising rapidly, the false night darkening almost to pitch black, while overhead a sense of massive electric potential was building, accumulating, great enough to—

It struck.

White lightning blazed downwards—

Time . . . to live.

—and struck the flat rock.

But did *not* dissipate.

And then another bolt.

Yes.

A third.

But the lightning remained: glowing bolts connecting earth to heaven, upward-flowing electrons coruscating as they rose. Hissing and crackling, rippling white fire pillars reared up into darkness.

Another crack.

Fourth.

Again, again: fifth and sixth.

I'm going to live.

Grimly, Ro forced herself to stand.

And then, incredibly, she laughed.

While all about her, on the flat-topped rock, white lightning played and danced, glowed and cracked.

I'm going to live, my father!

And blazed.

Hissed, steam rising.

And burned.

<<MODULE ENDS>>

31

NULAPEIRON AD 3420

Brother Tom began his prayers early.

First, the dynamic warm-up devotions. And then he ran: day one of forty-nine, pacing himself for a forty-nine-klick offering before the Way. Along a dark, clean tunnel—he moved; the world flowed past.

Logos, I devote myself to thee.

For it is the world, the universe which thinks.

I *do not exist.*

The ego, the *I*, is an atom of self-awareness: one cog in the cosmic mechanism, a unit vector in the infinite nöomatrix by which the universe perceives itself.

Beyond thought . . .

I am nothing.

. . . he ran.

Back in the refectory, he drank deeply from a bowl. Then he sat back, eyes closed, and shuddered in ecstasy as electrolytes flooded through him, replenishing the muscles, while zentropes recharged his mind.

"How goes it, Brother Tom?"

"Well, Brother Thrumik."

Tears sprang to Tom's eyes.

He was so lucky, being here . . .

Thrumik laid a reassuring hand upon his shoulder.

"I know, my brother."

And so it continued, the seven-squared sequence, until the forty-eighth night arrived.

It was the eve of his final run in this extended devotion, and he remembered Brother Alvam's spiritual glow when he had completed the *novadecenovena* runs. And wondered if, with a night of fasting and no sleep, he himself might gain a fraction of that grace.

Neither eating nor drinking, Tom meditated alone in his cell.

But drowsiness caused his head to nod, so he rose, walked to the Outer Court—exchanging bows with the guardian-monks—and passed through the bronze doorway to the deserted marketplace beyond.

The nightwatchman, in his tattered surcoat, leaning on his staff, observed without comment.

One with Logos.

Tom began to run: slowly, silently, emphasizing heel-to-toe.

Logos is one.

For a time, he moved at an easy pace. Then, after passing through a series of quiet residential tunnels, he slowed to a walk. Tomorrow's devotion would require energy.

The footpath led into a long cavern, bisected by a dark stream running arrow-straight along its centre. At a curved footbridge, Tom stopped.

The bridge flows.

He stood there, contemplating.

The water does—

Something.

No. That's not right.

It floated past: a small pale corpse, tiny hands cupped palm upwards as though in supplication.

"Sorry, brother." An uncouth voice echoed from upstream. "Missed the bugger."

A big-bellied youth with dull eyes was hurrying along the bank, bearing a long-handled scoop. Moving marginally faster than the small, furry, drifting body.

The nightwatchman had two burly sons: Baze and Taze. This was one of them.

Making a tiny mudra of blessing, Tom watched as the youth—whether Baze or Taze, he was not sure—fished the dead marmie from the black waters.

But then another voice called out—the other brother, leaning against a stone bollard to catch his breath—and on the cobblestones, by this one's feet, a heavy burlap sack lay still.

No . . .

Lay *moving*.

Tom's skin prickled. Then something snapped behind Tom's eyes, a red rage filled his vision, and when his senses cleared he was standing above the second youth—now prone, stunned, beneath him—pressing his foot into a fragile throat.

"What are you doing?"

Without waiting for an answer, he reached down, opened the sack just a little—enough to see the wide amber eyes inside: six or seven trapped, fearful marmies—then sealed it shut.

"Taze! Taze!" Gasping, the brother was running up. "Let him go, brother . . . He ain't done nuthin'."

Tom stepped back, releasing him. "You're Baze."

"Yeah, I—" He stopped, puffing, bent over in agony. Then: "We's doin' the Abbot's bidding, brother. No messing."

On the cobblestones, a tortured gurgle was the only sound which came from Taze's throat.

"Don't try to talk," Tom told him. "In an hour, drink a little cold water."

Inside the sack, the marmies struggled without hope.

"You said"—his own voice came from far away—"this is the Abbot's bidding?"

Sack in hand, he headed towards the public cavern where he had first seen marmies. At this late hour, only a few pink glowglobes moved

through the shadows, casting weird ripples across the green translucent turing-block at the far end.

"*They squeals, see,*" Baze had told him. "*Disturbs the Abbot's meditations.*"
And the other elder monks', apparently.

Taze had nodded emphatically when his brother added: "*Our Pa
says, it must be right an' proper, or they wouldn't—*"

But Tom had cut him off.

Now, at the cavern's edge, he gently knelt down, and pulled open
the sack. At the same time, the resident troop of marmies, ranged high
up on the cavern wall, grew still. Then one of them called out, high
and chattering.

And, at Tom's feet, the freed captives swirled into motion—
bounding towards their fellows—save for one. A single marmie looked
up at Tom, gave a small grimace, a headshake, then loped away, using
foreknuckles sparingly on the flagstones, and then sprang up the wall
with admirable agility.

You're welcome.

Tom thought back to what he had told the two brothers, the nightwatchman's sons.

"*The rules have changed.*" And his thoughtful addendum: "*But don't
tell your Pa just yet.*"

He walked out of the cavern without looking back.

The novitiates' personal belongings were kept in a dank storage vault,
until they became full monks, expected to remain for life. Would his
things be here, or had too much time elapsed since his de facto ordination?

Tom looked along the shelves, until he saw a small folded pack
which looked familiar: a dark-green travelling cloak folded in a neat
bundle. Still uncertain—it was a generic cloak, nothing special—he
poked around with his fingertips, brushed something formed of metal.

Tom lifted it forth. It dangled from the neck cord: hooves upraised,
mane wild, in an endless striving for freedom.

Father . . .

He had not even realized his talisman was gone.

How can I follow the Way without my father's gift?

Sliding the cord over his head, Tom secreted the metal stallion within his orange jumpsuit robe. Then he pulled out a small disk—the travel-tag given to him by Trevalkin: he remembered his dislike of the man—and tucked it inside his clothes, beside his talisman.

He slipped out of the vault without a sound.

For the sake of the Way, I do this . . .

Repeating the sentence in his mind, over and over like a mantra, Tom made his way along the darkened cloister. By the time he reached the kitchen-lab, the monastery appeared deserted: it was four hours before dawnshift; no-one save the guardian-monks would be awake.

The travel-tag was a high-privilege access-request, tagged specifically to Realm Boltrivar. But the lab's semisentient scanfield, as Tom had hoped, recognized the implied authority.

Membrane dissolved, and he slipped inside.

He ran. It was incredible, wonderful—coming into the last few tunnels, knowing the monastery was in reach, then pouring into the Outer Court, standing there swaying, scarcely believing he had completed the Intermediate Devotion.

Forty-nine klicks: the forty-ninth successive day.

The courtyard was not crowded, but a few elder monks watched approvingly as aides took him to a recovery chapel, and laid him on a pallet. Soft waves of warmth rose through him, and a physiologist-monk came in to take readings, nodded, and left.

But when they brought in his meal on a tray, Tom passed his hand across the bowls in an unobtrusive motion, sprinkling fine grains like dust across his food.

For the sake of the Way.

That night he dreamed of Paradox.

At first it was true memory: of the white neko-kitten, mother killed by cruel youths, living wild. Of sneaking from the Ragged School with Zhao-ji, taking the poor thing fishbloc. The tiny buzz as the small body purred, little pink tongue lapping up food.

Or later, in a gilded travelling cage, in comfort like a Lord, tended to by Zhao-ji's officers . . .

But then those sea-green eyes became impossibly huge . . .

"Why have you stopped looking for me, Tom?"

. . . became grey . . .

"Don't you love me?"

. . . were Elva's eyes.

"I—"

He snapped awake, reaching into darkness.

It was a day of recovery-prayer—a solo run, light-paced—but he departed from the expected route, into a deserted cavern he knew was there, and bent himself to a different kind of devotion.

For the Way.

Slowly, crouching low, he threw a palm-strike against empty air; followed with a slow spin: reverse elbow to an imaginary face. Claw, hammer-strike.

Faster.

Knee-strike, moving smoothly now, low kick, drop to the gravelly ground, fire a knife-hand upwards, targeting a groin . . .

No, faster.

Leaped high: a spinning kick. Landed in the midst of invisible enemies, let rip the killing blows, the implacable dance of death.

Faster.

Cramps and vomiting came that night, but he hid the symptoms from his brother monks. A few stares followed him the next morning, as he left for his devotions.

Do I not emanate a holy glow?

But he was no better than his brothers.

Dead marmie floating . . .

No better.

On black waters, like Elva's death cocoon.

Edelaces dropped in his memory; barriers fell in his mind.

"After tomorrow's devotions," Thrumik told him on his return, "you're to attend Penitents' Chapel."

"Thank you, my brother."

It was no punishment, despite the name, but an honour to pray in the tiny chapel filled with deepscan fields and physiotropic processors. A place for receiving guidance.

The strongest guidance.

For the sake of the Way.

No-one stopped him when he went to run that night.

But it was a short-lived devotion, as he left the prayer-route, slowing to a walk, and made his way among the darker entertainment tunnels until he found the tavern he sought.

The holo still flapped virtual wings above the entrance, but there was no housecarl on guard at the House Of The Golden Moth.

Inside, the clamour lessened only slightly at the sight of a monk in the doorway; a confused-looking serving maid took him quickly through the main tavern, and sat him down in a quiet, low-lit chamber at the rear.

Shortly afterwards, the owner—Master Lochlen, Tom recalled—came inside, sat down opposite Tom, laying his hands flat on the black gloss tabletop.

"What can I do for you, brother?"

Strange patterns began to spark and swirl inside the tabletop.

"I'm looking for Kraiv. I—"

Beguiling patterns.

Calling to me.

Tom wrenched his gaze away, and looked at Lochlen.

"How very interesting, that you can resist . . ." A smile creased Lochlen's lean face, and he made a control gesture. "But Kraiv and Draquelle have left."

The patterns faded, were gone.

"I need . . ." Tom turned away, blinking tears.

"*Stokhastikos.*" Lochlen had been tugging his goatee in thought; suddenly he looked at Tom's shoulder, then up at Tom's face. "I should've known—"

"I'm sorry." Tom began to rise. "It was wrong of me to come here."

Thrumik's words: *you're to attend Penitents' Chapel.* That would sort out his confusion.

"No, my—" Lochlen stopped, then continued. "I can find out which way they went. I know something of their purpose. Can you come back tomorrow?"

After Penitents' Chapel?

"Perhaps they . . ." Tom frowned, trying to think. "Perhaps they went home, to the Hong."

"The Bronlah Hong?" Lochlen was looking at him strangely. "In the Bilyarck Gébeet?"

"Yes, that's—"

"The last place they'd go. Haven't you heard?"

Tom stared at his features, not quite processing the words.

"It fell," continued Lochlen, "to the Blight. That whole sector—"

Words like fading echoes, like roof-fall in distant caverns, crashing down where no-one waited to hear.

I must get back.

"—is Dark Fire territory now."

For the sake of the Way.

Keeping that mantra in his mind, making *use* of the deepest principle of his conditioning.

The Way . . .

In the darkest, quietest hours, Tom slipped from his cell, and returned to the kitchen-lab once more.

32

NULAPEIRON AD 3420

Tom was no logotrope designer.

He lay on his mat, alone in his cell, writhing beneath the tortured images—surreal, bloody, sexual, morbid—which tore at him, dragged him through a place that was neither sleep nor waking but more akin to a blistering, morphing, confused and agonizing hell.

And snapped awake, wide-eyed and drenched with sweat.

Outside, the sound of running footsteps.

A yell, a clatter.

And a scream, high-pitched as a woman—suddenly cut off.

Followed by a cold and heavy silence.

No logotrope designer . . .

Tom stepped out of his cell, and into Chaos.

Dressed in ordinary clothes, long dark cape across his shoulders, he walked through the refectory, among rows of writhing monks who tore at their skin, their eyes, each other.

Saw the Abbot face down in a bowl of clear broth. Ignored him.

"Help us, brother!"

A splintering sound.

Goodbye, my Brothers.

Passed into the Outer Court where two guardian-monks stood in an agony of indecision: whether to remain at their posts, or investigate the yells from inside.

But then one of them collapsed writhing, foaming at the mouth—

halberd clattering to the flagstones—and there was no decision to be made. The other monk ran.

For the Way.

Tom was no logotrope designer . . .

Retrieving the fallen guardian's control-bracelet, he caused the great bronze door to swing open.

. . . but sabotage is easier than design.

And stepped through, into freedom.

Inside the darkened, empty tavern Tom sat alone—sipping indigoberry daistral Master Lochlen had served himself—while Lochlen made arrangements out of sight. Low voices, words indistinguishable, drifted back from the rear chambers.

"It's hardly your fault," said Lochlen, returning.

He spun a floating seat the wrong way round and sat down, forearms draped over the back.

"What do you mean?"

"A man with your background . . . Zentropes. Sweet Fate. It's surprising the treatment didn't kill you. Bad enough for someone who's never had 'trope infusions at all."

"I don't—" Tom closed his eyes, opened them. "Are they dead?"

"The monks? From what I hear"—Lochlen glanced towards the tavern's rear—"they'll mostly recover."

Mostly.

For the Way . . .

Tom shook his head.

"I'll help, my Lord." Lochlen made a recognition-mudra, a flickering gesture like a conjuror's sleight of hand. "For Freedom's sake."

Surely the old ways of LudusVitae had been forgotten.

But there was a dark enemy within the world—he must remember that—and perhaps the movement, the alliances, still had their part to play.

". . . and Kraiv," Lochlen was saying, "have been travelling for several days. But with a few judicious shortcuts, and a bit of luck"—with an ironic smile—"you'll catch them up, my Lord."

"Call me Tom."

The next night he found himself inside a sealed, darkened cargo bubble—in the middle of a two-hundred-bubble train—floating along a black canal.

Bonded, their contents—theoretically—inspected and officially guaranteed, the bubbles floated through two checkpoints in as many days without being opened.

Tom passed the time in isometric exercise, used the gelblock sanitation with distaste, ate sparingly from the food satchel Lochlen had given him.

And let his thoughts slowly coalesce from the zentrope trance he had been trapped in for far too long.

On the fourth night he drifted through another border, after which the tunnel walls grew opalescent. Some ten hours later, at the start of morningshift, the bubbles slowed.

It was his cue to disembark.

Up ahead, beneath armed guard, stevedores were marshalling clawdrones, lifting cargo out. But there was a subtle green mark upon the bank nearby, before a narrow exit; Tom climbed swiftly ashore, spun into the darkened gap, waited for a shout or a burst of graser fire.

Nothing.

He followed the dark horizontal shaft, ducked through an opening at its far end, and came out into the middle of a group of men, dressed in heavy workers' surcoats stained with black grease and worse.

They were chatting, and appeared to take no notice of the stranger who suddenly stood in their midst. But Tom was holding out a sigil which Lochlen had provided, and he was under no doubt of their reaction had he failed to produce it.

No energy weapons were visible, but each man bore heavy steel tools, and had the strength to use them.

"This way," someone muttered, and they began to walk.

Tom stood at the top of a ramp which led down onto a wide platform, beneath a square-edged archway decorated with dull gold. People were milling down there, trying to get through; but membrane had been stretched across the archway's width, leaving just a narrow portal at the centre, through which mirrormasked soldiers let people pass after checking authorization.

The tunnel beyond was hundreds of metres wide; in it, a multitude of floating vehicles—lev-platforms, some levanquins, half a dozen stub-winged flyers—massed in readiness, preparing to take the escaping refugees.

Tom's contacts, the heavyset men, had provided him with a travel-tag, fastened a fake ID-stud in his ear, and left him here.

Still, Tom could not see how so few soldiers could control such a large crowd, liable to panic. Obviously, there were rumours of the Blight's spreading this way, and any freedman of means would try to—

Chaos.

On either side, scarcely visible, a slender monographite pillar rose. Each supported a small, transparent platform; and on each one stood a Jack.

Tom's skin crawled. He could not imagine a threat so great that *two* Jacks were required.

Don't worry . . . Not wanting to call attention to himself.

In their dark sleeveless uniforms, the Jacks looked small from here. But their senses could detect Tom's fear pheromones, listen to his sub-vocal mutterings as if he were talking aloud . . . and could pick out any individual, even from this crowd of thousands.

A Jack had been hunting for the Pilot, when Tom was young . . .

That was long ago.

But it was not just their sensory capabilities which made Jacks a breed apart. Either one of the two individuals overhead was capable of laying waste to this entire platform, and all the people on it, and that would have been true even if the mass of panicking civilians were magically replaced by professional enemy troops, armed and armoured, and looking for a fight.

A tingling spread across Tom's entire skin. He grew aware of the mass of people behind him, jostling and muttering; of the soldiers pressed against him, weapons cold against his throat; of the two Jacks high overhead. Of the glistening, hardened membrane which separated the restless throng from safety.

His ear grew hot. The fake ID-stud sparked ruby red.

Tom held his breath.

"OK. Let him through."

Pressure behind him, as the membrane pulsed. The force of it spat him through, and he nearly fell flat on the dock beyond.

"Over here, friend." Someone reaching down.

He clambered aboard the dangerously overloaded levanquin—filled with wide-eyed families who did not yet believe themselves safe—and stared around at the rest of the flotilla, wondering when they would begin to move.

Almost as if that were a signal, the first lev-platforms rose higher, then forwards, and the great evacuation commenced.

Three days later, in an inn called the Lair Of The Silver Slug, Tom was reunited with Kraiv and Draquelle.

"I prayed to Rikleth you'd be safe, my friend."

"Come here, Tom, and let me kiss you."

They hugged him simultaneously; he squeezed his eyes shut, determined not to cry.

33

TERRA AD 2142

<<Ro's Story>>

[10]

When Ro walked into the village from the desert, the notion of salvation took a moment to register. There was orange-red sand still beneath her feet. A small tan dog ran towards her, barking with impossible energy in the blistering heat.

Her skin was burned, her tongue parched; but she was walking, buoyed up by the water from yesterday's storm, and her memory of the power inside her.

"Come inside, girl."

It was a flat-faced Navajo woman, her grey hair bound in braids, wearing a man's shirt knotted at the waist. She gestured back towards her home, a pale peach ceramic hogan. Behind, a tiny robot crabbed its way along her neat vegetable plot.

This was a long way from any sizeable town, but the woman was already speaking into the silver-and-turquoise bracelet on her left wrist, then pointing it at Ro: transmitting her image.

If they've got scanAgents in EveryWare—

But she had to leave the burning desert—regardless of who "they" might be.

It was an hour later when she jerked awake, sitting in a hard-backed rocking chair—she had refused to lie down—and saw, through the polarized window, a whitish desert-stained flyer kicking up dust clouds as it descended.

There was a red cross emblazoned on the hull, but it wasn't until the hatch slid open and Sergeant Arrowsmith poked his head outside that she—

<<MODULE INTERRUPTED>>

A woman's scream, oddly attenuated by distance and the twisted rock channels—a klick away? More?—echoed around the small cavern. Tom, sitting, wiped the holo.

He was sealing up his stallion talisman, mu-space crystal secreted within, when Draquelle stumbled into the cavern.

"Tom, did you hear?"

"Of course I—"

"It came from that direction. The way Kraiv went."

After five days hiking through raw, interstitial territory, their supplies were lasting well; but Kraiv had offered to scout ahead for water while Tom and Draquelle put together a makeshift camp.

Crouching down, Tom unsealed Kraiv's discarded pack—heavier than anyone but the huge housecarl could have carried—searching quickly for weapons.

Found none.

Doesn't matter.

He stood up, noted Draquelle's compressed lips, the paleness of her skin.

"Show me."

34

NULAPEIRON AD 3420

He hurdled a fallen, shattered pillar, ran on across the broken ground. Hoping that Kraiv was far from danger; praying—somewhere inside— that there would be trouble. Because some part of Tom needed action, massive and immediate: to rip and tear more than imaginary enemies; to work out his rage with blood, not some prissy logotropic sabotage.

He ran.

For the . . .

No. Not that.

For Elva.

And then he was past the camp's perimeter—so much for the sentries—and skidding to a halt on shale almost before he realized that he was in the renegade band's midst.

They were seated, drinking, around a large thermoglow. None of them, not even the sentry standing on an outcrop overhead, wore his uniform correctly fastened; they looked like deserters, probably marauders.

Too late, Tom saw that Kraiv was sitting among them, on a flat rock with a large flask in his hands—the morphospear laid aside, out of reach—and deduced that the carl's strategy had been more subtle than frontal attack.

Behind them lay a black cave where fluorofungus did not grow; that would be where they kept any prisoners who still lived.

"Stranger!" It was a warning, not a greeting.

But the sentry's words—as he fumbled for his graser rifle—were unnecessary. Exploding from their places round the thermoglow, the men grabbed weapons without hesitation, swinging them round to bear on Tom.

Then it all happened very fast.

Kraiv was on his feet—big and ursine—smashing two soldiers' heads together before anyone knew he had moved. Another stepped into his path; Kraiv banged him in the centre of his forehead with one great fist: he dropped like a marionette whose lev-field had crashed.

And Kraiv now held the morphospear.

Three soldiers split from the group—two youths, and a veteran who probably knew of the carls' prowess—and ran towards Tom. A scything kick took the first one down, but the others kept coming . . .

Move.

Sentry, overhead.

The air cracked. Graser fire blew apart the rocks beneath Tom's feet. But he was already going down, snatching the fallen man's graser as he rolled, and came up on one knee taking careful aim upwards, and pressed the firing stud.

An explosion of blood ripped the sentry's body in two.

Tom spun back towards the camp—and froze.

What took place next defied any description he might later give, awestruck before an exhibition of warrior spirit such as he had never imagined, nor ever hoped to see.

For few men witness true berserker rage and live to tell it.

Two dozen soldiers—more, thirty—came for him in a pack, but Kraiv's great figure moved fast—massive muscles sliding beneath glistening black skin: a warrior—as the great opalescent morphospear slid and moaned through the air like a living thing.

As a wide flat halberd, it sliced through limbs. Then it snapped into a cupped, parabolic configuration, shielding Kraiv from spitting graser fire, before lancing out, long and straight, to impale the shooter through his soft throat.

Huge, heavy, blood-hungry: only Kraiv could have wielded such a weapon.

Roaring, he swung in a great arc, and four men fell before his long —now scimitar-bladed—morphospear. Then a group of their comrades, armed with entrenching cutters and bare hands, fell on Kraiv— and died, as he appeared to shrug his huge muscles, threw them in all directions, then sliced them down.

Two soldiers had graser rifles but they looked in fear as Kraiv reared up before them, swung down, and then their butchered limbs lay streaming blood upon the stones beside their fallen weapons.

More of their comrades turned and ran.

But three men, lean-faced and lupine, now circled Kraiv with monopole daggers drawn: quiet, coordinated, knife-fighters used to working as a team. Even the briefest exposure of a limb, his torso, would gain Kraiv a tendon-slicing cut, an organ-piercing thrust—

He yelled as he advanced, but they fell back towards the cave, a feint, then spread out. With blades, they could attack from all angles with no risk of crossfire; and they could deliver tiny, progressively weakening cuts, before stepping in close for the kill.

They sprang at Kraiv—

No!

—who whirled, arms wide, in what surely must be a fatal mistake—

Do it.

—except that the morphospear had cleaved in two, into blazing blades which cut infinity symbols into the air as Kraiv spun through their midst, then stepped back, chest heaving.

Splashed blood, dying moans.

There were two more left, two soldiers with weapons drawn, who looked at the dark cavemouth, at each other, then turned to run.

Each of Kraiv's weapons became hatchet-shaped as he hurled them, spinning through the air, burying their heavy blades with a thud in the fleeing soldiers' spines. Two corpses fell, arms outstretched towards lost salvation.

Kraiv held out his hands, palm upwards, as though in prayer.

Both hatchets' hafts elongated—grew impossibly long and thin, stretching towards their master—then looped themselves round his massive wrists, and tugged their blades free with a liquid slurp. Fat burgundy blood drops spattered and gobbet-stained grey vertebrae fell aside as the twin weapons sucked back into shape, merged into one, and the great morphospear was whole again, sharp and ready.

Kraiv turned towards Tom, death shining in his eyes.

"My friend. Kraiv."

The huge carl stopped, breathing hard, veins like cords prominent across black iron muscles, until slowly the tension and berserker rage attenuated, faded to nothing, and he was human and civilized once more.

From the small dank cave at the camp's rear, Kraiv led forth two women—careful not to touch them, even when they stumbled—whose torn clothes, bloodied skin and shrinking posture told Tom everything he needed to know about what had happened here.

Neither woman gloated at the evidence of vengeance all around them. Instead they shivered as they passed the corpses—the taller woman weeping silently—granted no release by the sight of hot ripped meat which had so recently been real and powerful, revelling in power to brutalize their victims, to tear fragile humanity to shreds.

It took nearly three more tendays to reach the Dorionim Goldu.

In a marketplace, among holosprite tables and narl-egg vendors, they found the leaders of a local Urdikani community, distant kin to the two refugee women—Hani and Ravi by name—who agreed to find them shelter, and who listened with saddened sympathy to a too-familiar tale of families gone to war and not returning, of armed invaders who crashed into ordinary lives, turned peaceful Aqua Halls into blood-soaked scenes of horror, left children dead, and stunned survivors with fractured lives.

Tom and his companions bade them a short farewell. Tears tracked without shame down the trio's faces, as they followed the directions they had been given, and headed for the Blue Lotus Hong.

"*Nǐ hǎo.*" Tom's words echoed oddly in the low, misty cavern. Behind them, their rented skimmer was already departing from the flat dock. "*Lǐ xiānsheng zài ma?*"

Five cloned enforcers, black hair braided pit-fighter style, stared at him with eyes like stone. But behind them, an older Zhongguo Ren in a robe of black and gold bowed to the three strangers.

"Master Lee," he said, "has been expecting you."

Overhead, a tiny holo flower with cupped azure petals slowly revolved.

The shaven-headed oriental man was old, and his hands looked unsteady when he showed them the lamina trap he intended to use on Draquelle. But Tom gave Kraiv a tiny nod: he trusted Master Lee's ability to remove the silver-scaled dragon which slithered endlessly across Draquelle's slender torso, sliding between the soft layers of her skin.

Trusted him to remove the femtautomaton; after that, there was Draquelle's indenture and their safety to consider.

"Leave the chamber," Master Lee told Tom and Kraiv. And, to Draquelle: "Remove your tunic, please."

"No." Draquelle reached out to hold Kraiv's hand. "He stays with me."

Tom went outside, into a holoflame-lit foyer, and stood with silent footsoldiers to whom exquisite politeness and passionless killing were two sides of the same professional coin. But he did not have to wait long before they called him back inside.

"Master Lee says . . ." Draquelle hesitated, still fastening up her clothes.

Tom watched the old man drape black velvet across the flat laminar trap, hiding the silver movement within.

"The Bronlah Hong," said Master Lee, "no longer exists. We make no claim on this person's indenture."

Tom wondered if he would have made the same decision without a towering, ebon-skinned housecarl standing in the chamber, giant morphospear slung across his broad triangular back. Nevertheless, Tom bowed to Master Lee with punctilious correctness, and delivered the most courteous formal thanks he knew:

"*Xièxie . . . Zhù dájiā̄ wànshì rúyì.*"

The old man bowed, palm covering fist.

"*Zhù gè wèi yílù shùnfē̄ng.*"

It was a traditional farewell to travellers.

Tom walked ahead, along a gloomy, cold, square-edged tunnel whose floor curved slightly upwards, sparsely lit by fluorofungus contained in baskets, not allowed to grow free across the damp stone. It was not a cheerful place.

Their next destination was the Manse Hetreece, where Kraiv would offer reparation, perhaps his life, to atone for young Horush's death.

But despite this, Kraiv and Draquelle—a freedwoman once more —walked hand tightly in hand, unable to look away from each other, skin tingling, their eyes filled with a sudden hope they did not dare to name.

35

NULAPEIRON AD 3420

The Manse Hetreece was a great, grey-blue, square-columned building, lined with copper, standing proud and strong atop a great cliff, in a black-shrouded titanic cavern where winds whistled eerily among strange rock formations.

It was late evening when Tom and his companions stood on a flat outcrop, the end of a winding causeway, on the other side of the dark abyss. Between here and the towering Manse, a single bridge stretched: shining gold and violet and flame-orange, shimmering above the drop—a bridge of light instead of dull, base matter.

"The sentinels," said Kraiv, nodding towards the distant watchtowers, "will be tracking us already."

"I can't—" Draquelle stopped, staring at the bright, glorious, insubstantial bridge.

"Stick with me, and you can."

And so they passed along the fiery bridge's length. Hissing and sparkling, every hue in the spectrum blazed in random patterns, and the travellers waded through that viscous, brilliant light—up to their ankles at first, then their knees, and finally, at the centrepoint above the now-invisible abyss, hidden by brightness, they walked hip-deep in shining bridge-stuff—and Tom was shaking by the time they reached the portal at the far end.

"The Bifrost Gate," Kraiv announced as they walked through.

Then they were in a courtyard tiled in shades of blue, surrounded by carls with deep-blue cloaks and helms of shining copper, and morphospears to match Kraiv's own.

A phalanx of carls escorted Kraiv—trailed by Tom and Draquelle—to the Great Hall. On the way, from dark stone corridors, Tom glimpsed gymnasia—saw female carls practising acrobatics—and schools. At one point, they passed two women, glowing with sweat and breathing hard as they left a training hall together, unfastening the sparring straps which bound their fists.

The taller woman, black-haired and athletic, caught sight of Tom, and sudden mutual attraction leaped between them—caring nothing for appropriateness of time or place.

But then the moment was past, a memory, and Tom was entering a huge hall already filling with boisterous housecarls looking forward to their evening banquet.

What happens now?

Tom had no legal arguments prepared—*Call yourself a logosopher?*—or rhetoric with which to plead for Kraiv's life. He knew little of the Manse's laws inscribed in Sèr Koedex Rechtenstein; he knew everything about a warrior's willingness to die for honour.

For if there were to be a trial, it would surely involve blood, endurance, and a stoic resistance to pain.

Long tables were set out in rows and tiers. Round copper shields hung vertically in mid-air; rosy glowclusters drifted among them, sliding warm reflections across the burnished disks.

On the dais, a central chair, surmounted throne-like by a carved blackstone canopy, stood conspicuously empty: it belonged to the clan chief who was currently away from home, with a fighting company of carls.

But the woman who sat to the vacant throne's right bore herself with a warrior's grace, limber and strong despite the grey which streaked her copper-bound hair. From time to time, her gaze would travel to the back of the Great Hall, where Kraiv ate nothing, waiting for the meal to end.

Plentiful food, hot and fragrant, accompanied by humorous boasting, by tall tales and word-puzzles, rounding off the day's hard work. But there were too many vacant seats, and every now and then the merriment would fade to silence; then someone would call out a warrior's name, and they would toast a brave housecarl fallen in battle in some far demesne.

When the last course was removed, the woman upon the dais rose, and beckoned Kraiv.

He stood up, muscular and impressive as a statue.

Then he walked among housecarls suddenly grown silent, along the central aisle. Before the dais he stopped, went slowly down on one knee, and bowed his head.

"Kraiv Guelfsson yclept am I, of the Clan Vachleen. And I caused" —looking up, he held the woman's gaze—"your son's death, which I regret."

Beside Tom, Draquelle jumped, gave a tiny sound, then forced herself to stillness.

Chaos, my friend . . .

"Reparation, your Highness, is yours to command."

The ruler's skin was paler than Horush's had been, but Tom could see the resemblance now: his mother, indeed. Would she call on Kraiv to fall upon his own morphospear? Or would the punishment be long, drawn out?

For an age, she regarded Kraiv.

Then her gaze lifted, and she pointed around the Great Hall, at the clusters of empty places. In a carrying voice, she said:

"We are short of honourable warriors, proud carl. An you pledge yourself to Manse Hetreece, we know brave Horush's spirit would be satisfied."

No-one breathed.

What's wrong?

Kraiv's own clan would already have accepted his loss. Surely that was not the—

Draquelle's fingers were digging into Tom's forearm like claws, gripping hard. For she had already realized: the danger arose not from the mass of armed and deadly warriors, nor even from the iron will of the proud, bereaved woman who was strong enough to rule them.

It was Kraiv's own sense of honour which placed him in peril.

"Do you accept"—the woman's voice was soft—"brave warrior?"

Kraiv frowned, hesitating, while inside Tom every nerve screamed. *Give your allegiance!*

But that was not the carl's way.

Do it, my friend.

Breathing fast, Kraiv squeezed his eyes shut, examining his soul for signs of cowardice. Honour-bound, he could pledge allegiance—but not fear-driven.

He scrutinized his feelings with ruthless self-honesty, ready to pay the price of weakness with his own blood. Beside Tom, Draquelle bit her lip, to prevent herself crying out.

Kraiv's eyes snapped open.

"By Axe and by Flame—"

Fate save him.

"—I bind myself to thee, wise Lirna, to the safety and welfare of thy Manse. I fight beside my broth—"

Suddenly every carl in the Hall was upon his or her feet, cheering loudly as they stamped feet and smashed metal goblets upon stone tables, roaring their approval, drowning the final words of Kraiv's blood oath in wave upon wave of glorious sound.

On the seat beside Tom, Draquelle hid her face and wept.

Two days later, on the far side of that blazing bridge of light, Tom looked back, eyes squinted almost shut against the brilliance. He raised his hand in farewell, though he could not see if they still stood beneath the Bifrost Gate.

Be well, my friends.

Then he turned his attention to the causeway, and carried on alone.

He travelled light and fast.

For three days, he ran like a monk performing ultra-endurance devotions: at an unstoppable, distance-eating speed. There was no logical reason to hurry; it had taken two Standard Years to get from his entering the Aurineate Grand'aume to here. But it felt as though time was running out.

At the border of Realm Boltrivar, they scrutinized Tom's travel-tag very carefully, and for a moment he wondered what that bastard Trevalkin might have encrypted in the tag, but then the membrane dissolved and he was through.

For an hour he walked among corridors and tunnels which knew nothing of distant strife. Eventually, Tom found himself in a market chamber filled with spice and fabric vendors, so perfect that he might have stepped back into childhood in Salis Core, with Father and old Trude, the other stallholders, the throng of market-goers . . .

Except that one of them was pointing at him.

And another, as growing whispers circled the chamber.

"It's him . . ."

An old woman, head covered with a plain dark shawl, confided in her neighbour: "I'd know him anywhere."

Repeated, the whispering grew louder, becoming a refrain.

"Lord One-Arm!"

By the time Tom reached the chamber's centre, beneath the broad silver disk inset upon the ceiling, there were soldiers hurrying towards him from every entrance. The nearest group was led by a running officer in a brocade-edged half-cape, hand upon his sword hilt.

Tom's travel-tag sparked ruby.

Overhead, the silver disk slowly turned.

No escape.

Troops on every side.

Overhead, slats descending . . .

But then the young officer, breathing hard, knelt down on the flag-stones, held his ceremonial sabre so it would not rattle, and made obeisance.

"My Lord, we have great need—"

A *snick* as the stairway slotted into place.

"—of your abilities."

Tom smiled at the officer's perfectly clean, pressed uniform, in contrast to his own rough-cut, dust-stained clothes. "Thank you"—checking the man's insignia—"Lieutenant."

"General d'Ovraison—"

"Is expecting me. Quite."

Then he set foot upon the first rung, paused for a moment, half-seeing expectant faces among the crowd, and began his ascent.

36

TERRA AD 2142

<<Ro's Story>>

[11]

Holo, with soundtrack by Borodin:

It is in the depths of icy winter—Ro kept the narrative as text: she could read it ten times faster than listening to voiceover *beneath a crust of fresh white snow, that Moscow (more properly, Moskva)*—she touched the word: it sounded from the speaker as *"Maskvà"*—*paradoxically reveals its character.*

Layer upon layer of history: like winter clothing, peeled off in the warmth indoors, we reveal a proud people—superstitious yet secular, intellectual and family-loving—who have suffered greatly . . .

Leaning back in her cushioned seat, Ro regarded the smartcart in the aisle beside her.

"Quelque chose à boire?" The device had noted her Swiss citizenship; Ro's canton-reg mistakenly listed her primary tongue as *français*: a piece of misinformation destined to spread through EveryWare.

"Non, merci."

To her other side, the window overlooked blue skies, with grey cloud cover nestling below, hiding the winter-bound countryside.

. . . fodder for gulags, when the secret police would knock upon the doors at night, arresting innocents for sedition. In the one country which suffered most in the TwenCen war against the Nazis, where every family was touched by bereavement, a national paranoia ironically replicated the worst of—

She minimized the holo, maximized the other: the message she had read no more than two dozen times since boarding the flight and checking her h-mail.

Bronze warrior face, the too-long black hair.

"I'm sorry," he said again, in re-play. *"I think you're expecting too much of our, ah, friendship. Forgive me if I'm out of line, but I'm not comfortable with this."*

Her stomach contracted once more.

"Tomorrow, I leave for Saarbrücken, for two weeks' initial training." He mispronounced the narrow "ü." *"If I've misunderstood, you can contact me there, before I go on to Tehran."*

Sick inside, skin tightening, Ro touched the miniature Luís Starhome: just an insubstantial holo, pure light and quite intangible.

Can I lose what I never had?

Was this the way poor Albrecht suffered, when she rid her life of him?

"Otherwise, I think it best"—his warrior's face was grave, rather than contrite—*"that we not talk again. Endit."*

The holo stilled, winked out of existence.

Endit. Yes, he had ended what he had never started.

Ro blinked rapidly, re-started the other holovolume.

. . . wide imperial streets, cupolas and minarets still prominent, stolid kremlins rubbing shoulders with the latest in leading-edge bioarchitecture—

Ro checked the aisle, tempted to summon the smartcart back. Something to dull the pain . . . No.

There were few other passengers. Up front, the big payers in luxury class were partying or working: too blasé actually to enjoy the flight. Under other circumstances, Ro would have been thrilled; now she felt dislocated in space, unnerved by despair.

—though Sakharov's statue has been removed, and the site has reverted to its former name of Dzerzhinski Square, the dark ghosts of Beria and Dzerzhinski himself have thankfully not returned. The iron fist in the iron glove no longer

haunts Muscovites. Where a grim dark cube once stood, headquarters of the feared Komityet Gosudarstvennoi Bezopasnosti—KGB—now grows the magnificent flowering bioarchitecture of XenoMir, home to alien ambassadors and UNSA's finest research scientists. It is situated opposite the well-known—

The hypershuttle banked, arced down into the cloud layer.

Sheremetyevo spaceport, and the whole of Moscow's grandeur, were laid out beneath her.

UN troops, armoured with flak jackets and bearing sonar-scoped lineac rifles, escorted her to a waiting TDV. Their boots crunched through the heavy snow.

"*S'il vous plaît.*" A sergeant gestured her inside.

"*Merci.*" She slid onto the cold bench seat as the heavy gull door swung down, clicked shut.

"Welcome to Moscow." The onboard AI spoke in English. "We will shortly be—"

"Shut up."

A smartcart slid her luggage—two carryalls—into the TDV's stowage compartment. The soldiers nodded, stepped away: apparently, their duty was fulfilled.

The vehicle slid into motion.

She had a glimpse of her fellow shuttle passengers, all queuing for taxis like normal civilians, and wished she was among them. Not important enough to be escorted all the way, but not allowed to remain anonymous.

. . . of the recent outrages, UNSA personnel are required to follow code-orange safety protocols at all times. She tapped on her golden-wire infostrand, cranking up the audio. *Please keep EveryWare-Assist in permanent pre-load whenever you are travelling out of . . .*

There had been anti-xeno demonstrations in Tehran, Dublin, Saigon and Reykjavik. Ro shook her head, and silenced her infostrand. She hoped that Sergeant Arrowsmith and the forensic scientist,

Hannah, were safe: both had taken indefinite leave, and gone to stay with distant relatives.

As for her, if there was some conspiracy which threatened her, she was safer surrounded by UNSA security, in a city where paranoia had once been a way of life, than wandering around the desert, exposed.

Outside, Moscow's wide snow-bordered boulevards slipped past.

Among the grand old granite buildings—bigger and more imposing than Ro had expected—was something new: a glistening black corporate pyramid, large enough to contain maybe two thousand employees, visibly reconfiguring itself. Ro pressed her face against the TDV's blue-tinted armourglass, watching the biobuilding slowly recede into the distance behind her.

Then she flopped back into her seat, let out a long breath, and smiled despite her dark mood. Perhaps this was going to be interesting, after all.

Outside, a cold grey rain began to fall, mashing at the snow.

Over glistening wet cobbles, the TDV hissed into Red Square. Crimson reflections—from the giant floating holo: <<КРАСНЯПЛОЩАД>>—dripped across the ground, and the soaking membrane which coated St Basil's Cathedral. The largest of its cupolas was striped with the exact shade of mint-green that the scarp slopes showed in the Painted Desert—

Ro shook her head.

The TDV slid past the Kremlin's long red walls, behind which golden cupolas brightly shone. Then the vehicle hissed across a wide boulevard, circled an imposing block of grey architecture, and settled to the ground before a building such as Ro had never seen in person.

It was approximately globular, rearing high overhead: a myriad black window facets embedded in a motile white web. The biobuilding was slowly but—as Ro slid out from the TDV—visibly deforming, morphing. Endlessly cycling through its configurations.

There was a policeman, in green thermal suit, with wide Slavic features beneath his heavy helmet.

"XenoMir?" Ro wondered whether she should have used the older name: XenoDom.

"*Da.*" He looked pleased. "*Vyi rabotayetye zdyes?*"

Ro shrugged, with an exaggerated grimace. Embarrassed at her linguistic limitations, though she did better than most.

And we expect to understand offworld species?

Behind her, the TDV disgorged her luggage, and whispered into motion.

She picked up her two bags and, while the policeman benevolently watched, carried them up the broad granite steps, through the immutable stone entranceway, and into a gleaming foyer furnished with polished marble.

That evening, in her private room in the Residence—part of the ancient university, situated north of the city proper, above the Yeltsin Hills; there was a bus to shuttle UNSA employees back and forth between campus and XenoMir—Ro tried to relax, could not. Despite the time lag, sleep would not come.

Her bed was built into the wall fittings: everything of rich, panelled wood. Old, heavy, sliding doors separated her study-bedroom from the bathroom, and the whole suite from the corridor outside.

The indoor warmth was comforting, if intense. Beyond the windows, grey-looking snow fell like silent ash in the gathering darkness.

She tapped her infostrand—currently the golden wire was wrapped necklet-wise round her throat—and directed it to pass images to her desktop. Sitting at the wooden desk, she smiled as its crystalline surface inlay cleared, and presented an image which seemed to stretch downwards, inside the desk: virtual holos, rather than real.

"Play the seminar." Her voice sounded tired. "Start from bookmark two."

It loaded at the point where she had stilled it. Professor Davenport's image was static for a split second, then the replay began:

"... like Lord Kelvin, in the nineteenth century, declaring that there was nothing remaining for physicists to do, except add the last decimal place to all that had been measured.

"Similar hubris was invited two centuries later, by cosmologists who believed they had deciphered the history and future of the universe. This, at a time when the Hubble 'constant'—essentially what we now refer to as the Dullaghan bubble-function—had never been satisfactorily measured; when every theory assumed that at least ninety per cent of all matter was invisible quintessence (or "dark matter" as they charmingly termed it) which had never been observed, and whose nature no-one knew."

There was laughter from the corridor outside. For a second, Ro was tempted to investigate. But she did not feel like company.

"And the lambda function was assumed to be a cosmic antigravity-repulsion constant, even though observation showed it must be smaller than its theoretical value by at least one hundred and twenty-three orders of magnitude ... No other estimate in the history of science has been so badly ..."

She sat down on the bed, killing the lights with a gesture. In the desk, Prof. Davenport's image was no longer visible, but his comforting voice droned on.

"... flatland, for example, by considering a polka-dot balloon. Inflate the balloon, and every dot appears to be the centre of cosmic expansion. Yet no-one considered that, though the balloon-surface inhabitants are two-dimensional beings, the balloon must exist in a three-dimensional context. For those charming fictitious characters, so too for us.

"When Gus Calzonni finally made her 'intuitive' leap from quintessence-matrix brane-harmonics (and inflationary cosmic evolution) to mu-space theory, wherein the realspace multiverse itself was draped across the fractal landscape of the mu-space continuum, it caused a shockwave through the scientific community.

"It was not just that the values of every fundamental constant were derived from a single fractional coefficient. Gus herself knew from the very beginning, *though it took decades and hundreds of researchers to prove it, that mu-space was more than a mathematical construct: in fact, an underlying and immeasurably greater reality through which we might travel.*

"Popular biographers, as she became an immensely rich and influential public figure (though not daring to publish until after her death), picked up on her rumoured but highly unlikely genealogy—that Gus, known more formally as Augusta Medora de Lauron (using the surname she preferred, taken from her seventh and final husband), was descended via illegitimate lines from Ada, Countess Lovelace, the world's first programmer, and therefore from Lord Byron himself. Despite all evidence to the . . ."

At some point, Ro drifted off to sleep.

When she woke, a tiny scarlet flag seemed to be drifting above her: a newswatch netAgent, signalling an item of personal interest in EveryWare. She waved the holo away, unwound the infostrand from her neck, and dumped it on the wooden bedstand on her way to the bathroom.

Afterwards, showered and dressed, she shoved the infostrand into her jumpsuit pocket, and went to look for breakfast.

Perhaps I'll see an alien today!

Ro hurried down the broad stairs, into the ancient dining room.

"Hey, Ro! How're ya doin'?"

It was Zoë, the teaching assistant who (slightly drunk) had told Ro about the Zajinet, on the day one of the xenos had disappeared . . . For a second, Ro's disorientation increased, as though she were back in Arizona.

"Er, hi, Zoë. I didn't realize you were going to be here as well."

But Ro could not remember having seen her in DistribOne recently.

"Pulled some strings. I'm not living here, though." She gestured at the crowded dining hall. "Too noisy. I've an apartment in Strugatski Prospekt."

"Very impressive."

Ro looked for coffee, could not see any. People appeared to be drinking black tea. There was a samovar on the counter, along with the cooked dishes.

"I need some breakfast." She started to head for the queue. "Have you already had . . . ?"

But Zoë had not moved. Gravely: "You haven't checked the news, I take it?"

"No." Ro looked at her, feeling suddenly cold. "Should I have?"

"Saarbrücken Fliegerhorst"—Zoë's voice dropped almost to a whisper, but Ro clearly heard every dreadful word—"was destroyed by a micro-tak last night."

"That's awful." She did not know what to say.

"I'm sorry . . . Security-reg confirmed . . ." Zoë swallowed. "Luís Starhome was there. He—"

"No, he's in Tehran."

Denying reality.

It can't be.

But she remembered his h-mail, his stopover for initial training.

No . . .

"You're saying he's dead." Flatly. As though there were no emotion great enough to cover what she felt.

"God, Ro. I'm sorry. I know you're . . ."

Luís is dead.

How could she lose what she never had?

The room spun around her.

Oh, my love. My Luís—

But he was not hers, and never would be.

Not now.

Luís . . .

<<MODULE ENDS>>

37

NULAPEIRON AD 3420

It was a return to noble life. Everything was the same; everything was different.

The physical surroundings brought back memories of Palace Darinia: vast halls and galleries on many levels (though contained within the Primum Stratum), walls and ceilings of dark lustrous mother-of-pearl or softly luminescent jade. Deep carpets of royal blue flowed through long hallways, carrying the noble-born effortlessly along, allowing them time to appreciate the precious works of art they passed, the intricate crystalline glowtrees which floated overhead. There were series within convoluted series of fountains and ponds, labyrinthine sculptures in their own right, within which fantastic artificial lifeforms swam and glowed; colonnades and quiet quadrangles, where small moss gardens provided places for silent meditation, isolated by quaint anti-sound hushfields from the sounds of young scholars and older folk engaged in logosophical debate; airy malls, formed of clean utilitarian lines at one moment, but whose walls would flow viscously, perhaps creating intricate spars and buttresses, extruding dainty footbridges, or sinking inwards to form niches in which noble statues stood. Gargoyles lurked playfully at odd junctures within the moving architecture.

Even the air seemed purer, to energize with every breath.

It was strange, and it was wonderful . . .

But he felt no closer to finding Elva.

Six soldiers escorted Tom along a gold-chased boulevard, and into a transverse hallway patterned in deep brown and crimson. At the end, they stopped before a silver membrane.

"Your quarters, my Lord." The officer-in-charge bowed formally.

"Very good." Tom heard the patrician tone which had resurfaced in his own voice, and hated it. "Carry on."

"Sir."

As the escort left, Tom stepped inside, and found himself in a round, marble-floored foyer where a young man in servitor's livery was kneeling, head bowed, soft black cap in hand.

Oh, Fate.

"Who are you?"

"Adam Gervicort, sir. Beta-plus servitor."

At that, six women filed in between nacreous pillars from the next chamber—bright and airy, filled with holosculptures—and lowered themselves to their knees on the silvery marble. They bowed in full forehead-to-floor obeisance.

This, to a man born beside a humble market chamber, who had lived more recently in fearful squalor for two Standard Years, out of his mind, surviving by drunken cunning and the pity of strangers, sleeping by day in derelict tunnels where nights were dangerous . . .

"Just get up."

They rose quickly, like soldiers called to attention, and stood frozen in blank-faced acceptance: awaiting punishment for an infraction whose nature they did not understand, but for which they accepted responsibility.

Chaos . . . I've forgotten so much.

Softening his tone: "I'm not . . . very big on ceremony. Are you all, er, assigned to me?"

"Yes, sir." It was Adam Gervicort who spoke. "Your personal servitors."

Tom looked around at the richly appointed antechamber. A platinum-inlaid glowcluster floated near the ceiling—decorative rather than utilitarian, for the wall panels glowed with a softly pervasive, diffuse illumination—and elegant statuettes filled small niches between the panels.

It was sumptuous, decorated with objets d'art whose price could feed entire families for lifetimes, and it was merely the entrance to his apartment.

"How many other chambers," he asked, "does this place have?"

"Thirty-five, sir."

Tom quelled internal laughter.

"I suppose . . . I'll be able to make do."

A wide green lake nestled in a crystalline cavern, only a few minutes' walk from Tom's new home. Nature and artifice combined in frosted-mint intricate pillars, joining gentle emerald waves to the sculpted ceiling above. Brightly coloured sailplanes floated just above the water, and even from here the laughter of carefree lordlings at play was audible.

There were even some swimmers, bobbing among the waves.

Leaning against a pillar on the marble shore, Tom watched. Beside him, his new chief servitor, Adam Gervicort, stood stiffly to attention. Adam was maybe twenty SY old—two-thirds of Tom's age—and suddenly that seemed awfully young.

There was a shout above the waters, then good-natured name-calling, as two sailplanes narrowly avoided a collision.

"The nobility at play," Tom murmured.

"My Lord?"

"Nothing. Who are they?"

There was a group of twelve runners further along the shore, dressed in olive-green long-sleeved leotards, running to a cadence.

"Soldiers, sir. From General d'Ovraison's Akademía del'Guerro."

"It's a military school?"

"Um . . ." Adam's shoulders stiffened, as though he had been about to shrug, but servitor reflexes stopped the gesture. "Everyone calls it the Academy, but it's more than a training school. It's Strategic Command for the sector."

"I see."

Tom wondered just what he was doing here. Change was not necessarily progress.

"Listen, Adam . . ." He hesitated, then: "In private, why don't you
just call me Tom."

"OK, I—" Adam reddened. "Sir."

Tom sighed. What kind of ulterior motive did Adam suspect him of?
Yet if Corduven has lovers, they're surely not female . . .

He put that thought aside. If the local mores were anything like
the noble milieu he was used to, his knowledge of Corduven's prefer-
ences was a dangerous secret.

Tom was sure—pretty sure—that Corduven was not the kind to
abuse servitors; but that could not be said for all nobility.

He looked Adam in the eyes.

"I was born a long way down, my friend. When the authorities sold
me to Lady Darinia, I entered servitude as delta-class. I'd ask you to
drop my title in public, as well as privately, except that it would
rebound on you. They'd find a way to make you suffer."

Adam was silent for a moment. Out on the lake, youthful Lords
and Ladies dived from sailplanes into the waves, and struck out for
shore.

"I knew you'd been promoted . . ." Adam swallowed. "But to rise
that far . . ."

Tom nodded.

"All the way," he said.

He had lunch at the apartment. Surprisingly, no-one batted an eyelid
—two servitrices came at Tom's summons—when he ordered gripple
yogurt mixed with soycheese.

"I'm not one for fancy food, either."

After lunch, Tom washed in his bath chamber's minty aerogel-pool
—he stayed submerged for nearly twenty minutes, breathing directly
from the gel—then padded into the master bedchamber, where Adam

had laid out clothes for him to wear: dark tunic and trews, black cape lined with emerald silk.

Good taste. And he's got the sense to make himself scarce.

There were noble-born High Lords who required servitors to help them dress. They might revel in the power they held; to Tom, it revealed a childish dependence on others.

But everything we perceive, he reminded himself, *is content within context.*

And his background was rather different from that of other nobility.

Halfway through dressing he stopped, noticing a small floating bedside table. On it, atop a small cushion, a sapphire-decorated thumb ring lay.

From Corduven?

It was a Lord's signet ring, and Tom's original—as presented by Lord A'Dekal—had been lost for years. Mixed emotions washed through him as he slid his thumb inside, and the ring adjusted itself to fit.

There were no messages from Corduven. Yet this apartment had been made available, according to Adam, on Corduven's direct order.

Tom tagged his cloak fast, then left the chamber. He passed by a series of angled mirrorfields, noting that the cloak billowed though there was no breeze.

Smartfibre: he would disable it later.

"My Lord?" Adam was waiting in the antechamber.

There were six servitrices present—Adam had been double-checking their inventory—so Tom did not complain about the honorific.

What the Chaos am I doing here?

But, "Come on," was all he said. "I want to see this Academy."

A silver-lined tunnel. Tom's ring sparked blue as he passed through a membrane-barrier; Adam's earstud winked ruby light.

"Is this part of the Academy?"

Adam shook his head. "Not yet, my Lord."

The Academy must take up some two-thirds of the previous Palace Boltrivar, and extend beyond its bounds.

"Wait here, would you."

There was an archway off to the right; a discreet floating tricon warned that entry was for nobles only. Beyond an antechamber, in a golden hall, stood fine-gowned Ladies, and Lords in formal half-capes, conversing.

Tom slipped into the antechamber. The murmur of conversation grew louder, accompanied by soft flute music.

"Some orthoplum wine, sir?" A majordomo, trailed by junior servitors bearing trays, gestured with a white-gloved hand towards the selection. "We have the finest—"

"Is there any gripplejuice?"

In answer, the majordomo merely looked at a servitrix, who departed at a run.

Damn. Why couldn't they just say no?

But that, of course, would never do.

When the servitrix returned, Tom took the glass directly from her, before she had a chance to present it to the majordomo.

"I appreciate this. Full of antioxidants, you know. And no side effects."

She blushed, curtsied, withdrew.

Tom nodded to the majordomo—who bowed—and headed inside.

". . . gestalten successfully," a young Lord was saying, "as a way of decoding perception-processing: pattern against backdrop. But when they founded a school of psychoanalysis . . ."

His companions laughed.

But Tom wondered whether archaic self-actualization cults were as ridiculous as scholars thought. What if the few surviving texts were satire or parody?

Silently, he moved to another group.

". . . Valerron's conjecture." The speaker was a dark-haired Lady of some thirty SY, and her glance flickered in Tom's direction. "Only a millionth of the nervous system's processing is conscious; even contemporary humans are a mix of competing personalities and cognitive daemons. In the flow, in the midst of writing poetry, defining a logosophical model—there's no self-awareness involved."

This was elementary; Tom wondered what her point was.

". . . millennium and a half ago, measurements showed electric potential changes in the brain a third of a second *before* conscious volition takes place."

A nice paradox: the illusion of autonomous self.

"But Lord Valerron concludes," said the Lady, "that true consciousness itself may be a recent phenomenon, *post*dating culture. Perhaps not even the world's founders thought as we do now."

Tom looked at her.

"Are you saying we don't think like Terrans a mere thousand years ago?"

"Did they have logotropic integration, or even cognate-daemon mapping?" Her blue eyes brightened as she conjured a billowing holo manifold into existence. "My own model suggests that Terrans rarely experienced hyperego formation during the third decade of life."

Murmurs of appreciation arose among the onlookers. Rigorous tesseracts and proof-dendrimers backed up the Lady's analysis.

Tom gave a small, exact bow. Then he went to stand by the wall—unconsciously like a servitor—and frowned, wondering why her hypothesis disturbed him so.

She sought him out afterwards, as the other Lords and Ladies drifted away. Tom, not wanting company, angled his body, allowing his cape to fall open on the left.

"It's OK, my Lord Corcorigan." Her smile was mischievous. "I recognized you immediately. I'm Brekana."

"Honoured." Tom's bow was punctiliously correct. "But why would you recognize me? I don't—"

"My cousin Sylvana's told me all about you."

Tom's breath caught. "Lady Sylvana, of Darinia Demesne?"

"Of course. It's a shame she's not here. Normally, she can't resist our little conversaziones."

Sylvana.

With a tiny smile, aware of her words' devastating effect, Brekana bobbed a curtsy and moved away, catching an elder Lord's gaze and waving a greeting.

Sylvana's living here?

Tom took a goblet of gripplejuice out to Adam, who started with surprise, but seemed pleased enough with the drink.

"Thank you, my Lord."

Sylvana. You, for one, always had an interesting way with servitors.

After Adam had drained the goblet and tossed it into a recvat, Tom indicated a long white tunnel. "That leads into the Academy proper?"

"Just so, sir. I have access permission."

They passed through a membrane which took longer than usual to liquefy—while its deepscan procedure completed—before allowing them inside.

"This way, sir."

Tom came out on a high balcony, having left Adam far below on the winding stone staircase, struggling with the climb. The cavern ceiling, knotwork-decorated, was close overhead. On one side, a stubby stone gargoyle, missing half its teeth and a portion of one wing, leered at Tom.

Down below, among exquisite formal gardens, perhaps a hundred men and women were running in time or performing group calisthenics.

Tom was not alone. An athletic-looking man, perhaps a little younger than Tom, had been observing the training; now he turned, and bowed.

"Pleased to meet you, sir." And, in a moment of mutual recognition: "We can always do with another fighter."

Tom smiled. "I'm Tom Corcorigan."

"Jay A'Khelikov yclept." Obviously noble-born.

They clasped wrists, but alertly: each aware of the other's capabilities.

"Sorry," the man added, "but I must go back to—"

Danger.

A soft sound, behind.

Tom started to spin, forming a knife-hand, but then he recognized Adam—puffing, out of breath, oblivious to the danger—and straightened up.

Beside him, Jay A'Khelikov's gaze flickered over Adam, dismissed the threat.

Treating him like something inanimate.

No.

Sounds of training cadences drifted up from below.

"This fellow"—there was steel in Tom's voice—"is called Adam Gervicort."

A person, not an object.

A'Khelikov's face was like stone: a warrior's mask, betraying nothing, ready for anything. But then he did something which astonished Tom, and would continue to astound him on reflection.

"Your pardon, sir." Jay A'Khelikov stepped forward and grasped Adam's forearm. "I'll not make the same mistake again."

Chaos . . .

Then he nodded, to Adam and Tom both, made his way to the staircase, and descended from sight. Adam looked stunned.

A Lord, apologizing to a servitor?

What kind of a place is this?

38

NULAPEIRON AD 3420

That night he dreamed he was before the traders' tribunal. The other boys from the Ragged School—the real thieves—had escaped; but the security mannequins held Tom fast.

Tom still clutched the purloined tunic which Algrin had pushed into his grasp. In a moment of sickening insight, he realized that he was guilty by the traders' laws, and that the punishment was mortal.

"My Lady—" He stops, unable to plead before Lady Darinia, visiting this stratum on a whim, with only an academic interest in such administrative matters. The Lady, unconcerned, turns to her young daughter, seeks her opinion.

"It should be quick. The boy should not undergo cruel or unusual punishment."

Until that moment, Tom has known nothing of the nobility, save that they are lovers of paradox and wordplay, masters and mistresses of logosophy.

Sylvana has endorsed his execution.

"Very well," says the Lady Darinia. "Take him to a holding—"

And that is when his words burst forth:

"But that's cruel."

The traders exclaim angrily, one of them rising to strike down this impudent boy. But Lady Darinia stops the tirade.

"Explain yourself, boy."

He knows the executioner is away, due to return in three days' time. They will hold him in a cell, as though leniency were his due—saving him mental torture—until the true extent of his punishment is revealed.

"The wait itself is cruel and unusual punishment," Tom argues desperately, half aware that he is recapitulating classical allusions, archaic principles all logosophers must know. "By your own logic, you have to pardon me."

For a second, there is stunned silence.

Then the traders erupt in anger—but Lady Darinia raises a finger, and they stop.

"He argues prettily, Mother." Sylvana is pale, with golden hair, as youthful as Tom himself. "And we need more Palace servitors."

Thus did Sylvana save his life.

Then the inevitable coda:

"An arm, perhaps?" suggests Sylvana.

"Very well." Lady Darinia, ruler of this realm, rises to her feet. "Before you deliver him"—grey gaze sweeping over Tom—"remove an arm."

And, with no change in expression: "Either arm will do."

So did she change that life forever.

In the morning, there was still no word from Corduven; but a message from Lord Jay A'Khelikov invited Tom to a nearby daistral house for breakfast.

And does Sylvana live nearby?

His endurance run was on a laminar-flow pad in the study: running hard to nowhere. He drank a litre of water beforehand, another afterwards. Then he sat at the wide quickglass desk, and read the invitation again.

This chamber, he realized suddenly, was similar to the study in his own palace, during his brief reign: too similar for coincidence. And of all his former noble acquaintances, only Lady Sylvana had visited him there.

Was the apartment's very layout a subtle message?

What else have I missed?

Tom sighed. He had been away from noble life for too long.

Or not long enough.

Over daistral, Jay quizzed Tom about his intentions.

"The war effort is gearing up." Jay poked at a bowl of cold rice and sliced dodecapears. "And, er, tactically trained Lords with real battle experience are not exactly plentiful."

"I'm not—"

But Tom's attention was caught then by a complex holo, like a golden net, floating above the next table.

Tac simulation.

And he noted that other diners in the daistral house, male and female, looked lean and fit. In fact, they exuded robust vitality in a way that suggested everyone, like himself, had already pushed themselves through extreme physical training, despite the early hour.

". . . them hard." One of the young men was pointing into the simulation. "And continuously."

"Right," agreed a colleague, as she gestured for the holo to rotate. "Pound 'em here and here, until they give it up."

A smile was hovering on Jay's lips. Tom looked at him, then returned his attention to the young officers' strategy discussion.

Then he asked a quiet question which stilled their voices and caused them to turn their lev-stools to face him.

"You're targeting civilians, is that it?"

One of the young men looked at Jay—a flickering glance, as though seeking permission; Tom noted Jay's minute nod in reply— then addressed Tom directly: "An outmoded concept, surely. An entire culture supports a military action, regardless of some members' noncombatant status."

"So everyone in a culture is identical in outlook, are they?"

There was a pause, then a young woman—the one who believed that pounding the enemy was called for—spoke up.

"Definitely not, sir. That's why isolation and continuous bombardment will make the general populace give up their military leaders, and revoke allegiance to the enemy."

"After Flashpoint," one of them said, smirking, "perhaps they'll be all the more willing to engage in revolution."

Tom shook his head. "If someone—some external power—destroys your home, uses blockades to cut off food and other supplies, does that weaken your community spirit and allegiance to your Lord, or does it strengthen it?"

They were silent for a moment.

Then another young officer, who had been silently regarding the model, pointed to the heart of the glowing network. "Penetration," he said, "is what we need. Feints here and here, then a lancing strike, straight to the core."

"Taking out their strike capability." One of his colleagues nodded. "Nice. And effective."

There was a chorus of agreement. Then, with an air of expectancy, they looked at Tom.

Across the table, Jay smiled.

"It could work." Tom spoke slowly. "Say that it does. What do you do next?"

"Send in massive occupying forces." It was the fellow who believed all targets were legitimate. He pointed into the model. "Spread them out, keep the population under the thumb. The iron fist, I mean."

"No . . ." The young woman beside him shook her head. "Give them aid. Rebuild the med centres and the schools." She looked at Tom for approval.

He smiled gently, and said: "And if you're dependent on an outsider for handouts—for your very existence, I mean—what do you feel towards them? Love and gratitude?"

"Ah." She understood immediately. "Bitter resentment, more like."

"Especially if the outside force," said her quiet colleague, "is a former enemy."

"Bloody Chaos," said the belligerent one. "How do you ever win a war?"

Tom looked at Jay.

"I believe," said Jay A'Khelikov, "that was Lord Corcorigan's point."

Before the young officers left, Tom called to them.

"You want to learn how to think strategically?"

"Why we're here, sir."

Their faces were expectant.

"Here, tomorrow, same time." Tom paused, then continued, "You can each present a poem entitled 'Freedom,' which I'll expect you to write tonight."

One of the young officers laughed.

"Yes, sir," he said.

"Sir."

The group bowed to Tom and Jay, then filed out quietly, failing to hide their dismay.

After they had left, and the daistral house was deserted save for a few older officers breakfasting at the rear, Jay chuckled.

"You're an evil bastard, my Lord."

"And you, my Lord"—Tom raised a daistral cup in toast—"set me up very nicely."

I am not a soldier.

Nor had he ever wanted to be one. But Tom felt strangely isolated, sitting in a rear booth in a tavern that evening, as he watched carousing troops, smiling at their songs—traditional melodies, with words their composers would not have recognized.

The bar counter was circular, surrounding a thick round pillar of raw grey stone decorated with a collection of flasks and decanters of every hue. Around the bar, the crowd was a mass of energy; at least half of them were belting out the lyrics of "The Sergeant's Weapon Is Fully Charged (Fastened to a Sticky Tag)" to the tune of "The Ducal March."

In an alcove on the far side, Tom glimpsed Jay A'Khelikov, hunched over a solitary holodisplay.

But then, as Tom stood up, a grizzled old sergeant-maximus called Gieson—a few people murmured his name—rubbed his big square hand across his scarred face, the stubble on his scalp, adjusted his eye-patch, then put down his tankard and began to sing in a soft sweet voice which carried through the tavern and brought every conversation to a standstill.

It was a ballad—a young man sickened by horror, his comrades fallen and his best friend's blood still warm upon his tunic, remembers the soft white arms of his true love as she ladles out rations in the Aqua Hall back home—and even Tom, threading his way through the crowd, stopped and held his breath as the sergeant drew his song to its bittersweet conclusion.

In the silence, Tom blinked away moisture from his eyes.

Then thunderous applause echoed around the tavern, delivered by soldiers young and old, of both sexes, who were unashamed of the tears which ran glistening down their faces.

A hubbub grew then, as the emotional release spilled over into raucous conversation and renewed bouts of drinking. As the crowd's boisterousness returned, Tom reached Jay's alcove.

"Greetings, my Lord A'Khelikov."

"Tom!" Jay looked up hurriedly, wiping the holo with a cutting gesture. "I'm surprised to see you here."

"May I?" Tom gestured towards the seat opposite Jay. "Or should I leave you to your inspiration?"

For he had glimpsed the verse which Jay was writing. From choice?

Perhaps it was just that he would not have his officers-in-training put through anything he could not achieve himself.

"Ha. See him?" Jay pointed towards a scowling, blocky-shouldered sergeant-minor. "His cadets call him Bastard Benjil, especially after punishment runs."

"A charming fellow."

"Yes? Well, compared to you . . . What do you think my young officers are calling you right now?"

Tom picked up a decanut from a bowl on the table.

"Well, so long as they're doing it in rhyming couplets"—he popped the nut into his mouth, and spoke while chewing—"I really don't give a damn."

His dreams that night were haunted by desires unfulfilled, hopes un-realized, through which eerily paranoid images flitted: women who called to him but slipped away through solid stone; crowds of pale strangers feasting on corpse-grey fleischbloc; inhuman high-shoul-dered warriors, taller than a man, with granulated faces and fiery ver-tical-slit eyes, behind whom butchered humans hung from ceiling hooks, their pale glistening torsos axed open to drain the blood . . .

When he jerked into wakefulness next morning, he recalled nothing save the touch of women's fingertips, their fading cries, and the febrile beating of his own heart.

On black smartsatin sheets which folded back as they sensed his waking, Tom lay there, reflected in the bronze-tinged smoky ceiling-mirrorfield. His pale image stared back: a one-armed warrior with haunted eyes, and an air of not knowing where the Chaos life was taking him.

He felt exhausted.

It was early, but he dragged himself outside to run, knowing he would feel worse if he slacked off in training.

Tom passed through a glimmering, milk-white membrane, along a short round tunnel, and came out onto a long esplanade. Beyond, the small sea's mint-green waves gently lapped against shore and pillars, their reflections swimming upon the high cavern ceiling.

But it was not the tranquil water or the clean, energizing air which stopped Tom dead.

He was used to being the solitary runner, the obsessive athlete training in deserted corridors and caverns; but here, now, there were two hundred—no, three hundred or more—men and women running hard in small teams beside the waves, throwing themselves through gymnastic groundwork, scrambling across obstacle courses or climbing the cavern walls.

Interesting place.

Then he stretched lightly, jogged onto the esplanade, and began to run.

Afterwards, as he stripped off his sweat-sodden clothes, Tom waved his bedchamber's holodisplay into life. He was certain there would be no message from Corduven.

Yet the minimized tricon which hung there was enough to make him shiver.

When he pointed, the intricate knot of multi-hued light magnified, unfurled to deliver its many-layered semantic content, full of ironic overtones: exquisite topography, for a message which was so simple at its heart.

The Lady Sylvana would be taking breakfast in one hour's time, in the Wyvern Gardens off Promenade Excandior, and she hoped he would be able to join her there.

Elva . . .

But the image he saw in his mind was of a pale-skinned noble beauty with upswept golden hair, who moved with a soft and easy grace, and whose blue eyes sparkled brighter than any sea, alive with intellectual energy and a subtle humour which could never fade.

There had been times, when climbing, that Tom had thought he was about to die. But the body, flooded by adrenaline from the suprarenal glands, can deal with such emergencies on the spot.

It would be hard to reconcile the image of that fast-reacting athlete to this dithering man, fidgeting before his wardrobe-alcove, trying to decide what he should wear.

Get a grip, will you?

And then he was rushing to get ready, having left it strictly too late; perhaps it was a subconscious strategy to get his body moving fast, to deal with the heart-pounding fear.

He practically ran out of his apartment, black cloak billowing, servitrices dropping into startled curtsies as he barrelled past them, and was outside.

Streams of water arced overhead, forming silvery arches in the air through which tiny pastel-coloured fish with attenuated tendrils swam. There was soft sweet music, a mossy fragrance which hovered at the edge of one's perceptions—and, seated amid the elegance, the Lady Sylvana.

Her skin was pale ivory beneath the platinum glowglobes' light, her long golden hair bound up with silver cords and fastened with ruby clasps. She wore a morning gown of silver and cream which left bare her arms and flawless throat; a tiny faux-moth of silver and diamonds fluttered above each shoulder.

"Tom."

She held out her hand without rising, and Tom touched her fingertips with his own as he bowed and softly kissed the back of that smooth, perfectly formed hand.

Then he sat down on the floating soft-cushioned chair opposite her, and for a long moment they regarded each other without speaking.

Sylvana had lost a little weight. Unfashionably thin: it served only to enhance the ethereal quality of her presence. For Tom, she was suddenly the world's focal point, as if all reality led inwards to where she sat: real, tangible, around whom the air almost vibrated with excitement.

Elva . . .

But this was here and now.

"You saved my life, Tom."

Even her words were mellifluous song, liquid and beguiling.

"Good, my Lady . . . If you had not saved mine, so many years before, I'd not have had the opportunity."

Sylvana shook her head.

"But at such cost . . ." She did not look at his left shoulder. "I'm so sorry."

"Ah, Sylvana."

"You know . . . I can't forget the way you looked, when you dropped from nowhere onto the cruciform where I *knew* I was going to die. There were things I realized, in that moment, that I had never allowed myself to think before."

Tom swallowed. He did not know what to say; could not have spoken if he did.

"Well, then." Sylvana leaned back and gestured a column of small tricons into being above the tabletop. "What would you like for breakfast?"

"To tell you the truth"—Tom took a breath, released it—"food is the last thing on my mind."

"Some daistral, then."

"That would be nice."

They sipped from jewel-ringed cups, and when Tom shivered at the sweet taste overlaid by whiganberry and drime, it seemed that Sylvana did the same.

He had not realized that the simple act of taking daistral could be so sensual.

For a time they talked about history, engaged in wordplay as innocent as in their youth; they might have been back in the Sorites School, during a break between Lord Velond's exacting tutorials.

Finally, when the daistral was finished and Sylvana made as if to rise—Tom stood quickly, and the majordomo appeared from nowhere—he thought his heart might break: the ending of a perfect moment.

Then, "I need to go back to my place," she said. "Will you walk with me, Tom?"

"I—Of course."

A tiny smile touched her full rose-pink lips.

"My Lord Corcorigan, I take nothing for granted."

He walked alongside her, on her left, as they passed through a lemon-tinted glassine tunnel, then a stone garden with slowly morphing gargoyles, and came out upon the esplanade.

Sylvana slipped her arm through his.

Finally, they rose up a polished golden ramp, walked the length of a marble gallery, and stopped before tall doors of gold and rubies, where a discreet tricon indicated this was Sylvana's home.

Tom looked at her.

"Thank you. I'm—"

She stopped him with a gentle smile.

"Don't you want to come inside?"

On a diamond table at the side of her bedchamber stood a tricon cast in white metal: Epimenides' paradox—*this statement is a lie.*

Tom remembered the day Corduven had given it to her.

Her dress slid from her shoulders as she turned to him, arms outstretched, and old memories slipped away as he took her incredible softness in his arm and kissed her. Her lips were silken, absorbing him.

Her nipples were button-round, pink as though blushing; these, too, he softly kissed.

"Oh, Tom . . ."

It *was* a dream; it was reality.

"My love."

His tunic degaussed, shed in segments onto the floor.

Fell on the bed together.

Her fingers were in his hair, and she whimpered, and he was inside her, a miracle. Their very cells cried out for merging, fusion into one transcendent entity, pulsing together, united with the universe, the cosmic expansion—*yes, my darling*—and the nova explosion which blasted all history apart—*now, yes, now*—and brought them into a new and different world.

Staring into each other's eyes.

"No-one, Tom, has ever *focused* on me like that."

"Years of pure thought." He kissed her nose. "Self-discipline, logo-sophical—"

"Ha." Her smooth, perfect arms enclosed him. "Come here, my pure-thinking Lord."

Later, entwined upon the bed:

"It's serious, Tom." Suddenly solemn, the music of her voice. "The Blight, I mean."

"Is it?" Dreaming, still.

"I mean"—with her fingertip running down his sternum—"its incursions are spreading. More than—Ah, no. Yes. No. Not now . . ."

"What?"

"Oh, Tom . . ."

And later still:

Tom was standing naked beside a floating table, drinking water, when he heard footsteps, and hurriedly pulled on his trews. In the bed, Sylvana laughed prettily, though she tugged the smartsatin sheet up around herself.

"There's no need," she said, as a short grey-haired servitrix came into the chamber, and immediately headed for Sylvana's discarded clothes.

"Just the robe, Alystra." Sylvana gestured. "Leave the rest."

Quickly, the woman folded the robe, draped it across her forearms, and left. At no time did she look up or address Sylvana or Tom.

"No need for modesty." Sylvana patted the bed. "Come back . . ."

Tom stared at the doorway for a moment, then sat beside the Lady he had dreamed of so often, for so many years.

"You've no idea," she murmured, stroking Tom's stump with her fingertips, "how hard it is for me to see this."

"*Remove an arm.*" Lady Darinia's words. "*Either arm will do.*"

Tom exhaled, letting the memory go.

"You saved my life, Sylvana."

She smiled, and Tom closed his eyes, fixing this instant forever in his mind.

"Darling Tom . . . You'll join the Academy officially, won't you?"

"I'm sorry?"

"The Academy. I know Cord would really like you to."

"I haven't seen Corduven." Then, deliberately softening his tone: "Sorry. I didn't realize this was a recruitment operation."

"Perhaps a little more than that?" Sylvana laughed, but pink spots grew on her cheeks. "Ah, Tom, I've missed you."

"And I can't believe you're real, my love."

He kissed her.

But that was not the end of the subject.

"It seems a low-key position," she said. "Trainer and adviser. But they'll expand the role as you gain—"

"Sylvana. I'll place my expertise at the Academy's disposal, all right? It's what I've been doing since I got here."

"Tom, don't be . . . I'm glad, anyway."

"OK." He reached out and touched her long golden hair. "What is it you're really trying to say, Sylvana? I'm out of practice with multi-layered conversation."

"Been slumming it, my darling? Ah, it's just . . ."

"Just what?"

"You know they ship combat casualties back here, some of the worst ones."

There had been no reason for Tom to visit the med complex, but he had heard something of its renown.

Nothing like a war to improve medical techniques.

"I know," was all he said.

"As an attached officer, you could . . . You see, their regrow-vats are second to n—"

Tom was off the bed and standing.

"No."

"But—"

An unwanted vision flashed across his mind:

A one-armed black-clad figure leaps through an archway, kicks low, hits a second trooper with a rapid combination, throws a high spinning kick . . .

"Elva. Didn't you know I'd come back for you?"

He turned away.

"Don't ask, Sylvana. Just do not ask."

"Ask what?" Petulance insinuated itself into her silver voice for the first time. "Ask you to heal yourself?"

Tom took a shuddering breath, trying to calm himself.

"What is it, Tom, that won't let you take the chance to finally look normal, for Chaos' sake? Don't you think th—?"

Her words slammed into him like a sickening blow.

"Normal? Me?"

Tom's harsh laugh bounced back from the chamber's elegant walls, and she shrank away, staring at his face.

"Do you know half the things I've done, Sylvana?"

But that wasn't it.

It was not the little-girl twist to Sylvana's normally flawless mouth, the frustration in not getting her own way, nor the arrogance with which she had assumed he would automatically fall in with her plans. Nor was it the way she had ignored the servitrix's presence, treating the woman like some inanimate tool, no more worthy of consideration than a chair or a lev-tray.

It was not even the way she acknowledged Tom now as a peer because of his title, where formerly he had been chattel, purchased and utilized for his owners' benefit.

No, it was his own stupidity which galled him: that, and the harsh realization that nothing—nothing at all—had changed.

Elva . . . I've betrayed you, again.

There was no fever to blame this time, apart from his old fiery obsession with a noble beauty forever beyond his reach.

Not forever.

But had he not already identified the one constant factor in his life?

"I know what you've done, Tom." Quietly: "And so does Cord."

Redmetal poignard, sinking in to the hilt . . .

"How he deals with that"—Tom hardened his voice, remembering everything the Oracle had done—"is up to him."

He bent to retrieve his tunic.

"Sylvana, I'm sorry. This was perhaps not a good idea."

She watched silently as he fastened the seal, then shook her head.

"I should have known better," she said, "than to show you pity."

And that was the barb which finally got through.

"Pity? What *was* this? An exercise in charity? *Noblesse oblige*, my Lady?"

He looked for his cape, found it.

"I didn't mean today, Tom. I meant—"

"What? Come across for the cripple, and he'll be so grateful he'll—"

"Damn you to Chaos, Tom Corcorigan!"

And then it was too late to clarify misunderstanding, to look for justification.

"I'll see you around, Sylvana."

He stormed out of her bedchamber, out of her apartment, stalked down corridors with rage and self-disgust pounding in waves. Nobles and servitors alike stepped aside at his approach, reflexively sensing the volcanic madness swelling inside him, huge and uncontrolled, threatening to burst forth in torrents of hot, sticky blood.

39

TERRA AD 2142

<<Ro's Story>>

[12]

Saarbrücken Fliegerhorst—the words were blurred by tears—*war heute mit einer Micronuke teilweise zerstört. Die tödliche Explosion hat am wenigsten zwölf Offiziere und Studenten niedergemetzelt, und vielleicht mehr als ein hundert anderen verletzt . . .*

She halted the display.

Why?

The conference room was empty, unsettling; she sat at an unchanging desk beneath a slow-morph green-tinted window. Outside lay Moscow's ancient grandeur.

But Luís—

Hot tears as she confronted the thought: Luís would never see anything again. He did not *exist*.

It was implacable reality; it was the great terrible truth which could not be denied.

Details: lime-tinged sunlight falling on the desk; a tiny greenfly (escaping the building's nanocleaners), legs splayed, upon the desktop terminal-pad; from somewhere, a soft white-noise macromachine hum; the faint traces (to Ro's preternatural hearing) of distant conversation.

The physical world, surrounding her.

Reality.

Luís was dead.

There was a knock and her heart leaped—*Luís!*—while the small rational part of her knew it could never be.

When the door concertinaed open, it was Zoë who was standing there. Her normally youthful face was solemn, revealing hard lines Ro had never noticed before.

A black armband circled her left sleeve.

"Ro? Are you OK with this? If you're not up to—"

"I'll come with you."

"We're using an official vehicle, but unmarked. Leaving from the basement garage."

"Security?" Ro glanced at the news feature again, at its dry description of the airbase's devastation. Its content, its enormity had not changed. "All right. I'm ready."

She waved the holo out of existence.

"There are new security protocols." Zoë led the way along a winding corridor. "We'll talk about them later."

They came out into an atrium; grey evening lay upon the slowly deforming skylights high above.

Something flickered.

It rolled then: elephant-sized, it walked/flowed into the atrium. Like a collection of stony blobs hastily thrown together into an organic sculpture, the ungainly mass lumbered past a group of workers in civilian jumpsuits. It might have slowed as it neared Ro.

She focused her unusual vision; at small scale, the Zajinet still seemed to be formed of many components: pebbles and (squinting into the microscopic region) grains, all shifting and vibrating within the overall matrix.

<< . . . node is reinforcement: interference joy . . . >>

<< . . . deadly, like the other sweetened death . . . >>

<< . . . visual field prey/predator fascination . . . >>

<< . . . swift ambivalence in roiling calm . . . >>

Ro snapped her senses back to normal as the big thing lumbered past, turned left into the lab area, was gone.

"Are you all right, Ro?"

"Did you—Never mind."

Because she knew, suddenly, that what she had just seen was for her eyes only. For a fraction of a second, as it had rounded the corner, the Zajinet's gross form had grown insubstantial, and its true core had flared with brilliance.

A tracery of burning crimson, touched with fiery sapphire.

Demonic fire.

It was not the only memorial service.

Dislocated impressions. Hymns echoing back from the old stones, fading. The bearded, dark-robed priest intoning his prayer to the standing congregation. Incense upon the heavy air.

No, this was not the only service. There would be mourners at UNSA centres across the world, wherever there were people who had known Luís, or any of the others who had died in Saarbrücken.

Stained brass candelabras hung on soot-blackened chains from the shadow-wrapped vaulted ceiling. It was an ancient church. There were no pews; in this chill climate, no-one sat or knelt.

"Mi spaminaem Luís Starhome"—the priest's words, in any language, were meaningless: symbols devoid of referent; maps of a nonexistent territory—*"maladoy muzhchina, talantliviy y energichniy . . ."*

Zoë, wrapped in heavy coat and scarf, looked frozen. Her skin, always pale, seemed brittle and bloodless.

Death is waiting for us all.

Zoë joined in with the congregation's prayer responses. Her command of Russki, to Ro's untutored ear, seemed perfect.

It seemed to drone on forever . . . And then it was over, and Ro did not know what to do. The local babushkas and younger folk had gone, save for one old woman standing in prayer, her wrinkled face screwed up with concentration: a tense and private communication with her God.

The remaining UNSA staff filed out.

"Come on." Zoë touched Ro's arm. "We'd better go."

Darkness was gathering. Patches of snow looked blue-grey, surrounding the basilica.

Everything was cold as death.

There was a cemetery: iron-black trees stark against the fading sky; square dark mausoleums; narrow pathways. Before one grave, shocking against the monochrome world, a bright red bloom.

Ro, ever the mathematician, mentally plotted the equations: the straight-line geometries of the graves, the blossom's fractal spreading. But in the vaults and cathedrals of her mind, her grief was harder to map: an absence of feeling, a black sink absorbing emotion.

An absence with a name.

Luís . . .

A gentle touch upon her arm.

"Ro?"

Ro shook her head.

For a moment there were two white disks in the dark sky. Blinking . . . She wiped away cold tears she had not known were there. One moon, with Venus (higher, this evening) a small bright steady light.

"There's humanity out there." Zoë, looking up at the stars, might have been addressing herself rather than Ro. "Only a few of us, but a beginning."

But still we die.

"We have an embassy of our own, you know"—Zoë's breath steamed on the air—"on the Zajinet homeworld. If it *is* their homeworld."

Ro turned away then—*I'm not interested*—and trudged alone

through the snow, climbing to the top of a small ridge. Below her, the lights of Gorky village were a distant invitation.

Finally someone, not Zoë, called Ro's name, so she plodded back down to the UNSA bus which was waiting to take them back: to Moscow, to the mundane environment of work.

To a world without Lufs.

Seven days a week, Ro threw herself into her routine.

It kept her busy: rising at dawn, she would drink half a litre of water and go outside, running sprint-intervals along the Yeltsin Hills while Moscow proper lay below, to the south, as though rising inside an ancient impact crater. She used kali sticks against the proud birch trees, in her weapons drill. She alternated: fighting skills one day, strength training the next.

Occasionally, an early riser would see this slender woman performing chin-ups from a tree branch, or deep knee bends with a small boulder clasped hard against her chest, though it was midwinter and bitterly cold. Inevitably, such an observer would stop a moment, then shake themselves—no sane person would perform *zaryadka*, morning exercises, in the freezing outdoors—then quickly hurry on across the campus cobblestones.

However hard Ro tried, she was never too fatigued to think, and to remember.

He didn't want me.

A knowledge which did not help.

We would never have been together.

And so, her real work: banned from direct xeno access—however good she might be, she was still only an intern—she correlated all the data she could garner, talked to the researchers in the so-called coffee lounge (where the real brainstorming inevitably took place, over disposable cups of lemon tea more often than coffee), and spent long solitary hours immersed in holo phase-diagrams in the cramped, tiny office a grumpy administrator had allocated her. (In fact, she suspected that it was Zoë who had persuaded the man to grant a private office to a lowly intern.)

Her weekly messages to Mother and Gramps were always about work, never about her feelings.

Though Ro had turned away from other people, she was not blind to those around her. While they could be arrogant, the researchers were generally pleasant enough among themselves; but they had a tendency to treat the other staff—the security officers, the low-grade clerks, the cleaners—as though they did not exist. The nearest thing to friendship Ro was capable of right now was chatting in the early mornings with Andreiev (a white-haired military veteran, her favourite among the older security men) or Lucinda (the big Jamaican overseer of all the cleaning staff, who had taught herself to program maint-bots) before the researchers came into their offices and labs.

In the academic brainstorming sessions she kept strictly to business.

Two evenings a week, thanks to Andreiev's intercession, she trained at a hard, no-nonsense gym in *rokupashniboi*, a branch of the brilliant, evolving combat *sambo* practised for two centuries by Spetsnaz and airborne special forces. The warm-up routines (as in all Russki athletics) drew from gymnastics and ballet; the fighting techniques flowed effortlessly from striking to grappling; the sparring was heavy-contact. Every session resulted in at least one new cut or bruise on Ro's ever-healing body.

She had never known there were so many ways to break an attacker's neck.

In the dusty street, silence.

Lean and rangy, with lank, greasy hair, the gunslinger stands straight. His long coat, a travel-stained duster, stirs slightly in the breeze. Beneath his stetson, his eyes are narrowed against the glare.

"Hey!" The shout is from an alley on one side of the street, designed to distract. An accomplice.

[[In reality, Ro jumped with surprise.]]

But Ranger Shade's Colt leaps from his holster almost by itself, and he drills a scarlet hole through his opponent's heart before the gunslinger's pistol is half drawn.

The man spins and drops.

In the alleyway, his accomplice freezes for a moment, then turns and flees.

"Stone cold dead," murmurs Shade. "Another one for you, my love."

Beside him, a swirling coalescence of light. Juanita's ghost slowly forms. Solemnly: "Thank you, my fine man."

Blood, leaking from the gunslinger's splayed corpse, soaks into the dust.

The observer [[Ro, her actual hand movements matching the moment]] *unhitches reins from a rail, grabs the pommel as she inserts her pointed boot in one stirrup, swings herself up and mounts Querelle.*

The ranger does not look up as the observer trots past.

Piotr, a senior researcher, stopped outside her open office door, mumbling into his full beard.

"Hey," said Ro. "You got a real coherence problem, *da?*"

He flashed a grin.

"No kidding, queral-girl." Piotr knew her research's direction. "I'm in two minds about everything, myself."

"Ha. I mean, *da.*" Her Russki was a long way from Piotr's command of English.

He nodded and carried on, tugging at his beard, sinking back into his own thoughts.

Decoherence. To queral-net designers, it was merely an engineering problem: keeping a true quantum system, unitary-processing components (working through reversible algorithms: to a quantum bit, qubit, time is a two-way street) occupying many states simultaneously, isolated from the macroscopic world, until it was ready to collapse quantum weirdness and provide the computation's result to its human users.

"But queral computers," muttered Ro to herself, "were designed, not evolved."

It meant that Zajinets' decentralized nervous systems were messy. It also meant that, as far as she could ascertain, every Zajinet possessed a minimum of sixteen simultaneous consciousnesses: emergent properties of smaller daemon personalities—all thinking and emoting at the same time—whose numbers ran into thousands, maybe even tens of thousands.

Ten thousand semi-personalities in the same mind.

Yet they were complex, overlapping: a Zajinet neuron-analogue (strictly, one of the parallel states of that one microscopic component) could be part of many semi-personalities at the same instant.

Ro shook her head.

"I've got to work this out."

When I talk to myself, who the hell am I talking to?

Unsmiling, she kicked back her chair, stood, and headed for Zoë's office.

Trying not to think of Luís.

<<MODULE ENDS>>

40

NULAPEIRON AD 3420-3421

Half a Standard Year passed very quickly, with Tom's own re-training as well as teaching, as he delved deeply into the logosophical disciplines, relating them to the theory and practice of warfare—something which caused him many sleepless nights—in ways he had never done before.

There were times when he could pretend he was no more than an academic, for he was a scholar-dozent without military rank, and this was an educational establishment of far higher standards than he had expected: equivalent to the highest streams of the Sorites School which had set his mind alight.

But sometimes, when the talk turned to a weapon's blast-penetration characteristics or a cipher-logotrope's self-erasure command, he would look at his students' young, earnest faces and realize that he was asking them to blow apart human beings, or to wipe their own memory under interrogation by an enemy who would show no mercy.

Yet the more he learned of the Dark Fire's spreading, the Blight which dotted the world of Nulapeiron like some dread disease, the more he feared that he was witnessing the end of human culture, and the beginning of an age in which homo sapiens submitted to a power far more evil than any they had served before. Perhaps humankind's Destiny was to carry out the Blight's implacable, indecipherable will; perhaps there was no other choice.

In the meantime, Tom sent his young students off to war.

To die.

But there was another campaign, in parallel with the more obvious military actions, and that was a covert world: of penetration agents and clandestine support lines; of entanglement codes and suicide thana-totropes; of long-term sleepers-in-place, gathering intelligence in occupied realms, feeding back snippets whose overall import they would never comprehend; of paramilitary snatch-and-interrogate missions, of sabotage, of strategic assassination.

It was a shadow war which played by its own rules, or lack of them.

And in that war, the most heroic actions would go forever unrecorded and unrecognized: the heart-pounding run through dank shadow-wrapped tunnels with military installation schematics encrypted in a semi-crystalline tooth, while the Blight's dark dragnet inexorably closed in; the delicate conversation steering and eavesdropping, smiling and nodding at the occupying forces' stone-faced officers, in polite dinner parties and soirées where a misplaced word could spell disaster.

Or the lonely death: face down upon broken flagstones, or shuddering beneath the suicide implant's pain before the interrogators could get to work.

It was a war within a war, of which Tom caught only glimpses; but those snatches of detail drew him with a terrible fascination.

During his second half-year at the Academy, he steered the course of his work in a different direction, making it known that he could help in the briefing and training of agents. He had been a LudusVitae senior executive, after all.

At the same time, he trained when he could with the special instructors—those who taught penetration agents disciplines where physical arts and covert tactics merged: tailing techniques, situational gymnastics (with particular application to escape-route vectors), stealth climbing, silent killing.

He even learned to swim.

Even to himself, Tom pretended his reasons were something like Jay A'Khelikov's, that time when Jay wrote a surprisingly lyrical and emotional poem: to understand what the operatives were going through.

But there was a part of him that knew that self-serving rationalization rarely tells the whole story: that teaching frustrated him; that he was no closer to finding Elva.

And it was Jay, for reasons which had nothing to do with military advantage or tactical gain, who finally enveloped Tom in that shadow war.

They were deep inside the Labyrinth, an extended cubic multi-level volume within the Academy's core, where corridors were uniformly grey, square in cross-section and carpeted in the same dull blue.

It was a place for hushed voices, for drawn-out planning sessions behind sealed doors: a hive in which code-makers and -breakers worked in solitude or quiet teams; a warren where plans could be hatched—the assassination of a once-friendly ruler, the kidnapping and interrogation of a noble Blight sympathizer—which would never stand up to public scrutiny.

Bleak tactics: but they were all that stood between civilization and the darkness, in a world where everything was sliding into Chaos, and even the Academy's own Oracles—under heavy guard at the Labyrinth's core—were unreliable.

In Jay's depressing cuboid office, Tom sat down to have a chat, sensing that Jay had a favour to ask, not dreaming where it might lead.

Jay leaned back in his soft lev-chair, hands behind his head.

"Have you seen my Lady Sylvana recently, Tom?" His tone was a shade too offhand.

"No."

"Right. Forget I said anything."

It was not the first hint that she might like to talk to him, merely the least subtle.

"How're your spacetime hackers doing?"

"You wouldn't believe the budget for coupling resonators, but otherwise, great."

"Glad I could help."

"My codebreakers think you're a genius, Tom."

"No." He shook his head. "I've only ever met one true genius. There were some big brains at the Sorites School."

"Fat minds?" Jay sketched the tricon for "phospholipid" in the air.

"I'll say."

It was a biochemical pun, for minute changes in fat chemistry— the brain being largely structured fat—separate human sentience from Terran chimpanzees.

"But Avernon's the real thing, Jay. I mean it."

"Subject closed. Although I hear"—with a wink—"you gave the general a hard time on the matter."

"That I did."

Tom had met with Corduven on three occasions during the past year— each time in crowded meetings with little opportunity for private discussion, where matters of strategy, and the creeping Blight, hung too heavily for badinage.

But Tom had taken the opportunity to remind Corduven of Lord Avernon's coup in developing metavector theory: such a mind was the most valuable resource they could gain.

"I'll think about it," was all Corduven had said.

Perhaps Tom's latest work would make him reconsider.

When Tom—still a servitor—had been facing the Review Committee who held his future in their hands, his presentation had at first been stumbling, halting. But Avernon, in excited private discussion— needing someone to talk to—had given Tom a preview of his new approach; and Tom used that to dazzle the three Lords Academic with his own extrapolations, spun off from the basic theory, and helped gain his ascension to noble status.

Tom applied metavectors to cosmic timeflow, in a rush of enthusiasm which barely registered the Lords' Academic lack of surprise. For *they already knew* his findings—and more—despite the new techniques in his derivation. It was Tom's first hint that whole areas of logosophical endeavour were forbidden, even to most Lords.

For history and cosmology were always restricted: kept hidden from a populace who ought not to dwell on thoughts of other worlds, nor on the dramas of Nulapeiron's founding, lest they wonder how things might have been different, or could become so.

So, yes, Tom knew the difference between ability and obsessive drive on the one hand, and genius on the other. For he had glimpsed the magical workings of Avernon's mind, and remained in awe at the flashes of poetic insight such an intellect delivered.

I'm no Avernon.

And yet, and yet . . .

Something about the Academy's atmosphere, despite its warlike purpose, had reawakened in Tom the fire of logosophical exploration. Perhaps the clandestine nature of the Labyrinth's operations lent extra plausibility to Avernon's vector-on-vector approach, which invoked yet another layer of indirection between *qualia*—perceived reality—and the underlying stuff of the universe-as-is.

It allowed Tom to treat entangled particle-pairs as twin pointers—hidden variables of a very particular kind—to the same underlying state in ur-space: a concept which had nothing to do with other space-time continua and everything to do with reality's deepest nature.

At any other time, such musings would be purely intellectual games. But in the world of espionage and quantum cryptography, the ability to hack reality, using metavector iterators to tease apart entangled states, was a useful technique indeed.

In the arcane subculture of the codebreakers, Tom was something of a hero.

But, on this particular day, it soon became clear that Jay's reasons for talking to him had little to do with logosophical expertise. It was his newly upgraded security rating that interested Jay.

"You're cleared for code-gamma ops now, aren't you, Tom?"

"But this is code-alpha"—Tom delivered the old joke with a straight face—"so now you have to kill me."

"Right . . ."

Tom had already taken more than one pensive agent through tactical scenarios, using intricate holo models of distant locations with observation points (or in one case a sniper's kill-zone) clearly marked and annotated.

"I've a favour to ask."

"All right, Jay. Whatever you need."

Behind his desk, Jay doodled in the air, creating abstract holos, while Tom waited. But it was not until Jay had caused the garish, morphing shapes to float around the chamber—appearing to bounce off the stark walls—that he sighed and came to the point.

"There's a woman . . ." Jay began. "Chaos. You've no idea how hard this is."

Tom managed not to laugh.

"If it's advice you want, old chap, I'm not sure—"

"I'm talking about a mission briefing, if that's all right with you."

Tom looked at him carefully. "Go on."

"Her name is Lihru. Her target zone is Jephrin, and she's due to go in within the tenday."

"I'm sorry? Jephrin?"

"In Realm Ruvandi, about twenty klicks inside the border."

"But that's—"

"Deep in Blight-occupied territory, yes. It makes the access routes complicated, but they're all worked out, and there's a network in place . . ." Jay's voice trailed off.

"You're involved with this woman," said Tom.

"Yes, I—"

"And you don't want to be her briefing officer."

"I don't think it's appropr—Damn it, Tom. I can't send her in, knowing . . . I just can't, that's all."

Tom wondered what Elva was doing now. Was she, too, in some occupied realm, in constant danger of discovery by forces of the Blight?

"Of course I'll do it."

"Thank Fate."

Later, Tom found himself brooding on the notion of hyperego formation, as mentioned by Sylvana's cousin, Brekana, when he had just arrived at the Academy. Surely it was no conceit to consider modern people superior, better integrated than their ancestors. Yet perhaps they retained their capacity for self-delusion. For some part of Tom was surely aware there was more to Jay's request than a prematurely ended love affair, or a natural concern over a comrade's safety.

Back in the more open parts of the Academy, an unusual melancholy settled on Tom. There was a seminar he was supposed to prepare for, but instead he sat in a deep lev-chair at the edge of the instructors' common chamber, where gentle holoflames flickered with simulated warmth in illusory braziers, soft music played, and a solitary glass bird circled slowly below the ceiling.

Tom brooded over the first, tentative stanzas of a new poem:

> ENTANGLED LOVE
> *Where deep beneath the strongest crests*
> *Of wave-equation Fate creates—*
> *The startled glance, the love that binds—*
> *Two souls in matching eigenstates.*

". . . with us, Tom?"

"I'm sorry? What was that?"

When Fate without remittance splits
The tangled pair a world apart;
Yet links them true with bonds so great
That each one beats the other's heart.

"We're going to a conversazione. More like a historical lecture, really."

It was Anrila, a young Lady who was a fast-track instructor in psychomanipulative strategies, and her perennial companion, Zebdinov Krimlar. He was bearded, with wild red hair—and a commoner by birth.

In any other milieu, their open association would have been unthinkable.

"Forbidden knowledge," said Krimlar. "History and stuff."

"Like what us commoners"—Tom pretended to snort in a disgusting way—"ain't supposed to know, like?"

"That kind of thing, yeah." Anrila let out an exaggerated sigh, then giggled.

Tom forced himself to smile. "It sounds irresistible."

Historical Society though this might be, the speaker's sources seemed to draw more from fanciful ancient literature than any objective account.

Seated near the back of the small lecture hall, among an audience of some two dozen people—mostly young, but with a handful of older, watchful men—Tom allowed the words and holos to drift through his awareness, ignoring minutiae.

This Lihru—I wonder what she's like.

It was foolish of Jay to have become involved with an operative, but what recrimination could Tom give? He himself was staking everything on a remembered vision granted by a dead Seer whose true nature remained enigmatic.

Elva . . . What are you doing right now?

She could be in any realm of Nulapeiron; any realm at all.

What can you see? What do you feel?

He shook his head.

"Xiao Wang's commentary"—the speaker, a smallish grey-bearded man with an excitable manner, moved around the low stage—"is an exciting mix of factual account and dramatic narrative. This marriage of forms, while both intriguing and compelling, makes it difficult for the serious scholar to . . ."

Tom tuned out the words.

Among the audience, only Zebdinov Krimlar, his red hair prominent, seemed to be of common origin, like Tom himself. Tom would bet that the rest were noble-born.

"For those not familiar with the text . . ."

To himself, Tom smiled.

Aged fourteen, within the parochial, inward-looking Salis Core, in a humble stratum of Darinia Demesne, he had read a bootleg copy of Xiao Wang's *Skein Wars*: a riveting account of distant events one thousand Standard Years before. He had worked his way through that massive work in a single rest-day.

Seventeen years later, he could recite it almost word for word.

They were the Luculenti élite, small in relative numbers, but the controlling force on the rich, half-terraformed world of Fulgor. Their brains—using archaic pre-logotropic femtotech—were enhanced via plexcores: processors implanted in their bodies, initially as *tabulae rasae*, into which their minds extended.

They knew the dangers of too-large plexcore-arrays, even though emergenics had not yet developed into a mature discipline. The number of plexcores per individual was strictly regulated by law.

But every epic needs a villain, and the deadly Rafael fulfilled that role.

Vampire-like, he preyed upon living minds, and the plexcores of the dead: sucking out their private thoughts and memories, their deepest feelings; deepscanning into his own array, heisenberging the originals to Chaos.

His plexcore array was vast—secreted processors scattered across Fulgor—and his abilities grew accordingly. And yet, he was killed, by an unknown Terran whose name did not survive.

But dead Rafael's plexcore array—networked by mu-space comms —was not destroyed. Some—or all, depending on the account— remained undetected.

My talisman . . .

Tom touched his chest, feeling the stallion beneath his tunic. In some ways, it formed a link to that ancient tale, in ways he had not considered before.

"After the disembodied Rafael's two centuries of slumber"—the speaker cleared his throat—"it was, as Xiao Wang says, time for the Dark God finally to awaken . . ."

At the time of Rafael's birth, Fulgor was a bright and shining republic, an intellectual utopia, where commercial empires flourished and died in seconds—inside Fulgor's rich, consensual alternate reality: the virtual Skein.

And the Luculenti reached levels of intellectual ability which would never be seen again—or at least, not until Nulapeiron's nobility refined their logotropic techniques in a distant place and time.

But, although it took two hundred Standard Years, the strange, dark fragments of the former Rafael's distributed consciousness slowly resurfaced in Skein. Slowly, slowly, they began a process of malevolent rebirth: the central theme of Xiao Wang's epic work.

From strange, fractured, dislocated beginnings, those shards of evil linked together, spreading and growing in Skein, eventually to coalesce into something infinitely blacker, more mysterious, and totally implacable.

Small numbers at first, then large groups of Luculenti fell under its sway, were absorbed into darkness, as the days of the eponymous Skein Wars began.

There was heroism, among the élite and ordinary people both, as they fought back against the spread of evil. Many sacrificed everything for the sake of the greater good, so that utopian days might be seen again by others.

Xiao Wang chronicled their valour, the outstanding intellectual effort of their campaigns: the days of the counter-Skein, brilliant twin to the corrupted virtual world; of the de-programming viruses they unleashed in Skein and in reality.

His work, as a commentator's foreword said, *speaks to the warrior spirit in us all.*

But, ultimately, it was about the tragic fall of a once-bright society, a doomed struggle, as decades-long campaigns failed one by one, and whole populations died or melded into a vast *something* that was not remotely human, a planetwide blackness Destined to remain forever.

It was the Fulgor Anomaly.

Then a strange alteration came over the speaker's manner. He stood taller, his fidgeting ceased, and when he spoke his voice was softer but more commanding.

"My real name is Strostiv." He looked around the chamber. "And I have a particular reason for inviting you today. Everyone here has been carefully chosen, according to criteria I will not discuss at this time."

Tom sat up straighter, and looked at Anrila who winked, before returning her attention to Strostiv.

"You will already have noticed"—a smile flitted across Strostiv's face, was gone—"broad similarities, as well as important differences, between the Anomaly's genesis and our own situation. Of course, we have long abandoned the dangerous and ultimately corrupting practice of immersion in artificial realities."

Strostiv's gaze tracked across his audience.

Tom could have mentioned zentropes—on the subject of corrupt technologies—but held his silence.

"That closes off one potential weakness. But the Blight has many more techniques at its disposal."

Everyone was paying rigid attention, now that myth was explicitly linked to contemporary menace.

"My Lord Corcorigan, some years back, you delivered an interesting exposition on the nature of timeflow. Would you care to repeat that now?"

Tom grew very still.

He had been almost too frightened to see straight at the time, but this Strostiv could be one of them: the trio of Lords Academic who had recommended his promotion to Lordship.

"Yes," he said, rising. "It would be my pleasure."

There were people with stronger logosophical backgrounds than Tom Corcorigan in this chamber, for sure . . . But none that would have meddled in the forbidden areas, or brought a clumsy energy to inquiries unhindered by the complex, careful scholarship which had gone before.

This time, he would make his exposition shorter and to the point.

It was no longer logosophy, but military strategy, which was important now.

Quickly:

"Assume that space is flat—just pretend it's a disk, all right?"

A holo almost-sphere, elongated towards the ends, appeared at his gestured command.

"This is the lifetime of the universe: starting at a point"—Tom indicated one end—"then growing to a maximum"—the middle—"and shrinking to the Big Crunch."

He looked at Strostiv, who gave a small ironic smile.

I'm working from incomplete knowledge. I didn't know that eight years ago, but I do now.

Tom continued:

"The Sakharov-Gold Principle, from ancient times, links the direction of time with cosmic expansion. Therefore, by symmetry, there are *two* Big Bangs, and time flows towards the Centre Time, the phase transition. And there's no way to distinguish which half of the cosmic history we're in."

The audience were giving him their full attention. These were areas that bright minds must have speculated on, for all that discussions were discouraged.

"The interesting thing"—he looked to Strostiv: no reaction—"is that Centre Time. In fact, even if the cosmos continued to expand forever"— Strostiv shook his head: that could not happen—"the principle remains."

Tom caused a vertical plane, through the centre of his holo model, to sparkle with pinpricks of scarlet light.

"Does time flip over in one instant of contextual metatime? Or are there seedpoints of time-reversal, spreading out to engulf the cosmos?"

This was more than the young Tom Corcorigan had talked about. But it was something he wanted people to know.

"If you could emulate the Centre Time conditions, then you would produce regions, perhaps micro-regions, of negative timeflow, such as . . ."

Tom paused here—some speculations were most definitely forbidden—but Strostiv made no comment, so he pressed on to make his final point.

". . . such as obtains inside Oracular minds."

He sat down amid a heavy silence.

"I'm not going to comment," said Strostiv, "on the processes which produce an Oracle."

It sounded as though he could, if he chose to. That made Tom wonder what Strostiv did when he was not interviewing nervous young would-be Lords.

"But the Blight is most certainly interested in those procedures."

Then the lecture hall grew dark, and the true point of this gathering became apparent.

Black space, and a roughly cylindrical richness of stars: a section of one galactic spiral arm. One star glowed amber: Nulapeiron's own system.

It reminded Tom of the ancient joke. A bystander, during a scene in Ro's Story, wore a holo-emblazoned sweatshirt depicting the galaxy. At the edge, a tiny insignificant point was labelled *You Are Here*.

Strostiv's words came from the darkness.

"Nulapeiron, yes. And this"—as a distant star flared baleful red—"is Fulgor's sun. And over there"—green—"the homeworld of Terra."

More systems were highlighted, all in blue.

"Other so-called first-wave worlds: Coolth, Vijaya, Sivlix III . . ."

But then two more stars flared red, like Fulgor.

"And these are the hell-worlds of Siganth and Molsin—you'll recall the children's stories."

Even *Skein Wars* probably survived because it was a cautionary tale.

"Extrapolating . . ."

A spiky flat polyhedron grew, solidified to three dimensions, metamorphosed to projected 4-D—using the faux-perspective of hypergeometric trompe l'oeil—then flickered again . . . and each of the highlighted stars now lay on a pointed projection from that single, impossibly faceted shape.

"You'll see how the so-called Anomalous Worlds"—more stars shone scarlet—"can be topologically linked through this one geometric construct."

In Tom's flat-space, had he touched the disk-shaped universe with his thumb and fingertips, there would be five spots of intrusion in 2-D space. But in 3-D, it would be obvious that there is only one hand.

Could these spreading intrusions, these Anomalous Worlds, really be linked through some analogous process? A mathematical fiction, with the extra dimension representing the richness of communications links? Or something more . . .

That they are all one?

But finally, the stars were replaced by a single globe—Nulapeiron itself —with scarlet spots springing up throughout, highlighting the Blight's incursion. But, in the rotating globe, three locations were marked in blue.

"The Collegium Perpetuum Delphinorum," said Strostiv, "is normally referred to in the singular. But there are three Collegiate locations in the world, and each one, as you can see, is the focus of concentrated Dark Fire expansion.

"It is imperative that none of them fall beneath the Blight's dominion."

Another detail: Tom had not realized how close the Blight was to this sector. And Strostiv's next words made that chillingly explicit; it seemed obvious, too, that he foresaw no halt to the Blight's annexing of territory.

"The Academy's sphere of interest is threatened here"—Strostiv pointed—"and here. Accordingly"—everyone blinked as holo diagrams snapped out of existence and the lighting grew bright—"an evacuation order from General d'Ovraison will be circulated within the next few days. That fact is not to leave this chamber."

Consternation erupted, then faded as Strostiv held up one hand.

"If the Academy regrouping is successful, then fine. If the evacuation fails, then make your way to another Sector Command, and divulge what you've learned today to the highest-ranking officer you can reach."

And, with a grim smile:

"This briefing is concluded. Thank you for your time."

Tom slept little that night. But early the next morning he was in his assigned briefing chamber, taking a dark-haired young woman called Lihru through final checks: entangled-crypto protocols and keys; passwords and paroles for every contact along the complicated access route; secondaries and fallbacks.

She reminded him a little of Jasirah, but more composed, and he could see why Jay would have fallen for her: anybody would.

Tom kept things strictly business—it was her life on the line—and made no mention of Jay, or the fact that Jay was originally assigned to be her briefing officer. But at the briefing's end, Lihru thanked Tom quietly for taking the time to instruct her.

"And you can tell Jay . . . I understand. Tell him to take care."

"I'll . . . pass it on."

After she had gone, Tom stared for a long time at the blank stone wall, seeing nothing except the fading afterimage of a beautiful young woman whom—he was suddenly sure—he had just sent to her death.

The next morning, a new general order was posted in every corridor, wrapped up in one tiny tricon whose minimal size belied the heavy import of its meaning:

BY ORDER OF THE C-IN-C: STRATEGIC COMMAND

*All personnel are hereby advised that Evacuation Plan Gamma
is to be implemented immediately. Fully urgent: invoke immediate
save-or-destroy procedures for all repeat all material classified
level 7 or above. Section heads cf. standing orders: deadline schedule 2 alpha.*

Final evacuation date: Chameleon 173

May Fate preserve us all.

Authorized today 27th Quintembral Chameleon Year (Chameleon 145)

GENERAL LORD CORDUVEN D'OVRAISON

Command-in-Chief

41
TERRA AD 2142

<<Ro's Story>>
[13]

December. Bathed in white, Moscow stretched wide.

Below Ro's feet, concave snow-covered slopes—of the Yeltsin Hills—dropped to the flooded grey river. On the opposite bank stood the rebuilt stadium, formed of dull granite. Beyond, the great old buildings, like powerful square-shouldered prole workers, stood hard and strong amid the wide, clean geometric boulevards.

Patterns within patterns.

Behind her reared the university campus, with its broad, grand central building. Among its turrets, the central spire rose; its apex cupped, as it had for centuries, a bright golden star.

Ro's mathematical analysis sense, always active, mapped the conic sections and fractal details of the frozen snow's gradient, the trajectories of homemade sleds as bright-clad students, shrieking with laughter, belted downwards at hazardous speed towards the churning waters.

White within white . . . variations even in the texture of soft snow.

Patterns—

To Ro's left, Zoë shifted her feet.

"Cold." Her breath steamed as though in evidence. "Damned cold."

"I hadn't noticed."

—within patterns—

"Ro . . ."
—*and this one with meaning.*
"Look, Zoë, I'm sorry I screwed up, OK?"
Mortal danger.

There had been no flash of inspiration, after all the pressure she had put on Zoë to grant direct xeno access.

In a penrose-tiled observation room, its glass roof revealing the dull grey sky above, Ro had sat on a cushion, watching the elephantine moving sculpture which was the Zajinet's external form.

"First test." She thumbed a holopad into life. "What do you make of this?"

There was a secondary psych team—*sed quis custodiet ipsos custodes?*—keeping watch on her. Or rather, on the human—Zajinet interaction considered (in traditional psych fashion) as a third entity, separate from the individuals involved.

Ro's second holo—an intricate geometry puzzle—provoked the xeno's interest:

<< . . . multi-flange: the transform . . . >>
<< . . . rotate, translate before inverts . . . >>
<< . . . fond beginning, reinforce potentiation . . . >>

"You mean"—Ro smiled at her own intuition—"it's like a toy, from your childhood."

The Zajinet's body-granules whirled and spun.

<< . . . is-is-is . . . >>
<< . . . transaction double emit/receive . . . >>
<< . . . standing wave for true . . . >>

Ro looked at the psych team.

"Lucky guess," she said.

On the skylight above, a sudden rattle of hailstones.

"Christ. What about this weather?"

No! Damn it—

Too late, she realized what she had done.

The Zajinet was frozen.

"*Merde.*" She dragged herself upright. "*Scheiss!*"

It was totally immobile.

"Never mind." One of the psych team pushed back his chair. "Happens to everyone, sooner or—"

Storming from the room.

"Not to me, it doesn't."

"You did all right," said Zoë. "Everyone falls into the rhetoric trap."

"Not if they do their jobs properly."

"They said"—Zoë smiled to take the edge off her words—"that you might be a perfectionist."

Psych analysis. That's all I need.

"Could it be a weapon?" The thought struck Ro. "If we ever need one against the Zajinets, I mean?"

Zoë shook her head. "They freeze into analysis-catatonia only if they take the question seriously. They have the choice of ignoring it entirely, from what anyone can tell."

It might remain in stasis for an hour or two; it might be longer. The record was nine and a half days without movement, after the British ambassador to Iceland, at the Reykjavik xeno centre, had held a hand out to a Zajinet and said: "How do you do, sir?"

Ro's breath steamed.

Patterns. Always patterns—in the cold air's movements, in the lightly falling snow. In the games and duplicities of human beings in general, of Zoë in particular. Finding her in Moscow had been one coincidence too many.

"Can I ask *you* a question, Zoë, without dire consequences?"

Zoë made an adjustment on her cuff—turning up her coat's thermal filaments—before answering.

"If you like."

"Just how old are you, Zoë?"

"Ah. I wondered when you'd get to that."

Ro's jumpsuit was lent a touch of European elegance by her velvet scarf, indigo on one side and teal green on the reverse, draped casually round her throat. Her ears, though, were freezing, for she had thrown back her heated hood.

Sounds carried badly through the muffling snow. It was important to remain alert.

"My husband, ex-husband"—Zoë coughed—"used to feel like a child molester when we went out in public. So he said."

It was hard to believe, but she claimed to be forty-two years old. Up close, it was obvious only that Zoë was too tough to be eighteen, however girlish she looked.

Hardly a grad student, then.

There was a point they had skirted around: Zoë's exact role. But observing—or manipulating—Ro McNamara was obviously a part of her assignment, whoever she was working for.

Just as we're being watched right now.

Ro said nothing about the hidden observers. If it was not Zoë's people but some kind of enemy team secreted in the snowbanks, then she would have badly miscalculated. But the tiny patterns within patterns of Zoë's body language, to Ro's alert senses, suggested knowledge of their hidden positions.

And there was tension strung throughout Zoë's body; it took no genius to figure out that she was expecting some kind of action.

"Christ, I hate the cold. But Moscow"—another cough—"in December, of course it's friggin' freezing."

A shriek as a sled tipped up, spilling its two riders. Other students laughed.

"Shame the labs are off limits." Ro did not look in Zoë's direction. "Stupid time for a shutdown."

"Nice to see the hills, though." With a sniffle: "At least the air's fresher than my apartment."

The lease on Zoë's place, on fashionable Strugatski Prospekt, had allegedly been arranged by a long-term Muscovite friend whom Ro had never met.

And she's sticking to her cover story.

Ro's suspicion was that the "friend" was a colleague in UNtel—the UN's covert intelligence and xenology arm—and that Zoë herself was some kind of intelligence officer. Not that Ro had ever met a spy . . .

Another probe: "I haven't seen any security recently."

"They pulled off the teams." Zoë shrugged, indicating a lack of worry. "No trouble for two months, no anti-xeno demos. Nothing."

That's almost convincing.

If it weren't for patterns in the snow.

Seven men . . . No.

They were hidden superbly well.

Nine of them, and armed.

"Are you going home for Christmas?"

"Home?" Distantly, as though Zoë hardly recognized the concept: "No . . . No, I don't think so."

Snowflakes, falling heavier.

Awaiting phase-transition, the pattern-shift . . .

Are mathematical minds made vulnerable by their abilities, or is it that, seeing so deeply, the arbitrary and ephemeral nature of consensual reality becomes too flimsy to hold on to?

Ro thought of Cantor: periods of deep insight into the nature of infinite sets, invariably followed by incarceration—amid black depression—in the Nerveninstitut von Halle.

Are thoughts, then, so fragile?

Nash's Nobel Prize–winning one-page paper, founding the concept of game-theoretical equilibria, highlighting the nuclear madness of Mutual Assured Destruction—the product of a mind about to be torn apart by schizophrenia.

Or is infinite truth so dangerous?

Of the first four Kabbalists, conjuring up a group vision—of God's manifestation upon Mount Sinai—one was shocked into permanent disbelief, and two died insane, before the blazing glory of *Ein Sof*, of infinity glimpsed—

Transition.

It's starting.

"Behind you," murmured Ro, "at three hundred degrees."

Transition *now*.

She saw: *gunman, eleven o'clock.*

Despite the gloom, pale silver light washed across the weapon's transmission face, a bulky figure kneeling, aiming at her and Zoë, and Ro knew she had a tenth of a second, no more—

Evade!

Zoë was fast, but not fast enough. Ro used a scissoring sacrifice-sweep, kicking Zoë's feet from under her, as she herself dropped prone.

"*Tarapityes!*" Zoë screamed into her bracelet. "Go, go, go!"

Tracer beam, cutting the air above them.

And the pattern: white shapes rising silently from the snow.

"Damn it—" Zoë rolled over to elbow-crawl.

Too late.

Ro could see the gunman: rising to his feet, taking new aim—

Acceptance:

I'm going to die.

Then there was a blur of motion, a white-suited figure arcing through the air—flying thrust-kick with perfect extension—and the crunch of snapping vertebrae.

The gunman dropped, neck broken, into the snowbank.

Other white-clad soldiers fell on him, bayonets glinting on their magThrow rifles, and stabbed downwards, making sure.

Laughter.

Zoë, on her knees, retched into the snow.

But the students, dragging their sleds upslope, had seen nothing.

"Let's go." Ro helped Zoë to her feet. "This—"

"No, this way."

Trudging through drifts, they headed directly to the residence block. Beyond, in a slush-bordered courtyard of black wet cobblestones, white-jumpsuited soldiers were sliding a body bag into a TDV.

My God—

Ro recognized the corpse.

The would-be assassin's movements had been altered by his thermal suit, but suddenly she was sure. Moving quickly, taking them by surprise, she palmed the membranous bag into transparency.

Soldiers, grabbing . . . They stopped at Zoë's soft command.

"I know him," Ro said to Zoë. "And so do you."

Coffee-coloured features, broad cheekbones. Nothing out of place: this country's historic Sovietski empire had once been bigger than AmeriFed's.

"I don't—"

Ro remembered: the bare-headed Mexican in the burning early sun, staring at her with dark impassive eyes as she ran at the desert's edge, where red sand met cultivated greenery.

"He was a gardener at DistribOne."

The TDV's door descended, clicked shut. The vehicle murmured into motion.

"Christ." Zoë. "Someone will pay."

Soldiers moved off at a noiseless, loping run, disappearing among black-limbed trees, as thickening snow fell, then gushed, from the bone-white sky, enveloping the world in heavy silence.

"So we're safe," said Ro.

"Not yet. Let's go."

<<MODULE ENDS>>

42

NULAPEIRON AD 3421

The long balcony was exquisite—rose-pink flagstones with platinum borders, floating lev-tables of clearest crystal—in contrast to the shadowy training cavern it overlooked. Though antisound deadened the clamour of unseen manoeuvres below, odd highlights spattered across the raw, jumbled cavern ceiling: reflected graser fire.

Beside Tom, Corduven looked more highly strung than ever, his pale skin taut across prominent cheekbones, his narrow body angular with tension.

"You're sure about this, aren't you, Tom?"

"Going into the field? Yes, I am."

Lihru was the last agent he would send into danger; it was time to do something active himself.

They walked in step, pacing along the balcony. Corduven's hands were clasped behind his back, hidden by the dark-blue half-cape he wore over his plain uniform.

Daistral and minrasta cakes waited on a nearby table, untouched.

"It would be a tragedy," Tom said, "if Avernon were dead. Have you tried to—?"

"He's safe." A fleeting half-smile tightened Corduven's features. "Which means, he isn't here."

At the balcony's end they stopped. Tom leaned over the balustrade, staring down upon the dark crawling figures of troops on the cavern floor. The terrain was jagged, and they used every possible concealment: broken outcrops, shallow craters half-filled with dirty water.

"I'm sorry." Corduven's voice tugged Tom back. "We don't spend any time together."

His skin looked almost translucent, blood vessels visible as pale-blue shadow lines.

"You've enough on your plate, old friend."

"Too much, perhaps." For a moment, despair webbed Corduven's features. "I don't—There's something I've been meaning to ask you."

Here it comes.

Tom was not sure he had faced up to his own feelings; he did not want to discuss the Oracle Gérard d'Ovraison's death with Corduven.

I killed your brother.

But the question was: "Why did you really join us, Tom?"

Caught off guard, he answered, "I'm not . . . sure. I needed a purpose. I couldn't just stand by, you know? I'm looking for . . ." His voice trailed off.

There was so much he had left out of his debriefing, after he had offered to describe his experiences in the Aurineate Grand'aume. He had been interviewed by a single portly man in civilian cloak and tunic, whose timid manner belied the astuteness of his questions. Tom had furnished descriptions of the Grand'aume's torture chambers and the names of his interrogators; he had passed on his speculations about the Seer's origins and capabilities, and everything he knew about the Dark Fire's manifestation and the manner in which the Seer died.

Tom had lied, though only by omission and misdirection: he had worded his account so that it sounded as though Elva had perished at the same time as the Seer, during the Blight's strange attack.

Was it natural paranoia?

Perhaps they could help me.

But he had access to many levels of the strategy net, could query the intelligence results and perform interpolations/extrapolations (assisted by tactical AIs whose inductive/deductive capacity obeyed the letter, if not the spirit, of the anti-Turing laws).

Internal security officers, who monitored all Labyrinth personnel, must surely have noted his obsession; and Corduven was too thorough not to have acquainted himself with the contents of Tom's dossier.

Perhaps it was just a reluctance to appear insane, to share his belief that the woman whose body had long been consumed by teloworms in a black burial lake was still alive, in another person's body.

"They've taken you through the implications, Tom?"

Corduven began to walk again, back along the balcony, and Tom moved to keep pace.

"Of becoming an active agent, you mean?"

"Exactly. With your knowledge—"

"I need triple-redundant fail-safe thanatotropes. Of course. And the will to use them."

Because it was strategically inconceivable that he should survive capture long enough to be interrogated.

"You're not doing enough here, is that it?"

"You know my background. And I've nothing more to gain, training people, giving hints to codebreakers."

Sending people off to die.

They paused, halfway along the balcony's length.

"But so much of this"—Corduven's gesture took in the richly appointed balcony, the small group of servitors who waited quietly at the far end—"is what you wanted to destroy, isn't it?"

Tom said nothing.

"The noble institutions, the . . ." Corduven looked at Tom, continued: "The world's founders used pre-logotrope memetic engineering, yet I think they got the social design essentially correct. But you . . . Surely you don't agree."

"If any system lets human beings be bartered or sold, Cord, then there's something rotten in its foundations."

They stared at each other.

"Maybe." A flicker of sympathy, or maybe amusement, crossed

Corduven's taut face. "So why fight for it? Because your revolution failed, and you need a cause? Any cause?"

Tom took a deep breath, let it out slowly.

"Corduven, my friend, you know how many realms the Dark Fire has taken." His fist was clenched; he forced it to open. "Do you really think, once this war is over, your precious Lords and Ladies will still hold power?"

I've said it now.

Tom felt his own face mirror Corduven's expression: a small, hard smile of recognition—of positions taken, of battle lines being drawn—while down below, amid the jagged, broken rock, soldiers crawled beneath tracer-fire cover, breathing musty air replete with the stink of battle, of sweat and fear, laying down desperate skills to be tested soon for real, wincing when a practice beam harmlessly struck clothing, seeing instead the last spurt of blood, hearing the silent cry, feeling the infinite heavy blackness closing in forever.

The evacuation began: three thousand personnel, many tonnes of materiel, to be transported to a distant demesne, the Academy's new home.

But I've made the right choice.

For Tom would not be going with them.

Corridors grew packed with vast, squat arachnargoi; they teemed with lines of troopers bearing wrapped bundles: cargo for the great thoracic holds. Pale drawn faces. Excited children, running among the troopers' feet, playing beneath deadly black arachnabugs: one-person military bugs, armed and fast, hanging by their black tendrils, watching and ready.

Beyond the Outer Courts, Tom found other folk. Faces pinched with worry, local non-Academy inhabitants, ordinary people—the sort who, on a lower stratum, would recognize Lord One-Arm by sight—watching the preparations with dismay. Occasional glares of silent anger flashed in Tom's direction, as he walked the stark corridors in his black velvet cloak lined with silver.

If you only knew.

But they would assume he was running away, with all the others.

Here, the children were too cowed to play, hushed when they tried to speak. More aware than their parents: they had no rationalizations with which to combat realistic fear.

There was a toy, a fastclay model lev-car, bent out of shape upon the flagstones. Tom picked it up, handed it to a wide-eyed girl watching from inside a small—but very clean—dwelling alcove.

"Is this yours?"

She took the toy from Tom, and opened her mouth to speak—but a heavy hand, her mother's, descended on the girl's shoulder, and she remained mute.

Tom nodded, walked on.

"Sir . . ."

Behind him: the mother.

"Yes?"

"My daughter." She was a large woman; when she swallowed, her jowls shook. "Would you take her with you, please?"

"I can't. I'm . . ."

The little girl's eyes were blue and calm, as Sylvana's might have been at that age.

". . . sorry."

It was Jay who conducted Tom's final briefing, in a blue-grey chamber devoid of decoration. Both the table and the too-hard chairs were square-edged extrusions of the same featureless stone. Half-light came from dimmed glowglobes floating near the ceiling.

It might have been an interrogation chamber: a reminder of failure's price.

But Tom's healed skin remembered the open cuts across his stomach, the pain weals from the Grand'aume's dungeons, the toxin-laden stings of the glistening red paraflesh which lined the—

He forced his attention back into the moment.

"No-one, old chap"—Jay's glance flickered towards Tom's left shoulder—"has done better in training. You've all the makings of an effective deep-cover operative."

Tom waited.

"I've got to ask, though," Jay added, "why you're doing it. Your tech skills are first rate, you can plan and—"

"I've been over this with Psych."

Not to mention Corduven.

"Your father was an artisan, is that right?"

"A stallholder, many strata down, old chap."

"But he made things, too?"

"Yes."

Like his stallion talisman.

The white-hot graser beam, the spattering of liquid metal and the strong smell of burning grease and oil. He could see it right now: *Father's strong, stubby hands manipulating the cutter, removing metal from the plain block, bringing forth the stallion's magical form.*

"You're asking"—Tom, with a faint ironic smile, raised his one hand palm up—"whether I've a sublimated desire to make things with my *hands?*"

"What I'm getting at is—"

"All I ask, Jay, is that you use me effectively. Send me into a network where I can make a difference."

Not into betrayal.

The subtext was obvious, and Tom had made subtle enquiries to verify his suspicions. Though not everybody agreed, it was known that Jay considered the Jephrin network in Realm Ruvandi to be blown: the agents-in-place sending back their encrypted reports under their captors' supervision. Which meant that, for the sake of those captured men and women, he had allowed his own lover Lihru to meet her rendezvous.

I'm no better than he is.

For Tom had known, some part of him, that there was more to Jay's shirking of responsibility for the final briefing than he had claimed.

"Maybe that's why I'm conducting *this* briefing, Tom."

Had Lihru failed to make contact as arranged, the Blight's security forces might conclude that their subterfuge had failed; at which point, there would be no point in delaying execution for the agents already in their hands.

Jay's own superiors disagreed with his assessment of the Jephrin network's status. But that did not excuse—

"This particular assignment," Jay continued, leaning his elbows on the stone table, "carries an extra risk. If anyone—or any scanfield—recognizes you, they'll shut down the surrounding tunnels immediately, before closing in."

"But the Aurineate Grand'aume is a large realm." Tom shifted on his hard stone seat. "I'll be nowhere near the Core, or any of the upper strata where I was before."

Jay nodded, then tapped the tabletop for the briefing models to be displayed.

"Just make damned sure of that, old chap."

Travel plans: itinerary, temporary cover ID. Once in place beyond the local realms' borders, his short-term "legend" would be switched for a new, deep-cover persona.

"Your access phase," said Jay, "will take a little time. We've recruited some help, who are inclined to be a little, shall we say, spectacular. But they'll get you there safely."

"All right."

Tom checked through multifaceted parole/countersign tricons; tight-beam ciphers (for short-range use) and entangled-crypto keys;

ingress and egress of the holomapped target zone, until he was certain of every safe chamber and code drop location.

Can I really maintain the subterfuge?

In the past, as a Palace servitor, he had hidden his ambitions and plans for vengeance from his noble-born masters; but he had relied on his legal status rather than a fictionalized biography for his protection.

"Here are your incidentals." Jay waved open a membrane-covered wall niche. "Check them through."

Tom fingered the garments: convincingly aged Grand'aumique clothing.

"There are some crystal-stored personal messages," Jay added, "in convincing idiom, I'm told. You're OK with tunnel-slang?"

"No problem."

His cover persona's first language was Belkranitsan, in the Middle Lintran dialect.

"Corporal Wilnasz sang your praises." Jay smiled bleakly. "I don't need to tell you how rare that is."

Wilnasz was Lintran-born, and she made a point of talking to both transient Lintran refugees and the local resettled populace, keeping up with current linguistic usage. She was a stickler for exactitude.

"Please thank her for me. Have we finished the preliminaries?"

"Very nicely."

The briefing's final phase:

A holo-tesseract shone steadily in the chamber's gloom.

"Let's review objectives."

This was the crux of things.

Under Tom's direct local command would be two dozen agents, divided into two overlapping teams. The smaller team comprised resistance-fighter types (led by one Tyentro Liushkasz: a hard, driven man) whose role would be to take care of the rough stuff.

The others were undercover agents-in-place: those who had infiltrated strategically useful positions to glean intelligence. Among them were a police officer, two demesne-administration servitor-bureaucrats, a baker, several cleaners, and two prostitutes.

They could be classified in another manner, which cut across both groups: those who were Academy-trained, and those who were locally recruited inside the Blight-occupied Grand'aume.

"Your first formal mission will be risk assessment of a potential defector."

When Jay gestured, it was a familiar image which hung above the blue-grey tabletop: a blond, bearded man with an amber ovoid inset below his left cheekbone.

"Ralkin Velsivith?" Tom shook his head. "This is a trap, I can tell you now."

Glistening blood-red, the torture chamber's slick acidic walls—

"Don't make this personal, Tom."

With the man responsible for his arrest? But . . . No, this was a mission.

"There's no chance of that. He's passed preliminary vetting?"

"Correct. Your number two, Tyentro Liushkasz, has already made contact."

"An infiltration attempt . . ."

"Our—*your* people have taken full precautions."

Quietly: "They better have."

There was a strange air in the cavern. Masses of movement, yet the huge crowds of people were quiet, disciplined: loading cargo, boarding arachnargoi and lev-transports. Emptying the Academy.

"We always seem"—Sylvana's voice sounded strange—"to be saying goodbye."

It was a line from a holodrama, but she meant it.

I couldn't leave, he wanted to tell her, *without seeing you again.*

But, "I know," was all he said.

"Tom—"

Gently, he took hold of her soft hand and kissed it.

He pushed his way through the throng of people, holding his plain blue cloak tight around himself, hood pulled forward. Past queues, past crying children and the adults who tried to calm them.

"Excuse me."

Then he passed into a narrow tunnel, where the air was cold, and the rough path led him into raw, natural caverns. He walked beneath an archway beside a ceramic guard-booth, but the place was empty, and the booth was unmanned.

Abandoned, like the Academy itself.

Tom pushed back his cloak's hood. There was no-one here to recognize him.

Pebbles scrunched underfoot as he walked on. Small echoes, answering back from broken stalagmites, sounded like a tiny distant marching army; but Tom Corcorigan was journeying to war alone.

43

TERRA AD 2142

<<Ro's Story>>

[14]

There was a crump of sound. Over the roof of the old granite residence, a column of dirty smoke rose into the cold leaden sky.

A military TDV, very long and low to the ground, swerved into the courtyard, spattering slush, whipped into position and hovered, quivering: a hound straining to be loosed. A side door snapped upwards.

"Inside, now!"

Zoë's hands pushing against her back, Ro threw herself inside, landing sideways on a hard black bench, with Zoë following.

Who was he working for?

And why would the gardener be trying to kill her?

They were already in motion as the door snapped downwards, locking, and the residence—pale watching faces of faculty and students at the windows—was fast receding behind them.

"Could've done without the audience," muttered Zoë.

Up front, the driver spun the TDV hard around, while the four soldiers—sitting in the central outward-facing seats, between the driver's control seat and the rear bench where Ro and Zoë crouched—snapped their helmets' flash-visors down, ran through capacitor-status and micromissile-mag checks on their lineac shoulder guns.

The driver looked back—a dark red dagger symbol upon her cheek: special forces tattoo—and fired a sentence in rapid Russki.

Zoë nodded, gave a clipped command, of which Ro picked up only one word: XenoMir.

More than one assassin, then.

Ro was not as scared as she ought to have been: things were moving too fast.

Who are they? And now what?

They were on the snow-laden Yeltsin Hills. Moscow lay to the south, on the other side of the icy river, as though nestling in a titanic crater.

"Jesus Christ!" Ro clutched her seat as the TDV tipped nose down, on the same slope where students had been sledding, and gunned downwards, accelerating hard, as the river's churning metal-grey waves grew larger at sickening speed.

I'm going to die.

Waves, growing impossibly close . . . then there was a swerve to the right, smashing into water with a white cloud of spume, jolting Ro's spine as the TDV shot downstream, spewing water in all directions.

Another swerve, and they were tearing upwards, into the city.

Beside Ro, Zoë was clinging to a grab handle, white-faced, tears of fear unnoticed upon her bloodless cheeks.

Someone's trying to kill me.

Past the stadium. Armoured bikes, strobing blue, fell into place beside them, matching the TDV's velocity.

"Police escort." Zoë stared at them. "If they can keep up."

As though responding to the challenge, the TDV's driver maxed her controls, red-planing the output, zipping past pedestrians. Streets and people looked static—flicked past, were gone—like momentary snapshots, frozen glimpses of the world.

Dzerzhinski Square, and they took the turn at frightening speed.

Ground traffic used the centuries-old no-left-turn rule: use a designated U-turn gap, go back, turn right. But the TDV ignored the niceties, hooking across a hover-bus's path, sending it into a panicked swerve.

Then the bus was behind them—they had lost the police bikes—
and an entranceway was looming.

Slam of jet-brakes, a hard turn which sent Ro sliding across the
bench, then snapping downwards, into the tunnel ramp which led into
basement bunkers beneath XenoMir's vast bulk.

White lights strobing.

Then a howling screech as they whipped into the floodlit under-
ground garage and spun to a halt.

A heavy clang, echoing: steel doors closing off the basement. But the
sound failed to mask Zoë's muttered: ". . . a Zajinet, sighting confirmed."

Clamour of soldiers running to their guard positions; but Ro's
hearing could be finer-focused than a normal person's.

". . . saw its light traces, for sure." Zoë touched her throat: upping
the volume of her embedded mike. "The escaped one, yes. It really is a
renegade."

Then she caught sight of Ro observing her.

"We're going to talk to the ambassador, what else? Out."

Zoë beckoned Ro. "As of now, you've all-areas access. Come with me."

"Not until you tell me what—"

"You'll recall there's a rogue Zajinet, one that's loose outside the
embassies without authorization?"

Zoë was walking at a rapid clip; Ro hurried to keep up.

"That story," Ro said, "was part of the bait that got me here."

"But very real. And it wants your life, girl, though I've only half
an idea why. It has more than human assassins in its employ."

They stopped before a lift-tube.

"It has something," Zoë added, "to do with mu-space, we think.
All right? Now come with me."

The lift-tube door slid open. Stale warm air drifted out.

"OK," said Ro.

They stepped inside.

Piotr, overweight and gasping, was waiting for them on the top floor.

"The ambassador," he said, "is a little agitated."

Zoë grimaced. "Wait till we've had a word with it. Then you'll see agitated."

Piotr handed a resp-mask each to Zoë and Ro, then pulled his own from a voluminous pocket.

"We can take the quick route."

Through low-lit labs, to a background of gentle susurration, and bubbling from the long liquid-filled tanks. A whiff of ammoniac vapours, and Piotr's cough was a sudden barking intrusion among the shadows.

Inchoate purple shapes drifted in the tanks, but it was the crystalline sediments, growing and reconfiguring too slowly for human eyes to register, who were the Felakhim: the intelligent, dormant species of their world.

Only stop-motion analysis revealed the coral-like pattern-language which greeted the first exploration station, and deciphered the initial question once the basics were established: *Do you not hum the Earthstones' song, and dance the waltz tectonic?*

Twelve years later, semantic arguments among Terran translators and philosophers continued to rage.

"This way."

The next zone was worse.

Some rooms were dark, others brightly lit, but each was unsettling: whispers just beyond the edge of hearing, a sense of not-touch upon the skin—hairs rising—of almost-caresses upon cheeks, of brushing lips.

When they exited, through an ultrasonic vibrashield, Ro felt as though she were being stripped clean, yet still felt violated. In the corridor, she stopped and looked back inside, trying to catch a glimpse of the Ephemerae, ghost-rulers of the world called Limbo, seeing nothing until she turned her head away. Then . . . something.

Hint of—No.

"Come on, Ro. We're in a hurry."

Nothing like that could exist.

They made a detour around the Floaters zone—it would take too long to pull on the necessary env-suits—and left Piotr, wheezing, leaning against a pitted glass panel. Behind it, an eye sphere drifted among corrosive clouds.

"I'll catch you up," he said.

"Take it easy." Ro thought of calling medics, but Zoë was already hurrying on. "You've got a strand?"

Piotr nodded.

Feeling slightly less guilty, Ro ran along the curving corridor until she caught up with Zoë.

Vibrations in the floor. The zone beyond the wall was high-g: a maglev centrifuge cylinder some fifty metres across, spinning at immense speeds, to keep the squat Veraliks in shape.

At the corridor's end, Zoë stopped before a ceramic door.

"This is Fyodor's apartment."

"Fyodor?"

"Pet name. The Zajinet you've already studied."

"Hope he's not still frozen."

The entire building shuddered as the door was sliding open. It jammed halfway—and sirens began to whoop and wail, with a calm woman's (automated) voice declaring: *Please evacuate calmly but immediately*, repeated in eight different languages—and Ro and Zoë had to squeeze through the gap.

The Zajinet was not frozen, but in chaotic disarray: the macrocomponents of his body, from granules to small boulders, were spinning and shuddering, changing shape, pulling apart far enough to reveal the Zajinet's inner form: a tracery of electric sapphire-blue, along which sparks of agitated white light burst and spattered.

<< ... danger ... >>

<< ... danger ... >>

<< ... danger ... >>

Every part of its group consciousness, for once, was in agreement.

<<MODULE ENDS>>

44

NULAPEIRON AD 3421

The carapace was scarlet speckled with black, and the tendrils, too, were shiny red.

"What's the matter?" Its rider swung her black-clad leg over the saddle, and slid to the stony ground. "Ain't you never seen a 'sprite before?"

Tom shook his head, admiring the thing. "Never."

"Chaos." She crouched down, picked a shard from the floor, and idly tossed it away. "What a boring life you must've led."

The stone skittered across the ground; small echoes started, died away.

All around, the cavern was vast, unfinished and natural. It was interstitial territory, belonging to no realm—neither Blight-controlled nor otherwise. On foot, Tom had descended fifteen strata, and made three hundred klicks' horizontal progress, since leaving the Academy.

He sketched a tricon—no holo, just fingertip movement in the air—and waited for the countersign.

"For Fate's sake." The rider rose, slapping dust from her shining black membrane-suit. "I'm Thylara, of the Clades Tau, and if you're not the man I'm supposed to meet, then you're dead. All right?"

There's a vast chasm between theory and practice—as Maestro da Silva used to say *when your life is on the line.*

Tom smiled.

So bridge that gap.

"What, then, do I do?"

"Climb aboard, my friend."

He slid onto the saddle behind Thylara, and carapace extrusions encased his legs, looped round his waist.

"Are you sure this is—?"

Acceleration jerked him back, knocked air from his lungs.

Sweet Chaos!

The arachnasprite whipped into motion.

Tendrils were a scarlet blur as they sped towards the cavern wall and, still increasing speed, hurtled *upwards*, gravity and acceleration tugging together, and then they were speeding across the ceiling, the *thwap-thwap* of tendril pads a constant percussive refrain, with the broken floor far below/above Tom's head.

Thylara whooped as she kicked the 'sprite into overdrive, and Tom yelled once, hard, and then their wild laughter was conjoined as they tore along maniacally, upside down amid the convoluted cavern system's myriad twists and turns.

TauRiders' camp.

They swung into view, rapidly crawled down the wall, leaped— tendrils flicking to maximum extension—onto a broken series of marble pillars, danced downwards. Outriders circled overhead, but Thylara waved them away.

Adults, running children—dirty faces, but mostly clean enough. Parked arachnasprites, most of them dark blue, some scarlet like Thylara's. A handful of bigger, older arachnargoi: brown/black cargo models, with holds sufficient to carry all the clan's belongings.

Tethered glowglobes, string-tied and sticky-tagged to pillars, provided patchy light. Cooking smells rose from thermopots.

"Home"—Thylara slid down from the saddle—"for a day or two. Then we'll all be gone."

"How—ah." Cramp—after a full second day of riding as her passenger—hit Tom's inner thighs. "How many of you are there?"

Getting awkwardly to the ground, he rubbed his legs.

"Two hundred and f—no, two hundred and three, as of next move. Tomorrow."

Tom frowned, but his legs hurt too much to decipher that.

Stripping off her gauntlets, Thylara waved to somebody, then turned back to Tom.

"Let's eat."

They were too poor to eat fleischbloc more than once a tenday; Tom had no problems with the food. Only with the ragged kids, who ran circles around the eating adults until Thylara clipped one around the ear. They scampered off laughing, unhurt.

Across one pillar, someone had daubed a glowing dragon, all fiery breath and shining eyes, and Tom remarked on it.

"One of them, at least, has talent."

"Baz." Thylara turned aside and spat into the dirt. "Pity he can't ride worth a damn."

That's all that counts here, isn't it?

He understood, then, the appraising glances of the women, and the negative hand-sign Thylara had given. He might look all right, but—like the unfortunate Baz—Tom Corcorigan could not ride, and so was useless to the tribe.

After eating, he curled up inside his cloak, and rested.

"Hey!" Thylara's fist was thumping his thigh. "Wake up. You like wrestling, don't you?"

"Huh?" Tom sat up. "What's wrong?"

"Come on. Don't dawdle."

In a half-natural amphitheatre, some of the men had already stripped off their jerkins. There was a beefy woman, in a laced-up vest, among them.

"Fate," murmured Tom, as the first match began and a sweeping ankle-hook took a wrestler down. "That's madness."

There was nothing unusual about their grappling technique, but they were competing on solid stone, without mats. Tom watched, enthralled, as a bearded man threw or locked five challengers in a row; then the big grappler looked around, disappointed.

"Hey, Valdur," Thylara shouted down to him. "You've got a live one tonight."

"Who's that, then?"

Tom felt Thylara's elbow nudge his ribs.

No.

"Don't worry about his name, Valdur. Or his lack of an arm. This skinny guy's going to kill you, you big bugger."

Afterwards, everyone save Tom got drunk, and he was more tempted by the booze than he had been for years. Every burgeoning, needless bruise spoke to him, taunted him with pain.

I could've talked my way out.

But he had not.

Valdur had not been fooled by Tom's apparent disability, and they had stalked each other like neko-felines, until Tom attacked.

He had no idea how long they had grappled, and no-one seemed to have declared a winner, just finally decided to drag the bloodied fighters off each other.

Then each had grasped the other's forearm, and they laughed like madmen together.

Next morning, very early, he forced himself to run. Easy pace, through tunnels which had been deserted for centuries.

Damn, it hurts.

But he ran from more than stubbornness. Experience told him that resting would make it worse, stiffening his body until he could scarcely move.

It still hurts . . .

On his return, the tribe was up and about. Even the children were helping to load panniers and cargo pods. Thylara waved at him, a white knife in her hand, inviting him to breakfast.

"The tribe's migration," she said, "will swing closer to the Grand'aume than we ought. But"—spitting onto the ground—"that's what we've been paid for."

"Don't take risks."

"With the tribe's safety? I won't." She slit open a food pack, passed it across. "We'll travel together for three days, then I'll take you to the drop-off point alone. OK?"

"OK."

Fascinated, already mounted behind Thylara, Tom watched the Tau-Riders breaking camp.

I'm privileged to see this.

This was his time, his own one-way journey through life . . . He suppressed the thought, forcing himself merely to watch.

They moved with practised efficiency.

Within a quarter of an hour, they had struck camp: all cargo hauled up into thoracic holds, dark arachnasprites taking up escort formations around the great arachnargoi. Scarlet and blue 'sprites leaped ahead, forming scout and vanguard, while others fanned out.

The TauRiders were ready to continue their migration.

And then the last of the children was aboard, adults waved, and the first arachnargoi unfastened tendril pads and moved.

From a hanging vantage point near the cavern's ceiling, Tom and Thylara observed the motion.

The entire formation flowed towards a wide exit.

But—

A person?

Tom turned in his seat as Thylara kicked their 'sprite into motion, crawling easily along the ceiling above the migrating tribe.

"I saw someone." He tapped Thylara's shoulder. "We've left someone behind."

A shake of her head.

"That's Kayla," she called back. "Too old."

They're leaving her? Deliberately?

A wizened woman, stoically watching her extended family leave, knowing she was not fit to migrate with them.

"Comes to us all, speed-boy." Thylara reached back and thumped Tom's thigh. "Comes to us all!"

A last glimpse of the old woman.

Then Thylara leaned forwards, hands sunk inside black control organs, and the 'sprite shot into accelerated motion, faster and faster until the passing rockface was a blue-grey haze, tendrils becoming insubstantial scarlet mist, as slipstream blurred the world with stinging tears.

45

TERRA & BETA DRACONIS III AD 2142

<<Ro's Story>> [15]

Turbulent, churning: the Zajinet's external form.

<< ... crux is ... >>

<< ... danger ... >>

<< ... nexus-node-now ... >>

Alarms still wailed.

There was another shudder in the building, as though XenoMir itself was falling. Components whirled, and the Zajinet's internal tracery sparked brighter.

"Sir?" Zoë had to shout above the noise. "It's your former colleague, isn't it? We need your advice."

It seemed to shrink, the Zajinet, as though its external chunks were being drawn together.

<< ... danger ... >>

<< ... yes ... >>

<< ... it comes ... >>

Even above the sirens, a screeching sound pierced the room. Ro and Zoë turned.

The jammed half-open door was crumpling . . .

Then a blocky brown three-fingered hand, close to the ground, ripped the metal door away.

"Jesus."

Ro was unarmed, but Zoë had a pocket lineac—abandoning any remaining pretence at being a civilian—and she snapped its laser sight on.

It was a Veralik, the intruder—brown, squat, and cuboid—and it stumped into the room on short legs, thumping its vox-box into life.

"*THE FEMALE.*" With a wave of its thick stubby pseudoarm in Ro's direction: "*HOLD HER.*"

Ro stared at it, then at Zoë, who shrugged.

"Why are you—"

But, from the corridor outside, a gasping voice, half unheard beneath the sirens: "The centrifuge hab . . . fail . . ." A wheeze, then: "Energy drain . . ."

It was Piotr, leaning against the twisted doorjamb.

Behind Ro and Zoë, the Zajinet ambassador had withdrawn into a tighter form.

"*HOLD THE FEMALE. IT WILL ATTEMPT TO TAKE HER.*"

Ro circled away from the Veralik, using aikido footwork, knowing that to close with the blocky creature would be deadly.

"*ZAJINET, THE RENEGADE. IT STOPPED ROTATION. ENERGY—*"

Avoiding, Ro changed direction.

And stopped.

Blinked.

For a moment, she thought she had seen another Zajinet, but different: whorls, hexagonal convection cells, an hypnotic study in blue-grey movement.

"*STOP HER.*"

Unbelievably complex, that flow. Enthralling, as the room began to fade.

"Ro!" Zoe's distant voice. "What's happening?"

Strange perspectives, twisting.

A ghostly grasp on her sleeve.

Slipping . . .

"Ro, take my hand!"

Slipping away.

Transparency, a shrinking in all directions, a turning inside out: it was all of these, and more. Implode/explode, twist and elongate and shrink simultaneously: the world commanded, tore her apart, *pulled* her.

Help me . . .

Spacetime's unbraiding, the freezing-burning explosion/transition, the ripping apart of all she was.

Please . . .

Obliteration.

A moment of lucidity.

Chamber: ovoid, glistening blue. A Zajinet with her.

Its outer form, a thousand rocks and grains, slipped to the floor. Only a floating network of scintillating light remained.

Scarlet light.

Sparking—

Blackness.

Aching stiffness clasped every limb, tightened around her ribs, as she squinted against blue-tinged light, waking on a cold hard floor.

"You're awake." A woman's voice. "Jared, call Lee. Our visitor's waking up."

"Ugh." Ro sat up, pain clenching her back.

"You'll be all right, I think."

The woman had cropped royal-blue hair, was dressed in black and burgundy.

"Where . . . ?"

The blueish corridor, round in cross-section and shining like glass, looped to the left. Two men were hurrying into view. Everything seemed different from XenoMir.

Like a giant artery.

Ro shook the thought away, trying to focus despite a pounding headache.

"She needs the 'doc." The woman.

"No way, Lila." One of the men stopped, hands on hips. "Not till we . . . Just where the devil have you been hiding, young woman?"

"I don't—"

Help me . . .

She remembered the strangely twisting maelstrom which had enveloped her.

"For God's sake, Josef. Look at the state of her."

"Until we find out what's going—"

A large hand grabbed her wrist, and Ro reacted as she had been taught. She rose to her knees, twisting, as the big man rotated and thumped heavily to the floor.

She stood up and backed away.

"Who the hell are you people? How did I get here?"

Danger . . .

They stared at her, at each other; even the man who was on the ground was watching wordlessly.

"Are you saying"—the woman, Lila, spoke slowly as though to a child—"that you've only just arrived here?"

"Here? I don't know where on Earth I am."

"In the Central Bone," Lila began. "Downslope from—"

But the big man, climbing painfully to his feet, suddenly laughed. "Hardly on Earth."

Someone said: "But "where on BD3" sounds terrible."

Laughter fading.

Ro began to shake.

Help . . .

"What"—with teeth chattering—"is BD3?"

"My God. She really doesn't . . ."

A pause, then Lila softly spoke:

"Beta Draconis III, my young friend. You're on the Zajinet home-world."

The strange, metallic blue surroundings seemed to spin around her.

<<MODULE ENDS>>

46

NULAPEIRON AD 3421

The long shapes hung like stripped carcasses amid the gloom, eerie and threatening. Odd echoes of sound—plashing waves, from the canal outside—dissipated among the shadows.

There was a soft footstep.

Holoflash . . . A virtual tricon was beamed into Tom's eyes. Silently, he clenched his fist, and the steel ring on his middle finger sparked back the countersign.

"We can use lights." A square-chinned man, older than Tom, stepped into an area of lesser gloom amid the hanging shapes. "I've watchers posted."

Glowglimmers drifted up from his hands, casting eerie, demonic highlights across his face.

"You're Tyentro. I'm—"

"Honoured, sir."

Canoes . . .

Now that he could make out the shapes, hanging vertically in the glowglimmers' friendly illumination, they were no longer threatening.

"How many watchers?"

"Five. My main team, Stilvan in charge."

From the dossiers, Tom had thought this Stilvan too gung-ho, likely to jeopardize too much for too little gain; but Tyentro's tone was approving.

He's survived here.

All of them had developed instincts to live amid the occupying regime without detection. Tom could learn from them.

"We can sit down at the rear." Tyentro pointed.

"Lead on."

They walked among the canoes, careful not to touch one and set it rocking into motion: if they had to depart in a hurry, they should leave no obvious traces.

Earlier, at midday, Tom had been outside: walking by the long straight canal, where the arched ceiling bounced back the musical wave sounds, the reflected ripples of light. There had been a family, taking a picnic on the flat stone bank; a matronly fruit vendor; some young revellers canoeing for pleasure on the placid, gentle waters.

But at some point a patrol had walked by, scarlet flashes on their grey uniforms, and at that moment the laughter faded. Even afterwards, when the Tunnel Guard militiamen were gone, a subtle sober change remained in the atmosphere.

Another sound, and Tom dropped into a crouch.

"That's Rilka." Tyentro seemed to be inspecting the back of his hand: lasing-gel, a his-eyes-only display. "And all's clear. We can debrief now, sir, if you're ready."

"Go ahead."

Rilka was Academy-trained, working in the local constabulary as a trusted cleaner. Somewhere, she kept a concealed lab kit, and was adept at reconstructing flash-burned or reinitialized crystals.

"And then," said Tyentro, as Rilka's voice trailed off and it was clear she had nothing more to report, "there's Ralkin Velsivith . . ."

He held out a crystal.

"I'd better leave." Rilka nodded to Tom and Tyentro. "Take care."

She rose and slipped away, into the shadows beyond the hanging canoes.

Was gone.

"It was my wife they threatened." In the holo, Velsivith stopped. *"You know my Vhiyalla's blind, don't you?"*

Rustle of cloth. Out of view-field, Tyentro must have nodded.

"A morale officer"—a humourless smile, the amber ovoid inset beneath his cheekbone suddenly catching the light—*"had a little chat with me. About the importance of rooting out the realm's enemies. And, just as I was leaving, she asked whether Vhiyalla was being treated right by the Service's benefits scheme. 'Given her circumstances,' he said."*

"And that was a threat?" Tyentro's voice.

"Yes, and none too subtle."

Tyentro paused the playback.

"He's edgy, at this point. I don't think there's real friction between us."

Tom wondered if that was a veiled hint. Did Tyentro know of his past encounters with Velsivith?

"Carry on."

"At first . . . we really arrested criminals, made the corridors safer. People we'd suspected but didn't . . . Well. We were told they were conspiring against the realm."

He sank back, shadows darkening the amber ovoid and his eyes.

"But then . . . Complaining about food rations, during a residents' meeting—that became a crime. One that carries a five-SY sentence. We've shipped out hundreds, thousands, of prisoners for such 'treasonous' activities."

A pause, then:

"And who knows whether any of them will ever be sent back?"

This time it was Tom who halted the re-play.

"Stress analysis?"

"Seems genuine." Tyentro waved open a secondary holovolume: phase spaces gently rippling, colour-coded sheets of lights a gentle green, within normal parameters. "But I wasn't using sophisticated equipment."

"Takes some training, all the same, to lie without detection."

"I've been fooled before."

Tom looked at him, then nodded.

"It's a memetic virus. People informing on their neighbours, on their friends. Even family.

"So we take them from their homes in the middle of the night, hold them for a while, ship them out. Some of them . . . Their sentences should be up soon, and then we'll see."

Tyentro: *"See what?"*

"Whether they come back."

Pause.

"There are more stressors here." Tyentro pointed. "I think he's seen people he knows—maybe even friends—being loaded onto deportation trains."

"Fate."

Tyentro glanced up. "You sound sympathetic."

"That only goes so far."

"When you take them from their homes . . . there's no fuss, you see. No disturbance. It's in their eyes: terrified, but convinced it's a mistake. The world has tipped upside down but they're sure that someone in authority will see it's a cruel misunderstanding, and set everything to rights."

Another pause.

"It's why," Velsivith added, *"they never fight."*

"Never?" Tyentro.

"Not . . . until the torture cells." Blinking. *"Sometimes then, too late."*

Stress indicators flared orange, then scarlet.

"Are there visitors?" asked Tyentro.

"Family members." Looking up, towards the out-of-view Tyentro: *"They'll do anything for news, never mind the hope of leniency."*

"And?"

"I'm sorry?" Velsivith's face looked raw. *"What do you mean?"*

"Are they ever successful? The family members."

Turning away: *"It's always too late for that. For any of them."*

Halting the display once more, Tyentro said: "Visiting family don't always reappear either. Pleading on a prisoner's behalf can be construed as treason, if the interviewing officer decides."

Tom let out a breath.

"Where are the camps? Do we know anything about them?"

"Far away." Tyentro shook his head. "A thousand klicks or more. If anyone's infiltrated them, it's not our network."

They played it a second time through, in silence.

"The problem"—Tyentro shut down the holo, concealed the crystal in his surcoat's flash-pocket: ready to wipe the crystal at a tapped command—"is that Velsivith is a pro."

Even the questions which Tyentro asked could be used to gauge his knowledge.

"We'll work him gently," said Tom. "And slowly."

"Sir? I don't want to expose your cover, but a safe-chamber, with you sitting in darkness, perhaps—"

"Velsivith and I have a personal history."

A pause. "I see."

"Slowly, then?"

"Agreed."

There were parts of the following tendays which were pleasant, almost intoxicating: strolling through the market chamber in the early morning, buying fruit from the Belkranitsan mother and daughter who ran a modest stall, strolling past the canal when the canoeists were at practice, getting deep into the language so he could eavesdrop on serving girls' gossip, bright with the promise of youth when love's promise was everything, even now, under the occupation. In the evenings, there might be picnics by the fresh-smelling canal, where the families' laughter was softened, yet made more piquant, by the gentle wavelets which trapped the ceiling's light, rippling with blue and golden reflections, lapping gently at the clean stone banks.

Or perhaps it was the constant awareness that informants and the Blight's Tunnel Guard militia were everywhere, and that life's quotidian pleasures could be snatched away instantly and without warning by the human representatives of a vast distributed power which cared nothing for individuals, which saw no pleasure or purpose in the smiles of a teenage couple walking hand in hand through a world of bright awakening, or in the simple warmth of a communal meal spiced by light-hearted gossip.

Almost half a Standard Year passed, faster than seemed possible: gathering snippets of information, gently wooing Velsivith—he handed over confidential crystals of increasing significance—and every courier got through without mishap.

And Tom, in his role as merchant-trader Quilvan Nyassen, slowly settled into the local community, on the outskirts of the Seventh Stratum in the Aurineate Grand'aume.

Then one morning, buying his usual breakfast from the fruit stall, Tom noticed that young Rosa's face was stiff with the onset of a bruise. There was a difference, too, in the way she had tied her pale green shoulder scarf, but Tom had not yet deciphered the full significance of the various knots which local women wore.

"Where's your mother, Rosa?"

"At home." Her inflection was flat.

"Is anything wrong?"

After a moment, "My father's back."

"I see."

But he saw nothing.

It was later, when he watched Rosa's mother walking by the canal, stone-faced, arm in arm with a tall narrow-shouldered man whose pot belly hung over his tunic's belt, that Tom understood. There were few other folk by the water's edge at this time, but they moved back unnecessarily, without a word or sign of recognition, giving the couple more than adequate room to pass.

For the returned husband's tunic was grey, as were his trousers, tucked into combat boots. And the cravat inside his collar was scarlet: the only insignia necessary to identify him as a member of the Dark Fire's armed forces, home on leave with his human family.

—

47

NULAPEIRON AD 3421

Once every tenday, Tom ascended two strata—the highest his cover-ID would allow him to go—and dined in the Club d'Anderquin. Sometimes with business contacts, where conversation would proceed in the strangled jargon of commerce (which Tom had perfected in the Bronlah Hong) unless it turned to personal matters; most often, Tom would take dinner alone, and watch the local bourgeoisie relaxing.

While burghers and military officers dined in restaurants, alongside bright, airy promenades where polished glowclusters floated, most ordinary folk would still be working; the luckier ones would be trudging home through service tunnels to their tiny alcoves.

On the evening after he had seen Rosa's returned father, Tom sat by himself at his usual table by the wall, picking at a light salad, listening to the soft Kaznin folksongs. The musician was a traveller—these days, a dangerous occupation—and he was surprisingly skilled, perched on the tiny stage at the chamber's rear, picking at his aerolute, his soft melodious voice somehow reaching throughout the club.

Among the rich gowns, the formal uniforms—the officers' braid prominent in the bright light—marked the occupying forces' highest representatives. But they sometimes behaved in unexpected ways.

Kaznia was a distant realm currently besieged by the Blight. Famously (as though the authorities knew they had no hope of suppressing the news), the inhabitants of one small outlying community had committed suicide—parents taking their children's lives before their own—rather than surrender. That was only six tendays ago, but the blockaded realm's core was on the brink of falling, as Duke Broyse and his subjects starved.

It was the officers who surprised Tom.

As soon as the musician had begun, his first sweet ballad threaded with the unmistakable harmonies of the Kaznin ten-point scale, the uniformed men had laid down their tine-spoons, ignoring both food and the brittle conversation of their female paid companions, and turned their attention towards the music.

They did not applaud when the song ended—a few scattered claps sounded, then fell away to silence, as other diners followed the officers' lead—but they watched and listened attentively throughout the next song, and the next.

One of the officers, lean and grey-haired with a rigid back, was sitting in profile; Tom saw the bright glitter of unashamed tears upon the man's cheek as the musician's ballad drew to its soft, sweet, haunting close.

Have I misjudged these people?

Tom's impulse was to leave, and think over what he had seen.

But then a waiter-servitor stumbled slightly, spilling some water from the carafe he was carrying, and brushed against the grey-haired officer's sleeve. Without taking his gaze away from the stage, the officer whipped his tine-spoon across the apologetic waiter's cheek, ripping three parallel welts just below the eye.

Blood was already welling as the waiter-servitor backed away, hurrying towards the service membrane-door, while the other waiters stood and watched, not daring to help.

Tom picked a slice of gripplefruit from his plate, and slowly chewed, tasting nothing.

After the musician finished, glowglimmers brightened and the ambient noise grew to a hubbub, over a low background of recorded zeitdeco chorales. The grey-haired officer resumed eating, using the same tine-spoon which had raised blood in the servitor's cheek.

Then, as the music softened, in one of those sudden unpredictable lulls, a woman's voice carried clearly: ". . . Chaos-damned occupation ends, and we'll all be free."

The music rose, in counterpoint to murmured conversations' fading away to silence.

She was dark-haired, the woman who had spoken. Slowly she replaced her goblet upon the table where she sat, as her companions unconsciously shifted in their seats, distancing themselves from her remark.

Then another woman's laughter—too brittle: bright and intoxicated—cut through the silence, and an officer made a coarse remark, and gradually diners began to converse once more.

But there were watchful gazes trained upon the dark-haired woman.

Excusing herself, she left her table and walked, a little unsteadily, to the exit, where a servitor fetched her cloak and draped it around her shoulders: royal blue and lustrous, with a spray of silver flecks fanning out across the shoulders, and a brocaded hem which brushed along the marble flagstones as she passed through the glistening membrane and was gone, the membrane vitrifying to milky hardness.

Tom, still seated, used his cred-ring to pay the bill, touching it to the tabletop sensor.

His black cloak was folded on an unused chair beside him, and he picked it up, carrying it across his forearm as he stood. Near him, on the wall, an area of liquid texture was subtly different from the polished stone surrounding it: a servitors' doorway. No-one—he verified with a casual scan across the restaurant—was looking in his direction.

Tom crouched down so that the covered table hid him, rolled sideways through the membrane, and came to his feet in a dank service tunnel.

His heart beat faster.

In a dank, cobbled piazza shrouded with black shadows, Tom finally caught sight of her spectral shape, wide cape sweeping the dark glistening cobblestones. She was heading for a square archway—but, in the tunnel beyond, he saw silhouettes move. Outlines of three militiamen standing out of the light, on purpose.

Alerted by someone from the Club d'Anderquin?

"Sweetheart?" Tom called out.

His black cloak was still draped over his forearm, but he was able to give a half-wave in the woman's direction.

She paused.

Tom moved quickly, taking long paces to hide the urgency.

"It *is* you, darling. Fancy seeing you here."

Doubt reached her eyes, and she began to turn away, but Tom was close enough now to murmur: "You're in danger. I can help."

"Danger?" Her voice was quiet.

He took her arm, redirecting her—"Don't turn your head, but can you glance to your left?"—until he was sure she had seen the watchers.

"Who are you? A friend of Yano's?"

"Talk later." Tom was already leading her towards a different exit: rounded, black with gloom. "Right now, you've attracted some unwelcome attention."

She gave a small, silent nod.

Either she was less drunk than he had thought, or fear had sobered her, for she matched his pace with no further argument. Accompanying him into shadows.

And stopped with him, when they were hidden in the exit tunnel. Like Tom, she held her breath, and listened.

Footsteps.

The militiamen were following.

Tom felt the entire mission, his secret world, collapsing in around him because of the impulse to help a weak embittered stranger, who might turn out to be detestable.

"Take this." He shoved his folded cloak into her hands. "And give me your cape."

At the next intersection, half-lit in sombre blue, Tom stood briefly where the following men might see him from a distance—clad in the woman's long cape—then stepped into the shadows and slapped his own face.

"Swear at me now," he said in a low voice.

And the dark-haired woman delivered a loud blistering curse—the sound would surely carry back to the militiamen—using a wealth of vocabulary which surprised him even in the circumstances.

"Now go," he said when she had finished. "Meet me in Skandril Market at dawnshift."

She started to move.

"And don't return home."

A hesitation, then: "I was with *friends* at the club."

Bitter undertone. Friends who would likely have betrayed her, by now.

You betrayed yourself.

"Go on," said Tom. "Get out of here."

Into a side tunnel's shadows—

Go with freedom.

—and was gone.

Militiamen, making more noise as they drew near, no longer bothering to conceal themselves.

Tom made his move.

Swimming was the least of the new skills drilled into him at the Academy. But he was going to have to count on it to save his life.

Deep breath, silent dive—it was a mental rehearsal—*and push like Chaos.*

Tom was walking fast, but not too fast, with the cape billowing slightly, and three militiamen following. But in his mind, he was already in the cold, black canal, taking the only way to freedom.

Focus now.

The teachings of fine, honest warrior-instructors—from Dervlin and Maestro da Silva, to Sergeant M'Kalnikav and his Academy comrades—lived on in Tom. Defining the nature of reality: that it bends to human will, to the power of imagination.

Hold the objective in mind, consider it achieved, keep that image despite all pain and all confusion, hang on to it with frenzied energy, and it becomes—finally—real.

More footsteps, ahead as well as behind him.

Another patrol.

Tom turned left, into a grey stone corridor, but there were voices at the far end.

They're closing in.

But the soldiers' mental objective was to capture a lone, somewhat drunken woman, who might curse and scratch but offered no serious threat to uniformed males at the height of their power, with the strength of their comradeship and teamed desire, their polished weapons in their hands, and the knowledge that a prisoner was in no position to complain about anything that might occur between here and the cells, after they had finished with her.

There was an alcove, too small to hide a person, but sufficient to conceal a bundled cape of lustrous blue, in the shadows where its sprinkled silver flecks would not spark with reflected light.

Then Tom climbed up and hung motionless, like some three-limbed silent arachnabug, splayed against the tunnel ceiling.

After they had passed, he descended easily, retrieved the cape, and broke into a loping, soundless run.

He had spent little time here on the Quintum Stratum, but the design was replicated through several levels and he had memorized the topological differences. The canal was where it would be near his current home, two strata down, and he ran harder than he ever had, heel to toe, in utter silence.

Black water, glistening.

He cast the cape, and it fluttered to the waves then floated, where it began a slow rotating drift, like a discarded blossom whose purpose was to spread genes by the power of its beauty. Silver flecks scintillated, grew dark.

Distant shouts, as the militiamen, angry now, retraced their steps.

Tom crouched down at the stone bank's straight edge, controlled his breathing as he extended his arm, and rolled forwards softly into darkness.

Cold black water enveloped him.

48

BETA DRACONIS III AD 2142

<<Ro's Story>>

[16]

It was a world where nothing made sense.

The human settlement was like a tangled pile of silver bones; but, from the lip of a balcony extrusion near its apex, it seemed an island of stability amid churning chaos. The sky was a van Gogh madness, purple blood swirling in turbulent turquoise waters; the cracked ground lay still, but its hues shifted—always at the edge of Ro's vision, whenever she looked away.

And the buildings . . .

They changed. Sometimes, flickering, it seemed that multiple images overlaid each other. Staring at the Zajinet city for more than twenty seconds at a time caused migraines. Beside Ro, also beneath the balcony's protective membrane, even Lila periodically closed her eyes, readjusting: a protective habit after two years' sojourn on BD3.

And the beings . . .

Foot traffic, and unsettling flying things, passed among the fractal avenues. Their shapes morphed, flowing as they moved; sometimes, briefly, just a fiery tracery remained, before some new external form clad the bright-glimmering inner core.

"We don't even know," murmured Lila, "whether they're all Zajinets. One species, or a full ecology."

Ro squeezed her eyes shut.

I don't like this place.

A Zajinet—the renegade on Terra—had somehow brought her here. After the events in Moscow, the Mexican gardener who was really an assassin, attempting to kill her—or had the target been Zoë?—her presence in this place seemed simultaneously unremarkable and a massive, cosmic joke.

Why did the Zajinet leave me here?

She felt as though she was going to be sick. Even Zoë had, in one sense, betrayed her. For it seemed obvious now that, though the Zajinet or one of its human servants might have stolen the crystal-cassette of Anne-Louise's work from her room in Arizona, it was more likely that Zoë had been the thief. Working for her masters in the intelligence services.

Protecting Ro from a threat they only half comprehended? Or using her as bait?

She wondered if the renegade Zajinet was acting on its own, or whether it had allies—or enemies—here on BD3.

Why did it let me live?

Somehow it had transported her across the light-years; it seemed that not only human Pilots possessed the secret of mu-space travel. Yet the Zajinets had kept their capabilities secret all this time.

"Come on, Ro." A gentle touch upon her arm: Lila, smiling softly. "Let's get inside."

The corridors were blue-silver, tangled hollow tubes—occasionally widening out into rooms—which formed no discernible pattern. Sometimes, if all the humans happened to sleep at the same time, they would awaken to find the configuration altered: old rooms disappeared (sometimes with the equipment and sparse furnishings they had contained); new rooms came into existence. Occasionally long-lost equipment made a reappearance. Most times, it was warped beyond easy recognition; sometimes—though formed of solid metal—it seemed to have been twisted inside out.

There were forty-four people living in the settlement, and they called it Watcher's Bones.

Ro woke in the middle of the "night," and made her way to the current designated relaxation lounge. There was a bar (complete with cocktail-mixing AI) installed by the wall, and a tall, bulky, florid-looking Englishman named Matheson—usually called Fluffy—was making practised use of it.

"Delighted to see you, old girl."

"I couldn't sleep."

"Take a pew."

Ro fetched herself a fruit-juice mix, and took a reclining seat facing Matheson—in her own mind, she could not bring herself to use his nickname.

"It's a strange place," she said.

"No more so"—he quaffed some of his fluorescent cocktail—"than the manner of your arrival."

She sighed. "I couldn't agree more."

Everyone in the settlement had seen the tape of her interview, with Lila and Jared asking the questions, and AI-physiometry displays indicating that everything Ro said was true. Or at least that she believed it.

There were still stares: hers was the first new face here for two Terran years, and it was nearly six months before the next relief vessel was due to call.

"Y'know, on Earth"—Matheson, old-fashioned beyond his years, never used the word "Terra"—"an alien visitor would sample grass blades, penicillin growths, mushrooms and human beings, and see that we're all outgrowths of the same DNA chemistry. Even oxygen is a byproduct of life. It would be obvious, y'see"—with a wagging forefinger—"that we're all of the same world."

It was an old speech, Ro could tell, but with a new audience. And she was interested.

"Lila said no-one knows how many species live here."

"Or even if it really is their homeworld. The eco relationships appear senseless. But my research leads me to believe—well, never mind."

"Tell me."

"That they've travelled here. That the Zajinets possess the ability to travel through mu-space. And your appearance here forms my vindication, old girl." He held up his glass in salute, and drank to her.

"I guess it does."

It was hard to believe that another species had the means to enter mu-space, and bring a frail human captive all this way through that strange, fractal continuum, without her being conscious of the journey.

If that's what really happened.

She hunched up in her chair, and shivered. All was confusion. For she could not interpret recent events' significance, any more than her eyes could make ordered sense of the shifting, random, chaotic cityscape outside, where her kidnapper must even now be living, plotting its next indecipherable move.

"I don't know," she murmured later, "whether Zoë's still alive, even."

Matheson shifted in his chair—startling Ro: she had thought he was asleep—and spoke without opening his eyes.

"Spook training, old girl. She's bound to have got out intact."

"I'm sorry?"

"Scholar-diplomats are we." He made it sound like the words of a song. "And we get around a bit. I've come across your friend before, and she was an UNtel agent-in-charge during a little, er, difficulty in Lhasa. Years ago."

"I think the renegade was trying to kill Fyodor." Ro had taken to using Zoë's pet name for the Zajinet ambassador which was living in XenoMir. "But it might have been after Zoë."

Matheson opened his eyes and slowly shook his head. "I really don't think so."

Ro stared at him. "What do you mean?"

In answer, he slowly levered his bulk from the chair.

"Either you're being disingenuous, old thing"—he stood surprisingly steadily, after all he had drunk—"or it's yourself that you're fooling. It's time you opened those rather distinctive, unsettling eyes of yours."

But if it wanted me dead, why did it bring me here?

Then Matheson steered himself towards his quarters, leaving Ro alone in the lounge to contemplate his words and the formless thoughts boiling in her mind, like a chemical spill in a troubled ocean, fermenting explosively in the shark-haunted, shadowed depths where she had not dared to look.

<<MODULE ENDS>>

49

NULAPEIRON AD 3421

Some things had not changed, even under the conditions of the Dark Fire's occupation. To move between strata, it was still far easier to descend.

The dark-haired woman, Shayella, was waiting in Skandril Market, in a dusty annexe away from the stallholders setting up. Her face was webbed with tension, pale beneath the glowclusters' primrose morning light.

Tom, still dripping wet, had rousted one of the local agents-in-place from his bed in the small hours. Apologizing for the intrusion, he had taken away a fake ID and one-off scan-unit.

By a dusty pillar, he scanned in her DNA, handed over the ID.

"You're coming with me," he told her.

Two strata down, in a deserted former warehouse hall where ciliates rustled unseen, she sat with Tom and Rilka and Tyentro, and told them what she knew.

"A thousand artificers," she said, "constructed and upgraded the Seer's chamber, up on the Primum Stratum. When the—enemy— came, they took it over, by all accounts. Lately, they've searched for anyone who worked on those projects. My . . ." She looked at them. "My brother Yano was one of them."

For two hours they talked, about conditions since the Blight's forces had arrived, the strictures on speech and social life, and about her brother. It all spilled out of her, as the tension of holding in her opinions and feelings broke open, in a cathartic relief which was helped rather than hindered by the fact that her audience consisted of three strangers. But there was no other information of immediate tactical benefit.

Except in the negative: Yano was no dissident, had no personal enemies, yet the Tunnel Guard had arrested him. But he had worked on the Seer's chamber, perched on one of the flexible catenary walkways which led to it, dangling over the dark chasm in which it was suspended.

Finally, Rilka took her away to a temporary dwelling alcove, leaving Tom and Tyentro to decide what would happen next.

"The thing is," said Tyentro, "while you were gone, Rilka came back with some interesting data."

The constabulary where Rilka worked had assisted in a raid, taking the autodoc files from a local med centre and imprisoning two of the medics. One of those medics, with travel authorization spanning eight strata, had an unusual range of patients.

"His name wouldn't be Xyenquil, would it?"

"No." Tyentro shook his head. "Any reason it should be?"

"Just wondering. So who was the most interesting patient?"

Tyentro brought a holo to life in the gloom, and rotated the image of a woman's head. Her eyes were milky, her complexion unlined, and it took a moment for Tom to realize where he had seen her.

"That's Velsivith's wife."

"Just so." Tyentro smiled. "Lieutenant Velsivith neglected to mention—and I knew he was holding something back—that wife Vhiyalla has serious problems."

"She's blind." Tom frowned. "He told us that."

"But he didn't mention that she's dying."

"Ah, Chaos."

"And now his intelligence superiors know it too. She's the one hold they really have over him."

There was movement at the old warehouse's edges, and Tom wondered how the ciliates fared with only dust to eat. It was one of those moments when the small realities assume importance, before the arbitrary process of decision-making commits an entire human life to one course of action.

"It's time that Ralkin Velsivith and I had another little chat, Tyentro."

"I can arrange that, sir."

Shaven-headed children walked—no, marched—in ranks along the wide corridor. Tom felt his face stiffen into a mask as he saw the matching tunics, the bright expressions somewhere between solemnity and buoyant enthusiasm. They wore half-capes of blue, lined with red, and they walked straight-backed and proud behind a small banner bearer who could not have been more than eight SY old.

Adult gazes slipped away as the procession passed.

But it had been worse, earlier that morning, when the tunnels had been quieter and Tom had seen the column of prisoners, thirty men, women and children tied together, walking barefoot, under guard. There had been six soldiers escorting. *Only six.* The prisoners should have fought back tooth and nail like vicious animals, accepting the risk of death. But their attentions were focused inwards, full of muddied confusion (just as Velsivith had described), and the conviction that this was a bureaucratic error which would surely be rectified as soon as they could talk to someone in charge.

On each forehead, a motile sigil—slapped on during their arrest—cycled through changes, from red diamond to blue spot: a prisoner brand, which would have deterred escape had they even perceived the extent of their own danger; but they did not allow themselves that madness. Not consciously.

Only one small girl, too young to deceive herself, stared at the soldiers with open mouth and fear shining in her eyes.

While passers-by, whose former neighbours might have been among the prisoners, oddly carried on about their daily business, walking to market or godown. Unable to look, as though they could not quite perceive what was happening in their own quiet residential tunnels, in the clean stone corridors with well-kept alcoves, among the small, tidy moss-gardens and scrubbed piazzettas of a modest, well-ordered community.

Tom was trembling when he reached the safe chamber, passing by Stilvan—Tyentro's lieutenant, hawk-nosed and dangerous—and two other team members, on silent watch.

I should have done something.

But the Blight's forces were everywhere, implacable, as though the very air was heavy with its essence.

Something . . .

In the small, curtained-off chamber, Velsivith sat on a low stool, heavy russet cloak pulled round himself. There was a chill, and a musty smell rose from the old drapes. When he saw Tom, he gave a thin, tight smile.

"Well met, my Lord."

A flicker of a glance from Tyentro, well concealed. Surprised at Tom's rank? Neither had told the other much of his past; their meetings were always brief, for safety.

"Lieutenant Velsivith, I'm sorry for your wife's troubles."

"You saw us that day, from the balcony." The amber ovoid in his cheek looked dark, almost brown. "But that's not what you're—Her illness. Who else knows?"

"We were the second interested group to find out."

"Who . . . You mean my superiors. Chaos!" Velsivith looked away. "Ah, Vhiyalla. What are we going to do?"

"Accept our help," said Tom.

"Oh, that. As I recall our last meeting"—with more than a trace of self-disgust—"I left you to the interrogators' mercies in one of the pain chambers. Why should you help me?"

"Common enemy."

"Not good enough. Why should you *trust* me?"

Tom stood with his back against the cold stone wall. He could feel the heat being leeched from his body, despite his cape.

"That day, I did see you and Vhiyalla. What I saw could not be faked."

Tom heard the longing in his own voice, fell silent.

Neither of the other men looked surprised or amused: too many people, nowadays, had tragic stories of their own to carry with them.

"Have you got courier lines?" Velsivith glanced at Tyentro, then back at Tom. "Enough to take us into a friendly realm? Away from the Blight."

Is that what you're after? Infiltration, after all?

Taking down an enemy courier network would be a big feather in any intelligence officer's cap. Or more immediately, security forces might already be converging on this rendezvous.

"She wouldn't go by herself," Velsivith added. "Not that I want to remain."

Tyentro made a silent shift in stance. This was between Tom and Velsivith; Tyentro's job was to kill Velsivith if things went wrong. Should Stilvan raise the alarm, Tom would attempt to escape—his duty as a local control—while Tyentro dealt with things on the spot.

Anybody can kill anybody.

Not true, but Tyentro was very capable.

"What are you offering," Tom asked, "to pay for passage?"

Velsivith hunched forward on his stool. "Not many people have seen the Blight manifest a portion of itself—but you have, my Lord. And so have I."

Tom felt a chill that was nothing to do with the stones he was leaning against.

"You mean the people who killed the Seer."

"People." With a faint smile: "If you can call them that. I think of them as *substrate*."

"But you didn't see them."

"Not then. But later. I've travelled, closer to the power centres, where there are more non-people like that. Their eyes . . ." Velsivith shook his head, very slightly. "They're *part* of the Blight, just components, and that means they're no longer human."

Tyentro unfolded his arms, recrossed them, without tucking in the upper hand: ready to strike as soon as it became necessary.

"What can you give us?"

"Locations of two of their High Commands. And biometric data on every prisoner who's passed through the Grand'aume Core."

Tom stepped away from the wall. "Biometric data?"

"Every prisoner is deepscanned and analysed. Of the ones who are deported, some are directed to camps near the High Commands, the power centres. There are tales of what happens there"—with an almost violent headshake of denial—"but I don't know. I do know that those camps' prisoners are chosen from the multitude that pass through."

"From bio-analyses?"

"Oh, yes." With a bitter smile: "You didn't think they'd actually committed a crime or anything, did you?"

Tom's eyelids fluttered as he shifted into logotropic trance, analysing and synthesizing, allowing gestalten to form themselves against the background of his own experience, and his consciously constructed model of the Dark Fire's nature and intentions, matching with the scant information he already possessed about the ongoing arrests.

Finally, he breathed in deeply, snapped his eyes open.

"You've a prisoner called Yano," he told Velsivith. "I'd like you to release him."

"And that"—Velsivith's voice was suddenly subdued—"is the price of my passage?"

"With the biometrics. And one other thing."

"Which is?"

"Something we'll discuss later."

50

NULAPEIRON AD 3421

When Yano was released, Tyentro himself tagged along through the crowded tunnels, following the dazed man as he stared with wonder at homely sights he had thought were lost to him forever. With experienced tunnelcraft strengthened by natural paranoia, Tyentro was excellent at spotting human surveillance; there was none here.

Femtotech was more dangerous, but that would have to wait till they could get to a safe chamber for screening.

Finally, before Yano reached his sister Shayella's dwelling—she was with Tyentro's lieutenant, Stilvan, two strata below; up here, notice had been given for her arrest—Tyentro intercepted him.

Dismay shut down Yano's expression when Tyentro showed a crystal copy of Shayella's arrest notice. He agreed to go along with Tyentro, though he feared trickery, and a return to the Grand'aume's dungeons.

Tom learned all this as he debriefed Tyentro.

"Let's get him down to his sister," he said. "Then he'll be more forthcoming when we ask questions."

"All right," Tyentro answered. "But I thought his release meant nothing, tactically. Just a way of bringing Velsivith further into our camp. Strengthening our hold on him."

"That's part of it. But I want to know more about the Seer's chamber."

The way Tom remembered it, the Seer's chamber was a great ovoid hanging in a vast darkened shaft, its catenary walkways like transparent capillaries linking it to the tunnels beyond the abyss. When he had last seen it, row upon row of arachnabugs had been crawling on the shaft wall, guarding the Seer.

Yano had helped to build the walkways. Beyond confirming Tom's impressions and adding architectural detail—the exact number of walkways (twelve), the materials used (moldoil softglass)—he had little tactically significant information.

"Thank you," Tom said finally. "Make yourself comfortable. Two more days, and you'll be far away from here."

Yano began to reply, but his mouth twisted and suddenly he was sobbing, and he sat with his hands clasped between his thighs, rocking back and forth, staring at the grimy flagstones, seeing only the jailers coming for him once more, and the glistening red of the pain chamber's flesh-like toxin-laden walls, while his skin shrank beneath the piercing screams of tortured prisoners only he could hear.

They used a different location for Tom's next meeting with Velsivith. It was an art gallery, its owner absent; the walls and ceilings were burnt orange, composed of flat planes but in a jumbled maze of polygon-faced tunnels, and the floor was a single continuous turquoise crystal.

It reminded Tom of the Arizona realm in Ro's Story, but he tried not to take that as some kind of omen.

He sat beside Velsivith on a wide bench, and watched a deep-burgundy smartglass sculpture slowly morphing through liquid, abstract configurations.

"Tell me," Tom said slowly, "about the Seer's chamber."

Velsivith twitched. "That place."

"It was under heavy guard when last I saw it. Not that it helped at all."

"No-one"—the amber ovoid pulsed alternately dark and light as Velsivith shook his head—"would dare attack it now."

"Why's that?"

"There are no guards, except in the ordinary access tunnels outside. But the mausoleum is haunted, my Lord. I mean it."

"Mausoleum?"

"It—We kept the Seer there. Froze the—remains. Council orders."

Haunted.

Dark Fire manifestations?

Then, "That's the other thing I want to ask of you, Ralkin," he said quietly, using Velsivith's forename for the first time. "Can you get me inside there?"

It was like dark, coagulating blood: the burgundy smartglass, slowly changing shape upon its shelf.

"No," said Velsivith finally. "Not you. The scans will remember you, still recognize you, and I can't override that."

Chaos . . .

"Tyentro, then."

"If you get Vhiyalla to safety, yes."

"I'd say we have a deal."

They sent Vhiyalla, along with Shayella and her brother Yano, via the long-prepared escape routes, stage-managed by some of their deepest-cover agents-in-place. A bland-faced courier went with them, carrying a crystal in his tunic's flash-pocket, set to heisenberg the crystal to oblivion if the pocket was incorrectly opened.

But the biometrics data which Velsivith had provided might be very important. Unknown to the others, Tom sent a duplicate with a second courier.

Deep-lined face and whipcord-thin, with long wispy white hair: the man was in his seventies, but ramrod-straight and obviously fit.

That's how I want to turn out.

Tom and the courier bowed, each recognizing a kindred spirit. Then the old man was gone, and Tom knew they were unlikely to ever meet again.

Three nights later, Tom moved through a district of prosperous but depressing tunnels: black, with steel dragon-sculptures—fangs bared, neck cowls flaring open—sprouting from purple pillars. Archways were decorated with black tangled wire on which blood-blossoms sprouted, their wispy rust-coloured air-roots gently waving.

Passers-by smiled or laughed rarely; when they did, their humour had a predatory, self-satisfied aura, congratulating themselves or their cronies on the power they held.

Tyentro's team had already swept the rendezvous for surveillance, but Tom's skin prickled all the same. This was some sort of crux: if Velsivith had been setting them up, now was the time for him to spring the trap.

The rendezvous was a tavern, with half-enclosed booth-alcoves along the rear wall. In the third alcove from the left, with tiny flames flickering inside, two glasses of fire-brandy were waiting.

Tom squeezed into the alcove, painfully aware that it made a perfect cage, and sat down opposite Velsivith.

Sparks, cast by the fire-brandy, danced in the warm amber ovoid inset upon Velsivith's cheek.

"Well, my Lord?"

A rippling privacy-screen now blurred their view of the saloon outside, but Tom wished Velsivith had not referred to his rank.

"They're in neutral territory, beyond the Grand'aume, and still travelling. I received word."

"Right." Velsivith's lean face looked diabolic through the flames. "There's Internal Security surveillance on my home again, but I had a chat and joked with the team leader: we went to school together."

"They'll wonder why there's no sign of Vhiyalla."

"I said she's not well, but that won't last for long. If they deepscan—"

"Tomorrow, then." Tom's real internal demons stirred at the rich brandy scent, enhanced by the flames' flickering warmth. "And you'll be done here."

Velsivith snuffed out one glass's flames, then took a deep swallow, and put the glass down with careful control.

His eyes were unreadable.

"Tomorrow."

51
BETA DRACONIS III AD 2142

<<Ro's Story>>

[17]

Twenty-two humans attended the event; afterwards, there were twenty-two theories about what, exactly, had occurred. Some said it was a trial, a criminal prosecution; others considered it merely a political debate between opposing Zajinet parties.

A few thought it some kind of entertainment or joke, or else a manifestation of alien cognitive processes whose full nature no human being would ever be equipped to understand.

They stood confused amid the flickering, overlapping occurrences of Zajinets and the dome-shaped hall—mostly dome-shaped, though other forms (a horizontal pyramid, a series of stone needles, even a patch of sere green sky that looked like nothing on this world) flipped into existence, were gone.

Each individual Zajinet seemed at times to split apart and overlay, shimmering, in superimposed images of differing configurations, as though they somehow existed in simultaneous, parallel realities which could be concentrated together in one place, though never for longer than a moment.

The human visitors wore tight env-suits, though they stood on a stable dais in a hemisphere of Terran atmosphere; it was the craziness around them which they needed to shut out. At any time during the proceedings, two or three humans were likely to have matt black helmets, darkened for a moment's respite to hide the random chaos which bubbled through the air, rippled through the ground.

Two Zajinets manifested, unclothed: that was how Ro thought of it later. They were not clad in the granules and stones and boulders which formed the aliens' normal, outer forms, like huge elephantine sculptures. Instead, these two individuals comprised raw traceries of light: scarlet fire, and blazing sapphire.

Bursts of white agitation scintillated around their peripheries.

Were they prisoners before the dock? Speakers before a gathering of peers?

<< ... preserve ... >>
<< ... in finding, hold on to ... >>
<< ... converse manifests ... >>
<< ... obliterate ... >>
<< ... a focus ... >>

Then the first Zajinet's opponent—in Ro's interpretation they were opponents, judging by the strange overlapping waves of light, the pulsing interference pattern—blasted its reply:

<< ... single thread! ... >>
<< ... saved softly in confusing dark ... >>
<< ... their only hope ... >>

Lila, her hair a shining violet today, examined a small disk embedded in the palm of her glove.

"One of them"—Lila pointed—"we've dealt with before. The other Zajinet's a stranger."

I know him.

It was the one who had broken into XenoMir, had somehow brought her to this world. Ro was—almost—sure of it. But she kept her mouth shut as Lila tapped her palm disk, downloading the defendant's (as Ro mentally labelled the Zajinet stranger) energy signature for later reference.

Some kind of resonance? Ro was sure she could steal a palm disk, now she knew of their existence. *A way of detecting particular individuals?*

Or of tracking them down.

Already Ro was thinking in terms of tactics and weaponry. And revenge.

Between the two Zajinets, a complex wave pattern built: a form of communication so beyond humans there was nothing to do but analyse the ebb and flow of brightness. It was like trying to decipher a person's speech by looking at the blaze of neurons firing within the brain: devoid of semantic content. But it surely was an argument, between two minds.

Then the pattern slowly faded.

An expectant air hung over the hall, and for a moment the walls seemed solid, devoid of the flickering overlays which normally characterized this place.

Find him guilty!

Nothing.

If it was a trial, the defendant was not being punished.

And then the conclusion, which no-one among the humans fully understood.

The individual that had kidnapped Ro blazed brightly—in triumph, she thought. Then both of the opposing Zajinets seemed to *slip sideways* into the liquid air, somehow folding the atmosphere and themselves into narrow lines, then collapsed to points, then nothing at all.

Is that what it did to me?

Was it teleportation?

Whatever the mechanism, it was the disappearance into thin—if unusual—air of two alien beings which captured people's imaginations. Not the workings of the Zajinet legal system, if such a thing even existed.

The others were muttering excitedly to each other—"Did you see that?"—but Ro tapped her glove's wrist controls to silence her helmet's audio input.

Can they teleport across the light-years?

But a strange memory came to her then, a flickering glimpse of *a hollow ovoid chamber, glimmering with eerie light, with the Zajinet, her shining captor, hovering above a white glowing brightness at the chamber's centre. Then a twisting, a blaze of amber.*

And somehow she knows the Zajinet's attention is upon her, though it is no more than a jumbled tracery of scarlet light. Then a tendril of lightning reaches out—

Blackness.

Ro drew a deep, shuddering breath.

It's short-range, the teleportation, if that's what it truly is. But it's not how they travel among the stars.

Because she knew what the shining chamber must have been. And that glimpse of amber . . .

They have mu-space ships!

She knew, but she was going to keep that knowledge to herself. At least for now.

All around the humans on the dais, the remaining Zajinets, clothed in a variety of abstract-sculpture conglomerate forms, began to depart, drifting outwards from the hall's centre. Each timed its egress with a wall's flickering out of existence, so that no actual openings were necessary.

There was an air of anticlimax.

Behind the dais, the humans' large personnel carrier, a blank-windowed converted TDV, opened its opaque doors. Quickly, they began to move inside with a shivering eagerness, desperate to return to the settlement they normally despised.

You should've killed me, Zajinet.

It brought her here, but let her live. To avoid a murder charge, instead of kidnapping, in the strange trial they had just witnessed? The trial from which it had gone free.

But it was responsible for Anne-Louise's murder.

And for the death of Luís, the man she loved.

You really should have killed me.

A woman called Anita—normally to be found in the company of Oron, a skimpy-bearded sociologist—pushed her way through the noisy gathering to Ro's side.

"Did you feel it?" Her dark brows, which almost met in the middle, were raised in amazement. "Their prayer energy. It was seventh level, at least."

"Amazing," said Ro.

"Would you like to talk it over?" Anita's face had grown flushed, as though the invitation were sexually illicit. "Oron's waiting in my room. We could—"

"No, thanks."

"But you're simpatico, Dorothy. I can sense it."

Only Mother calls me that.

"I need to meditate on it," said Ro. "I'm going to pray alone."

"Ah, ah. I see." Anita withdrew, confused. "Talk to me later."

Much later.

Ro stood at the periphery, until the excitement began to die down, and the group broke up slowly of its own accord, as people began to drift back towards their work.

But there were some diehards for whom the distraction had been too much. There was boisterous laughter, and a booming voice called along the silver corridor's curved length:

"Hey, Fluffy! You up for a game of ping-darts?"

Matheson shook his head. "Sorry, old thing." He started to clap a hand on Ro's shoulder, stopped himself. "I'm going to buy this girl a drink."

In the otherwise deserted bar, he fixed two drinks in plastic cups, and he and Ro sat down on opposite sides of a small round table.

Both drinks were juice-mixes.

"On the wagon?" asked Ro.

"After this morning, no chance. But it's a bit early, still."

"You've been out in the city before."

"I didn't like it then, either." He blew out a long breath. "And they weren't discussing the welfare of one of my friends, that time."

"I'm sorry?"

"You, old girl"—he raised his cup: a mocking toast—"were the focus of today's proceedings. Couldn't you tell?"

"That's not true."

Not from the energy flows. But their implied regard—inasmuch as they had focused attention: their entire minds were also their sense organs—had indeed been directed at her from time to time.

"Bit of a blistering argument, among those two fiery Zajinets. I'd love to know what was really going on."

Has he worked it out?

Ro set her cup down, and spoke very quietly.

"It was a trial." And, with bitterness: "But the guilty party went free."

She was sure of it.

That night, Ro prowled the empty corridors of Watcher's Bones, until she came to the area known as Sparks. There was a lock system, but Ro spent only seconds examining it. She stood before the sensor panel.

Golden scintillations.

It was more complex than the locking plates she had subverted in Arizona, but she could feel the ebb and flow of energy, the tiny flux-knots of power—

A blaze of golden light.

Yes.

Fading . . .

Then her eyes were shining jet once more, a glistening black, and the security door was folding open.

In a long cupboard, six empty env-suits hung like shadowed spectres. None of the gauntlets bore a processor disk, though each palm held an empty socket.

Damn, damn.

But she analysed the layout, saw in her mind the quiet movements of the senior researchers, Lila among them.

If I were a disk, where would I be?

She waved open a lab-bench drawer, and found the disk. She pocketed it.

Then a strange sound/not-sound pulsed through the air.

There was a folding/unfolding in the shining wall before her, as her surroundings began to reconfigure—

It's not supposed to happen when someone's watching.

—and, galvanized, she took the opportunity and pushed with all her might, impossible strength in her narrow frame, and the spacetime disturbance caught hold of the lab bench and sucked it into presumed oblivion, while Ro leaped back to safety.

She laughed quietly, surprising herself, as the wall shivered into its new configuration and solidified.

Now no-one would know she had stolen a palm disk.

Off to one side lay evidence of an experiment in construction: a jumble of processor blocks, a pile of narrow copper tubing. It seemed an omen, for Ro had been thinking that a metallic conductor would make the best weapon.

There was a length of copper which was the right size for a *bo*, the fighting staff of aikido with which Ro had trained since childhood, and that was the one she picked.

Forgive me, Father.

She did it occasionally: talked to Dart, to the dead father she had never known, who had sacrificed himself in mu-space—subsumed within the quasi-sentient energy pattern which had held his ship and threatened Mother's—to save his lover and his unborn child.

It was the only form of prayer of which Ro was capable.

You would not approve of this.

No answer rang back from the empty metal corridors as she broke into a silent jog, the copper pipe held horizontally in her hand, like a spear-carrying warrior who was used to moving long distances, fast, while conserving her true strength for the waiting battlefield.

<<MODULE ENDS>>

52

NULAPEIRON AD 3422

Scarlet banners. Armbands on the civilians who marched in rows through the boulevards and galleries, their febrile manic excitement washing through the air, bouncing back from stone walls which had seen everything over the passing centuries.

Soldiers were everywhere.

In the quieter residential tunnels, there were people who turned away from Tom as he passed by, not wanting to lock gazes. They were the rationalists, the scared ones who could not openly share their fear.

It was the first day of Phoenix Year, and the community was giving birth to itself in a new guise, with new loyalties. The occupation had continued for long enough. Something in the cultural psyche had given way with the passing of the old year, and acceptance of the new order (with the over-enthusiasm of new converts) pushed its insistent way through every corridor, inserted its self-serving images into every family and social group.

And blocked out memories of deportation: the disappearance of former neighbours and friends enveloped now by an overarching wave of desperate optimism.

At the first checkpoint, an officer had insisted on chatting in Lin-tran, and Tom had made it through the interrogation-by-gossip, careful not to over-use his memorized trivia of that region. But he had been sweating heavily by the conversation's end.

Finally, a waiter-servitor showed him to an expensive restaurant table, on a semicircular grey balcony which overlooked a wide passageway below. Bronze glowclusters floated near the silver-decorated ceiling.

Tom took the chair nearest to the railing, so that he could watch the expected parade pass by. The waiter complimented him on his choice, and waved a command at the table.

Menu-tricons floated meaninglessly before Tom.

The waiter leaned close.

"Phase One complete. We've just had word."

Tom picked a dish at random.

And, as he brought the silver carafe—"A nice gripplewine, sir?"—another whispered update: *"Phase Two. They're in."*

Tom nodded his thanks.

Tom pushed food around on the plate with his tine-spoon, watching his fellow diners—there were occupation officers among them, and willing dining partners to share their jokes and bonhomie—and, occasionally, looking down, over the balustrade, at the crowd which swelled below the balcony. A tunnel party had expanded into the main broadway, and the laughter was both coarser and more genuine than the brittle affectations up here in the restaurant.

Tyentro's team had set up tight-beam comms along an old service tunnel. In places, it was scarcely wide enough for maint-drones to pass along; it seemed safe enough from eavesdropping. The control end was here, behind an access panel in the kitchen; for now, Tom preferred to maintain his merchant-trader cover and stay outside, pretending to eat alone, while two agents among the kitchen staff listened carefully.

By now, in any case, Tyentro and Velsivith would be out of contact.

Tyentro's lieutenant, Stilvan, was manning the comms at the other end. He would have watched them using cling-gloves and slippers—formed of gekkomere, covered with fine, invisible fractal hairs, like arachnargoi tendril pads—to crawl along the outside of the catenary walkways, until they reached workers' entrances (as revealed by Yano) and slipped inside the former Seer's headquarters: the great chamber which was now the mausoleum holding his remains, suspended above a dark abyss which seemed to fall away forever.

At the restaurant's far end, the waiter caught Tom's gaze and blinked slowly, three times.

They're inside.

And then the waiting.

Unpredictable, this phase, but there was that Clausewitzian principle related to the role of chance in war—which normally brought a grim smile to Tom's face, but not this time. He would count this mission a success if all his agents, and Velsivith, returned alive.

I'd make a poor general.

For a former revolutionary, it was a strange thought. A fragment of half-formed poetry came to mind—and it had been a while since he had written anything—but he pushed it gently to the back of his mind, letting his subconscious daemons nurture the idea before trying to pull it forwards into the limiting constraints of language.

Then the waiter, having brought another table's main course, threw a white towel over his left shoulder as he headed back towards the kitchen, and Tom slowly put down his tine-spoon, swallowing hard.

It was the signal he had been hoping not to receive.

There were skaters below, using smooth-boots as they glided through intricate dance steps: a hundred people in approximate coordination, while a makeshift band played music, and onlookers laughed—without malice—if anyone slipped or fell. For they were amateurs all, and this was supposed to be a celebration.

But Tom was a merchant-trader, too grand for mixing with the commoners, and his face twisted at the aftertaste of his food as he stood self-importantly, and strode with a determined glare towards the restaurant's rear.

"I've got a complaint to make."

Play-acting came naturally, but it was real fear which thickened his voice as he stepped through the membrane, and let his complaint die away.

Inside, they ushered him straight through to a dark grimy service tunnel, where he crouched down beside a narrow-faced man who sat on an upturned box, manipulating a holopad.

"I don't know." The agent shook his head. "There was graser fire, then we lost contact."

"Chaos." Tom closed his eyes.

"I think . . . Stilvan was hit."

"Hazard and perdition." Tom spat the curse. "I should've been with them."

After a moment: "Perhaps you should go back inside, my Lord."

"No. I'm staying here."

The waiting now was worse.

The access panel opened, and light from the kitchen flooded in, along with the tail end of an argument: ". . . the sorbet this way. Then serve across the person's *right* shoulder. Got it?"

There was a mumbled reply, lost as the head waiter poked his head into the tunnel and said: "The intelligence forces have a guest. Not here, I mean, but at their HQ. Tortured and eventually turned, someone from another network. I can't believe they're discussing it openly."

"Who is?"

"Officers." He grimaced. "At table seven."

"What else?" Tom checked the holopad: still no contact. "Any hint of this man's identity?"

"Not a man. Someone called Lihru."

The ground seemed to shift beneath Tom's feet.

Coincidence?

Could it be some cruel joke of arbitrary Destiny that the woman he and Jay had betrayed, had sent into a compromised network and almost certain capture, had been transferred from distant Revandi into the realm where Tom was undercover? And on this particular day.

She could certainly identify him.

And maybe, by now, that would give her a fierce joy, a satisfaction that her tortured pain might be shared by those who had wished it upon her.

"Wait a minute . . ."

In the kitchen, a disturbance.

"Quick! They're here . . ."

They came along the dark tunnel: Velsivith limping, Tyentro with his tunic dark-stained and torn.

"We gave them the slip, my—"

At that moment the spit of graser fire sounded from the corridor outside, and Tyentro's face paled. Everyone in the kitchen froze in place.

We're blown to Chaos.

It was a prime tenet: not to keep a rendezvous with local control unless the locale was clear. Tyentro had broken a basic rule, but that was not his main concern.

"*Rilka*," he whispered.

It was obvious that she was dead or captured. And that Tyentro had feelings for her which Tom had not known about.

Perdition . . .

She was not supposed to be part of Stilvan's cover team, and a bitter curse rose to Tom's lips. But he stilled it: if they survived, guilt would be Tyentro's punishment.

"Quick." One of the waiters gestured towards the access panel. "Inside."

There were three ways out: to the corridor, where graser fire spat and hissed once more; to the narrow maint-shaft which looked like a trap to Tom; and the membrane which led back out into the dining area.

"No," he said. "This way."

And, with a bitter smile:

"Is anybody hungry?"

Velsivith and Tyentro sat down with Tom at his table. They had no choice: the exit-membrane was flanked now by armed troops. Their dress uniform—of scarlet and silver, with white capes and gauntlets, polished sabres at their hips, absurdly plumed helms—failed to conceal the functional grasers or their steady predators' gazes as they scanned the diners.

The whole place is a trap.

Down below, on the broadway beneath the balcony, a gentle gavotte was playing, and commonfolk were dancing its steps with none of the intricate irony-laden choreography of Lords and Ladies, but with a more robust enjoyment. One pretty girl glanced upwards—copper curls beneath a scarlet scarf—then whirled away, caught in the dance.

Am I going to die here?

"There's a substance," murmured Velsivith, "on which the Seer's power depended. It was part of—"

But one soldier's gaze had lingered on Tyentro a half-second too long, and now his lips were moving silently. Communicating with an officer.

The trap slammed shut.

"We've had it." Velsivith had seen it too. He rose from the table in one smooth movement, a graser pistol in each hand. "Tom, get away!"

And fired.

Chaos!

There was a tiny moment when it was possible to see what was happening: Velsivith's aim swept across the officers' table, ravening beam cutting through torsos and necks, while his other hand fired towards the soldiers near the door.

Then Tom was ducking as webs of graser fire cracked and spat, burning the air.

Yells and screams accompanied his elbow-and-knees crawl across the floor.

"*Here* . . ." Tyentro tossed a crystal in Tom's direction, then pulled his tunic open to withdraw . . . something.

Blue glow.

A strange peacefulness in the midst of chaos and death. It shone, sapphire then electric-blue, and Tyentro's face was demonic in the shadows it cast.

Sapphire blue . . .

The sphere was small, palm-sized, and Tyentro rolled it across the floor to Tom. He grabbed it. The small globe was neither warm nor cold, yet its touch both burned and numbed Tom's hand.

A sudden vision racked him—of *once-bloody gobbets in their containers, inert upon filter pads, while electric fluid slowly dripped through to the collectors*—and he shook his head to clear it.

"The Seer's body?" Tom mouthed the question, but Tyentro understood.

He nodded, thin-lipped. Whatever he had hoped to find in the mausoleum, that had not been it.

Extracted from the Seer's corpse?

Time was moving slowly. The music, from below the balcony, was only now beginning to die away as the revellers realized that something was happening.

Slowly . . .

Then Tyentro rose, spinning, and his graser was out, beam cutting a wide swathe, and soldiers fell before lancing light impaled Tyentro and he dropped, inert, splayed across the tabletop.

Dead.

Tom clutched the glowing sphere and held it to his chest, wondering if it was worth the cost of blood.

When it seemed that all graser fire had ceased, the diners—most of them frozen in place, hunched forward on their chairs—slowly, shakily, returned to movement. They stood, staggered, trying not to look at

Tyentro's or Velsivith's ripped bodies whose glistening intestines had spilled forth, or the dead soldiers' blasted remains, or the wounded man who softly mewled, clutching his torso, his leg graser-torn, blackened, twisted half off.

In the confusion, Tom pulled his cloak around himself, concealing the small glowing sphere. He began to make his way among the panicking, sobbing diners, towards the exit.

"That one."

Officer's voice.

For a moment Tom thought he might make it, but then three of the soldiers in dress uniform—helm-plumes gone awry, sabres missing and tunics torn, but grasers in their hands—blocked the exit and one of them looked straight at Tom, hand rising—

"Yes, him."

They've got me.

Peripheral vision, as Tom spun behind a knot of stumbling civilians, showed him more soldiers coming from the kitchens, and he knew that every exit was blocked.

It glowed, eerie and wondrous, blue and strange.

Tom judged the throw carefully: as it arced high, the soldiers' gazes tracked its trajectory while Tom was already moving fast. There was a table in his way but one of the chairs was empty and he used it as a springboard—*jump*—then two sprinting paces across the tabletop—*careful*—and a leap over a rotund man's shoulder, and then the acceleration.

Graser fire.

Emerald beam splitting the air.

Balustrade, and Tom's palm hit just right, and then he was over.

The Academy called it situational gymnastics, and they learned to do it without rehearsal. The sheer drop would have broken his legs—ultimately fatal, in this place—but Tom used the balcony's external carvings, its baroque stone swelling fruit and heraldic symbols, as the pivot points for a series of swings and vaults, and then the final drop and roll.

Suicide. The soldiers are everywhere.

The crowd was a swirling mass of confused revellers, and most people would not have seen him as he hit the flagstones, rolling. He was almost to his feet when sapphire-blue shone at his vision's edge and he threw himself forwards to make the catch.

But there were too many people and something, someone, tripped him and his fingertips made contact but he was already falling.

No!

He tried to hug the sphere to himself but it was too late and there was a pointless crack as it smashed beneath him, and momentary despair flooded inside. Knowing that he had failed those who had died.

Whatever the secret of the Seer's power—more than he had expected them to acquire: the infocrystal was surely the scanlog which had been Tyentro's objective—Tom had just broken it beyond retrieval in a moment's clumsiness the Academy instructors would have deplored.

Did they die for this?

But he would be joining them soon—

A wordless agony.

It burns.

Crawling, trying to move.

And then he stopped, as his body turned to ice.

What's happening to me?

Shivering . . .

He was freezing now.

There was a crackling in the air, a shaking in the ground. Yet the half-seen crowd just stood there, staring at him. Cold flames flickered blue, were gone.

Concussion?

Come on.

Then he was on his feet again.

Get moving.

Stumbling . . .

People, tunics and surcoats—dark and pastel, plain and fantastically patterned—and a blur of faces. A glance back.

Broken shards upon the flagstones, obscured now by the shifting crowd.

Scarlet banners, hanging.

Distant martial music: a parade, and the promise of a thousand troops and militia, the impossibility of escape. An advance guard, perhaps a hundred soldiers, at the crowd's edge, already scanning, calling the officers above, and searching for the figure which had dropped from the balcony and into the crowd.

But in that glance . . .

Shards on the flagstones, yet nothing more. Not a single drop which might have glowed electric blue.

It's in me.

Extracted with care, over a period perhaps of two Standard Years. Distilled with exquisite delicacy from the Seer's decomposing corpse. That sapphire fluid, once subsumed within the Seer's entire being, was gone, absorbed.

Inside me . . .

A shudder of revulsion passed through Tom.

Mother . . .

He remembered the day she died, having briefly come back to life, in her crystal sarcophagus in the Oracle's home. Blue fluid, fluorescing with internal light, had spilled from her mouth and ears, pooled inside the sarcophagus as she . . .

What's it doing to me?

The memory faded, but all around him the world blurred, growing double.

Soldiers. Get away.

He stumbled through the crowd, aware of half-glimpsed uniforms, the glint of weapons.

Hurry . . .

But something strange was happening.

This was the theory:

In the context against which time flowed—a motion in meta-time—a strange splitting might occur. The interaction between any cause and effect is bidirectional in time, like a handshaking protocol of reinforcing waves.

And any wave can be refracted.

When Tom had changed the Oracle's perceived future, it had been (it seemed) a programming trick. It took mu-space processors to generate an *imagined* reality, and make that the future which the Oracle perceived.

A swap-over: everything the Oracle had predicted, had seen in his personal future beyond a certain moment in time, was an illusion of Tom's creation. The Oracle's real future was very different in length and in quality: short and brutal, ending on the point of Tom's blade.

And yet . . .

An unexpected blue fire, a barrier igniting the air, had tried to prevent the process—as though reality itself resisted the incursion. And then, that hallucinatory episode . . .

Exiting the Oracle's terraformer floating high in Nulapeiron's sky, Tom seemed to see *himself*, leaping suicidally to his death.

It was hard to say when the split occurred.

There was the pushing and shoving—*get out of here*—forcing a way through the crowd, and suddenly the empty coolness of a dank tunnel. Momentary respite: but a hundred soldiers were in immediate pursuit, and there were thousands more behind them; already they would be closing in from all directions, from above and below.

But in the ephemeral peace of the moment, he turned to his left to face . . .

He turned to his right and saw . . .

Not alone.

It was Fate, and it was beyond surprise: the features which were so familiar and yet so startling, seen every day in a mirrorfield. Yet neither was surprised: it was an implacable phenomenon, so unexpected it struck beyond their capacity to absorb shock.

There was Tom Corcorigan—

Brother . . .

—and there was Tom Corcorigan.

And the shared recognition in their eyes, that death was almost upon them. Each soldier would want to be the first to drop the escaped terrorist; there would be no mercy, no taking of prisoners.

Does sapphire blood run in my veins? In ours?

Prisoner, singular. They were looking for *one* person.

Laughter, conjoined, identical in pitch, dying fast.

"You should go."

A pause, a shake of the head: "I'm nearest to the door. You go on ahead."

For a moment, each Tom Corcorigan regarded the other: the more-than-twin, sharing not love but mutual self-knowledge.

"I'm not suicidal, so neither are you."

"It's random chance"—with an ironic smile which brought forth its reflection on the other Tom—"that you're closer, by one pace, to escape. Divergence, my brother."

"The blue stuff—"

"Needs investigation, by Avernon."

"We can both—"

A shake of the familiar head. "No, we can't."

They clasped forearms, then he made the hardest decision of all and turned to run, while he knelt and faced the door.

He ran.

He stayed.

He stretched lightly, loosened limbs, controlled his breathing. Regarded the stone tunnel, dank and unlovely—and saw a tiny golden spider apparently in mid-air. Its web, invisible, suspended it near a splotch of pale, grey-green colour on the wall: a patch of lichen. It was life, spreading everywhere, even in these surroundings.

And it was somehow fitting, somehow appropriate, that the end should come in such a place.

Elva. I would have liked to see you again.

But in a sense, he would.

He was sure of that.

Running, with the tears unnoticed upon his cheeks, shutting down his thoughts by act of will, focused now on sheer survival.

Take them with you.

The Enemy's forces would be upon him soon.

Take them, my brother.

Thighs pumping as he ran.

Take out as many as you can.

53

NULAPEIRON AD 3422

It is there: the untouched potential for every long-term fighter to transcend, to achieve that graceful state beyond the immediate, messy, bloody business of combat, to reach a place where the flow and the spirit are all that matter.

He fought.

As they spilled into the corridor, Tom leaped from a hiding place halfway up the wall, knocking a graser rifle aside with a descending crescent kick as his elbow hooked into the soldier's neck, pinpointing the carotid, and even as the man fell Tom used him as a stepping stone, knee to throat and fingertips to eyes, taking out two more before they even realized he was upon them.

It was ferocious and it was unexpected, and they could not deal with him at this range.

He kicked, used a palm-strike—aiming for a chin, missed, using a knee and whipping the hand back as a hammer fist and this time he got it but pain exploded in the back of his head.

Then he let loose his animal spirit, the ravening predator inside us all, and blood-lust curtained his vision as he kicked, swept a man's legs from under him, grabbed a weapon-bearing hand and twisted, breaking fingers—moving, always moving, confusing his enemies— and stamped upon the fallen soldier, a sharp crack audible even amid the Chaos.

Faster.

Smoother . . .

Graser beam, and it scorched his shoulder but the pain was *nothing* and he took his revenge, kicking another man into the weapon's path—shocked features, drained of blood: the soldier killing his own comrade-in-arms—but there was no chance to follow up as others were upon him.

Untrained men would have fallen back but they were used to working as a team, to strive for their comrades' welfare above their own, and Tom used that to his advantage, taking out those closest to him where they could not bring weapons to bear.

But their numbers—

Transcend.

Fight faster.

He was a blur, he was violence incarnate, and he danced among them like a demon, dispensing death and pain, and he was flooded with a joy such as he had never known, that no civilized being should experience.

Elva!

Father's blocky hands, graser tool, molten metal spitting as he drew the stallion's form out of a featureless metal brick. Mother's cupric tresses, her dreamy smiles. Golden hair and creamy skin, and Sylvana's blue eyes regarding him in Lord Velond's classroom, as the joys of logosophy blossomed at last. The simple shore and the tranquil cavern sea, and the Pavilion School where for a while he taught and knew some peace.

And Elva.

Fluid on his hand, hot blood and worse, and the bodies were one Chaotic group-mass of limbs and torsos, a vast target, and he smashed and impaled and twisted in his death-dance and then the bodies close to him were fallen and there was no time left to reach the soldiers who knelt at the rear and the mirror transmission-faces of their graser rifles shone like rainbows, shimmering spectra of diffracted colours, blue the colour of the homeworld's skies and red as of the dark blood which runs through us all, a vast extended river passed on and ever on which flows along the mainstreams and into the tiniest tributaries of human history, billions and eventually trillions of actual physical existing feeling thinking individual people—real warm smelly wonderful healthy dirty loving hating depressed and disappointed with joy-moments and the high transcendence and the thousand hidden fears and petty details, the colour and the texture of those curtains and the taste of today's breakfast and floating dust which catches the light and another's touch and the countless sensations too easy to overlook which form a universe for every human and every being alone along that tiny capillary flow of history until suddenly one day with unforeseen abruptness ends.

And nothing.

Running.
    Nothing in his mind but a prayer of hate, an oath which spreading virus-like was imprinting itself within his molecular structure, rewriting every cell, as the animal-organism simply ran for life.
    Empty tunnel after empty tunnel, as though none would dare oppose him.
    I will kill them.
    Running.
    My brother . . .
    Running harder.
    For you—
    Harder.
    —I will kill them all.

54
NULAPEIRON AD 3422

It took forty-two days to reach the wild zones.

At the second tenday's start, he finally left Grand'aume territory, carefully picking his way through jumbled broken tunnels—a battleground of two SY before, still shattered but without the stink—to avoid the border patrols.

In Khitaliaq, the atmosphere was different; though the Blight's forces were still everywhere, the occupation rested more easily upon the local inhabitants.

Because, he realized after a while, *they offered no resistance to the takeover.*

If there were deportations, he did not spot any, and he did not dare to ask. Though he had an emergency cover-ID, his description alone might throw up an alert in even a routine security check.

There was a store, on the realm's outskirts, where he tried to buy some food.

"I'm sorry." An expressive shrug of the shopkeeper's shoulders. "No cred-spindles accepted. Not since the . . . you know. Only scrip."

Which, as a non-citizen, Tom did not possess.

"I see."

But, as Tom was leaving, the shopkeeper stopped him, and handed over a small bundle: baked rolls and a small bottle, wrapped in cloth. Tom bowed, expressing thanks beyond words.

Avoiding patrols, he slept in deserted corridors, wrapped in a thin cloak taken from a storage bin—at an almshouse, intended for the needy—and curled up on cold stone. Sometimes, older folk took him in, fed him, let him sleep on a mat or a spare cot; always, he left silently before dawnshift, sans farewell.

If there was an organized resistance here to the Blight's occupation, Tom had no way of contacting it.

A large woman, smiling at his accent, gave him freshly made broth. But she left him, saying she had a neighbour to visit, and something about her expression—a hint of determined scowl, quickly hidden—alerted him.

He slipped away as soon as she was gone, regretting the loss of warmth and comfort, but afraid that soldiers would soon be descending upon her spotlessly clean chambers.

There were patrols, but the border into interstitial territory was extended—with thousands of tunnels and caverns to cover—and the place Tom chose had been another battleground.

Quiet now, air redolent of old slaughter, the cries of dying men and women embedded in the shattered stone, the blackened ceilings and the riven floors, though their bodies had long since been hauled away by grieving civilians: family members reclaiming their dead.

He moved through the caverns, silent and grim, as though he were a ghost himself.

It was the monks who saved him.

Am I forgiven?

There were times, as he ran, that it seemed he was not alone: that orange-robed spirits ran alongside in soundless encouragement. It was their zentropic drugs, not designed for someone like Tom, which had caused his psychotic breakdown.

Tom ran on, disbelieving.

The sounds of monks collapsing, perhaps dying.

But they saved him, nonetheless, for the training was deep, part of his body now: a remembered discipline of ultra-distance runs with very little food. The physical organism reverted to that state, and his spirit kept him going when medically his body should have failed.

And the need to revenge the other Tom Corcorigan's death.

Kill them all . . .

For his brother's sake.

It was in the fifth tenday that he reached the wild zones. After that, he lost track: it might have been two days, it might have been twenty, thirty—he fed on wild fungi, which sometimes brought lurid dreams even as he ran—before he saw, beyond a raw, unfinished cavern, the smooth marble of a boulevard, the polished copper archway and the glistening protective membrane, and the welcome faces of startled guards.

Help me.

He tried to speak the words aloud but nothing came out, just gasping, then blackness crashed in as the floor rose up to meet him, hands catching him at the last moment before the world dwindled, slipped away into the distance, and left him for an extended, welcome time.

55

BETA DRACONIS III
AD 2142-2143

<<Ro's Story>>

[18]

She did not find revenge that first night.

Could Luís's killer have escaped, travelled in its mu-space vessel back to Terra? But that would make her quest a futile one, and she could not accept that. For all she knew, Zoë had also died, her broken corpse stretched out in that ruined lab in XenoMir, while the other Zajinet, the ambassador, looked helplessly on.

The renegade had a lot to answer for.

In Watcher's Bones, day and night were artificial periods of light and darkness: the irregular world outside maintained its own non-rhythms where flickering overlays failed to conceal the unsettling core reality. Though the odd-shaped planet's centre of gravity followed an elliptical orbit, the world itself tumbled chaotically through the other degrees of freedom.

Ro's "nightly" excursions were surreal: sometimes taking place beneath a sky of blazing white, though other realities seemed to whisper of gentler worlds, before disappearing. At other times, the night sky was a black dome in which the stars' constellations occasionally flickered into new patterns: a phenomenon she had not reported and could not explain. She wondered if she was becoming attuned to the impossible contradictions of this place.

Her own routine became fixed. Inspired by an account of life in Spain two centuries before, she slept twice a day, four hours at a time, using solo study-time for sleep. She would awaken late, take her copper shaft and her palm disk, and hunt for resonance traces of the Zajinet who was responsible for Luís's death.

No-one looked for the missing recognition disk; the disappearance of the lab bench accounted for everything.

In the weeks which followed, she came to suspect, then grow certain, that she was not the only one to leave the human settlement when everyone was supposed to be asleep. One night, finally, she tracked two human figures beneath a quasi night sky banded with violet aurorae. Then she caught sight of their faces, just for a moment, as they turned beneath an archway of white light and entered the ever-shifting maze of the Zajinets' city.

After a while, into the third month (now February, back on Terra, had there been a way of returning there) of nocturnal explorations, her once-frequent migraines began to lessen, and finally to stop altogether. Sometimes it frightened her, that the flickering van Gogh surroundings should no longer upset her perceptions.

And, inside Watcher's Bones when the humans there were gathered, playing out their little social vignettes as though to shut out the vast strangeness which surrounded their insignificant enclave, she watched Anita and Oron, listened to their near-evangelical interpretations of Zajinet sociology, and wondered where they went, in an alien city, at the dead of night.

There was an overweight biologist called Bruce, who led a group of co-workers through daily t'ai-chi, at whom Ro privately laughed till the day he slapped her lightly and sent her spinning across the room. Then she buckled down, learning the hidden complexities of the art with a rapidity which dismayed—patience being a virtue—her new teacher.

In her room, she rigged punchbags and horizontal bars, practised kickboxing and Irish kempo, aikido footwork and pentjak silat tactics: analysing, comparing, modifying.

Synthesizing.

She did not know why.

But she knew it was something she had to do.

"I'm going to retire," said Fluffy Matheson over the usual drinks, "when we get back to Earth."

"Terra." Ro smiled.

"I've got something to show you."

For once, there was a tremble in his voice, and Ro made no joke. "What is it?"

Later, she minimized her display and said:

"You made me cry, you bastard."

Matheson swallowed, all facades slipping away. "Is it good enough?"

"I'm no writer." She killed the display. "But I think it's wonderful." She could see, in the story, where some of the characters had come from. But his *Settlements & Separations: An Embassy Tale* was all his own, and it was funny as well as sad. "Go for it."

He made no reply as she left the room, quietly.

Copper arc.

Matheson's finding himself.

Stab, advance, retreat.

But what about me?

Circle, redirect, and strike.

Who is Ro McNamara?

Shining thrust.

Who am I, really?

"Three weeks left." Lila practically sang the words, as they stepped into the communal shower. "I can't wait to see a real sky again."

Ro almost slipped, but caught her balance.

"What do you mean?" She raised her voice above the hissing, the clouds of steam.

"Relief," said Lila, but she was not talking about the shower. "The ship arrives in twenty-one days and seventeen hours. Not that I'm counting."

"Oh, right." And Ro laughed, but not wholeheartedly.

Three weeks to go.

Nervous as kittens on moving day, the humans moved about their settlement, checking crates in the corridors, keeping watch (lest they disappear) on the most valuable items, and making handover preparations for their replacements.

No-one was staying for a second tour.

It was the final night, and Ro's final chance, when the metallic tubular tunnels dimmed. She had thought it would be hard to slip out, but in fact the muddle of crates and unpacked belongings made it all the easier to sneak through the protective membrane.

Easier, too, to follow the two figures moving through the glaring whiteness outside. Between them, they held a case which was not big, but too heavy for them to carry easily.

A leaving present for your xeno friends?

There was bio-research, including Bruce's analysis of samples he had taken from Ro, which had been held in a case like that; Ro had seen Bruce's assistants put it at the centre of their team's pile of crates.

This better not be anything to do with me.

But she was the one who had been brought here, yet not killed.

Whose roommate had been murdered. And Luís—even if his death had been unintentional, if it were anti-xeno terrorists and not the Zajinet who had attacked the UNSA airbase, still it had been the renegade who sparked off the most recent wave of anti-xeno sentiment.

Patterns, falling into place.

Even as she followed through the blazing city, shadow buildings flicking into existence and disappearing, momentary flashes of green—solid sheets of it—decorating the sky, she saw the influence of opposing forces back on Terra. More than individuals? Two factions of Zajinets, or something more complex?

Yes: *two factions* among the Zajinets.

For every individual in this alien place was perpetually in two minds—if not two hundred minds—on any matter you could think of.

Why me?

The question burned through her mind, a counterpoint to the surreal slipping and sliding of artefacts and sky, of Zajinets' bulky external forms gliding through the chaos, the half-glimpsed images of other worlds or times or dreams, whichever they might be.

Flowers of blood, ribbons of ink.

That was the sky which flowed overhead. Her footsteps, sounding back from the vermilion metal path running through the confusion, occasionally clanged, sometimes faded to disconcerting silence.

Her membrane-thin env-suit served only to detoxify the atmosphere; it could not hold back the madness of this place.

But, however much reality flickered, she kept Anita and Oron in sight. They were beginning to struggle with the case's weight.

Walking amid waist-high steel grass, being careful, Ro stopped suddenly. Crystal mosaics, with tessellae of a thousand hues, sang in the warm/cold pulsing air.

What if they want to remove the proof?

The mu-space ship was due—but if they faked a natural disaster, killing everybody, they could remove all traces of Ro's presence. And that would keep the Zajinets' mu-space travel abilities a secret.

Surely not. Surely no-one could be that insane.

Cobalt spheres, which might have been floating liquid, coagulated in the now-darkening air like frozen raindrops.

Ro shifted her long copper rod from her right hand to her left, and narrowed the distance to Anita and Oron. Then the disk in her glove's palm pulsed.

Found you.

Luís's killer was at hand.

She shrank back as a Zajinet passed. It might have been muttering threats:

<< ... ephemeral segment ... >>

<< ... most linear shard ... >>

<< ... blind and dark-burrowing ... >>

<< ... begone ... >>

Then, as she moved back onto the metal pavement, Anita and Oron slipped out of sight. But they no longer mattered, now that the disk was resonating with the target signature.

Very close now.

Following the trace, Ro slipped inside a grey moving structure, something like a Roman villa formed of lead, and at its centre two partially uncloaked Zajinets—fiery tracery blazing as their stone-like exteriors came apart, then coalesced once more—hovered, with the air between them beginning to burn.

Like awed children, Anita and Oron sat off to one side, watching.

"No, you can't—"

Anita's voice, but Ro was already moving.

For you, Luís.

Were they mating?

Air crackling now, as she moved closer. The Zajinets glowed, and there was a current of some sort in the air.

"Not now! They're re-forming." Anita was on her feet, hands out-stretched as though to push back Ro.

"It's a new being!" Oron was struggling to get up. "You don't know—"

A rebirth? A metamorphosis? Many beings change radically, make transitions from one life-stage to another . . .

Should that remove the guilt?

Closer.

Then the external forms came apart, and she was in a blizzard of whirling stones, every one flying with deadly momentum, and she squinted against the blazing inner forms as she moved, blending and avoiding, working by instinct—*irimi*: seeking the hurricane's centre, the eye of the storm—and then she was in the midst of blazing wave-forms, spiking and burning and glowing with reinforced energies.

Patterns.

Needing to make sense of . . .

She recognized the second Zajinet now. It was the renegade's accuser, the one which had gone up against it in the trial. But why—?

There. The pattern flicked into view, a visual paradox resolved—*now*—then she took her chance and struck.

Light flowed like liquid flames.

For Luís.

Her hands burned and she cried out, dropping the copper shaft, but a blackness was already rippling across the Zajinet's blue/red fire.

Done it.

Then they were two distinct forms again, stones snapping back into protective body-form, and they dropped to the floor and remained still, two elephantine sculpture-piles built of charred pebbles and boulders.

"Oh, Ro. What have you done?"

<<MODULE ENDS>>

56
NULAPEIRON AD 3422

Four more tendays he spent in a coma, floating in an autodoc's womb, flooded with nutrients and tranquillizers, muscles contracting against viscous fluid—stimulated involuntarily—in an effort to rebuild them.

Slowly, slowly, mind and body knitted together.

Healed . . .

In the early days of his waking convalescence, therapists and counsellors tried to work with the deeper wounds, until he raged at them and they were made—under Corduven's direct orders, Tom later learned—to leave him in uneasy peace.

Whatever Tom was becoming, or had become—he knew the darkness in his own spirit—it was nourished on hatred. And he wanted nothing more than to be a weapon, directed by Corduven to wherever it would do most damage to the hated Enemy's cause.

But it would be nearly year's end before they sent him out again.

The day after his final debriefing, he had dinner with Sylvana. The conversation was of intelligence matters: she was part of Corduven's strategy team, most of whom considered Tom's mission a striking success, despite the human cost.

He wondered how Velsivith's widow was coping.

Sylvana seemed easy in Tom's company. But at the meal's end, when he leaned forward to chastely kiss her cheek in farewell, she flinched.

That told him everything he needed to know about their relationship.

"Take care, my Lady."

He watched her walk away, along a rose-pink marble gallery, followed by a small retinue of servitors clad in ivory and black. They were colours he himself had worn for too many years.

At the new, relocated Academy, he trained decryption teams, helped design idiom-level eavesdropping AIs (Turing-capable and therefore illegal, but this was wartime), brainstormed organizational cell structures and messaging paths for penetration agents sent in to liaise with partisan resistance fighters.

And he trained hard, waiting for the day they would send him back into the field.

But his debriefing had been very thorough, and not all of it had been conducted while he was conscious. There were forces at work on his behalf, which he was not aware of until the night a clap sounded from outside his modest quarters, and when he waved open the membrane-door it was Adam Gervicort, his former servitor now in military uniform, who was standing in the corridor outside.

"Adam? What are you doing here? It's good to—"

But Adam sketched a bow, then quickly handed over a crystal.

"It's from High Command, sir. Tom. From Brigadier-General d'Ovraison himself."

Tom had scarcely seen Corduven since his return.

"Wants to see me now, does he?"

"Yes, sir."

Looking back at his crystal-strewn desk: "Well, I could—"

"I was told to say, it concerns a certain security chief. She's been located, alive and well."

Elva!

The world whirled all around him, and he had to grab at the doorjamb for support.

Elva's alive, and they've found her.

57

BETA DRACONIS III AD 2143

<<Ro's Story>>

[19]

Gritty-eyed, unable to sleep, they gathered in the main conference room: a bellied-out section of bluish tubular corridor. There was a ragged energy in the air, the unspoken communal thought keeping them awake: *We're going home.*

Lila was perched on a crate, holding the comms pad. Not long now.

Ro pushed her way through. "Lila, you're missing two people."

"I know." Anger darkened Lila's eyes, and she flicked back her hair—now lustrous green, and long—from her face. "Anita and Oron."

"They're staying in the city, they said. For good."

"They'll need—"

But just then the comms pad squawked into life.

"Pilot Vaachs to Diplomatic Settlement BD3. Confirming rendezvous as scheduled."

There were cheers as Lila answered, "That's terrific, Pilot. Our thanks. There will be twenty people boarding, with this cargo." She appended the manifest, sent it with a gesture. "We're leaving two people behind. Gone native."

"That doesn't sound like a good idea, BD3. Though I'm not sure about your arithmetic. Doesn't that leave nineteen personnel?"

"You know where they are?" Lila whispered. "Oron and Anita?"

Ro nodded.

"Well, then." She spoke into the comms pad. "Our replacements will have to dig them out. And there are twenty departing: this is not a mistake."

"Negative on the stay-behinds, BD3. There are no replacements. This is a full evacuation, as per your regulation X-nineteen. Orders file appended."

"Shit." Lila put down the pad, and looked around the room. "Any volunteers for an arrest party? We have two assholes to collect."

Ro led the way, with a sense of fatalistic acceptance: she would pay the price for her revenge. The others in the party, experienced though they were, had to concentrate, connected to Ro by smartrope and hanging on whenever the flickering overlays—white sky replaced by corn-yellow and blue stippling, smeared blood-red, then white once more—grew too surreal.

Anita and Orun, env-suited, came surprisingly easily. It was not just the news that all humans were being evacuated; they were subdued, and Ro sensed that the Zajinets blamed them in some way for what had happened. But the gazes they turned on Ro were liquid with dark malevolence.

"She damaged him irreparably," Anita said. "The new union, the remake of a being, and she spoiled everything."

"Your Zajinets"—Ro's voice was taut with bitterness—"are responsible for dozens of deaths on Terra. Why do you think we're being evacuated?"

"You—"

"No." Lila brandished a wrist-graser Ro had not seen before. "Shut up, everyone. Recriminations later."

"But—"

"Let's just get out of here alive."

So I didn't kill it.

She had aimed, with her mathematical intuition, to destroy only one pattern-within-patterns: one group personality, among the many, the supergroup, which comprised each Zajinet. But at a time when it was—mating? reproducing? reincarnating?—somehow re-forming itself, in conjunction with the other, its former accuser.

It made no sense.

But she had effectively lobotomized the one responsible for Luís's death. For Anne-Louise.

They hurried through the shifting streets, observed by hovering Zajinets who offered no greeting, but made no move to stop them.

Departure.

A wide space had been cleared before the twisted silver-blue tubes of the settlement, of Watcher's Bones, and the cargo was piled up ready to go. The gathered humans watched as autoshuttles drifted down in triangular formation from the dark rippling sky.

Cargocrabs loaded crates, while the people—one group led by Lila, the other by Bruce's imposing bulk—lined up for the two shuttles whose holds were made over as passenger cabins: lined with grey carpeting, filled with sleep-couches for the mu-space voyage.

"OK, everyone. Let's go home."

They were silent as they climbed aboard, casting glances back towards the shifting, changing cityscape, noting the absence of any formal deputation. No farewells; no replacements to be greeted.

Terrans were no longer welcome here.

She watched the others lie back. Fluffy Matheson winked at her, then placed his delta-band on his forehead and slid into immediate sleep. All around her, people were closing their eyes, relaxing.

But Lila and the slightly built but hard-looking Jared were watching Ro, and both of them were armed.

"See you on Terra," said Ro.

She lay back, thinking: *Twenty minutes. Remember.*

And slept.

And dreamed.

Of liquid golden space, of black spongiform stars embedded in infinite amber, with crimson nebulae, like streamers of blood, here and there amid the vastness.

Then, after twenty minutes (as humans reckon the passage of linear time) she awoke, and found what she had deeply known all along.

The dream was real.

There was something trance-like in the way she drifted through the shuttle, past Matheson's and Lila's and Jared's sleeping forms. Golden space seemed to overlay everything, as though she swam in a fractal sea, while the shuttle's rectilinear outlines seemed faded, a little transparent, and softer to the touch.

But the door mechanism worked, and it rose up, revealing the great cargo hold beyond.

Amber warmth pouring out to the infinite beyond.

It was a siren-song and she ignored it, concentrating on her purpose so that she did not lose herself in beauty.

Her hand, as she waved it before her face, seemed to replicate itself in series, until she held it still and there was only one hand, and she was herself once more. A small private joke: her stay among the Zajinets, her enemies, had helped to prepare her for this.

But why were they her enemies?

Golden space.

I'm home.

It was a feeling which sank down to the very heart of her.

This is where I belong.

And was this the reason behind everything? Was she, the first human born in mu-space, the first to feel truly at home here?

Was it me they were trying to kill?

But there were two Zajinet factions involved. Perhaps the one which had taken her here had not been trying to murder her.

Have I hurt the wrong one?

Could it be that the renegade had taken her here to *save* her? That the official ambassador was behind Luís's death, and Anne-Louise's murder?

No . . .

Amber . . .

She made her way forward to a bulkhead, and sought the passageway which would lead her to the great ship's control cabin where the Pilot would be working, interfaced with the vessel's systems.

The woman was slender, naked, lying on her couch, and silver cables hung in graceful catenary curves, linking her physical being to the ship's AI core.

"Pilot Vaachs?" Ro stood uncertainly.

The Pilot's head turned, and reflections slid across the polished bus-cables plugged into her eye sockets.

"A normal human being"—her voice drifted, oddly attenuated—"would have been driven insane within seconds, awake in this continuum. I guess it identifies you."

"I don't—"

But the Pilot must have given some internal command, for the cabin grew transparent to the ship's surroundings, and golden paralight flooded the place, became part of the ship, flowed through Pilot and vessel alike.

Amber space, and stars of black.

It was a realm of wonder.

"You are Ro McNamara, daughter of Karyn, and some of us have waited for this day."

Outside, it stretched forever:

A sea of infinite beauty.

The place where her father had died.

<<MODULE ENDS>>

58

NULAPEIRON AD 3422

They were waiting for him in the briefing chamber: Corduven, standing with his hands clasped behind his back; and Sentinel, his cropped white hair making him look as ageless as ever, his thick arms folded. Tom had not seen Sentinel since his abortive recruitment attempt, in the Aurineate Grand'aume.

"You sent a courier for me, didn't you? I mean, back in the Grand'aume."

Sentinel nodded. His square face, impassive, gave nothing away.

"I apologize," said Tom. "I disregarded his warning. More than that. I attacked him. I thought he was robbing a young woman, beside a canal."

"I've read the reports."

"He committed suicide . . ."

At the time, the notion of suicide to avoid torture had been an unreal abstraction; that was before Tom's own experience in Velsivith's acidic cells.

Velsivith. Another death . . .

There was more Tom had to say, but it evaporated from his mind.

Behind Sentinel and Corduven a crystal desk floated; in front of them hung an intricate network diagram, a tangle of brightly coloured arcs linking explanatory tricons, depicting the Blight's disposition of forces in some far sector.

But that was not what caught Tom's eye.

Is it true?

It was tiny, the holoportrait suspended in mid-air, but her features were unmistakable.

"That is her," said Corduven. "Isn't it?"

Elva!

Tom could only nod. It was the moment which culminated five years of doubt-filled searching, but there was no way to express the yearning and frightened joy which burst like a fragrant storm through his veins and set his soul on fire.

Elva . . . You really are alive.

In the head and shoulders portrait, slowly rotating, she wore a grey uniform with scarlet flashes on the high tunic collar.

What was she now? An officer in the Blight's forces?

"She's infiltrated their command at a higher level"—Sentinel coughed, then clasped his blocky hands together—"than we've ever been able to."

"Where did you—" For a moment, weakness swept over Tom.

Corduven gestured, and a lev-stool detached itself from the wall, positioned itself behind Tom. He sat down.

"Thank you. I . . . ."

What could he say?

It was Sentinel who broke the silence, softly. "We tracked down her brother, Odom."

"I met him."

"Attended his wedding, yes." Sentinel smiled briefly. "We learned that. But what you didn't know was, Elva had a twin sister. Natural twins, not clones."

"But—"

"She never mentioned it. Of course. Because her sister Litha was already working deep undercover, for an organization called the Grey Shadows. You remember it?"

"I . . . No."

"In LudusVitae"—Sentinel looked at Corduven, and Tom wondered for a moment whether Sentinel's allegiance to the revolutionary movement had been all that it appeared—"we came across them once or twice, but they were only ever loosely allied. Sometimes our objectives coincided."

"So they've been around for a while."

"Whatever their original purpose," said Sentinel, "the Grey Shadows have been implacably against the Blight for as long as we have. Every now and then, one of our couriers might receive warning of a Dark Fire interception. Twice, captured agents of ours have been rescued from captivity, though always as part of some other operation against the occupying forces."

Elva. You had a sister.

It was obvious that their nervous systems had been quantum-entangled since an early age. And that it was Elva who had expected to die, when Litha committed suicide and her consciousness made the transition to Elva's body, displacing the original Elva identity—her thoughts and feelings and memories: her soul—in the process.

And had Elva, too, held back from expressing her feelings towards him, because she had expected oblivion to strike at any moment?

Perhaps she had both loved and hated her sister, knowing that Litha, if she found information of sufficient value, would be prepared to make that sacrifice without hesitation.

". . . funding from," Sentinel was saying. "But it's always been effective."

"I'm sorry." Tom tried to focus. "I missed that."

Corduven smiled.

"You haven't," he said, "asked the question I was expecting."

For a moment, Tom could not think what he meant. Then:

"Does that mean you know where she is?"

"It's deep in Blight territory. In Realm Buchanan—if we can still call it that, five SY after the Earl's execution. Really deep in the heart of—"

"You have to send me in."

Real fear took hold of him, that after finding out this much he would not be able to reach her. But Sentinel relented then, transforming the floating diagram into a holomap into which he pointed.

"In any other briefing, you have to understand, Elva Strelsthorm's whereabouts would not be first item on the agenda." He held up a placating hand. "What I mean is, there's a news item which may be of immense significance, given the pattern spread of the Blight's invasions. There are places it seems unable to manifest itself directly inside, but now . . ."

Tom looked at Corduven, wondering if he understood any of this. It made no—

"The Dark Fire," Sentinel said, "has taken the Collegium Perpetuum Delphinorum. One of the Collegium's three sites has fallen; the other two are at high risk."

He gestured, rotating the display.

"There, near the place where Oracles are made"—Sentinel spoke without regard for Corduven's feelings: without realizing the emotional significance of the place which had turned Corduven's brother into something both more and less than human—"lies a place which appears to be a death camp. We have no agents in place around there, so our details are sketchy."

Tom shook his head. "I don't—"

"Captain Strelsthorm is there."

"*In the death camp?*" Tom was half out of his seat.

"Not as a prisoner." Again, the placating hand gesture. "She's infiltrated their command structure in a way we've never achieved. Her cover name is Herla Hilsdottir, and she's safe enough for now."

At the heart of Blight territory, in a camp where who knew what atrocities were being carried out, at this moment.

Elva. You really are *alive.*

"We want you to—"

Tom stood up. "I'm going to get her out."

Reservation Gamma was a vast series of interlinked natural caverns, never before used, to anyone's knowledge, since the colonists' founding of Nulapeiron twelve centuries before.

But now it was an assault-training area, purchased at minimal cost from High Duke Frendino (in whose realm it was nominally located), sealed off by opaque smartfilm while the men and women inside faced their fears and drilled their reflexes. And the training casualties sometimes included life-threatening injuries; everyone knew that sooner or later trainees were going to die.

A guard saluted as Tom stepped through the membrane. Inside, a black-visored sergeant bowed.

The cavern was gone, or so it seemed.

Open sky—

A holo-sky, lemon-tinged and grey-clouded, replaced the cavern ceiling, and troops crawled across the broken ground, as though they were on the world's surface. But, even as Tom watched—standing there without flinching, while the training officers stared at him, obviously unable to believe his lack of reaction—five soldiers, in catatonic foetal positions, were carried by aides from the battlefield.

Those aides, like the training officers, wore polarizing smartfilters to block out the nonexistent sky: to them, the rock above them was as solid and reassuring as ever.

"How goes it?" asked Tom.

"Poorly, my Lord." The sergeant, face hidden behind his visor, shook his head. "Perhaps we should increase the—"

"No. *Decrease* the duration"—it was the way Tom had conditioned himself—"but increase the frequency."

"Yes, my Lord."

"They will acclimatize." Remembering: his long hard climb up the terraformer sphere, the Oracle's skyborne home, with murder in his heart. "Believe me, they will."

Next day, when he returned from his run, a message was waiting for him in his quarters: an invitation from Lady Sylvana.

Tom wiped the crystal, reinitializing it with a waved command, then tossed it into a communal storage bin on his way to the mobilization caves.

Extract from an internal report: *Beyond the Academy zone, where veterans are billeted awaiting their return to the front, discipline grows increasingly difficult to maintain.*

Tom saw what that meant in human terms as he passed a grim scene: two cargo-levs smashed into one pile of twisted junk, and a torn bloody corpse.

Platoons from two rival services had been involved. One of them stole the cargo-levs—from their rivals—then drove the two vehicles straight at each other, diving from the controls just before they hit.

If it had been only a matter of wrecked vehicles, the situation would have been little more than an annoyance, a symptom of cooped troops, fearing uncertainty more than death, blowing off the pressure with an act of uncontrolled vandalism. But the man who had been guarding the cargo-levs had been tied by smartrope to the front of one of them, and when the two vehicles collided head on, he had been crushed into red pulp by the impact.

A hard-faced military proctor told Tom the story, while his colleagues used sting-batons on the now-sober perpetrators—already confessing their guilt; one of them was weeping—before taking them away for trial.

This was nothing which would appear in any propagandized report on the war's progress. It would remain yet another dark secret until the war was won, or until the failings and weaknesses of human civilization ceased to matter.

Tom pulled his cloak round himself, and walked on.

By a turquoise, mineral-saturated pool in another cavern, a small group of young bare-chested soldiers held up their dead trophy, posing for a holocamera-bead: a five-metre-long sealaconda, viciously barbed with long dorsal spikes. They had used knives for the kill, which was a local tradition though the soldiers looked to be from far away, and they pulled open flagons of gripplewine and drank a victory toast, the pale liquid running down their bare smooth-skinned chests, knowing that this was a moment of brief shared joy they would remember forever if they survived this long dark war.

But Tom knew that the sealaconda, for all its fierce appearance, was a gentle coward which fed on microflukes and fungi and the occasional ciliate-newt, and offered no threat to the band of bipedal killers which had hunted it down for sport.

He quickened his pace, nearing his destination.

In the final cave, a squad of quiet, watchful men was waiting, and their commander was Adam Gervicort. Tom's former servitor was now a battle-scarred veteran with a habit of holding himself very still, like a neko-feline with prey in sight.

"My Lord."

There was camouflaged smartfilm, and Adam led him through.

"Look at this, Tom." They were alone, in the membraned-off end of the cave, where he could ignore Tom's rank. "Talk about stripped for speed. What do you think?"

It was a low-slung arachnabug of mottled grey, with a collapsed sled and food bundles tied behind the seat. The vehicle's tendrils looked like faded rope.

"It'll burn itself out," added Adam, slapping the nearest tendril, "to get you there. Programmed to self-immolate when it can go no further, or at your command."

No comfort. Everything sacrificed for speed and endurance.

It'll get me to Elva.

"Is it ready to go?" Tom asked.

"Aye, it is. And"—Adam held out his hand—"sooner you than me, my Lord."

59

MU-SPACE CONTINUUM
AD 2143

<<Ro's Story>>

[20]

It had an aura of confession, amid the miraculous amber glow flowing like a viscous river through the cabin. Odd, fractured visual echoes stuttered around them, and when Ro spoke, her words rippled and reflected like waves breaking upon a shore.

"I think we're in danger, Pilot. I've made enemies among the Zajinets."

With silver cables depending from her eyes, the Pilot's smile looked grim, disturbing.

"I know."

Golden space, and the fractal stars of darkness.

"They're capable, I think, of mu-space travel."

"I'll say. There are two vessels following us right now."

Hunting me?

If they wanted to rid themselves of humans—of Ro McNamara—an accident in mu-space would place them beyond blame. She had placed everybody in danger.

No. It wasn't my choice to be here.

"Do we have weapons?"

"We thought we had no enemies." Again, the I/O cables drew unsettling curves across the Pilot's smile. "Not out here."

"Can you lose them?"

"I haven't managed it yet."

Damn, damn . . .

"Drop out into realspace?"

"We're still not armed. I suspect they are."

There was a control pad, used by ground crew for status checks and diagnostics, and Ro waved it into life, though her hands seemed to move through pale amber water.

Am I going to die here, Father?

But the place of his death was not exactly here: in fact it was some considerable energy-expenditure away. (Despite her grasp of fractal physics, there was no adequate labelling of spacetime separation, of length, in a milieu where the distance between two points grew larger the closer one looked.) For she remembered every detail of the story, told so often by Mother and Gramps that she could visualize everything that had happened.

"These coordinates . . ." Ro concentrated on setting fractional variables. "Is that location accessible from here?"

"Not easily. I'm going to have to push things hard, and the event-membrane may not hold back some of this continuum's odder phenomena."

It was another reminder that this place was very different.

Amber sea . . .

Magical beauty tugged at her.

It was so peaceful in this place, in the wondrous continuum where she belonged, that danger was hard to believe in. But the status display showed two sparks of light following, and the Pilot's word was good enough for Ro.

But how to persuade her to abandon any sensible route, and strike out for such a far location?

Yet already the quality of golden spatial flow seemed different, harder and more turbulent, and it came to Ro that perhaps the Pilot was already following her suggestion.

"Why are you—?"

"You didn't have to explain." The Pilot's body shuddered, then her voice grew dreamy, suffused with a reverent awe: "Any one of us would recognize those coordinates."

Once, when she began to lose focus, Ro felt herself drifting *into* the deck, while the cabin and the stars outside receded in all directions, and she snapped herself out of it before she was lost.

They continued to arrow through golden space.

Pilot Vaachs was deep inside herself now, one with the vessel, as she charted a course no unaltered human being could ever understand. Brain virally rewired to cope with this continuum, blind in the cold reality of her homeworld—yet here she was a bird in flight, mistress of the elements, at one with the golden flow of a universe that was not her own.

Amber, flowing . . .

And Ro was able to follow the Pilot's calculations, tracking through the infinitely recursive dimensions of the mu-space continuum, to the place she had dreamed of all her life.

Vessels, following.

Closing.

"Soon now."

The Pilot's voice was a prayer as much as a promise.

Closing . . .

Their destination was close, measured in the remaining effort to get there, when suddenly the ship shuddered. Violet lightnings splashed past outside, and Ro knew they were under attack.

"Whatever you're going to do"—Pilot Vaachs, her voice tight with tension—"now's the time."

Diving inwards, fractally smaller, but the enemy vessels were following.

"It's been an honour—" the Pilot began.

But Ro was already broadcasting, forcing the control pad to spew out its recorded message in all dimensions, pushing the transmission's gain all the way.

++ **HELP ME, FATHER** ++

The ships came closer.

Father . . . Am I insane?

Violet lightning fell again, but the Terran ship held, though it felt as though it would shake asunder.

Praying to a dead man I've never known.

Was her old delusion going to bring death to them all?

And then—

Yes . . . No.

Nothing.

Yes.

A presence grew.

It shimmered without light; it sang beyond sound. It coalesced, yet there was nothing to see or feel but an invisible blazing of energies, of a *presence* beyond understanding or the limited filters of human perception.

Golden space, mirage-like, twisting . . .

A sense of warmth.

"They're going to fire! Watch—"

Lightnings sparked towards them as their pursuers opened fire. Ravening gouts of violet and orange energy–

Faded, flickered.

Father?

Were gone.

The attackers' weapons no longer functioned.

"Oh, no . . ."

Was this what she had wanted? But it did not matter, as she watched the shivering of space itself, for the process which was occurring was implacable. And the power behind it was unimaginable.

The Zajinet ships rippled apart . . .

Oh, God.

And then they were gone.

For a moment, the ship hung there in mu-space, alone in the golden deep, until some power—not the Pilot, who yelped in surprise— thrust them through the deepest currents of the fractal universe. They whirled, they sang—and then the moment of transition into cold blackness, where stars like diamonds shone, and a blue world was hanging before them, clothed in puffy clouds.

They were back in realspace, and home was close.

Father . . .

But it was a home which would never be the same. Not for Ro.

There was snow in Reykjavik, cold and dry beneath a grey and lilac sky.

Everything seemed preternaturally real: immediate and minutely textured. She tasted the air's coldness, felt the landing field's reassuring solidity beneath her insulated boots.

TDVs moved like hunched beetles among the landed shuttles, retrieving the still-sleeping passengers, complete with the couches on which they lay, for transfer to the warmly lit reception domes.

"Are you OK?" Gramps leaned close, his face reddened by the cold, a bright hood enclosing his head.

"Of course she is." Mother, holding Ro by the elbows. Her blind metallic eye sockets notwithstanding, she could sense deeply in matters of mood and health. "She's fine."

Someone cleared his throat.

"There's been an official apology." It was the young UN officer, FO Neil, who had accompanied her at the Flight School. He shifted his weight from foot to foot. "Conspiracy among the Zajinets. The ones who tried to get you have been punished. Several ambassadors have been replaced."

No-one knew for sure, but the renegade might well have kid-napped Ro to protect her, hiding her in Watcher's Bones from the offi-cial delegation who wanted her dead.

Who cares?

Ro shrugged.

Everything was different . . .

"Gramps?" She looked over to where a crane, like a black scorpion in the gathering gloom, plucked the Pilot's cabin from the ship. "You know how the Pilots regard my father?"

Whatever else he might be, Grandfather was still a Jesuit priest: "Are we going to debate the nature of superstition out here?"

"Maybe later."

Dart Mulligan, subsumed in mu-space. Everyone knew that tale.

Thank you, Father.

"Good." It was Mother, Karyn, who hooked her arm inside Ro's. "Let's go inside and get warm."

The cold air felt good, but she was beginning to shiver. Ro and Mother walked on together, with Gramps, big and burly, protectively beside them.

Flight Officer Neil trailed behind. Would he have anything to report to Frau Doktor Schwenger?

I have my own goals now. Not UNSA's.

But to carry them out she would need help.

If I have the strength . . .

At the terminal building's entrance, Ro stopped and looked back across the night-shrouded space-field, at the great vessel which crouched like a bird about to leap into flight—a tenebral raptor in an umbral world—and wondered at everything that had occurred.

"He was a good man, wasn't he? My father?"

They answered her with hugs, and led her inside to a place of human cheer, where hot glasses of tea and clear strong spirits were imbibed with laughter, while orange flames danced in a fireplace which looked real, smelled *true*, with its crackling warmth and hint of raw smoke tasted upon the air, where the furniture was old, dark wood grown iron-hard with age, with soft cushions of maroon and chocolate brown, and where trays of pungent fish dishes were passed around with a gentle invitation or a witty joke, among people relaxing at the end of a day's work well done, celebrating their life near the axis of the world, unaware of the greater universe which lies beyond: that place where the stars are black and spiky, like negative snowflakes formed of darkest ink, where crimson nebulae like streamers of spilled blood in warm salt water gently elongate themselves and drift, where the stuff of space itself shines gold or amber, endless and forever, and the natural laws which govern humankind can hold no sway, and where even the miraculous can occur; a place which, once glimpsed, lures the spirit with a soft but all-pervasive siren-song, always tempting, never to be escaped.

<<MODULE ENDS>>

60

NULAPEIRON AD 3422

Death train.

He was a tiny clinging insect, buffeted by the crushing slipstream, held by gekkomere-clingrope to the brushed-brass hull. The cylindrical train powered its way through arterial tunnels, riding the shock wave of its own passing.

Just hang on.

Deep into trance, locking his body in position, an unthinking animal with only one objective.

Hang on.

And then the slowing, the welcome deceleration, and the urge to laugh as it shrieked to a halt, in a titanic hall arched with steel and stone, where red-badged soldiers were massed everywhere—on platforms, on raised walkways and balconies—and floatglobes trained their weapons ceaselessly on the people who passed beneath.

It was the heart of Dark Fire territory, a lifetime away from freedom.

There were no alarms, no spitting graser fire, as Tom slid slowly from the hull, gasping, and dropped to the safe side of the train, away from the disembarkation platform.

He crouched there, sunk deep inside himself—closed his eyes, but just for a moment—hearing as from a distance the clang of metal (not membrane) carriage doors lowering, forming ramps; the guards' shouted orders and the stunned absence of protest from the thousand ragged prisoners who shuffled from packed cargo holds onto the platform's breadth, and stood in starved and dehydrated fright: waiting for whatever Fate was going to throw at them next.

Tom shivered—and continued to shiver, unable to stop—remembering the Grand'aume's dungeons, afraid to move into the open.

This is insane.

But the edicts of the Blight assumed no notion of human normalcy, or showed any sign of treating individuals as anything more than meat.

It had taken three tendays, a massive trek through wilderness, and Tom looked as gaunt and starved as the prisoners. To any watching guards, he would seem as weak and dispirited as other captives—for lack of food stuns the mind into a state of sleepy helplessness, even as the body begins slowly to digest its own tissues.

But in his case the appearance of weakness was a deception.

The nearest he had come to death had been at the mission's start, as his arachnabug hurtled through friendly territory and a startled sentry had fired, graser beam missing by centimetres as Tom threw the 'bug through evasive spins, found an exit, whipped into it and was gone, the small vehicle's tendrils a fast-moving blur.

He had journeyed high, keeping to Primum Stratum-equivalent through the abandoned territories, then finally using a vertical shaft to ascend all the way to the surface.

Wide open skies.

The arachnabug functioned on the ground, moving swiftly across the landscape. It would have been faster to remain in habitable tunnels, but avoiding detection had become the primary factor.

And, finally, it had burned out totally, and Tom had left the 'bug collapsed and smouldering, as he tugged his sled behind him—smoothplate underneath, but still heavy, and hard to manoeuvre across the shale—and began the long trek on foot towards his destination.

The planet's surface had not featured yet during the war, but Tom knew its use was inevitable: if the allied forces did not use it first, the Dark Fire's would. And the Enemy's people could more easily lose their normal mental conditioning, for human restraints within their minds had long since been snapped by the power which had overwhelmed and then subsumed them. For Tom, it was a journey through mankind's history on the homeworld. Surely nomad wanderers, hauling their few belongings with them, had travelled and lived off the land like this. On Terra, they would not have needed a lab-kit for converting transplanted vegetation into food; luckily the apparatus was low-tech, unlikely to alert whatever surveillance systems the Blight might have in place above the surface.

One tiny being, in this wild and endless landscape, was effectively invisible.

There had been heathland, with long grasses whipped like waves by the wind. A range of low purple hills, harder to cross than Tom had thought; he lost half of his supplies down a ravine when the sled tipped and strapping tore.

Finally, he was reduced to carrying his dwindling food supply in a cloak tied packwise behind his back.

His body fat, already low, melted away with the long endurance exercise. Soon, he was sinew and bone, a starvation victim to anyone who looked—had there been anyone, in this lost, forgotten world.

But it was partly an illusion, for the figures went like this: his daily energy deficit was huge—a deficit which would match that of any dying famine victim—but those victims (*ipso facto*, as his tutor, Mistress eh'Nalephi, would have said) neither ate nor exercised.

But Tom's energy expenditure grew to twelve thousand kilocalories a day, and two-thirds of that was replenished by his ration bricks. He could survive drops in blood sugar and body fat which would kill someone who was eating nothing.

He was not in the peak of health; but he was nowhere near as close to death as his fat-stripped appearance might suggest.

And, in extremis, it is the mind which rules.

Tom's will—forged in hate, now focused on his lost love—had grown implacable.

There were clear, pale-yellow skies; there were days when creamy clouds covered the sky's vast dome from horizon to horizon. And once, amid the cloud cover, he glimpsed a high dark shape, tiny at that altitude, which might have been a floating terraformer.

But he trekked onward at ground level, alone and undisturbed.

And finally, starved and exhausted, he came to the green and purple dell which he had been aiming for, where the membrane covering the abandoned vent shaft had denatured to milky stringiness, unravelled by its own chemical decline. It revealed a shadowed opening which led to Nulapeiron's habitable depths, in the heart of Blight territory.

Slowly, shaking, Tom began his downwards climb.

And now the death train.

Time to take his place among the prisoners.

With no other access into the death camp itself, this was his only plan. He climbed through a gap between carriages, up onto the platform, and shuffled into the group's centre, inserting himself amid starved-looking children and adults who had aged decades in a matter of days: gaunt, emaciated and grimy. An air of hopelessness hung over them, heavy and unbreakable.

Tom's clothes, too, were torn and ragged, and his cheekbones, like theirs, showed gauntly through stretched skin. Even so, there was a minute ripple of motion away from him, as though they sensed that he was different.

Soon they would be too weak to care even that much.

Guards stood overhead on lev-platforms, and surrounded them on ground level, armoured and with graser rifles held at port-arms: on armed watch everywhere. The rows of prisoners moved slowly forwards, half stumbling towards a square black tunnel mouth, where even the air seemed too thick and solid to breathe.

"Faster, animals!"

Crack of nerve-whip, and someone fell, but no-one helped. Already they had learned that the price of humanity was death.

"Come on."

Beside Tom, a little girl stared straight ahead, her eyes big and round and grey. Her lips parted slightly, but she neither turned around nor looked up at Tom. A child, but nearing her life's end.

Another crack and another. The fallen man would never rise again.

"Move!"

They shuffled into darkness.

They found themselves in a long grey cavern divided into open barracks by toxin-laden membranes which glistened with putrescent, liquid malevolence. There were graser-blasted slit-trench latrines, their foul smells hanging heavily upon the fetid air.

Blood-red drones, armed and armoured, circled overhead, beneath the jagged ceiling.

The prisoners were segregated by gender, and Tom moved with broken gait amid a group of fifty men whose hopeless stares tracked the progress of their wives and children into other parts of the camp.

One of the women dropped, suddenly, like a pile of sticks. A beefy guard laughed, putting his micro-graser back into his pocket, while the other prisoners moved on, avoiding the corpse: now merely an obstacle in their path, a discarded object whose human spirit had been shorn away long before this moment of physical death.

Ignore it.

Tom was trembling, but that was so very dangerous when he was among captives too stunned to care, too hungry to think, too battered to feel emotion. If the guards spotted one who was different, they would single him out immediately, and that would be the end.

That could *not* happen now. Not with Elva so near, after all this time.

Slowly, he turned, head drooping forward with feigned weakness, disguising his careful scan of the surroundings. Far back from the newly arrived prisoners, the incumbents—captives who looked as if they had been here for decades, though it might only have been days—stood or sat upon the hard broken ground, their faces sunken where flesh had collapsed, their eyes too big and dull within prominent sockets. The skull behind each human face was obvious, an indication of the state to come.

Ignore . . .

Beneath their torn, ragged clothing, their limbs were narrow rods or sticks, and their shoulders were sharp corners, devoid of tissue.

One figure moved a finger, made a rattling sound in his throat before lying still. Tom knew he was looking at another corpse, a carcass.

. . . but don't ever forget.

The allocation of barracks by gender was arbitrary, designed to sunder remaining family bonds. The prisoners themselves were sexless, in that their wasted, skeletal bodies could no longer generate or accept desire; only an aching dullness, which drew fatigued eyelids down over too-prominent eyes, and a deadened memory of hunger survived in their moribund nervous systems. They were shutting down, accepting the inevitability of death because it takes energy to believe in life, and they had none.

"There." A grey-haired man with tangled beard raised a thin, trembling arm, pointing to the next barracks. "A way out for . . . some."

At the rear, near the wall, a queue had been picked out by the guards. They waited before a black opening into the solid rockface. From inside—Tom sensed it, even at this distance—came a strange hot sulphurous smell, like some titanic animated cadaver's rotting breath as it swallowed the hopeless human victims one by stumbling one.

"Where—?"

But the man had already dropped his arm to his side, and turned to shuffle away, exhausted beyond measure by that last pitiful spurt of communication. It came to Tom that perhaps they would be the poor devil's final words before he died, and even the vengeance anger smouldering inside seemed inadequate to answer the outrage perpetrated on these people, in a world that was supposed to be civilized.

Tom looked on as another near-dead woman moved into the dark opening, and then another, and then he too could watch no longer, and turned away as though he had lost the will to care.

Night was a time of quiet despair, when the fluorofungal colonies upon the cavern ceiling grew quiescent, shrouded in shadow as they replenished their energies from autotrophic bacteria within the solid rock.

Drones, the colour of an open wound, still circled overhead, weapons trained on prisoners who were barely strong enough to stand

Tom shifted painfully on his threadbare mat which did nothing to cushion the rough stone surface underneath. Then there was a whisper of cloth, a slight grunt and a stink of hot breath as a big man tried to lie down beside Tom, insinuating himself onto the mat—but Tom stabbed lightly against the eyeballs, pivoted up onto one knee, and slammed the edge of his hand down hard.

There was a snap, then a soft cry of pain.

One hand clutching his now-broken collarbone, the big man crawled away. In the darkness, wide eyes seemed to glisten as the other prisoners watched his retreat.

Tom lay back down, and pretended to drift straight into sleep. But he listened, all senses alert, in case another attack should come. But there was none; nor could he hear any trouble coming anyone else's way: few of the inmates had sufficient energy to abuse their fellows.

Somewhere, in the next camp section, a child began to sob. Then a sweet woman's voice, soothing, drifted through the night air, and men opened their eyes, wondering whether they dreamed this angel's presence or had in fact passed beyond life's end.

So fluid, so gentle—

There was a crack, the sizzle of graser fire, and the black night fell silent.

Sometime during the second day there was an inspection, with senior officers whose cravats and epaulettes shone crimson, trailed by heavily armed guards whose aggressive posture was for the sake of form. No-one expected the prisoners to rise up in revolt; had they tried, all would have died in seconds.

Tom, standing among his ragged fellow captives, weighed his chances of escape and found them to be zero.

"Very efficient." One of the officers congratulated a subordinate. "Minimal supply usage. Good work."

"Thank you, sir."

They walked on, past the standing, starving men who might as well have been inanimate rock for all the attention the officers and guards paid them.

After they had left, an air almost of anticlimax settled upon the prisoners. No-one had been killed; no-one had been granted the only release possible from this ongoing hellish punishment for crimes whose nature no-one could remember or imagine.

Third day. Fourth . . .

Lethargy weighed down upon him in a blanketing fog. Had all his vaunted plans boiled down to this? Starved into submission.

For his mind and body, without sustenance, were inexorably shutting down. Soon he would be unable to form the logotropic command sequence which activated his thanatotropic suicide implant; and beyond that point he dared not go.

I'll die when I decide.

It was the only option left open to him.

Not before.

But either way it marked his failure. Starving or the other thing: both marked the end of his quest for Elva, his fulfilment of the Seer's vision which was proving to be an illusion, a tortured and torturing dream. He would never see her again, never touch her skin, never kiss the soft warm lips of a woman who had died yet still survived.

Elva, my love.

Disappointment hurt more than torture, more than wounds.

I've lost you now.

Fifth day, and his eyes were closing of their own accord. He lay upon the broken stone—on a bare rock, though he could not recall his mat being stolen—and tried to conjure up the suicide code within the slow, restricted remnants of his mind.

An end, at last—

Boots, with polished toecaps, were standing in front of him. He squinted up at the inspecting officers. From somewhere, a woman's voice clearly carried:

"That one will do." With a note of disgust: "Clean it up. Have it sent to my quarters."

Hard prods against his back. The transmission ends of grasers.

I'm sorry . . .

Lice-ridden and filthy, he wanted to apologize for his own stink and lethargy. Were he a guard, he would not soil a hand on such as himself.

"Move, animal."

Stumbling, he somehow forced himself to move.

Gleaming floor. The sound of flutes. Soft rose scents . . .

Tom stood swaying, overcome by the soft air's cool embrace, waiting as he had been told.

A doorshimmer evaporated.

Then an officer walked into the luxury-filled chamber, and stopped in front of him. He squinted, trying to focus. His surroundings were a blur of platinum statues, a holo sculpture floating before a russet tapestry, a face—

Floor shifting.

A *familiar* face . . .

"Tom. Oh, my Fate, what have they done to you?"

Reaching out.

Elva.

Mouth opening, but no words came out.

"Tom . . ."

Her strong arms caught him as darkness closed in.

61

NULAPEIRON AD 3422

Wondrously soft, her hand in his. Glistening grey, her sparkling eyes he had thought would remain unseen. Those beautiful lips.

Facing each other across a low table, seated on comfortably upholstered lev-stools, holding hands in a deep communication needing no words.

It was her.

"Elva . . ."

She smiled, blinking away tears.

"I thought we were lost," she said. "Forever."

"That couldn't happen."

"No." Her grip tightened on his hand. "We won't let it."

Earlier, when he had come round, she had fed him: taste explosions bursting with liquid sweetness in his mouth. The physical organism, starved, fed without allowing talk; but his gaze had remained fastened on her even as he nourished himself like an animal, gripplefruit sticky with juice on his hand.

But when she had finally stopped him eating—knowing the dangers of gorging himself too soon after his extended fast—he had allowed her to take away the food for now, despite the urgency of his hunger's demands.

He trusted her.

Elva. At last . . .

Trusted her with everything.

Washed and dressed in clean pale-grey tunic and trews—the uniform of prisoners taken to act as vassals for a time—Tom felt his thought processes revitalize as his blood glucose rose. All sorts of barriers and barricades had fallen away in his mind: the inner defences he had shored up against fear and loneliness and disappointment, not daring to let his feelings out in case he never saw her again.

But Elva was here, she was real, a fantasy made fact, and this time he was going to hang on to her, despite the danger.

It was like hanging over an abyss, dangling from a solitary hand-hold, with only one chance for survival and happiness: never to let go.

"I'm not the woman you knew, Tom."

"We all change," was the only reply he could make.

"See here?" Letting go of his hand, she rolled up her tunic sleeve. "This wasn't me."

When she put her hand in his again, he raised it up and softly kissed the rippling white scar which ran up the inside of her forearm.

"It's part of you now," he said.

"But I saw Litha get cut, playing with a broken blue glass bottle when our parents weren't watching. I was *there*. I bandaged the wound. I can remember how her hot blood smelled like copper. We were seven SY old, my inseparable twin sister and me . . ."

When she turned away there was no sobbing, but soft silent tears trickled down her cheeks: in mourning for the sister she had effectively destroyed, displacing Litha's consciousness when the entanglement system decohered, and all of Elva's thoughts and memories slammed into Litha's brain, even as Elva's body dropped dead in Tom's arm and the Seer looked on, powerless to prevent the disaster he had just created.

What had it been like for her, suddenly to be in a distant realm, surrounded by strangers who thought they knew her, and knowing above all the price Litha had paid for her being here?

But it was what Elva said next that caused the hairs on the back of Tom's neck to rise, his skin to grow chill.

"Sometimes I dream," she told him. "And not always when I'm asleep: waking images of places I've never been to, of people I've never seen . . ."

Tom swallowed.

Finally, there was only one possible response.

"You *are* Elva. And I love you more than I can say."

"I was never really recruited into the Grey Shadows," she said later. They had moved onto a couch, in a chamber lit by glowflitters hanging close to the wall tapestries, and she sat on his right so they could hold hands. "Mother and Father were part of it. Litha and I just naturally, as we learned more and more of their purpose, became involved . . . Were we stupid, Tom?"

"No."

"I worked genuinely hard, as an astymonia officer and in LudusVitae. But the Shadows wanted to stay in the background, not openly commit themselves to LudusVitae's cause, even though their objectives were largely the same."

Tom nodded. The infighting between different covert groups had at times threatened to destroy any effectiveness the umbrella organization of LudusVitae might have had.

"But Litha . . ." She looked away, then back at Tom. "She was in deep cover, in Earl Draufmann's Palace Guards, rising through the ranks faster than me. The pact was, if we came across knowledge that looked vital to the Shadows, if there was any risk at all that we would not be allowed to bring it back without hindrance . . ."

"You were as willing to sacrifice yourself"—Tom shifted on the couch, staring hard at her: trying to convince Elva of her own bravery—"as she was."

"I don't know. How can I ever?"

"You gave up a huge amount, even so."

"I thought I'd lost you . . ."

Draufmann Demesne had been at the core of Blight territory, one of the original manifestations in the world: a seed-growth of malevolent influence which spread, eventually becoming the vast infection which now threatened everything. Elva had communications facilities—code drops and couriers, nothing high-tech and therefore open to subversion—but no means of leaving.

Not without abandoning her mission totally. Her *sister's* mission: that was what made escape unthinkable.

"But now you're here," she said, "we're going to have to get out."

It was what Tom wanted, though he had no illusions about the dangers they would face in trying to leave this dreadful place.

"What about your superiors?" he asked. "Can you simply drop out of the Grey Shadows network?"

"Perhaps. But I'd rather take back the price of my passage." With a bleak half-smile: "There's stuff here worth dying for."

But before that, Elva had a guest for dinner, and Tom could only watch and suffer as she flirted with an enemy senior officer who had a non-military conquest on his mind. All the while, Tom held back the trembling desire to lash out, to strike the throat and claw the eyes, bringing the bastard the Fate he undoubtedly deserved.

It started when a chime sounded, and Elva ran a hand through her hair and stood up, flustered.

"There's a . . . cleaning kit. In the kitchen chamber, there. Perhaps you ought to . . ."

"Don't worry." A too-tight smile stretched Tom's face. "I know how to be a servitor."

Elva closed her eyes for a moment, composing herself, then nodded abruptly and went to receive her visitor.

When the doorshimmer dissolved, a large florid man in dress uniform stepped inside. His greedy eyes, and the small wrapped present he handed Elva, were mere details: Tom hated the man on sight.

But Tom bent to his cleaning tasks with tense familiarity, remembering how to carry out menial tasks without ever looking his betters in the eye.

"Ah, Herla, my dear." It was Elva's cover name, and it sounded strange. The officer took her hand and kissed her cheek (as Tom winced, unseen, at the moist invasive sound). "Beautiful company, elegant surroundings. What more could a man ask for?"

"Careful, Major." Elva set the present down upon a crystal table. "You'll turn my head."

"That would be nice, if you'll allow it."

The urge to crush his throat was almost overwhelming. Tom moved on, polishing a shelf by hand.

"Hmm. I see your unit is damaged. I'll just send for a—"

"No, no." Elva laid her hand upon her visitor's arm. "It's quite efficient, and I find the asymmetry aesthetically pleasing."

She's talking about me.

"Symbolically? As a visible mark of inferiority? Interesting." The man gave a liquid chuckle. "Perhaps I'll commission a holosculpture, depicting them all in that light."

"You've more than met your targets, then." Elva gestured at wall units to deliver up the meal which they had been preparing. As the membrane-doors liquefied, it was Tom—having quickly stepped through a vibroclean field—who reached inside and carried them across to the dining table which floated at the largest chamber's centre. "Or you'd not be so willing to devote yourself to art."

"Well, it's amazing." With a self-conscious clearing of the throat: "We've instituted such productivity gains by utilizing short-life units that it's cheaper than mesobores, even as we get rid of the failed biomass."

It took a moment to realize he was discussing human beings: their uses as slaves, the economics of working them to death and bringing in replacements, as opposed to keeping them alive or using inanimate devices, which felt no pain, had never been equipped with the capacity for suffering.

"But I shouldn't bore you with details. Work, work, work. It's all I seem to do."

"Major, you push yourself too hard." There was a false caress in Elva's voice; Tom had to turn away to hide his distaste. "But I really am very interested . . ."

The dinner conversation was a masterpiece of emotional intrigue: the major's none too subtle attempts to entice Elva away from the table into a situation of physical proximity (neither noticing nor caring about Tom's presence); Elva's deft verbal parries and gentle avoidance.

Later, as she manoeuvred him towards the door, fending off a friendly pat which could have become much more, he said: "Ah, Commander Hilsdottir. You break my heart."

"Soon, Major," she promised him. Laughing, she pushed him outside, as though it was only for the opportunity to touch him. "I'll break your heart very soon."

Then she stepped back inside and waved the doorshimmer into being.

After a moment, her shoulders slumped.

"You can stop tidying up now, Tom." She would not meet his eyes. "It's not—"

"Elva." Very gently, he touched her shoulder, and moved to face her. "You are the bravest person I've ever met. And I love you more than I ever thought possible. All right?"

"Yes." Nodding, her eyes damp. "Yes, it is."

Tom decided, even in the miraculous shared warmth of their embrace, that there was a great deal he would never ask about—would never pass judgement on, should she ever call on him to listen.

Her voice was muffled against his shoulder, but her words were clear and spoke to his heart.

"We have to get out of here. Tonight."

Although Elva—or rather, Litha—had begun her military career as Herla Hilsdottir in Draufmann Demesne, she had been posted to five other realms since then. This place was formerly Realm Buchanan, and it had a very special significance beyond the human tragedy taking place in the death camp just a short walk away from Elva's chambers.

For at its heart lay the Collegium Perpetuum Delphinorum, creator of Oracles: one of three Collegiate sites in the world, and the first to fall before the encroaching Blight.

And Elva would not leave without retrieving the price of her passage.

"There. Not bad." She adjusted the large black satchel on his back.

"Thank you." Tom shifted inside his new, baggy outer clothes. "Where are we going?"

"You're my beast of burden. You're not supposed to ask questions."

"Anything you say, ma'am."

"There are some crystals I was planning to retrieve—duplicate—over time. Other things that I could never steal without blowing my cover. There's no point in leaving them behind. Not now."

"But how will you—?"

"Theft is easy, when you've rank and clearance."

There was a strange light in her grey eyes, simultaneously calm and vibrant: a look of centred energy.

"Good to know," said Tom.

"It's getting away afterwards that's going to be hard."

The Collegium.

The boulevard which led through the square archway was lustrous with age: arch, wall and ceilings all of grey polished mother-of-pearl, edged with jet and lightly decorated with gold-wire sculptures.

At the ancient black gates, a dozen armed sentries stood, and their eyes were watchful, almost reptilian. Tom wondered if they remained truly human.

But he and Elva, with an escort of their own, passed through unchallenged.

He shuffled behind her, moving neither too fast nor too slow. There were mesodrones overhead, armoured and armed, circling through constant scanning patterns; he did not attract their attention. Bare-headed officers walked by, in earnest conversation, while more troops, mirror-visored here, stood to attention in the shielded alcoves which lined every wall.

Once, Tom supposed, there had been statuary in their places; and he had a brief irrational wish that some benevolent magic might turn them all to stone, and let this place revert to its original purpose.

It was a purpose he had once feared and hated; but if the Dark Fire had suborned it, the Collegium Perpetuum Delphinorum might become—might already have become—a greater evil than anyone could have—*ha!*—predicted. Or were there Oracles at the Academy, even now, who had foreseen their birthplace's fall?

And did they know what might happen to him and Elva here today?

Irrelevant. Ignore.

A guard barked a question.

Elva gave an apposite countersign, spoke a coded phrase, and a mirrorfield darkened and collapsed. They stepped into a plush cosy corridor, carpeted in soft deep burgundy, with floating crystal glow-globes overhead.

Silver doors, opened, led to party sounds: clink of goblets, murmured conversations. Someone called to Elva as they passed the doorway.

"Back in a moment, General." She waved at someone, but Tom dared not turn his head to look. "If you've left some decabrandy, that is."

Laughter, but a recognition that the man's teasing greeting had an order buried inside.

Tom and Elva had an escort of six armed troopers. At the corridor's end, a transverse intersection, Elva ordered one of the soldiers to pull the satchel from Tom's back and hand it to her.

"And put that thing in a holding pen." She was referring to Tom. "I'll need it later, mind. Don't damage it."

"Ma'am." Hasty salutes.

And a hard boot kicking against Tom's buttock, as they indicated the direction he should follow.

The holding pen was a dank, black stone alcove: a far cry from the nacre and marble halls where the Collegium's Magisters had once socialized and deliberated. Tom sat on cold stone, hunched inside his voluminous prisoner's tunic, nursing the bruise to his lower ribs. The two soldiers had not damaged him significantly, but a final strike with a rifle butt had been irresistible.

Floating dust sparked, outlining the horizontal alarm beams' bands. It was the simplest security-tech imaginable, and for a starved prisoner barely able to stand, it would have been sufficient to hold him immobile.

But, after Tom was sure the soldiers had departed and the corridor outside was deserted, he rose slowly, and shrugged off his outer clothes. Underneath, he was wearing a skintight black bodysuit with integral friction-slippers, which had come from Elva's wardrobe.

He wadded up the discarded clothes—he would need them later—and tossed them over the top barrier beam. They flopped onto the flag-stones outside.

The stone was rough, with hand- and footholds which would have been child's play had it been dry, and Tom spider-climbed up to the ceiling, then slowly, slowly, climbed belly up over the waiting alarm beam, hauled himself—*careful!*—up to the outer corridor's ceiling, then dropped lightly to the floor.

Wait in the holding cell, Elva had told him, *until I come for you.*

But she was going to be a while, and when else would he have the chance to infiltrate the Collegium Perpetuum Delphinorum, cradle of the Oracles' power?

Solo infiltration is dangerous; but Tom was very good at this.

There was one tense moment when chatting officers were coming towards him and the only way to move had been upwards, to hang suspended between a Doric column's apex and the nearest wall, applying counterpressure against smooth polished pink-tinged marble while the officers passed underneath, oblivious. And then he slid down, carefully, to continue his exploration.

Took a turn at random.

And felt a strange change upon the air.

A sense of dread.

Once, in training at the Academy, Tom had been overtaken by a revulsion-driven need to kill a man: a small, odd-looking trooper with a crooked stance. The man had done nothing to attract Tom's attention, but at first glance Tom was seized with the impulse to stamp him out of existence like a toxin-laden insect, or to beat an immediate retreat.

He did neither of these things, but watched instead as a sergeant gave the trooper punishment duty, a long arduous run with heavy kit followed by acid-burning the latrines.

"Court-martial found him not guilty," the sergeant muttered later. "But if he gets accused of rape again, I'll shoot the little bastard in the head myself."

It was a chemical change, someone had theorized: a pheromone excretion which caused ordinary decent humans to react instinctively in the presence of a psychopath.

And, in a totally empty corridor, that was the kind of sensation—though many times more powerful—which washed over Tom's skin, and perversely drew him forwards.

He looked over a sill, into a round hall cupped like a giant hand: an amphitheatre, filled with row upon curved row of seated figures.

So many people.

They were clad in pale grey, and their breath filled the atmosphere, an incessant hum though no-one spoke, for there were ten thousand individuals down there and, as Tom watched, it seemed their breathing was in total synchrony: ten thousand chests rising and falling to the same rhythm.

Then, in the amphitheatre's centre, a strange blackness flickered: a negation of light, an inverse of warming flame.

Chaos . . .

It was something primal; it was something very dark and strong: powerful beyond resistance, implacable as death. A force was manifesting itself, here, below him.

Go back. Now.

But he could not retreat, could only stare down at the shape-which-was-not-a-shape twisting in an outgrowth of nothingness, a growing void in the centre of their regard, of the ten thousand watchers . . .

Stench of ozone.

No . . .

Suddenly it seemed that stars were rippling in the dark flames, and Tom wanted to take a step backwards but fear prevented it.

It cannot be.

And then, in unison, ten thousand faces turned upwards, towards the balcony where he crouched, and focused their myriad gaze on Tom.

62

NULAPEIRON AD 3422

Those eyes . . .

Tom sprinted, but with a prickling across his back, upon his entire body, as though ten thousand pairs of eyes were still trained upon him; and he knew with an absolute inner certainty that something—some *thing*—was fully aware of him.

Then a sense of relief, as though some dark deity had blinked, forgetting the human insect which had momentarily caught that near-omniscient regard.

Trembling, he found his cached prisoner's tunic and baggy trews, and pulled them on. Then he stumbled onwards, slowing to a bent-backed shuffle as a patrol—six troopers summoned by the gathering Blight: he was sure of it—hurried to block the corridor before him.

"Commander Hilsdottir," he mumbled. "Orders. Must find Commander Hilsdottir."

The patrol leader's lips moved, as he silently reported Tom's capture.

Tom's skin prickled again, just for a second, before the sensation faded to nothingness.

He swallowed in relief, not even minding the blow which thudded against his head and knocked him to the ground.

"The commander's in her office; I saw her earlier. Take the thing to her."

Boots against his ribs, not hard, and Tom forced himself to react slowly, pulling himself upright as though it took all his mortal strength merely to stand.

He moved at a stumbling pace, off balance, for there was a fine line: if he slowed too much, they would merely kill him and bring another prisoner, a replacement unit, to carry Elva's satchel for her.

Walls of lustrous mother-of-pearl, here a deep swirling blue, and big curved pillars of the same hue which bellied outwards, fat and richly decorated. Thick azure carpet beneath their feet. From somewhere, soft Aeolian music—

And a yell, cut short by the liquid spit of graser fire.

Elva!

He knew, with dread certainty, that they had caught her in the act of theft.

They left him, five troopers running towards the sound, with only one remaining—and his attention was not on Tom. A fatal error, as Tom added one more to the list of dead souls who would stand before him in his dreams; it took an ankle sweep assisted by a hand-edge throat-strike, then a knee-drop to the fallen man—an audible crack as the ribs went— and a foreknuckle collapsing the laryngeal cartilage to make sure.

Tom cast aside the baggy outer clothes and sprinted after the patrol.

A row of membrane doors extended beneath curved arches, one of them already dissolved, and that was where the patrol headed. Tom upped the pace, legs pumping, silent across the thick blue carpeting.

This is my future.

And then he was into it.

This is my Now.

Inside the chamber, a trooper was down and another on one knee, clutching his eyes and softly whimpering. Elva was grappling with another, using her teeth against his throat, while another tried to hook punches over his comrade and into the side of Elva's head.

The five reinforcements, sensibly, were holding back. Their leader gave the command to draw grasers—but Tom was upon them then, and it was too late to play a waiting game.

Spilled crystals scrunched underfoot but he kept his balance, scythed a shin-kick across one man's thigh—the trooper dropped,

muscles paralysed—used finger-claw, elbow and knee in quick combination on a second, and then, incredibly, Tom laughed.

He took out another man with a spectacular spinning hook-kick,
which amazed himself after the fact.

"Elva." Sidestepping. "Didn't you know I'd come back for you?"

Side-kick, and he bounced the patrol leader off the wall and met
the returning body with a throat-punch. A heavy blow exploded on the
back of Tom's head but he spun regardless, conditioned to hard contact, and his answering combination used knee and palm-strikes, and
then he was behind the man, and his arm slipped softly, serpent-like,
round the throat, grabbed the man's left epaulette, then a bend and
twist and he was out of it.

Elva's opponents, too, were down. With a grim efficiency Tom had
not seen before, she used a small triangular black knife to finish them.

"Quickly, now. They didn't call for assistance"—she was gathering
up a spherical grey bag (it might have contained a large children's
lightball, from its size) and a handful of crystals—"but we don't have
much time."

After Tom had pulled on a uniform over his bodysuit, they left
together. His was the lower nominal rank, so he took the black satchel,
now with the round grey bag and stolen crystals inside, and walked to
Elva's right, half a pace behind, keeping in step.

It was what the Seer showed me.

The fight in the office. The Seer-given vision of Elva which had
guided Tom for so long—but no longer.

We're in an unknown future now.

At an intersection, with a great round-domed hall beyond, a patrol
moved across their path, jogging at double-march, graser rifles at port-
arms, and Tom almost stopped dead. But he took his cue from Elva,
recovered his pace, and heard her murmur:

"If they'd found the bodies, the Eminence itself would look for us."

The Blight.

And it would find them. Tom had no doubts of that.

We're insects before it.

Or perhaps that was not it. Crazily, since their lives depended on acting calmly, Tom found his thoughts wandering, drawn to the intellectual puzzle.

Perhaps It, the Blight, is more like a sea of bacteria.

Ten per cent of every person's body weight is bacterial. At a deeper level, mitochondria, the powerhouse organelles of all animal cells—which drive all movement, all being—have their own DNA inherited solely, always, from the mother: evidence of a symbiosis between two bacterial species, one absorbed inside the other, which eventually became animal life.

We're just emergent properties of a vast bacterial sea.

On Terra, as in Nulapeiron, bacteria crawled, lived, reproduced, struggled and died on every visible surface, on the deep ocean floor, and inside the very world-stuff, inside both planets' crusts as far down as anyone had ever measured. It had been one of the first lessons Tom had learned in his emergenics studies at the Sorites School.

But bacteria could—chemically—communicate as well as fight, and could swap DNA across "species" so easily that the term sometimes became nonsense, in a vast planet-wide, microscopic-dimensioned, eternally uninhibited ongoing orgy.

And perhaps that was the natural way of things, as Terra's NetWars had given hint of, as the Fulgor Anomaly had possibly proved.

Vast communal beings, stretching across entire worlds, if not further.

Individual animal and human organisms, perhaps, were in the same boat as archaic bacteria. A stage in evolution, still existing, still contributing to biomass, but scarcely aware—except in the most peripheral way, when more complex beings' actions led to proliferation or extinction as a result of purposes and actions unknowable by simpler organisms—of the growth in intellect, in society.

What did a human global economy mean to a single bacterium? What could the powers and intentions of the vast Blight mean to a single human being?

Humans were a part of it, Tom was sure, only in the same way that *E.coli* bacteria are part of every person. Were its capabilities as far beyond human thought as intellect is above the simple chemical reactions of a bacterium or virus?

You can't fight a god.

Then Elva's soft words broke his reverie.

"Checkpoint ahead. Follow my lead."

They passed through the first checkpoint, and the next.

But the Blight-controlled territories stretched a thousand klicks or more in every horizontal direction, and they would never get away from here on foot through public tunnels. Or escape an extended search if they became the subject of a realm-wide manhunt.

Whatever they did next, it would have to be swift, imaginative, and undetectable.

"This way," said Elva.

63

NULAPEIRON AD 3422

Below the chamber's open portal, the walls dropped almost sheer to the bottom of the pit. Brass ramps spiralled down to the pit floor, where half a dozen flyers and cargo-bugs sat waiting, all with hulls coloured pale grey, zigzagged with scarlet lightning flashes.

Tom edged back from the opening, into the half-lit chamber.

Elva had been Tom's security chief, and a good one. Sneak-and-peek had been her favourite impromptu exercise, using burglary techniques to pass through smartfilms and avoid patrols, testing his demesne's defences which she herself helped to design and continually upgrade.

She's better at this than I am.

They were inside a cargo chamber, in a high-security section of this realm which, vertically, spanned seven strata: a military base within the greater occupied territory. And Elva had sneaked them inside as part of a general's entourage, following the bewigged burly man with the purple cape and ample brocade, splitting off from among the following junior officers, and bypassing every automated scanfield until they reached this hiding place.

Her eidetic memory helped, of course: she had visited here only once, had caught a single brief subsequent glance of the base schematics.

Now he waited among teardrop-shaped steel containers, while Elva worked on gaining access.

"Done it."

They crawled inside the dark container, exchanged a long mutual look while there was still illumination—the words of love unspoken—then Elva pulled the hatch shut behind them with a muted clang.

Darkness.

And the long wait.

They sat with backs against the inner hull, his hand clasped in both of Elva's, with the heavy satchel tugged round so it lay in his lap. And, in a soft murmur with lips held close to each other's ears, they talked.

"I know . . . as Litha, I know a thing . . . from nine years ago."

Nine SY? That had been an eventful year.

"What is it, my love?"

A long pause in the darkness.

Then, "They found a body on the ground, on the surface. Shattered. When they were searching for the Oracle's killer."

Poignard blade, hard into his body. Scarlet blood, splashed bright across the blue-white floor.

"Who did?"

"Grey Shadows, undercover. We—they hid the evidence."

And the escape. In the floating terraformer, high in Nulapeiron's skies, and the brief vision of himself, despair-filled with anger turning inwards, throwing himself suicidally from the balcony at the great sphere's apex.

But that was hallucination.

Except that more recent events suggested otherwise.

"They tested its DNA," whispered Elva. "Reconstructed the features. Litha saw it."

Her dead twin's memories, not fully displaced by Elva's occupancy of what had been Litha's body.

"What did they find?"

Dreading the answer.

Don't say it, my love.

Knowing the answer in advance.

"It was you, Tom." Her voice was eerie in the darkened container. "The dead body was you."

Take-off.

They clutched each other in the vibrating darkness, a tremendous roar pulsating through their bodies, hammering the air so that they could not even shout to each other. Their cargo container was in a flyer's hold, rising fast through the vertical shaft, heading upwards, bursting free into open air, shooting upwards into lemon skies whose nature Elva could perhaps imagine, but which she had never seen. Her grip on Tom tightened, hard.

Then freefall, arcing, and the landing.

Cargocrabs—they could tell from the scraping sounds, the sudden jolt of movement—carried their container outside, and stacked it against the others.

Tom and Elva waited till all was silent, then waited some more, until they could no longer stand it.

"Me first," said Tom.

It was night, and cloudy, but the black vault still showed distant stars and the wind, though soft, was in continuous motion, bearing the sound of dark leaves rustling and the grassy scents which no subterranean dweller would recognize.

Elva swallowed, stumbled, but did not cower: it was the most impressive reaction of a non-acclimatized newcomer Tom had seen.

But still she walked unsteadily, in the wide open spaces beneath infinite night skies, and Tom would have to lead for now.

They were on level ground, a gentle portion of a long slope, and its grass-covered surface looked silver by the light of triplet moons.

Tom led the way upwards, to a knot of trees and undergrowth near the ridgetop, and used Elva's small sharp knife to cut away branches, pulling them down to form a shelter.

They had no food, no water.

But they were used to waiting.

As false dawn lightened the night a little, Tom whispered, "Stay here," and crawled out from the shelter.

Elva remained crouched inside.

The stacked cargo pods still stood downslope. There was no sign of cargocrabs; the flyer itself had long departed. The diminishing night was clear, and—had it not been for the containers—he would have thought himself alone in a vast natural wilderness. Beneath him, a long plain led onwards from the foot of the ridge, spanning many klicks before reaching a range of low, dark distant hills, only just visible against the purple-grey horizon.

Woody scents, a sharp hint of some purple bush's fragrance—he recognized the plant but could not name it—made his nostrils flare. He took a long, deep breath, then slowly let the pure air slide from his lungs, bringing a momentary peace.

Then Tom turned and crawled upslope, to the ridge's apex, and looked down over the side.

Chaos . . .

And knelt there, unmoving.

Below lay a huge structure, all of crystal, like some titanic bloom which shimmered, ethereal in the fading moonlight, and its heart seemed twisted through extra-dimensional folds which Tom could not truly see.

There was a small clump of undergrowth, surrounding a stunted tree, nearby. Tom crawled to it, lay down beneath its meagre cover, and waited for the dawn.

And soon enough, the eastern sky was painted pale, washed-out lemon, and the grey clouds were tinged with yellow.

Then sunlight caught the vast spreading crystalline building, if that was its function, and it burned with the brightness of a thousand sparkling suns, a blazing glorious dawn-fire which hurt the eyes with its brilliance and made Tom want to crawl away and hide.

He waited, though, for the first of the big transport-flyers to glide overhead and settle down to land. He counted four hundred passengers disembarking down multiple ramps, and every person wore light grey edged with crimson.

More flyers touched down.

And then, from some membrane-covered shaft opening in the ground beyond the great crystalline construct, many more people began to climb into the open. And headed, like the others, to the vast stadium-like crystal flower.

Thousands, maybe tens of thousands, of Blight-subsumed individuals were converging upon the structure when Tom finally dared to crawl back through the long grasses, back to the knot of trees where Elva crouched alone, waiting.

Sunlight dappled the interior of their branch-covered shelter, and Elva squinted against it. She sat cross-legged, bulky black satchel in her lap, listening to Tom's description of what was occurring outside. For all her mental strength, there was no way that she—without conditioning—could move around on the world's surface in daylight. Agoraphobia aside, it was now too dangerous to leave this place.

"We made a tactical mistake, then."

Tom nodded. "I thought we could get far away on foot before I signalled my contact. But now . . ."

Elva touched the back of his hand. "Not with thousands of Eminence-Absorbed around us."

"Absorbed?"

"What it sounds like." Then she sat back, clasping her hands round her knees. "Signalled how?"

"What do you—Oh. Like this."

Tom reached inside his mouth with thumb and forefinger, steeled himself, then twisted. There was a *crunch*, and the tooth came free.

He held out the red-stained molar and spat warm blood.

"Transmitter seed."

"Not very big." Elva, with no hint of squeamishness or distaste, took the tooth. Her strong fingers split it apart. "Null-gel coated. Good. But no range to speak of."

"I know."

If only there'd been a way to set up long-range comms . . .

"But"—Elva held it up, checking its design—"it can feed off almost any energy-source, I'd say."

"I guess so." Tom frowned. "Does that help?"

"Tell me again about the crystal building."

In a lifetime of taking risks, Tom did something that scared him more than all the rest combined.

After waiting for the last of the marching crowds to disappear inside, through the ground-level entrances set all around the convex crystalline building, Tom crawled over the ridgeline and stood up.

He waited for a burst of automated graser fire, a shout of alarm, but nothing happened.

Then slowly he made his way downslope, walking as though he had every right to be here, heading down towards the place where tens of thousands of his enemies, or human components of the one Enemy, were congregated to carry out strange purposes of their own.

Blades of grass whipped around his feet.

Closer.

And then he was at the bottom, before a blank entrance, and the great convex building curved outwards, above his head, an improbably massive structure which surely could not hold its own weight.

Entranceway.

Tom closed his eyes briefly.
For Elva.
And walked inside.

64

NULAPEIRON AD 3422

A passageway like glass led onwards to what might have been a great arena. Massive waves of sound—no voices, but rasp of cloth and sound of breath from such a multitude magnified, took on a life of its own, became a deep inchoate roar of white noise—beat down upon him, froze him in place. People were standing up ahead—

But there was a small opening to his left and he slid into it.

It was a curved tubular shaft, twisting and curling, elaborate in shape, leading upwards.

Climb.

There might have been a flicker of motion outside the shaft— broken kaleidoscopic images shattered and refracted by the complex inner structure of this place—but Tom was already ascending. Counterpressure techniques allowed him to chimney-climb, faster than he would have thought possible, propelled by fear.

No shouts followed from below.

Climb.

It was glassine more than crystal: no sharp edges, but with an impossibly convoluted organic structure, as though it were some vast living flower through which the microscopic Tom Corcorigan was crawling.

Faster.

There was a tricky traverse, a junction between capillaries, and he slipped.

But he slid only a few metres before catching a lip, a junction, and then he was moving upwards through the transparent structure once more.

And came out, with the yellow sky blazing overhead.

Like an insect—and likewise insignificant, he hoped—Tom crawled along a narrow curving glassine ridge, part of the "roof" of the great complex blossom, and looked over the edge, into the hollow centre.

As he had seen earlier from the hilltop, the glassine pleats and petals folded and bent through strange, extradimensional axes which the human eye could not follow. When Tom tried to focus on the phenomenon, he felt vertiginously sick, clutched his handhold, looking away quickly before he fell.

Beneath, the blossom-building's core was hollow, and vast numbers of grey-uniformed people were already seated. Twenty thousand people, Tom eventually estimated, and many more were still taking up their positions.

Movement, overhead.

It was skyborne, a distant watcher-drone, and Tom slipped over the edge, and braced himself inside a capillary.

Foot pressure alone kept him in place as he adhered the tiny tooth-transmitter to the glassine material. If the energy focus was anything like he and Elva expected, the transmitter's nanosecond burst would reach clear to the Academy, thousands of klicks away. It would modulate some of the Blight's own radiated power, before the immense concentration burned the transmitter itself into a miniature smoking ruin.

Go now.

He swallowed, holding still. The feel of the crowd, the invisible vibration of those myriads of wills subsumed into one . . .

But a security drone was coming—perhaps it, too, was an infinitesimal sub-component of the Blight: that dark power surely transcended the organic—and Tom had to move.

He let go.

I'm scared.

Slid downwards.

There were few drones sweeping the sky.

From his hiding place, crouched at the glassine exit, Tom kept careful watch, analysing the pattern. Then, when he was sure—as sure as he could be—that he was in an observation gap, he broke into an uphill run. Running outright—no point in acting nonchalant—pushing hard, lungs bursting and thighs burning, deep in the animal joy of it, up to the top of the slope, then down over the ridgeline without looking back.

Nothing followed.

There was something hidden in the grass, a root, and he tripped without injury, turning his fall into a roll, and rolled again sideways and into the knot of trees. A laugh rose inside him, but he quelled it; despite his relief, the danger was not over yet.

He crawled, gasping yet feeling energized, to their makeshift shelter.

But it was empty.

NO!

He checked again, but it was true, the shadowed interior was empty.

Elva was gone, taken by drones.

He walked out of the tree cover, into the open, uncaring.

Drones . . .

He saw them, but they were heading away from him—no, away from the crystalline structure—flying as fast as their lev-units would allow.

Tom walked to the top, and looked down from the ridge.

It was glowing.

No . . .

White light, growing.

Greater than the sunlight.

A thousand suns . . .

It blossomed truly, a vast wave of white light.

A blazing globe: the Blight, gathering its power.

Shielding his eyes, crying inside, Tom rolled back over the ridge.

The strange impossible light continued, great beams of it thrusting through the sky, throwing strange, stark black-and-white shadows across the grassy ground. The crystalline stadium had become a giant spotlight, trapping the world in its blazing illumination.

Highlighting a trampled trail which had been invisible before.

Squinting.

It's growing brighter.

Tom moved with his eyes squeezed almost shut, following the trail.

White sky, burning now.

Elva, I won't lose you.

Half stumbling, half running, while his eyesight remained.

Not now.

Lost the trail . . . No.

There.

And found the membrane-covered shaft, an ellipsoid shining with reflected white intensity, and slid inside, ignoring security, just burrowing down into the solid depths of Nulapeiron, into welcome shade and safety.

White light still blazed at the bottom of the shaft, but a few metres into the horizontal tunnel beyond, he was able to open his eyes normally. Pale orange stone walls, dark floor. Utilitarian, clean. Though he was beneath ground, this was higher than the Primum Stratum: he had not descended far enough to reach normal depths, and the air still felt strange.

There was another shaft opening in the floor ahead, beyond which the corridor continued.

Which way, Fate damn it?

He ran forward.

There were doors to the sides, all locked and hardened to opacity. And farther on, a long chamber terminated the corridor. He stopped, panting, looked around, feeling desperate.

Damn, damn.

Ran back to the shaft.

This time he realized there was a descending tube, its interior coated with some viscous liquid which smelled faintly tart, and knew he had no choice. He lowered himself over the edge, felt the liquid cling to his black bodysuit—imagined a slurping sound—and then let go.

The transport-liquid propelled him downwards.

It was a climber's nightmare: falling into the void. But it was controlled, and as he hurtled downwards, breath torn away by the slipstream and trying not to yell, he tried to estimate the drop. One klick, maybe two.

Deceleration.

Tom's heart pounded as the slope curved gently and the liquid grew viscous, slowing his descent, until he slid out onto a horizontal chute and fell to the floor.

Blinking hard, he got up and walked, trying to focus on his surroundings: shining mother-of-pearl, swirling shades of grey. He was not just back in Realm Buchanan, but in the heart of the Collegium Perpetuum Delphinorum itself.

Part of him wanted to sit down and cry.

Elva . . .

Tom pushed on.

Somewhere above ground the titanic crystal structure was pulsing with energy, blazing brighter than the sun, but here the tunnels grew dank, some part of the Collegium which was long disused, with scraps of derelict machines—broken scrubdrones, the chassis of a burned-out levanquin—strewn across the cracked stone floor.

Tom stepped to avoid a filmed-over puddle from which acrid vapour rose ominously—

Something.

—and stopped dead, listening. Was something hunting him, or was it Elva and her captors?

The sound came again, from a black opening to his left. With silent steps, careful as a neko-feline stalking ciliate prey, Tom crouched low and moved inside.

He came out in a ruined square-cut chapel, ancient and deserted, lit only by mutated patches of wild fluorofungus which rippled with disease. In its shattered alcoves old worn-featured statues had collapsed, and lay at odd angles amid the rubble and broken shards. It was dank and unsettling, but it was not the place Blight drones would take a prisoner to.

Tom closed his eyes, cursing himself.

"*Ah . . . Cor-cor . . . igan.*"

A statue.

Against all his training, Tom was paralysed.

The statue *moved*.

"Who are—?"

But then he saw: in the shadows, a white fragmented face slowly twisting in his direction. A rainbow shimmered, as a pale shaft of light struck a diffractive microfaceted surface where one eye should have been—but the other half of that broken face was a blackened ruin.

It was a Jack, damaged beyond imagining.

In the past, when a fearful Tom had glimpsed them, Jacks were preternatural beings whose skins were laced with sensor tracery more sensitive than the best of scanfields and femtodefences, while their bodies enclosed weapon systems of legendary power, capable of blasting hugely superior forces into oblivion.

But this one . . .

Fear of the shattered half-human thing crept over Tom, until the Jack raised one hand, revealing ripped sinews and power cables, laid open to view with the flesh torn asunder.

It was a broken wreck, which some power had mostly destroyed and left here, propped up—immobile, statue-like—to suffer slowly, to wait out the years until its internal power plant finally gave up the ghost, and whatever passed for human in its core patterns finally dissipated into oblivion.

"I . . . hunted . . . you."

That brought the fear back. Jacks had searched for the Pilot's mu-space crystal, when Tom was fourteen SY old; years later, Jacks were part of the manhunt for Gérard d'Ovraison's murderer. Was that what it meant?

But the poor ravaged thing did not have the energy for prolonged conversation: Tom could see the agonized effort those few words had cost it.

"I'm looking for a woman. Held captive by the Blight."

Trying to enlist its sympathy, by naming the Blight as his enemy. For whatever had done this to a Jack was itself no human being. Such power: the ruined Jack's abdominal area, blackened, was melded into the chapel wall, part of the extended charcoal burn pattern which sprayed across half the chamber.

Slowly, it raised its shattered face.

And sniffed.

Tom's skin crawled in remembrance of childhood tales: those senses which could detect individual airborne molecules, the implanted weaponry which might destroy half a demesne in seconds.

"That . . . way." A minute nod indicated direction. *"Not long . . . Hurry."*

But Tom did not move.

"What can I—?"

"*You . . . know.*"

Tom had no weapon with which to end it. And a creature which could survive all that had happened . . . With his bare hand Tom could make it suffer, but he was not sure he could kill it.

Instead, he gave his deepest bow.

"I'll return, honoured Jack. You have my word."

"*Hurry . . .*"

65

NULAPEIRON AD 3422

It was vast: a wide circular arena, bathed in a pool of white ghostly light, shining from above. All around rose banked tiers of seats, filled with people: perhaps ten thousand, clad in grey, staring up into a searing glare too powerful for normal eyes.

Crouched in the shadowed entranceway, Tom held up his hand—a poor shield against that blinding white—and squinted, barely managing to see the shaft's walls rising vertically upwards, some two kilometres to the surface, and the great crystal stadium which blazed above.

And on those walls, all the way up, stood row upon circular row of people: a crush of entwined bodies, a seething mass like some vast communal hive. A quarter of a million people lined the shaft like jostling, crawling insects, waiting for . . . what?

But down here on the arena floor, at its centre, was a small figure ringed by armed human guards—not drones—whose attention was on her instead of the titanic presence growing overhead. One of them bore the bulky black satchel, proof of Elva's guilt.

The white light glowed stronger, nova-bright. Tom looked down and away, fluorescence crowding his vision, helpless as a crawling ant at ground zero.

At that moment one of Elva's guards saw Tom.

In unison, they turned in his direction. Simultaneously, every person on the lowest tier of seats stood up in perfect synchrony. Two hundred pairs of eyes stared at Tom.

"*Elva*," he called out.

"Fate, Tom! No!"

Only the guards looked armed, but it was irrelevant: no-one could survive the weight of such a huge crowd advancing. If he fled right now—he was in the exit-way, could save himself—but no. A strange calm descended on him.

Flight was impossible, without Elva.

And if death was inevitable, then he chose to face it here, with her—not by himself in some lonely future, whether hours or decades from now. He stepped out into the white light, onto the arena floor.

"Elva . . . I'm not leaving you again."

Hopeless love moistened her grey eyes.

Overhead, the blaze grew even brighter, though Tom had not thought it possible. It was huge, and its energy was growing: it was a manifestation of a great being, a vast power whose drives knew nothing of the two human specks who stood below it. And in that moment, flooded with a sense of his worthless insignificance beneath the Blight's overwhelming presence, Tom realized how much he and others had misinterpreted its nature, and underestimated its power.

For the Blight was not an extension or a limb of that distant Anomaly, but something more like a seed—or had been. For now it was mature, coming into its own as it gathered humans throughout the world into itself, almost *becoming* the planet: a true sentience beyond pitiful human understanding, which perhaps was evolution's goal as individuals were subsumed within the whole. While Tom and Elva were about to die, burned from existence in a flare of energy, like dust particles which drifted into incandescent flames, sparked briefly and were gone.

So this is death.

He tried to meet Elva's gaze.

Then a vast percussive clap slammed the air, and Tom fell down.

They swarmed inside.

Crimson arachnasprites with black-clad riders hurtled into the arena, up onto the walls, speeding sideways to the ground as their grasers spat ravening energy. Half of Elva's guards perished in that moment. Within seconds, as some of the riders caromed off the walls, causing their mounts to leap in a blur of tendrils over Elva, the other guards were down: two flattened by flailing 'sprite tendrils, the others drilled through with precision graser fire.

One of the riders stopped, flung back her helmet: Thylara, of the Clades Tau, with that familiar mocking grin and mass of flame-red hair. She held out her gauntlet-covered hand to Elva, who took a step towards the crouched arachnasprite.

But then Elva wheeled away, muttering, and crouched over one of the fallen guards, tugging at the black satchel which was caught in the corpse's grasp.

"Come on, Strelsthorm!"

While overhead, something new was taking place.

A great shadow fell across the arena.

Glimmers of white still shone around the shaft's edges—in the crystal stadium two kliks above, light still blazed—but immediately overhead a blackness was gathering. It roiled, it flexed: a twisting in space, a massive vibration of power so great that light could not escape its presence. It was the true Dark Fire, the Blight itself, coalescing into being above Tom.

Waves of dread washed down upon him.

The scarlet 'sprites sprang into action, firing at the massed humans in their tiers upon the shaft walls, but suddenly their coruscating fire was having no effect, as energy which could blast through stone spattered and burst from the Absorbed targets, fell away from those once-human beings as harmlessly as gentle water, leaving them unwounded.

Then darkness reached out, and half of the TauRiders and their 'sprites winked out of existence like snuffed holo images.

"Get out!" Tom waved urgently to Thylara, who had helped Elva to mount the saddle behind her, clutching the black satchel which surely could not matter now.

Her arachnasprite sprang forward, but even in that moment

human figures came from nowhere, a mass of them, jamming the exit from the arena, blocking the TauRiders' way. Tom heard Thylara's curse as she spun her mount sideways on and stopped.

The other riders, not wishing to present stationary targets, were moving, but such manoeuvres could have no meaning for the being coalescing above them, capable of reaching through spacetime itself, so powerful that it could not be termed anything other than a god.

But it did not strike.

For a moment Tom wondered why it held back, whether there was some awful torture it might have in mind for these tiny beings which had come to its notice, perhaps caused it a momentary annoyance; but then something strange happened which caused him to re-evaluate the wisdom of Elva's actions.

The satchel which she clutched so tightly *twitched*.

At that instant, in a circle around the arena's floor, black flames rippled in the air, and then there were nine scarlet figures standing there. Almost immediately, they began to walk towards Elva, and Thylara caused her 'sprite to crouch lower, ready to spring: sensing, like Tom, that these beings could perhaps be avoided but surely not defeated.

And the satchel twitched once more.

What the Chaos is it?

"Elva!" Tom made up his mind instantly. "Throw it to me!"

Startled, Elva stared at him—grey eyes wide with love—then tossed the satchel towards him.

Nine scarlet figures turned their attention to Tom as he snatched it from the air.

Overhead, the massive presence of the Blight stirred, but did not strike; that was more horrifying than if it had killed everyone outright.

Two TauRiders moved to flank Tom, guarding him, but *the air clenched* like a black fist and squeezed them from existence, and they were gone.

Why didn't you kill me?

Down on one knee, working quickly as the nine scarlet-clad Absorbed drew closer, Tom opened the satchel, drew out a spherical grey bag—spilling crystals: they were not the cause of the Blight's hesitation—and opened the bag.

He grabbed the wet, glistening contents by its long thin locks of sparse, blood-soaked hair, and stood up straight with the thing dangling from his hand.

The nine Absorbed stopped dead.

For in Tom's hand was a flayed human head, its blood-red muscles flensed and glistening, its sinews hanging intact, with prominent lidless eyeballs: white spheres in startling contrast to the bloody, stripped muscles. Its teeth looked long, for lips, like skin, had been cut away. The head ended at the severed, dripping neck: not neatly, but with a tangle of arteries and sinews, roughly hacked away from the long-dead body.

And then, as it hung from Tom's hand, *the thing's mouth moved*, forming silent words, and those dead eyeballs swivelled to focus upon Tom.

He was too stunned even to drop it.

"It's Eemur's Head." Elva's voice echoed oddly in the stillness. "She was a Seer, killed long ago, and they guard it like a treasure."

A Seer?

And even as he watched, two teardrops grew in that poor thing's butchered face: one drop swelling slowly at the corner of each eye.

But these were no ordinary tears, for they sparked with electric blue fire, glowed like sapphires in startling contrast to the black malevolence roiling overhead.

In silence, the blackness waited. The air chilled, as if solidifying, while the huge hive of Blight-absorbed humanity held its collective breath. Then the nine Absorbed continued their advance towards him—as though Tom had missed something, as though he could have struck back but failed—and he knew that mere seconds remained before he and Elva and Thylara and the other TauRiders were ripped from existence or, worse, invaded by the questing darkness with a sickening intimacy which could not be denied, as it inserted itself into body and soul, taking what it wanted, making human meat a part of its distributed self.

He could have run; he could have suicidally attacked.

Instead, in that moment of total desperation, Tom performed an action he would never be able to explain to himself or others, but which seemed simultaneously the strangest and most natural thing to do at the time.

Slowly, gently, he raised up that poor, bloody severed head . . .

"No! Tom—"

. . . and *kissed* dead Eemur on her bone-white teeth.

That flensed mouth parted, and for a moment an icy purple swollen tongue touched Tom's, cold and intimate, and he shivered with fear and another emotion he could not name. And then he kissed her twice more, gently, once at the corner of each eye where the fluorescent sapphire tears were waiting.

Fate . . .

Fear and joy—bittersweet emotion and a strange, acidic taste—accompanied the absorption of those electric, glowing tears into Tom's lips. He could feel their seeping numbness, then an odd sensation, like an internal itch which could never be scratched, slithering into his nerves, inserting and inveigling its way deep into his body . . .

And was gone, inside him.

"Tom? What's happening to you?"

Then, accompanied by angelic music only he could hear, white-hot fire began to sing inside his veins. The scarlet figures were advancing—slowly, slowly as though underwater—but Tom was no longer capable of fearing them.

For he understood his Destiny.

And a power was upon him.

$$\diamond\diamond\diamond$$

Gently—as though he had forever in which to act—he replaced Eemur's Head in the grey bag, and sticky-tagged it to his waist.

Then he waited.

Patiently.

There were nine of them, advancing.

Rip. A protest of sound.

Reality tore apart, and Tom crouched before his single opponent, aware of the Tom Corcorigan to his left, of the other to his right.

The blackness roiled overhead and spun, reacting—*It knows*—and then there were eighty-one scarlet-clad men coming towards him, before reality split asunder and once more each Tom Corcorigan faced one opponent, and the arena was becoming crowded now as the arachnasprites shuffled away, too close for comfort to the lowest tier of the Blight's other human components.

For I am become Legion.

Split again, and exponentially again, and they overlapped, were a multitude—more than should fit inside the arena, partially occupying the same space but without disaster—but Tom was there too and this time he struck.

And they fell, each of the Absorbed, as he—each Tom—struck once, hard, with killing concentration in the blow.

"Quickly, now!" one of him called to the others.

He closed his eyes . . .

Opened them.

He was by himself, the only Tom Corcorigan, standing at the centre of the arena, while scarlet figures winked out of existence one by one.

Thylara was the first to react, gunning her arachnasprite towards the exit tunnel. The people who had blocked it were fallen: unconscious or dead. Elva jerked back with the inertia, unable to look away from Tom, mouth open, her eyes sick with fear.

The other 'sprites moved to follow.

One of the riders paused, held out an inviting hand, but Tom waved him on. Above, the massive blackness gathered, yet he felt—he knew—it would not strike while he stood here, protected by the power of Eemur's tears.

The 'sprites left one by one, until only Tom was left, standing beneath the void.

But the void was darkening. Its capabilities were massive, godlike, as though the universe were gathering itself into one place above him, ready to wipe out Tom Corcorigan with the rest of humanity upon this world. And its human components, the mass of entwined bodies which lined the shaft overhead, sucked in a long collective breath, as though readying itself for one massive strike which would sunder reality and deal with this insect by flicking it into non-existence.

Roiling, it waited.

There was a twitch of crimson motion at the edge of Tom's vision, then Thylara's arachnasprite was hurtling across the arena floor towards him.

"Valnek's got your friend." She was panting as the 'sprite halted. "Come on."

With a glance upwards at the darkness, Tom swung himself up behind her.

"Can you do that trick again?" Thylara hesitated. "Make copies of yourself?"

"Not unless it attacks in the same way."

Tom did not understand how he had tapped into the Blight's own power; he knew only that he had subverted some kind of flow, blending with its channelling as it replicated its human manifestations.

I'm scared.

He had something of value to an entity whose evil and capabilities made it equal to any god of myth or legend. A power which had possibly subsumed entire worlds. And here he was, microscopic before it, frail and defenceless.

It can flick me from existence.

Instead, the ground shook with massive vibration, and a gout of dust rose from the exit as it filled with rubble, the tunnel collapsed in ruins.

Trapped.

"How do we ..." Even Thylara's voice shook as she looked upwards.

Gently, Tom's arm enclosed the sticky-tagged bag containing Eemur, cradling the long-dead Seer's head against him, knowing he could not lose her now. He locked the tension in his arm.

"There's only one way," he said.

Thylara whooped as the arachnasprite sprang upwards. It leaped to the wall, and they flew vertically up towards the surface, ducking as they sped past blackness.

No, no, no, no, no ...

Something clutched at Tom's heart but then they were past the void, hurtling upwards, the 'sprite whipping its tendrils in a blur across faces and limbs and twisting torsos of the boiling human hive. Between Tom's legs the arachnasprite shook and whined as Thylara pushed it far past normal limits, knowing they had seconds to live if she failed.

The shaft, the writhing people, flowed past.

A downward glance. The blackness was spreading, yet not pursuing.

Multitudes cried out, as the arachnasprite continued its hellish climb. The sound became a roar, a tidal pressure wave. Tom's ears popped.

The world grew silent.

Burst eardrums.

Tendrils a blur.

Half a million grasping hands fell away.

Whiteness . . .

And they sprang upwards into a place of blazing light.

66

NULAPEIRON AD 3422

Nova-bright, it shone around them. Thylara swerved the 'sprite, took a new course, and they danced upwards along the glassine structure. They were inside the great blossom which was now alive with focused light.

Five seconds to reach the apex.

The whiteness grew on every side. It was as though the crystalline structure was no longer the energy's source; instead, the very air seemed to be on fire, a pulsing white globe with a life of its own.

Then they were on the clear roof's outer rim where Tom expected Thylara to slow, but if anything the 'sprite moved faster as they tipped over, and danced down the convex outer wall until they reached the ground, and the temporary illusion of safety.

Tom's heart beat so fast he thought it might burst. In the bag he was still clutching, did long-dead Eemur feel fear of her own?

Now Thylara paused, checked her lased-in her-eyes-only display, then gunned her arachnasprite into motion once more, and the grass flowed by beneath them like an emerald torrent which rushes towards the wild and massive ocean, birthplace of life, saltwater cradle of all existence, something which Tom had never seen for real.

There was an invisible war, unseen but deadly: femtophages and pseudatomic lattices, borne in smartmists and virtual bursts, battling against each other. Attack and countermeasure formed a finely balanced conflict; with limits on evolutionary capability, to prevent wildfire leaps to unforeseen sections of morphological phase-space, the appearance of new forms which would prove as deadly to the human originators as to the intended targets.

It was self-interest, the ancient decision to limit the way femtotech was used for violence: a way of avoiding the immolation of the species. But everyone in the know among Corduven's forces had been afraid, since the Blight might have removed all restrictions and produced who knew what devilish creations.

But the war was waged, and fizzled out.

And the archaic forms of hand-to-hand conflict came to the forefront yet again.

The arachnasprite danced across a field of blood and mud, passed wounded soldiers—who reached out, might have called to Tom had he ears to hear them—and butchered corpses. Overhead, Corduven's flyers and the Blight's armoured drones, many hundreds of them now, filled the air with their own form of battle.

Down here, grey-uniformed companies of Dark Fire forces—human allies, not Absorbed, from what Tom could see—marched against the ground troops the flyers had landed. The élite forces, trained in holo-caverns to fight in the agoraphobic vastness of ground level.

I didn't expect this.

Only Corduven could have mobilized such vast numbers, and even then they must have been on instant standby. He must have been waiting personally for Tom's signal; had instantly seen the significance of the Blight's reaching out to Anomalies of other worlds—if that was truly the purpose of the great crystalline structure.

But Tom had not thought the agoraphilia-conditioned forces included the Clades Tau, or any 'sprite clans, and he wondered whether the nomad riders had made surface forays of their own, over the years. How else could Thylara function up here?

Graser-burst, and all the tendrils along the arachnasprite's right side gave way, and they fell.

Both Tom and Thylara rolled clear by reflex.

They were almost beyond the battlefield, and Thylara tugged Tom in the right direction, plodding now across unbroken heath, while the silent—to Tom—cacophony of light and death played out behind him. There was no point in looking back: if they were pursued, they were dead. Neither he nor Thylara had weapons to speak of.

They walked, and Eemur's Head in its bag banged against his right thigh on every other step, but Tom had a feeling that she would voice no complaint, even if she had the ability.

And then they were scrambling down a slope, into a small dell, where Corduven had set up a command post inside a transparent armoured bubble-tent. His strategy advisers clustered around him, and one of them was lean and cheerful—even in these circumstances—the light of magical genius dancing in his eyes.

Avernon!

Tom went to grasp forearms in the noble fashion, but Avernon embraced him like a long-lost brother, shouting words of joyful greeting which Tom could not hear.

Flyers passed by overhead, accelerating towards the battle.

"Can you hear me?" Tom pointed to his ears. "I'm deaf. Does my voice sound right?"

Avernon nodded.

Tom explained how he had summoned Corduven's forces, with a microtransmitter which utilized any power source it could: he assumed it had vaporized with the overload after the first message-burst.

I didn't think he'd send his entire army.

And accompany them. Tom glanced towards the tac-display, where Corduven looked like a living skeleton himself, taut-skinned and surviving on his nerves.

They must have interpreted the information in the same way as Tom. If the Blight was a local seed of an Anomalous form of life, restricted to Nulapeiron, and it was about to join with the Fulgor Anomaly and whatever counterparts existed on other worlds . . .

If the Blight was not already a dark god, then soon it would be.

"It was Elva's idea." Tom could not take the credit for the notion: she knew transmitter design better than he, for all his use of mu-space tech.

Avernon shook his head, not knowing who Elva might be. Then he asked a question, but Tom could not understand.

"We need to do the same again," he said, or hoped he said, to Avernon. "The most powerful signal you can imagine."

Tom reached inside his tunic, made a control gesture in front of his stallion talisman, and caught the small ovoid capsule as it slipped out of the metal when it split apart.

I did it before.

Spreading his hands, Avernon said something. An excuse, a reason it could not be done. Still, he accepted the capsule when Tom held it out, and split it open with one thumb to reveal the crystal inside.

If it doesn't work, we're all lost.

Avernon shook his head.

But Thylara moved before Tom could think of a reply, and dragged Avernon up the dell's slope—Tom followed—until they stood at the top with the battle zone a distant conflagration. She pointed, demonstrating why they had no choice.

We're lost, along with all humanity.

Beyond the battlefield, a white light blazed greater than the sun.

They flew, and they prepared to die, and it was magnificent. And Tom wept when he realized what was occurring.

It was a final, desperate move.

His idea. If he was wrong, brave young men and women were throwing their lives away for nothing.

Either way, for twenty flight crews, this spelled their deaths.

No . . .

Tom had not thought it possible, but the white light was growing, spreading . . .

Standing at the slope's apex, he suddenly fell to one knee, buffeted by a great wind which had sprung up from nowhere. All around, men and women were pitching over.

In the distance, thousands were engaged in hand-to-hand combat amid the blood and the mud, the churned ground a silent backdrop to desperate conflict where graser fire cut down distant combatants while others struggled close enough to inhale each other's stinking breaths, feel the opponent's heart beating beneath their ribs, using any weapons which came to hand: here, teeth upon the jugular, biting till bright hot blood spurted; there, the use of thumbs to wetly hook out eyes, then mercifully snapping the neck while the dying man screamed.

But all the time, that nova-glow was growing.

Tom knew—he had seen the confirmation in Avernon's eyes, and Avernon was a logosophical genius whose like had not been seen in Nulapeiron for a century or more—that the blazing white light indicated more than the burning of the atmosphere, the incandescence of a vast explosion to come.

Worse, much worse: those energies would rip through spacetime, twist apart its smallest structures, dive through the tiny extra hyperdimensions of the realspace continuum, tearing a pathway through the Calabi-Yau layers beneath reality, ripping open a channel which would stretch all the way to Fulgor, in a perverse exploitation of natural law which could breach the light-years between this world and the original Anomaly as though the universe's vastness were a mere bagatelle, a trick designed to separate lesser beings from their dreamed-of destinations.

We're going to die, all of us.

But worse, much worse, was the Fate of those who might physically survive, their souls lost forever as part of the expanded Blight: components of the Dark Fire, subsumed within a being so great its powers and purposes could never be comprehended by single biological beings, as far below awareness as bacteria within multicellular bodies.

Elva. Do I get to see you again before we die?

But he did not know where she was, whether Thylara's fellow Tau-Riders had managed to whisk Elva to safety along the deserted tunnels within the old Collegium.

The sky brightened.

Flickering in his vision—thinking for a moment that his retinae were damaged—black flames whose dimensions were impossible to guess danced across that whiteness, as the Dark Fire claimed Nulapeiron's skies for itself.

We expect to fight that?

Whirlwinds tore across the ground, spitting soil and people upwards into the air. Across the battleground, troops of both sides hunkered down, dug with their fingers into clay and mud, holding on for survival. Torn corpses and screaming soldiers—Tom could see their mouths distended wide, though the world remained silent and warm liquid ran from his ears—were whipped up into the maelstrom, were gone.

It was the Day of Judgement.

In the whiteness, there remained for now a core of greater energy, the blazing heart of the Blight's burgeoning connection which would soon explode in a crescendo of climactic joining as two Anomalies became one, merged their energies, pulsed together into a fusion whose urgent drives and godlike powers were beyond Tom's power to imagine.

There . . .

He could see them now: twenty tiny triangles, flying through the air, almost lost amid the glow.

Dead, for sure.

But Avernon was a genius, and he had networked the flyers together in a way which would heterodyne the signal that Tom had configured. On board, one flyer carried his mu-space crystal, which this time surely could not survive.

It was the Zajinets from Ro's Story who had given Tom the idea, with their ability to warp Calabi-Yau space in the near vicinity—the nature of the aliens' teleportation abilities had been clear to him, if not to the people involved in those historical events—as well as travel through mu-space using technology similar to the Pilots' own.

With his hearing gone and time running out, he had told Avernon only the barest bones of his theory; but Avernon had understood before Tom had half begun, and waved him away to get some peace, working on his calculations while Corduven had the task of deciding which flyer squadron he would send to their deaths.

And now the action was under way.

Raging storms tore the landscape, ripped vegetation and bodies apart, while energies lit the skies as the clouds became incandescent and the white-upon-white glow grew ever brighter overhead, and the entire atmosphere began to shiver.

It was indeed the Day of Judgement.

Do you remember, Dart?

But if Tom was right, it could become Ragnarok: it could be Armageddon.

Can you recall what it means to be human?

And if that entity, part of the mu-space universe itself, ever deigned to have such considerations, could It be moved to care? Would It worry about the species It formerly belonged to, any more than humans thought about the microbes from which they had once evolved?

For there was a difference: between the Last Judgement delivered by an omnipotent deity, and the Final Battle in which two such forces opposed each other . . .

Whiteness, as the atmosphere was ripped apart.

It was the moment space split open.

No . . .

Pressure waves slammed people to the ground, but Tom clung on, fingers entwined in grace, squinting against the wind to see.

The sky ripped apart, as a wide black ribbon tore through it from horizon to horizon, arching overhead.

Anomaly?

The world ended.

A foetus on the ground, a wet helpless embryo about to be squashed from existence, Tom wept, for the millions, the billions of people who would die, for Elva whom he would never see again.

He felt the dark, uncaring presence fill the void. He knew its malevolent drives, as though its hungers could resonate inside a human soul. Rising desire, the vast concentration of growing energies which were about to burst across spacetime, to explode in an orgy of merging with its distant Anomalous counterpart—

But there existed another power as far beyond humankind as it was possible to imagine, which existed in another universe, but whose origins were as human as those of the Anomaly itself.

And this was the moment for It to manifest Itself.

The air was sundered, but a new thought slammed into each person's awareness like a divine fist: a communication beyond words which burst through every mind, exploded in the soul.

##YOU DARE?##

It was the roar of an outraged god.

A cataclysm beyond human reckoning. A thunderous raging war beyond perception; a coruscating series of battles whose sequence and setting and very nature could never be comprehended by tiny mortals who see so little of their own universe—evolved to perceive only ten per cent of the matter which exists, only four of the dimensions—and whose capacity to imagine the fractal context on which it depends is insignificant.

They clashed, the Dart entity and the Blight.

They fought across the universes.

Flinging energies which could annihilate whole worlds, wringing subtle topological changes smaller than electrons in the stuff of space-time itself: they attacked each other on every level.

There was no way to understand their motivations: whether the being which had once been Dart held any loyalty to Its original species, or whether It merely resented the intrusion into mu-space of the Anomalous energies which Tom's summoning communication had allowed to bleed through into that fractal continuum, no ordinary human could ever know.

It was a conflict between two gods.

As they struggled for supremacy, miraculous changes in physical constants took place in a very special realm: the bridge between two continua which pulsed and expanded with fiery power, forming a universe in its own right. It became a battlefield, a chessboard, a comms link and a resonance cavity in which contesting deities duelled in ways which affected that universe's geometry, determined its future; and if stars and worlds and sentient beings rose and fell within the duration of that link-cosmos's existence, who was there to tell?

For when that war, that Ragnarok, was over, the battlefield which lay between them was destroyed—a universe which existed no more—and one of those two deities was gone.

And later analysis, led by Lord Avernon himself, would determine that the War Between Gods had lasted a little more than one picosecond—perhaps a millionth of a millionth of a single human heartbeat's duration.

Nothing of the Blight remained.

The sky was clear, fresh and tinged with yellow. The normal cloud cover, creamy and full, was wiped away. Distant dots—terraformer spheres, floating high above—looked dark against the peaceful backdrop. Below, amid toppled trees and flattened purple grasses, wrecked flyers seemed like abstract sculptures set in place to decorate a vast but neglected parkland.

Across the battlefield, nobody moved.

Then finally, a stirring.

Tom, by chance, was one of the first to awaken.

67

NULAPEIRON AD 3423

Fireworks exploded along the boulevard's length, starbursts along the golden ceiling: the welcome crack, and then the dying wheeze. Streamers and holos sprayed through the air.

Tom, in full nobleman's regalia, stood to attention on the balcony.

"Happy New Year." Avernon, at Tom's left shoulder, used the ancient benediction.

"To all of us," said Corduven, on Tom's right.

All three wore formal high-collared capes, and kept their position while the victory parade passed by below, and the swirling crowds of revellers laughed and cheered and hurled up their thanks, and their blessings.

"*Lord One-Arm,*" someone shouted. "*All hail!*"

There were answering cheers.

Tom's ears were fully healed; everything sounded closer, more richly textured, than it had before. He grinned at the mass of people below.

It was a long time before Corduven touched Tom's arm and said, "Let's go inside."

Tom had a silver cane to lean on, but his wounds were slight, and he limped only a little as they passed through the open archway, into a richly appointed chamber where Lords and Ladies from many realms were drinking, snacking on hors d'oeuvres delivered by lev-trays and drones—not servitors: an informality which some found gauche, while those with military experience appeared not to mind—and floating couches abounded. Corduven and Avernon watched, making sure Tom sat down, then fetched drinks for him and for themselves.

Their solicitude was beginning to wear him down, but he smiled his thanks all the same.

Next morning, a clap from outside Tom's sleeping chamber woke him early, and he struggled to sit up in the big comfortable bed.

"What—Oh, come inside. What is it?"

A servitor entered, swallowed.

"Brigadier-General d'Ovraison, sir. Sorry, I know it's early. But he's here, in the breakfast lounge. Says he has something you must see."

"I'll be right out."

Bare-chested and barefoot, dressed only in training trews, Tom padded out into the lounge where Corduven was waiting.

"Morning, old chap." He looked at Tom's stump, but without revulsion. "I thought we could go on a little trip this morning."

"Fine." Tom rubbed his face. He had slept well, could do with some more. "Where are we going?"

"You'll see when we get there."

In cloaks and heavy tunics, they walked along the boulevard, among the detritus of the previous night's parade. In one alcove, two men still in uniform were singing quietly. Here and there, unconscious figures were slumped, on benches or against the main wall.

"Premature, perhaps." Tom did not think they could afford optimism. "Perhaps the Blight's in hiding."

"I agree." Corduven had better access to intelligence. "But the other occupied realms are fighting purely conventional battles, and there seems to be confusion among their upper echelons."

The enemy officers appeared to be purely human. No-one had detected true Dark Fire activity since the War Between Gods.

"I've another thought for you, Corduven. A nastier one."

They walked in silence for a few more paces.

"All right, I'll bite." Corduven glanced at Tom. "What's the sting in the tail?"

"Two gods bumped against each other, and there was divine anger, and the dark one got burned. Isn't that what people think?"

"Don't you?" Corduven tapped Tom gently on the shoulder. "It was your idea."

"Not mine, not really."

"But—"

"Dart, or the 'system reflection' I talked to before, whatever—we used the Blight's own energies to blast a signal into mu-space, to the processor I used before. The Blight attracted the Dart-entity's attention, and they didn't like each other."

"That," said Corduven, "sounds like an understatement."

They stopped beside a floating bronze-encased levanquin, whose driver was waiting patiently, eyes ahead as though he could not detect Tom's or Corduven's presence.

"What if Dart destroyed Nulapeiron's Blight"—Tom's voice was very quiet—"but not before its signal got through to the original Anomaly?"

For a long moment, Corduven stood very still.

Then he stirred into life, but did not say another word as they climbed aboard, and the levanquin lifted and moved off.

They arced through a clear pale-yellow sky. Overhead, a tiny dark dot: a floating terraformer, spewing creamy heat-retaining clouds into the upper atmosphere, replenishing the storm-blown cloud cover.

Tom and Corduven sat behind the flight crew, looking out across the wild landscape. Mountains gave way to familiar heathland, and then the blasted muddy waste which had been churned up by battle.

None of it was Blight-held territory. Not any more.

They banked downwards, to the left, and Tom tried to look over Corduven's shoulder, but Corduven held up a hand, blocking his view.

"Not yet."

The flyer whispered softly into land.

Tom jumped down into the wild grasses, took a deep breath of pure fresh air, and walked up to the ridgeline. Trying not to remember the battle-Chaos of the last time he had been here.

He was puffing a little when he reached the top, and looked down. With amazement.

Where the great crystalline structure had stood, everything now was flat—and softly shimmering.

A lake of glass spread wide before him, cupped in a kilometres-wide natural depression, smooth and shining beneath the morning sun.

"Take your time," said Corduven.

A soft breeze caressed Tom's face as he descended to the glass lake's edge, and stood there.

For a long time.

Then he tapped the glass with the toe of his boot, satisfied himself that it was solid, and threw back his cloak over his right shoulder.

He stepped out onto the glass.

And walked.

Out across the smooth lake, taking careful paces so he would not slip, Tom did indeed take his time. Eventually he reached a point, smooth and perfectly flat like any other, which he judged to be the glass lake's centre.

Taking care, he went down on one knee, and leaned forward to splay his hand against the surface.

It was not heat, he decided, which had turned the glass structure to liquid, but some other force which had dissolved the molecular bonds only of that substance. He knew that, because the proof was visible, beneath him.

The girl was young, eleven SY perhaps, and she was frozen in the glass, hair trapped in a swirl which would remain in stasis. None of the bodies had burned: every one was intact, trapped forever at the moment of death.

Had there been children among the multitude? Tom had not realized.

She died, they died, to save us all.

But that was scant comfort.

Tom stood up, walked a little way, and stopped.

Lemon skies and creamy clouds, and air fresher than he had ever breathed.

But down below his feet, held frozen for eternity, were more intact people, hands raised upwards as though in helpless supplication, and it was at that moment that the enormity of his actions was made clear to Tom.

So many . . .

In there, down inside the vast lake of glass, frozen, were two hundred and fifty thousand bodies, every one a victim who had known what it was for a higher power to enter their minds, rape their humanity and take possession of the remnants, and each of those quarter of a million souls had once been a child, perhaps was one still at the end; had known life, their parents' love or society's cruel indifference, fallen in love, betrayed or been betrayed, bereaved, found happy fulfilment, hard work or indolence . . .

Each was a real, complete life.

An entire universe, if the truth be told, which ceases to exist when each person dies, with their perceptions, their thoughts and innermost untold fears and highest dreams—all turned to insensate dust.

For what can possibly matter, save people . . . people, and time, and love?

Tom knelt down, carefully, upon the smooth glass surface.

And bowed his head.

Oh, my brothers and sisters.

The magnitude of it all.

I am so sorry.

And wept for the frozen dead.

68
TERRA AD 2155
<<Ro's Story>>
[21]
Epilogue

Its slender body was silver; the delta wings were of shining copper, crossed with silver to match the fuselage. It hung, the mu-space vessel, high above a startling green meadow in the pure Alpine sky. White buildings shone beneath it.

A tiny drop-bug disengaged, floated downwards from the ship like a dandelion seed upon the soft spring breeze. Slowly, until it touched down lightly in a courtyard.

Its hatch puckered, opened, and a lithe dark-suited figure jumped out.

"Admiral." A young boy, also clad in black, was there to meet her. "Welcome, ma'am." He saluted, and looked up at her with his black-on-black eyes.

"At ease." Ro grinned, then tousled his hair. "How ya doin', young Carlos?"

"Great, ma'am." He grinned, revealing a gap where a front tooth was missing.

Then he turned and scampered inside.

Ro followed.

A passing nun nodded, walking swiftly by. Behind her, two Asian lay-helpers, their faces strained, hurried to keep up. Seven years before, they had come here as refugees, at the height of the Changeling Plague.

They look more worried, Ro thought, *every time I'm here.*

She walked from the courtyard to the meadow's edge. Beneath a spray of varicoloured flowers, a small grey headstone stood.

Father Michael Aloysius Mulligan, FSJ, PhD, DSc
13th April 2076—10th August 2154
Father of Dart and Ticky, husband of Angela.
Latterly a Jesuit priest and scholar.
Requiescat in pace.

So many deaths; so many family she never knew.

Gramps had died nearly a year ago, just before Ro's thirty-fourth birthday. She thought of Dart, the father she had never known, and wondered what it was that survived in mu-space. His soul? It was nothing she would ever discuss, here or anywhere.

Ticky was the younger son: the uncle who had never been, killed with his mother when he was very young; it was that tragedy, or Gramps' recovery from it, which had led to his ordination.

And he had been Mother's sensei.

I miss you, Gramps.

She bowed to the gravestone.

In the dojo, a small white-haired woman, in *gi* and split-skirt *hakama*, moved at the centre of a maelstrom. Beefy UNSA officers tumbled in every direction, and Ro winced as the tiny blind woman altered momentum and two heads collided with an audible crack and both men fell, stunned.

In a gallery, ten youngsters clad in black jumpsuits watched silently.

Mother. You just get better with age.

After she had led the cool-down and meditation, Karyn—Mother
—bowed formally from the kneeling position, forehead to floor, as her
trainees did likewise. Then they shuffled off the mat, covered in sweat,
faces drained.

"Mom!" Two children ran towards Ro.

She caught them around her waist.

"You're back." Karyn smiled, silver eye sockets catching the sun.
"For how long?"

"Long enough"—with a rough hug—"to put these two through
their paces."

"Ha. If you can keep up."

Towelling off, Karyn headed towards her quarters.

"Ten minutes, and I'll be showered and ready for lunch."

"Yes, Mother."

"And they haven't seen their father."

"Good. And we don't need his money, either."

They both knew that Colonel Neil was a father in name only, and
that his and Ro's disastrous liaison was long over. Anyone who performed a DNA check on the boys would soon find that out: they were
twin one hundred per cent McNamara clones, natural-born, with only
the gender chromosome altered.

They waited for Karyn to leave the dojo, then exchanged mutual grins.

"Colonel Neil"—Dirk imitated his grandmother's voice—"is
chasing lady officers in Pasadena. And we better not—"

"–grow up to be like him," finished Kian. "Of which there's fat
chance, right?"

"Right."

Ro could tell them apart, but only just. To everyone else apart from
their grandmother, the twins were indistinguishable, looking twelve
years old though they had just turned ten.

"So what have you two learned?" Ro glanced at the dojo mat: teal
green, holding the sweat of all that striving.

The twins slipped their shoes off.

And then they were into it, a sudden shift from stillness to blurred motion: jumping, rolling, using kicks and elbows, moving in for body-throws—a wrist-throw, begun but deliberately released (for both Ro and Karyn had decreed that locks and throws against the joints were too dangerous for growing bones)—and the use of confusion, attack-vectors which most fighters would never imagine, would have no reflexive defence against.

Dirk and Kian stopped, small chests heaving, and bowed in one motion towards their mother.

"Very good, my warriors." Ro bowed in return. "Very good indeed."

There were six hundred children seated in the assembly hall, wearing black jumpsuits, looking up at Ro. There was a lectern, but she ignored it. Instead, she stood with hands clasped behind her back, looking down at them all.

"Ma'am?" It was young Carlos, speaking from the wing offstage. "All clear, ma'am."

"Thank you, Carlos."

The nuns' surveillance cameras were now seeing images of Ro's devising: a pep talk just scandalous enough—by their standards—to stop them looking for a deeper truth.

Before Ro, the children waited. They were aged between seven and twelve, but even the youngest sat attentively, hands on knees, staring up at their leader with jet-black eyes totally sans whites, like Ro's own.

Pilots' eyes.

Only Dirk and Kian were her own progeny, but every child here bore a fragment of her DNA, her mitochondria, and the unique organelles collectively termed fractolons. Each child had been born in mu-space, to a host mother who had already signed her offspring's parentage over to UNSA, in the guise of a foundation headed by the still redoubtable Frau Doktor Schwenger.

UNSA trainees were still being virally rewired and stripped of their eyes, but the numbers per annum were diminishing, and in a few years the first of these new Pilots would be ready to take their place in the continuum they would make their own, at home in mu-space as no ordinary human beings could ever be.

Would they be alone there? No-one had seen a Zajinet for years: all ambassadors to Terra had been recalled, and the world of Beta Draconis III was devoid of life; no-one believed any more that it had been their homeworld. Among the higher echelons of UNSA, they knew only that the aliens—the faction in power, at least—had not wanted true Pilots in mu-space; and that encouraged them to back Ro's plans.

"Hello, everyone." Ro's voice carried clearly.

Above the ceiling, high above the buildings, her delta-winged vessel hung huge and silent, waiting. Though there were no skylights, Ro could sense its presence always.

"Today, we'll consolidate skills which we don't"—with a gentle emphasis "ever practise in public. Understood?"

Six hundred heads nodded in unison.

"Good. We don't want to frighten people."

In Ro's jet eyes, a small golden light softly glowed.

"After all . . ."

For a moment, nothing.

". . . they're only human."

And then, in every black orb, in six hundred pairs of eyes, an answering spark began to glimmer.

<<STORY ENDS>>

69

NULAPEIRON AD 3423

Corduven's uniform was cream and gold, and its decorations gleamed.

"Very polished," said Tom.

"Look"—Corduven waved a mirrorfield into existence—"who's talking."

In his reflection, Tom saw his own immaculate white uniform, its piping all of platinum, formal white half-cape thrown back carefully over his shoulder at just the correct angle. The lounge in which they were waiting, appointed in burgundy and gold with diamond inlays along the fluted columns, seemed appropriate.

"My servitor's outfit," Tom recalled, "was black and ivory."

"Lady Darinia's colours." Corduven laughed. "Terrible livery. I remember the day I first saw you, when you came to fetch my damaged clothes—"

"Buggy smartsatin."

"That's right. I nearly suggested you keep my garments instead."

"Chef Keldur," said Tom, "would've killed me."

They shook their heads, thinking of time's passage, and how it slips away from everyone. Then a discreet chime sounded.

Corduven stepped forward as an alpha servitor entered, and they exchanged muted whispers.

"Got to go," Corduven told Tom. "Details. Can't trust anyone."

"Don't be long."

"Just who's supposed to nag whom, today?"

There was a soft sound behind him, and Tom spun, hand raised. A service entrance, normally unused, was vitrifying into solidity.

The lean man bowed.

"I beg your pardon, my Lord."

But when he straightened up, he looked composed rather than apologetic. He was dressed as a courtier, a Lord-Minor-sans-Demesne, yet he stood with an easy warrior's grace, feline and watchful, and something about his olive-skinned features caused the back of Tom's neck to tingle.

"Do I know you?"

The stranger pulled a white poignard from his tunic. Tom readied himself, but the man held out the weapon hilt first, and the entwined archaic symbols, kappa and alpha, were visible upon the hilt's engraved end.

"Interesting weapon." Tom accepted it. "Nice balance."

He had used one like it, though cast from redmetal, to kill the Oracle. To murder Corduven's brother.

"A replacement." A tight smile crossed the stranger's fine features. "If you will, my Lord."

"I'm not sure what you mean. But I accept your . . . I *have* seen you before, I'm sure of it."

The smile left the stranger's face.

He turned away, reached up, dabbing at his eyes in a gesture which brought a frisson to Tom's tingling nerves.

"My name is Janis deVries."

When he turned back, his eyes—relieved of their cosmetic contacts—were of purest obsidian: totally black, devoid of surrounding whites.

"And I believe you knew my mother."

The Pilot . . .

DeVries cast a glance towards the main door-membrane.

"There are others coming. But we'll talk again, my Lord."

Tom turned as Corduven entered; when he looked back, the mysterious Pilot—unbelievably, the son of that other Pilot, the woman who had died before his eyes nineteen SY before—had disappeared, and the membrane was hardening once more.

"Was someone here?"

"Just a friend." Tom smiled. "Kind of an old family friend."

"Well, for Fate's sake. Are you ready? You know I'll be blamed if we're late."

"Relax," said Tom. "I'm ready now."

It was a low, wide hall, resplendent in white and platinum, and floating silver lev-disks formed a ceremonial stairway down to the dais at the far end, where a trio of shaven-headed priestesses waited.

Among the gathered guests were faces Tom had not seen for years: Lady V'Delikona, whom he had feared dead, smiled radiantly, her white hair gathered in an elegant coiffure and bound with platinum; Sylvana, in a shining gown, not looking in his direction; Sentinel, in a white and blue cloak of overstated magnificence; the housecarl, Kraiv—morphos-pear slung across his back, polished copper helm (in keeping with carl tradition) upon his head—with Draquelle beside him, grinning broadly; Avernon and, next to him, unexpectedly, a moustachioed Zhongguo Ren, thinner and frailer than Tom would have guessed—but Tom could remember him attempting to pummel the older praefecti at the Ragged School as if it were yesterday: his friend Zhao-ji.

And Eemur's Head was there, her flensed flesh gleaming red, in a five-sided box to screen the sight of her from delicate sensibilities, while giving her full unblinking view of the ceremonial dais.

Wind chimes sounded as Tom descended, and then the gathered faces became one inchoate blur as the great silver door swung open, to his left, and a new entourage came inside.

She was smiling beneath the veil.

The Antistita, the primary priestess, had a silver voice which carried clearly throughout the hall.

". . . have witnessed the marriage here today of Lord Thomas Corcorigan and Commander Strelsthorm, now Lady Elva Corcorigan—"

He could not believe she looked so beautiful. Or that she was here,
with him, a wedding bracelet twin to his own encircling her wrist.

Applause rose from the congregation as they stood.

"—before us now, sworn forever to be joined."

Tom raised her veil. *"My love . . ."*

"Forever." Elva tipped her face up towards his.

"Always," said Tom.

And kissed her.

the end

ACKNOWLEDGMENTS

Nulapeiron is an entire world: hence its multitude of languages. Here on Earth, one of our major languages is German; and in that tongue, the word "anders" means "differently" or "other." "Anders als jeder" means "different from everyone."

So, too, is Lou Anders, editorial director of Pyr, different from the rest . . . in his deep knowledge of science fiction, and in his energetic championing of the genre. I am proud and honored to be published by him.

So, too, are two people who are sorely missed: my late father-in-law, Jim Jenkins, who escaped from a POW camp; and my late father Tom (Pat) Meaney, who helped to liberate one. I learned everything from their silences, rather than their reminiscences.

Thanks to Paul Storer-Martin, Bob Bridges and John Dryden, for encouragement and great conversation. And to my beautiful web-mistress, Bridget McKenna: check out johnmeaney.tripod.com.

And to John Parker, agent and friend: mere thanks are inadequate.

JOHN MEANEY has a degree in physics and computer science, and is a black belt in Shotokan karate. He has been hooked on science fiction since the age of eight, and his short fiction has appeared in *Interzone* and in a number of anthologies. His début novel, *To Hold Infinity*, was published to great acclaim in 1998, shortlisted for the BSFA Award and subsequently selected as one of the *Daily Telegraph*'s "Books of the Year." *Paradox* is John Meaney's second novel.